PENGUIN BOOKS

Poseidon's Arrow

Clive Cussler is the author or co-author of a great number of international bestsellers, including the famous Dirk Pitt® Adventures, such as *Arctic Drift*; the NUMA® Files, most recently *Medusa*; the Oregon Files, such as *The Jungle*; the Isaac Bell Adventures, which began with *The Chase*; and the highly successful new series – the Fargo Adventures. He lives in Arizona.

Dirk Cussler, an MBA from Berkeley, worked for many years in the financial arena, and now devotes himself full-time to writing. He is the co-author with Clive Cussler of *Crescent Dawn, Black Wind, Treasure of Khan* and *Arctic Drift*. He lives in Arizona.

D1394570

Poseidon's Arrow

CLIVE CUSSLER
AND DIRK CUSSLER

PENGUIN BOOKS

PENGUIN BOOKS

Published by the Penguin Group
Penguin Books Ltd, 80 Strand, London WC2R ORL, England
Penguin Group (USA) Inc., 375 Hudson Street, New York, New York 10014, USA
Penguin Group (Canada), 90 Eglinton Avenue East, Suite 700, Toronto, Ontario, Canada M4P 2Y3
(a division of Pearson Penguin Canada Inc.)
Penguin Ireland, 25 St Stephen's Green, Dublin 2, Ireland (a division of Penguin Books Ltd)
Penguin Group (Australia), 707 Collins Street, Melbourne, Victoria 3008,
Australia (a division of Pearson Australia Group Pty Ltd)
Penguin Books India Pvt Ltd, 11 Community Centre,
Panchsheel Park, New Delhi – 110 017, India
Penguin Group (NZ), 67 Apollo Drive, Rosedale, Auckland 0632, New Zealand
(a division of Pearson New Zealand Ltd)
Penguin Books (South Africa) (Pty) Ltd, Block D, Rosebank Office Park, 181 Jan Smuts Avenue,
Parktown North, Gauteng 2193, South Africa

Penguin Books Ltd, Registered Offices: 80 Strand, London WC2R ORL, England

www.penguin.com

First published in the United States of America by G. P. Putnam's Sons 2012
First published in Great Britain by Michael Joseph 2012
Published in Penguin Books 2013

Copyright © Sandecker, RLLLP, 2012

001

PAPERBACK ISBN: 978–1–405–90988–4
OPEN MARKET PAPERBACK ISBN: 978–1–405–91411–6

www.greenpenguin.co.uk

MIX
Paper from
responsible sources
FSC® C018179

Penguin Books is committed to a sustainable
future for our business, our readers and our planet.
This book is made from Forest Stewardship
Council™ certified paper.

PROLOGUE
Barbarigo

October 1943
The Indian Ocean

The light of a half-moon shimmered off the restless sea like a streak of flaming mercury. To Lieutenant Alberto Conti, the iridescent waves reminded him of a Monet waterscape viewed in a darkened room. The silvery froth reflected the moonlight back to the sky, illuminating a bank of clouds far to the north, the fringe of a storm that was soaking the fertile coast of South Africa some fifty miles away.

Tucking his chin from the moist breeze that buffeted him, Conti turned to face a young seaman standing watch beside him on the conning tower of the Italian submarine *Barbarigo*.

'A romantic evening, Catalano, is it not?'

The sailor gave him a quizzical look. 'The weather is quite pleasant, sir, if that's what you mean.' Though fatigued like the rest of the crew, the seaman still held a rigid demeanor in the presence of officers. It was a youthful piety, Conti considered, one that would eventually vanish.

'No, the moonlight,' Conti said. 'I bet it shines over Naples tonight as well, glistening off the cobblestone streets. It wouldn't surprise me, in fact, if a handsome

3

officer of the Wehrmacht isn't escorting your fiancée on a stroll about Piazza del Plebiscito at this very moment.'

The young sailor spat over the side, then faced the officer with burning eyes.

'My Lisetta would sooner jump off the Gaiola Bridge than associate with any German pig. I do not worry, for she carries a sap in her pocketbook while I'm away, and she knows how to use it.'

Conti let out a deep laugh. 'Perhaps if we armed all of our women, then neither the Germans nor the Allied Forces would dare set foot in our country.'

Having been at sea for weeks, and away from his homeland for months more, Catalano found little humor in the comment. He scanned the horizon, then nodded toward the dark, exposed bow as their submarine sliced through the waves.

'Sir, why have we been relegated to transport duty for the Germans rather than the merchant raiding, for which the *Barbarigo* was built?'

'We're all puppets on the Führer's string these days, I'm afraid,' Conti replied, shaking his head. Like most of his countrymen, he had no idea that forces were at work in Rome that would, in a matter of days, oust Mussolini from power and announce an armistice with the Allies. 'To think that we had a larger submarine fleet than the Germans in 1939, yet we now take our operational orders from the Kriegsmarine,' he added. 'The world is not so easily explained at times.'

'It doesn't seem right.'

Conti gazed across the sub's large forward deck. 'I guess the *Barbarigo* is too big and slow for the latest armed convoys, so we are now little more than a freighter. At least we can say our *Barbarigo* attained a proud wartime record before her conversion.'

Launched in 1938, the *Barbarigo* had sunk a half dozen Allied ships in the Atlantic during the early days of the war. Displacing over a thousand tons, she was much larger than the feared Type VII U-boats of the German wolf pack. But as German surface ship losses began to mount, Admiral Dönitz suggested converting several of the large Italian *sommergibili* into transport vessels. Stripped of her torpedoes, deck gun, and even one of her heads, the *Barbarigo* had been sent to Singapore as a cargo vessel, filled with mercury, steel, and 20mm guns for the Japanese.

'Our return cargo is deemed highly critical to the war effort, so somebody has to act as the mule, I suppose,' Conti said. But deep down, he was angered by the transport duty. Like every submariner, he had something of the hunter in him, a longing to stalk the enemy. But now an enemy encounter would mean death for the *Barbarigo*. Stripped of its weaponry and floundering along at twelve knots, the submarine was more a sitting duck than a feared attacker.

As a white-tipped wave splashed against the bow, Conti glanced at his illuminated wristwatch.

'Less than an hour to sunrise.'

Heeding the unspoken command, Catalano hoisted a pair of binoculars and scanned the horizon for other vessels. The lieutenant followed suit, circling the conning tower with his eyes, taking in the sea and sky. His thoughts drifted to Casoria, a small town north of Naples, where his wife and young son awaited him. A vineyard grew behind their modest farmhouse, and he suddenly longed for the lazy summer afternoons when he would chase his boy through the sprouting vines.

Then he heard it.

Over the drone of the submarine's twin diesel engines, he detected a different sound, something of a high-pitched buzz. Snapping erect, he didn't waste time fixing a position.

'Secure the hatch!' he cried.

He immediately dropped down the interior ladder. The emergency dive alarm rang out an instant later, sending the crew scurrying to their stations. In the engine room, a massive clutch was engaged, killing the diesel engines and transferring drive power to a bank of battery-powered electric motors. Seawater began to slosh across the forward deck as Catalano sealed the conning tower hatch, then descended to the control room.

Normally, a well-trained crew could crash-dive a submarine in under a minute. But since it was loaded to the gills in transport mode, there was little the Italian sub could do quickly. With agonizing leisure, it finally sagged under the surface nearly two minutes after Conti had detected the approaching aircraft.

His boots clanking on the steel ladder as he descended into the control room, Catalano turned and scurried forward to his emergency dive station. The clatter of the diesel engines had fallen quiet as the sub converted to battery propulsion, and the crew mirrored the silence by speaking in hushed tones. The *Barbarigo*'s skipper, a round-faced man named De Julio, stood rubbing sleep from his eyes as he asked Conti if they'd been seen.

'I can't say. I didn't actually see the aircraft. But the moon is bright and the seas are relatively calm. I am sure we are visible.'

'We will know soon enough.'

The captain stepped to the helm station, scanning the depth gauge. 'Take us to twenty meters, then full right rudder.'

The submarine's chief steersman nodded as he repeated the command, eyeing the gauges before him as his grip tightened on a large metal steering wheel. The control room fell silent as the men awaited their fate.

A thousand feet above them, a lumbering British PBY Catalina flying boat released two depth charges that whirled toward the sea like a pair of spinning tops. The aircraft was not yet equipped with radar; it was the RAF plane's rear gunner who had spotted the milky wake of the *Barbarigo*, angling across the rippled surface. Thrilled with his find, he pressed his nose against the acrylic window, wide-eyed, as the twin explosives splashed into the sea. Seconds later, two small geysers of spray shot into the air.

'A bit late, I believe,' the copilot said.

'I suspected as much.' The pilot, a tall Londoner who wore a clipped mustache, banked the Catalina in a tight turn with all the emotion of pouring a cup of tea.

Dropping the charges was something of a guessing game, as the submarine had already disappeared from view, though its surface wake was still visible, and the plane had to strike quickly. The airborne depth charges activated at a preset depth of only twenty-five feet. Given enough time, the sub would easily dive beyond their range.

The pilot lined up for another run, tracking a marker buoy they had released ahead of the initial attack. Eyeing the remnants of the sub's fading wake, he gauged the vessel's unseen path, then gunned the pig-bellied Catalina just past the buoy.

'Coming up on her,' he told the bombardier. 'Release if you've got a target.'

The bombardier for the eight-man crew sighted the sub and flipped a toggle switch, releasing a second pair of depth charges stowed under the Catalina's wings.

'Depth charges away. Spot-on this time, I'd say, Flight Lieutenant.'

'Let's try one more for good measure, then see if we can raise a surface ship in the vicinity,' the pilot replied, already banking the plane hard over.

Inside the *Barbarigo*, the twin blasts shook the bulkheads with a deep shudder. The overhead lights flickered and the hull groaned, but no rush of water penetrated the interior. For a moment, the explosion's deafening roar seemed to be the worst consequence, ringing in each crewman's ears like the bells of St Peter's Basilica. But then the ringing was overpowered by a metallic clang that reverberated from the stern, followed by a high-pitched squeal.

The captain felt a slight change in the vessel's trim. 'Fore and aft damage reports,' he yelled. 'What's our depth?'

'Twelve meters, sir,' the pilot said.

8

No one in the control room spoke. A cacophony of hisses and creaks permeated the compartment as the sub dove deeper. But it was the sound they didn't hear that prickled their ears – the splash and click of a pair of depth charges detonating alongside the submerged vessel.

The Catalina had dropped wide on its last pass, its pilot guessing north while the *Barbarigo* veered south. The last muffled explosions barely buffeted the submarine as it plunged beneath the reach of the depth charges. A collective sigh was expelled as, to a man, the crew realized they were safe for the time being. Their only fear now would be if an Allied surface ship could be summoned to renew the attack.

Their relief was cut short by a cry from the steersman.

'Captain, we seem to be losing speed.'

De Julio stepped close and examined a bank of gauges near the pilot's seat.

'The electrical motors are operational and engaged,' the young sailor said, wrinkling his brow. 'But I show no revolutions on the driveshaft.'

'Have Sala report to me at once.'

'Yes, sir.' A sailor near the periscope turned to retrieve the *Barbarigo*'s chief engineer. He'd taken only two steps when the engineer appeared in the aft passageway.

Chief Engineer Eduardo Sala moved like a bulldozer, his squat frame churning forward in a blunt gait. He approached the captain and stared at him with harsh black eyes.

'Sala, there you are,' the captain said. 'What is our operational status?'

'The hull is secure, sir. We do have heavy leakage at the

9

main shaft seal, which we are attempting to stem. I can report one injury, Engineer Parma, who fell and broke his wrist during the attack.'

'Very well, but what about the propulsion? Are the electric motors disabled?'

'No, sir. I disengaged the main drive motors.'

'Are you crazy, Sala? We were under attack and you disengaged the motors?'

Sala looked at the captain with contempt.

'They are irrelevant now,' he said quietly.

'What are you saying?' De Julio asked, wondering why the engineer was evasive.

'It's the screw,' Sala said. 'A blade was bent or warped by the depth charge. It made contact with the hull and sheared off.'

'One of the blades?' De Julio asked.

'No . . . the entire screw.'

The words hung in the air like a death knell. Absent its single screw propeller, the *Barbarigo* would be tossed about the sea like a cork. Its home port of Bordeaux suddenly seemed as far away as the moon.

'What can we do?' the captain said.

The gruff engineer shook his head.

'Nothing but pray,' he said softly. 'Pray for the mercy of the sea.'

PART ONE
Poseidon's Arrow

I

June 2014
Mojave Desert, California

It was a myth, the man decided, an old wives' tale. Often he had heard how the desert's broiling daytime temperatures gave way to freezing cold at night. But in the high desert of Southern California in July, he could testify, that wasn't the case. Sweat soaked the underarms of his thin black sweater and pooled in a damp mass around his lower back. The temperature was still at least ninety degrees. He glanced at his luminescent watch, verifying it was indeed two in the morning.

The heat didn't exactly overwhelm him. He'd been born in Central America and had lived and fought guerrilla campaigns in the region's jungles his entire life. But the desert was new to him, and he simply hadn't expected the nighttime heat.

He gazed across the dusty landscape to a conglomeration of glowing streetlamps. They marked the entrance to a large open-pit mining complex spread across the hills before him.

'Eduardo should nearly be in place opposite the guard station,' he said to a bearded man lying prone in a nearby sandy depression.

He was similarly clad in black, from combat boots to

13

the thin stocking cap pulled low over his head. Sweat glistened off his face as he sipped from a water bottle.

'I wish he would hurry. There are rattlesnakes around here.'

His partner grinned in the dark. 'Juan, that would be the least of our problems.'

A minute later, the handheld radio on his belt chirped with two static transmissions.

'That's him. Let's move.'

They arose and put on light backpacks. Lights from the mine buildings were sprinkled across the hillside in front of them, casting a pale glow over the barren desert. They hiked a short distance to a chain-link fence that encircled the complex. The taller man knelt and rummaged through his pack for a pair of wire cutters.

'Pablo, I think we can get through without cutting,' his partner whispered, then pointed to a dry wash that ran beneath the fence.

The sandy ground was soft in the middle of the creek bed, and he easily pushed some of it aside with his foot. Pablo joined him in scraping away the loose soil until they had excavated a small hole beneath the fence. Pushing their packs under it, they quickly shimmied through.

A low blend of rumbling noises filled the air, the mechanical bedlam of an open-pit mine that operated around the clock. The two men stayed clear of the guard station, to their right, and made their way up a gentle slope toward the mine itself. A ten-minute hike brought them to a cluster of aged buildings crisscrossed with large conveyor belts. A front-end loader at the far end was shoveling piles of ore onto one of the moving belts, which transported it to a hopper on stilts.

The two men were headed to a second cluster of buildings farther up the hill. The mine pit blocked their way, forcing them to cut through the operations area, where ore was crushed and milled. Clinging to the shadows, they darted along the perimeter, then worked their way along the back of a large storage building. Reaching an exposed area between buildings, they moved quickly, striding past a semiburied bunker to their left. Suddenly a door flung open at the center of the building ahead of them. The two men split up, Juan ducking to the side and scrambling behind the bunker while Pablo sprinted ahead toward the side of the building.

He didn't make it.

A bright yellow beam snapped on, blinding him.

'Hold it right there or you'll regret taking that next step,' said a low, gravely voice.

Pablo stopped in midstride. But as he made an exaggerated stop, he deftly withdrew a mini automatic pistol from his left hip and concealed it in the palm of his gloved hand.

The overweight security guard walked slowly toward him, keeping his flashlight pointed into Pablo's eyes. The guard could see the intruder was a large, well-proportioned man, over six feet tall. His coffee-colored skin was smooth and pliant, in contrast to black eyes that burned with malignant intensity. A lighter band of flesh crossed his chin and left jaw, the souvenir from an ancient knife fight.

The guard saw enough to know he wasn't an accidental

trespasser and stopped a healthy distance away, clutching a .357 Magnum.

'How about you put your hands on your head and then you can tell me where your friend went.'

The rumble of a nearby conveyor drowned out Juan's footsteps as he sprinted from the bunker and plunged a knife into the guard's kidney. Shock registered on the guard's face momentarily before his whole body tensed. A wayward shot erupted from his revolver, whistling high over Pablo's head. Then the guard fell, his body kicking up a swirl of dust as it struck the ground.

Pablo thrust his gun forward, expecting additional guards to rush to the scene, but none came. The gunshot had been lost amid the rumbling of conveyor belts and the pounding of the rockcrusher. A quick radio call to Eduardo confirmed there was no activity at the front gate. No one else in the facility had realized their presence.

Juan wiped his knife clean on the shirt of the dead man. 'How did he spot us?'

Pablo glanced toward the bunker. For the first time, he noticed a red-and-white sign on the door proclaiming DANGER: EXPLOSIVE MATERIALS. 'That bunker houses explosives. It must be under surveillance.'

Blind luck, he cursed to himself. The explosives bunker wasn't marked on his map. Now their whole operation was jeopardized.

'Should we blow it?' Juan asked.

They had been ordered to disrupt the facility but to make it look accidental. That had suddenly become a tall order. The bunker explosives could be made useful, but it was too far from their actual target.

'Let it be.'

'Do we leave the guard here?' Juan asked.

Pablo shook his head. He unbuckled the guard's holster, then pulled off the man's shoes. He searched the guard's pockets and retrieved his wallet and half a pack of cigarettes. He stuffed those, along with the .357 Magnum, into his backpack. A growing pool of blood was dampening the ground around his feet. He kicked some loose sand over the blood, then grasped one of the guard's arms. Juan grabbed the other, and they dragged the body into the darkness.

Thirty yards away, they reached an elevated conveyor on which melon-sized chunks of ore whirled by. With a labored heave, the men swung the guard's body onto the moving belt. Pablo watched as the guard was carried up the conveyor and deposited into a large metal hopper.

The ore, a mixed fluorocarbonate known as bastnasite, had already passed through an initial crusher and sorter. The guard's body joined a second round of pulverization that smashed the ore to baseball-sized pieces. A tertiary crushing repeated the process, pounding the rocks into a fine gravel. Had anyone examined the rough brown powder that accumulated off the final conveyor, they would have noticed an odd red tint that marked the guard's last remains.

Though the crushing and milling were important stages in the mine's operations, they were less critical than the secondary complex up the hill. Pablo eyed the lights of several buildings in the distance, where the milled ore was leached and separated into a handful of mineral components. Spotting no moving vehicles in the area, he and Juan took off at a quick clip.

The men had to skirt the eastern edge of the open pit, jumping into a culvert when a dump truck rumbled by. A short time later, Eduardo alerted them that a security guard was making the rounds in a pickup truck. They ducked behind a mound of tailings, then lay frozen for nearly twenty minutes until the truck returned to the front gate.

They moved toward the two largest buildings in the upper complex, then veered right and approached a small shack that fronted a towering propane tank. Juan took the wire cutters and snipped an opening in the surrounding chain-link fence. Pablo slipped through, circled the big tank, and knelt before its fill valve. Removing a small plastic explosives charge from his backpack, he attached a detonator cap and placed it beneath the valve. He set the digital timer for twenty minutes, activated it, and scurried back through the fence.

On the ground a few feet away, Pablo scattered the guard's shoes, gun, and holster. The wallet came next, still containing its cash, then the rumpled pack of cigarettes. It was a long shot, but a superficial investigation might finger the guard for accidentally igniting a leaky tank – then being vaporized by the blast.

The two men scurried toward the next building, a large metal structure containing dozens of mechanized vats filled with leaching solutions. A small group of graveyard shift laborers monitored the vats.

The two intruders made no attempt to enter the building; instead they targeted a large pen storing chemical agents alongside one wall. In less than a minute Pablo attached a second timed charge to a pallet of drums labeled SULFURIC ACID, then escaped into the darkness.

They made their way to a second extraction building a hundred yards away, taking their time as the timers counted down. At the rear of the building, Pablo found the valve for a main water line. Monitoring his watch until just before the detonations, he twisted the valve, shutting off water to the building.

A few seconds later, the propane tank ignited with a boom that reverberated off the nearby hills. Night turned into day as a fiery blue glow enveloped the landscape. The top portion of the tank blew off like an Atlas rocket, screaming into the sky before crashing into the nearby open-pit mine in a ball of flame. Burning shrapnel flew in all directions, peppering buildings, cars, and equipment within a hundred yards of the tank.

The debris was still falling when the second detonation launched a mountain of barrels filled with sulfuric acid into the first extraction facility. Screaming workers fled the interior as the projectiles shredded the ore-leaching vats, releasing a nasty soup of toxic chemicals. Smoke billowed as the doors were flung open and the occupants staggered out.

Juan and Pablo lay in a ditch near the second building, dodging bits of raining debris as they watched a nearby door. At the sound of the explosions, a few curious workers poked their heads outside to investigate. Seeing the smoke and flames from the extraction facility, they called inside to their coworkers, then sprinted to the other building to help. Pablo counted six people rush out before he rose and moved toward the door.

'Stay here and cover me.'

As he reached for the door handle, it twisted from the other side. He jumped back from the opening door as a woman in a lab coat burst out. Her eyes focused on the nearby smoke, she never noticed him behind the door as she nervously followed after her coworkers.

Pablo slipped through the door, stepping into a brightly lit bay filled with dozens more extraction tanks. He turned left and moved to the far end of the building, where large storage tanks lined the wall. He studied their labels, then approached one of the larger tanks. KEROSENE. He tore away a bleed hose from its base, then opened its brass drain valve. A torrent of the liquid flooded across the floor and filled the bay with a gassy odor.

Pablo grabbed a bundle of lab coats from a rack and scurried through the building, stuffing them into all the floor drains. The thin liquid spread quickly, nearly covering the concrete floor. The arsonist made his way back to the door, then pulled a lighter from his pocket. As kerosene trickled past his feet, he leaned down and ignited it, then jumped from the building.

With a low volatility and high flash point, the kerosene didn't explode, instead igniting in a river of flame. As fire detectors erupted throughout the building, ceiling-mounted sprinklers kicked on – but only for a second, as the disrupted water supply ran dry. Unabated, the fire spread.

Pablo didn't look back as he ran to his partner in the gully.

Juan looked up and shook his head. 'Eduardo says the front gate sentry is on his way.'

Across the grounds, sirens and alarms wailed. But no one had yet noticed the swirl of smoke from the roof of the adjacent building. At three in the morning, no one at the facility was prepared to deal with multiple fires, and municipal firefighters were thirty miles away.

Pablo wasted no time watching the incineration. He nodded at his partner, then sprang off to the east. Juan had to scramble to catch up. They crossed the dirt road that led to the front gate moments before an approaching vehicle drew near. The terrain beyond the road turned to open rolling desert, and they dove to the ground as the first security vehicle roared by. Another chain-link fence appeared a short distance away. They cut a gap just big enough for one to slip under while the other pulled up the mesh.

In forty minutes of steady hiking, they reached the main highway two miles away, draining their supply of bottled water. They paralleled the highway east a short distance until spotting a black four-door pickup truck parked near a culvert, neatly hidden from easy view. Eduardo, the third partner, sat behind the wheel in a worn polo shirt, smoking a cigarette.

The two men dropped their packs and pulled off their black hats and sweaters, replacing them with T-shirts and baseball caps.

'Congratulations,' Eduardo said. 'It appears you have succeeded.'

For the first time, Pablo looked back at the mine facility. Billowing clouds of smoke hung over the complex, illuminated by streaks of orange flame that leaped from several sources. The mine's firefighting equipment was woefully inadequate to deal with the fires. By all appearances, the inferno was still spreading.

Pablo allowed himself a half grin. Except for the appearance of the watchman, everything had gone according to plan. The two main extraction facilities, the heart of the complex, would soon be reduced to charred wreckage. Unable to process ore, the entire operation would grind to a standstill for at least a year, maybe two. And if they were lucky, it might all go down as an unfortunate accident.

Juan followed his gaze, watching the pyre with satisfaction. 'Looks like we set the whole state on fire tonight.'

The distant flames glistened in the big man's eyes as he turned to Juan.

'No, my friend,' he said with a wicked grin. 'We have set the whole world on fire.'

2

Sweat trickled down the President's neck, dampening the collar of his starched white shirt. The mercury was hovering near triple digits, unusual for June in Connecticut. A slight breeze off Block Island Sound failed to cut the humidity, leaving the riverside shipyard a sweltering hothouse. Inside a massive green assembly bay known as Building 260, the air-conditioning fought a futile battle with the afternoon heat.

The Electric Boat Corporation had begun building diesel marine engines on the site along the Thames River in 1910, but ultimately submarine construction became the company's bread and butter. The Groton shipyard delivered its first submarine to the Navy in 1934, and had since constructed every major class of US underwater warship. Nearing completion inside the green building stood the imposing hull of the *North Dakota*, the latest fast attack submarine of the Virginia class.

From a scaffold stairway that led from the *North Dakota*'s conning tower, the President stepped heavily onto the concrete floor with a grunt. A large-framed man who hated confined spaces, he was thankful the interior tour was over. At least it had been cooler inside the submarine. With the economy a mess and Congress mired in another deadlock, visiting a shipyard seemed like the last priority on his agenda, but he had promised the Secretary of the

Navy he would go boost the morale of the ship workers. As a small entourage flocked to catch up with him, he suppressed his irritation by marveling at the sub's dimensions.

'An amazing feat of construction.'

'Yes, sir,' said a blond-haired man in a tailored suit who hung at the President's elbow as if attached by a string. 'She's an impressive feat of technology.' Assistant Chief of Staff Tom Cerny had specialized in defense issues on Capitol Hill before joining the administration.

'She's slightly longer than the Seawolf class boats, but downright minuscule compared to a *Trident*,' said the tour guide, a chipper Electric Boat engineering manager. 'Most people are used to seeing them in the water, where two-thirds of their bulk is hidden from view.'

The President nodded. As it lay on huge supporting blocks, the three-hundred-and-seventy-seven-foot-long hull towered over them.

'She'll be a great addition to our arsenal. I thank you for giving me the opportunity to see her up close.'

A granite-faced admiral named Winters stepped forward.

'Mr President, while we were happy to have you preview the *North Dakota*, she was not the reason we asked you up here.'

The President took off a white hard hat affixed with the presidential seal, handed it to the admiral, and wiped a bead of sweat from his forehead.

'If a cold drink and a touch more air-conditioning can be worked into the bargain, then lead on.'

He was escorted across the building to a small door

guarded by a uniformed security man. The door was unlocked, and the presidential group led in one by one, their faces captured by a video camera above the sill.

The admiral flicked on a bank of overhead lights, illuminating a narrow bay that stretched nearly four hundred feet. The President saw another submarine in a state of near completion, but this vessel was like nothing he had ever seen before.

Roughly half the size of the *North Dakota*, it sported a radically different design. Its unusually narrow jet-black hull tapered sharply at the bow. A low, egg-shaped conning tower rose just a few feet above its top deck. Two large streamlined pods were affixed close to the stern, almost in the shape of a dolphin's tail. But the most unusual feature was a pair of retractable stabilizers, shaped like triangular wings, that stretched from either side. A pack of four large tubular canisters clung to their undersides.

The design reminded the President of a giant manta ray he'd seen while fishing off Baja California.

'What on earth is this thing?' he asked. 'I wasn't aware we were building anything other than the Virginia class boats.'

'Sir, this is the *Sea Arrow*,' the admiral said. 'It's a prototype platform developed under a secret R & D program to test highly advanced technologies.'

Cerny turned on the admiral. 'Why wasn't the President informed of this program? I'd like to know how it was funded.'

The admiral stared at the aide with the warmth of a starving pit bull. 'The *Sea Arrow* was built with Defense

Advanced Research Projects Agency and Office of Naval Research funding. The President is presently being informed of its existence.'

The President ignored them and strode along the vessel, peering at the odd appendages along the hull. He studied a concentric circle of small tubes that sprouted off the bow, then made his way aft, noting the sub had no propellers. He gave Winters a questioning look.

'All right, Admiral, you have my curiosity. Tell me about the *Sea Arrow*.'

'Mr President, I'll pass that task to Joe Eberson, who heads up the project. You met Joe earlier. He's DARPA's director of Sea Platforms Technology.'

A bearded man with studious eyes worked his way to the front of the group. He spoke in a measured tone with the hint of a Tennessee accent.

'Sir, the *Sea Arrow* was, or is, being built as a multigenerational leap in undersea technology. We're bypassing the traditional development process by integrating a range of cutting-edge technologies and advanced theories directly into the construction. We started with a planned number of technical features that were purely at the conceptual stage. Through the crash efforts of numerous independent engineering teams around the country, I'm happy to report we are very close to fielding the most advanced attack submarine in history.'

The President nodded. 'So tell me about all these odd appendages. She looks like some flying creature from the Jurassic age.'

'Let's start at the stern. You'll notice she has no propeller.' Eberson pointed at the rounded pods. 'That's what these two external cases are for. The *Sea Arrow* will be powered by a shaftless propulsion system. The *North Dakota*, as you saw, uses a nuclear reactor to power a traditional steam turbine, which in turn drives a shaft-mounted screw. On the *Sea Arrow*, we've gone to an external drive system, which will be powered directly from the reactor. Each of these two flared pods will contain a permanent high-intensity magnetic motor that drives a pump jet propulsion system.' Eberson smiled. 'Aside from drastically reducing noise, the design frees up a tremendous amount of interior space, which has allowed us to shrink the vessel's overall size.'

'What are these permanent magnet motors?'

'They're an evolutionary, if not revolutionary, advance in the electric motor, made possible by recent breakthroughs in material sciences. A mix of rare mineral elements is synthesized to create extremely powerful magnets, which are then wound into high-performance, direct-current motors. We've invested a great deal of research in perfecting these motors – and believe they will revolutionize the way our future warships are powered.'

The President peered through a baffle on one of the pods and saw light shine through from above.

'It looks empty inside.'

'We haven't actually received and installed the motors yet. The first is due in next week from the Navy's research lab in Chesapeake, Maryland.'

'You sure they're going to work?'

'While we haven't fielded motors of this size, we are confident from our lab tests that they will provide the predicted levels of performance.'

The President ducked beneath one of the extended stabilizers, then glanced up at a pair of barrel-shaped protrusions fore and aft of the conning tower.

Eberson followed in his steps, narrating as he walked.

'The wing-shaped extensions are retractable stabilizers for high-speed operations. They automatically withdraw into the hull when speeds drop below ten knots. The tube-shaped box is a torpedo canister, capable of holding four fish on each stabilizer. The canisters can be reloaded quickly when the stabilizer is retracted into the hull.'

Eberson pointed to the two barrel-shaped objects above them. 'Those are subsurface Gatling guns. They're similar to those used on surface ships, which shoot depleted uranium pellets at rapid fire for last-ditch missile protection. Ours have been developed to fire underwater, using compressed air, for last-ditch torpedo suppression. Of course, we're banking that most enemy torpedoes will never come near us.'

He followed the President as he stepped toward the hull.

'The conning tower, you'll note, is of a slipstream design to accommodate high speed.'

'Doesn't look like she'll allow for much of a periscope.'

'The *Sea Arrow* doesn't actually have a periscope, at least not in the traditional sense,' Eberson said. 'She utilizes an ROV-type video camera that is deployed on a tethered fiber-optic cable. It can be released from a depth of eight hundred feet to give the crew a high-definition picture of what's going on on the surface.'

The President continued on to the tapered bow and

reached up to stroke one of the small tubes that jutted forward like a thin lance. 'And this?'

'That's the key link that will really make her go,' Eberson said. 'It's a secondary upgrade we hope to implement, based on a technological breakthrough from one of our contractors in California –'

Admiral Winters cut him off. 'Mr President, why don't we take a quick tour aboard, then we have a short presentation to show you that should answer all your questions.'

'Very well, Admiral. Though I'm still waiting for my drink.'

The admiral hustled the group through a quick tour of the interior, where they found a streamlined interior that contrasted with the *North Dakota* in its sleek modernity and scale of automated systems. The Commander-in-Chief remained silent as he viewed the high-tech command center, the small number of plush crew's quarters, and the odd assortment of padded seats with full safety harnesses that were positioned about the vessel.

After the tour, the President was led to a secure conference room, where he was finally given a cold drink. His normally jovial demeanor had turned hard, echoed by his aide Cerny.

'All right, gentlemen,' the President bellowed. 'What exactly is going on here? I see much more than some test platform for new technologies. That's a seaworthy vessel on the verge of launch.'

'Sir,' the admiral said, clearing his throat. 'What we possess with the *Sea Arrow* is a complete game changer. As you know, there has been a recent surge in the threat to our naval forces. The Iranians have acquired a host of new subsea technologies from the Russians and are working feverishly to add to their fleet of Kilo class subs. The Russians themselves have dramatically kicked up their shipbuilding efforts, with the help of oil revenues, to replace their aging fleet. And, of course, we have the Chinese. While they continue to claim their military expansion is strictly for defensive purposes, it's no secret that they've been rapidly expanding their blue-water fleet. Sources expect their Type 097 nuclear sub to go operational any day. That all makes for growing threats in the Pacific, the Atlantic, and the Persian Gulf.'

The admiral looked the President in the eye and gave him a grim smile. 'On our side of the ledger, we have a continually shrinking fleet as the cost of each new deployed vessel skyrockets. At a cost of over two billion dollars each, we all know there's just a limited number of Virginia class subs that can be squeezed out of an ever-tightening budget.'

'The national debt is still out of control,' the President said, 'so the Navy will have to take its medicine, just like everybody else.'

'Precisely, sir. Which brings us to the *Sea Arrow*. Eliminating the lengthy research-to-production cycle and piggybacking on some economies of scale with the Virginia program allowed us to construct her at a fraction of the *North Dakota*'s cost. As you can see, she has been built in utmost secrecy. We intentionally built her alongside the *Dakota* to divert attention and allow for delivery of components without suspicion. We hope to secretly launch her for sea trials when the *North Dakota* is publicly commissioned.'

The President frowned. 'You've done a splendid job of keeping her under wraps so far.'

'Thank you, sir. As Dr Eberson mentioned, what we have before you is the most technically advanced submarine ever built. The shaftless propulsion drive, the external torpedo tubes, and the torpedo suppression system are all state-of-the-art technologies. But there's an additional element to her design that truly sets her apart.'

Eberson had already loaded a disk into a projection player.

On a whiteboard, video footage appeared of the open stern of a small boat bobbing about a mountain lake. Two men lifted a bright yellow torpedo-shaped device from the deck and placed it over the side. The President could see by its winged appendages that it was a mock-up of the *Sea Arrow*, operated by remote control.

'That is a scale model,' Eberson said. 'She was built to the exact configuration and uses the same type of propulsion system.'

As the model was launched, the image switched to an onboard camera view. A row of tracking meters superimposed at the bottom of the screen indicated the model's speed, depth, pitch, and roll.

The model submerged a short depth into sage green waters and began accelerating. A flurry of lake sediments rushed past the camera as the tiny submersible gained speed. Suddenly, a surge of small bubbles filled the screen, obscuring the image. The video remained a snowy blur as the model continued to accelerate. The President's mouth dropped as he watched the speed gauge roll into triple digits. Eventually the model slowed and returned to the surface, where it was retrieved before the video clip ended.

Silence filled the room for a moment before the President spoke in a low voice. 'Am I to understand that this model attained an underwater speed of one hundred and fifty miles per hour?'

'No, sir,' Eberson replied with a smile. 'She attained a speed of one hundred and fifty knots, which would be on the order of one hundred and seventy-two miles per hour.'

'That's impossible. I've been told naval propulsion technologies can't get past seventy or eighty knots. Even the *North Dakota* only manages thirty-five.'

'Didn't the Russians develop some kind of torpedo that can run over a hundred knots?' Cerny asked.

'Yes, they have the *Shkval*,' Eberson said, 'which is a high-speed, rocket-powered torpedo. A similar principle is in play with the *Sea Arrow*. It's not the propulsion that allows the high rate of speed but rather supercavitation.'

'Forgive my lack of engineering know-how,' the President said, 'but doesn't supercavitation have to do with disturbances in the water?'

'Yes. In the case here, it involves creating a gas bubble around the object traveling underwater. The bubble frees up the water's drag, allowing for much higher speeds. The array of tubes on the *Sea Arrow*'s prow will be part of the supercavitation system we hope to deploy. Combined with the high-power magnetic motors, we fully expect to match those kinds of speeds – without the range limitations the Russians have with their rocket torpedoes.'

'Perhaps,' Cerny said, 'but there's a substantial difference between a torpedo and a two-hundred-foot submarine.'

'The differences mostly come in the way of control at high speeds,' Eberson said. 'The *Sea Arrow*'s Jurassic wings, as the President described them, will aid in providing stability. The supercavitation system itself will more directly affect control by manipulating the size and shape of the gas bubble. It's an untested theory on a vessel this size, but our supplier of the system is confident in its capability. I will actually be monitoring a final sea trial of their model next week.'

The President sat, rubbing his chin. Finally, he looked at the admiral with a knowing gaze. 'Admiral, if she works as advertised, what exactly does it mean?'

'The *Sea Arrow* will put us twenty years ahead of our nearest adversary. The Chinese, Russian, and Iranian buildup will be effectively neutralized. We'll have a weapon at our disposal that is nearly invulnerable. And with just a handful of *Sea Arrow*s, we'll be able to defend every corner of the globe on almost immediate notice. What it really means, sir, is that we won't have to worry about the safety of the seas for the balance of our lifetimes.'

The President nodded. The heat and humidity seemed to disappear from the room, and, for the first time all day, he smiled.

3

The customary Southern Californian early-morning gloom hung over the marina, the air damp with a misty drizzle. Joe Eberson hoisted himself from behind the wheel of a rental car and eyed the parking lot, then moved to the trunk, retrieving a tackle box and fishing rod. Both had been purchased the night before, shortly after his flight from the East Coast landed at San Diego's Lindbergh Field. Flipping on a battered bucket hat, he ambled into the sprawling marina at Shelter Island.

Eberson ignored the buzz of an E-2 Hawkeye surveillance plane taking off from the Coronado Naval Air Station across the harbor as he made his way past dozens of small sailboats and powerboats. The playthings of weekend hobbyists, Eberson rightly suspected, most of these pleasure boats seldom left their slips. Spotting a forty-foot cabin cruiser with a large open rear deck, he stepped alongside. The boat was pushing its fifth decade, but its gleaming white hull and polished brightwork revealed an owner who had long provided it loving care. A gurgle from the stern indicated the engine was already warming at idle.

'Joe, there you are,' said a man who stepped from the cabin. 'We were almost ready to leave without you.'

With his slight build, thick glasses, and white hair worn in a flattop, Dr Carl Heiland looked every bit the electrical engineer. His eyes danced and he grinned easily, exhibiting a near-constant state of high energy even at six in the morning.

Short on sleep and exhausted from his cross-country flight, Eberson oozed the opposite sentiment. He gingerly climbed aboard and shook hands.

'Sorry I'm late, Doctor,' Eberson said, suppressing a yawn. 'I took a wrong turn out of the hotel and didn't realize it until I pulled up to SeaWorld. I think even Shamu was still asleep.'

'It gave me time to get everything aboard.' Heiland nodded toward a mixed box of crates strapped to the bulwarks. 'Here, let's stow your tackle next to our gear.' He reached for Eberson's fishing rod, then caught a glimpse of his hat. He burst out laughing.

'You angling for brook trout today?'

Eberson pulled off his hat and examined the worn crown. A scattered band of brightly colored freshwater fishing flies encircled it. 'You did say fishing attire.'

'I doubt anybody else noticed,' Heiland snorted, then called into the cabin, 'Manny, go ahead and take us out.'

A dark-skinned man in cutoffs appeared and untied the deck lines. Moments later, he was behind the wheel, piloting the boat into horseshoe-shaped San Diego Harbor. They dodged an incoming Navy amphibious ship before clearing the channel and entering the Pacific. Manny kicked up the throttle and set a course to the southwest, rolling through a light swell stirred by an onshore breeze. Soon Eberson begin to feel queasy, and he ducked past Manny to grab a seat in the main cabin.

Heiland poured him a mug of coffee and joined him at

the galley table. 'So tell me, Joe, how are things back in Arlington?'

'As you know, we just spilled the beans to the President. Nevertheless, we're under the usual squeeze of trying to accomplish more with fewer resources. We'll be lucky to avoid a big budget reduction next year, I'm afraid.'

'I figured it was only a matter of time before the ax fell in our direction. Glad I've got five years' worth of work under contract.'

'You needn't worry, Carl. Your firm's work is of utmost importance. As a matter of fact, I've got approval to proceed with the Block Two retroactive upgrade – if you can prove operational ability. I assume that's why you called me out here on short notice?'

Heiland gave him a cagey look. 'That's some riverboat gambling on your part. You haven't even field-tested the Block One system yet.'

Eberson shook off a bout of nausea to return Heiland's smile. 'Carl, we both know it's going to work.'

'Did you source the propulsion components?'

'Yes, though there are some material issues going forward.' He looked at Heiland with an expectant gaze. 'But we're more interested in the Block Two mods.'

'We've had some similar materials issues, but I think we've made the breakthrough that we've been chasing after.'

Eberson smiled broadly. 'That's why I jumped on the first plane from Washington. I know you like to keep things light and tight.'

'Given the secure nature of the project, I don't like to draw attention to our field tests. Seemed to work for Block

One, so that's why we're just keeping it to a little fishing trip today.' He looked again at Eberson's hat and smiled.

'We've done our best to keep a lid on things at our end. Of course, you haven't exactly given us much in the way of specs.'

'The fewer eyes around, the better.'

Eberson took a swallow of coffee, then leaned across the table.

'Do you think we can really get to the theoretically predicted levels?'

Heiland nodded, his eyes sparkling. 'We'll find out shortly.'

A few minutes later, Manny cut the motor, signaling they had arrived at their test site. They had crossed into Mexican waters, almost twenty miles from shore and well off the path of the average San Diego day sailor. The water was too deep to anchor, so the boat drifted while Heiland went to work.

Ignoring a long rectangular case strapped to the bulwarks, he opened several smaller cases that contained a pair of laptops, some cabling, and connectors. Setting the computers on a low bench, he knelt and began configuring them.

Manny poked his head out from the wheelhouse. 'Doc, there's a freighter coming up on us.'

Heiland glanced over his shoulder. 'She'll be well past us by the time we're ready to go.' He returned his attention to the computers.

Eberson took a seat on the large crate and watched the ship approach. A midsized freighter, it seemed of recent build, by its streamlined design and lack of rust. Dark gray in color, the ship almost had a Navy look about it. The bridge windows caught Eberson's attention. Tinted black, they gave off an odd, almost menacing look.

A few crewmen in coveralls on the main deck worked behind a large container. As the ship drew closer, he could see they were adjusting a large dish-shaped object mounted on a platform amidships. The dish was painted a drab green and turned toward the sea, rising several feet into the air like a hardened sail. The men on deck soon disappeared, and Eberson noted the ship seemed to be slowing.

'Carl, I'm not sure about this ship.' He rose uncomfortably to his feet.

'We've got nothing for them to see,' Heiland said. 'Why don't you pick up a rod and make like you're here to catch a tuna.'

Eberson grabbed one of the boat's rods from a rack and cast a weighted hook over the side, not bothering with any bait lest he actually have to fight a beast from the deep. As the freighter pulled alongside a short distance away, he tossed a friendly wave toward the blacked-out bridge.

A burning pain shot through his hand, quickly tracking down his arm to his torso. He dropped his arm and shook it, but the sensation was already spreading across his body. In seconds, it felt like a thousand red ants were biting his flesh. The fire shot to his head, where his eyes seemed to boil in their sockets.

'Carl –' he cried. The words came out in a raspy gurgle.

Heiland felt the same burning sensation on his back. Spinning around, he processed two scenes at once. One was the dying Joe Eberson, still clutching the fishing rod

38

as he fell to the deck, his skin glowing scarlet. The other was the freighter's shield-like device, directed at him from a few dozen yards away.

Ignoring the burning that seared through his body, he staggered to the cabin. Manny was already on the deck, gasping a last breath as blood dribbled from his nose and ears. Heiland stepped past his longtime friend as his own pain became amplified. His entire body felt inflamed. Somewhere in his consciousness, he wondered why his skin wasn't falling off in chunks. A single urge drove him forward as he lurched to the pilot's seat. His head felt like it was going to explode as he reached under the console, his burning fingers grasping a pair of hidden toggles. He tripped them both, then took his last breath.

4

'Are you going to get wet with me?'

Loren Smith-Pitt stared at her husband. Just seconds ago, it seemed, he had risen from the pilot's seat and tossed an anchor over the side of their rented speedboat. Yet now he sat on the transom, clad in wet suit and dive tank, anxious to explore the depths below. Loren could only marvel at how the sea acted like a magnet to the man, drawing him in with an unseen force.

'I think I'll stay here and enjoy the sunshine and the clear Chilean sky,' she said. 'With Congress back in session on Monday, I could use a healthy dose of fresh air.'

'For Capitol Hill, earplugs might be a better choice.'

Loren ignored her husband's quip. A congresswoman from Colorado, Loren was only too happy to escape the partisan bickering of Washington, if only for a few days. Free from the pressures of work and an intrusive media, she felt more relaxed in another country. Dressed in a skimpy two-piece bathing suit she would never wear at home, she flaunted her curvaceous but firm body, kept trim through yoga and daily runs on a treadmill.

Stretching across the boat's bench seat, she hung a leg over the side and dipped her toes in the water. 'Yikes! That water is cold. I'm going to stay warm and dry up here, thank you very much.'

'I won't be gone long.' Her husband stuck a regulator

between his teeth, stared admiringly at his wife for a moment, then fell backward into the blue Pacific. He playfully kicked a spray of water onto his wife with a fin before he disappeared under the surface.

Toweling herself off, Loren tracked her husband's air bubbles for a few minutes, then gazed across the horizon. The afternoon air was crystal clear, the sapphire sky nearly matching the color of the ocean. They'd anchored the red speedboat a half mile off the Chilean coast, opposite a small beach called Playa Caleta Abarca.

A towering Sheraton Hotel stood on a rock cliff nearby, its outdoor pool crowded with sun-worshiping tourists. A short distance to the south lay Valparaiso, Chile's colorful and historic seaport long known by sailors as the 'Jewel of the Pacific'. Ancient buildings climbed the steep hills ringing the city, reminding Loren of San Francisco. She noted a large white cruise ship, the *Sea Splendour*, anchored in the bay, shuttling passengers ashore to visit the beaches of Viña del Mar or to trek to Chile's capital city of Santiago, sixty miles southeast.

A gentle swell rocked the speedboat as Loren turned her gaze to sea. A small yellow sailboat passed by, then tacked north toward an approaching freighter, its triangular sail fluttering. She leaned back on the padded seat, closed her eyes, and luxuriated in the warmth of the sun.

Sixty feet beneath her, Dirk Pitt had just shaken the ocean's chill that permeated the country's coastal waters due to the Humboldt Current. His breath rate eased as he slowed his descent. The visibility was good, about forty feet, allowing him clear view of a rocky bottom anchored with thick seaweed. Kicking his fins lazily, he glided over a coral-strewn ledge crowded with brightly colored urchins and starfish. A small school of jack mackerel eyed him for a minute or two, then darted away.

The sea relaxed Pitt in a way nothing else could. To some it was confining, but Pitt found the ocean depths produced in him an odd feeling of release that seemed to heighten his senses. It was an experience born decades ago, when he spent the better part of his youth exploring the coves along the Southern Californian coastline, free diving and bodysurfing. The allure was like that of flying, which had led him to the Air Force Academy and flight school as a young officer.

But the draw of the sea enticed him to leave the flight line and a promising military career to join a newly created federal organization, the National Underwater and Marine Agency. Created to study and protect the world's oceans, NUMA was the perfect home for Pitt, allowing him to work on and beneath the sea, all over the world. After years as its Special Projects Director, he now found himself heading the agency, which only fortified his sense of stewardship of the world's oceans. Loren often joked that she still competed with Pitt's first love, his mistress called the sea.

Pitt's quest for underwater discovery, along with a love of history, had led him to discover dozens of shipwrecks. But this afternoon, the object of his search was considerably smaller. Eyeing a thick ridge of jagged rocks that stretched into deeper water, he swam over and surveyed its crevices. After several minutes, he found what he was looking for. He plunged an arm between two boulders and pulled out a spirited brown spiny lobster that weighed

42

almost five pounds. He eyed its long, waving antennas for a moment and then stuffed the crustacean into a mesh dive bag and began a search for its twin.

Above the noisy rhythm of his regulated breathing, a faint tapping rippled through the water.

He held his breath to hear better. The metallic rapping repeated a familiar cadence – two short raps, two long raps, then two short raps. It wasn't exactly the Morse code distress call of SOS, which used three dots and dashes, but Pitt guessed the intent was the same. He could not determine its direction, only that the source was nearby. It had to be Loren.

He kicked toward the surface, angling for the position of the speedboat. He spotted the anchor line and approached it, swimming hard, surfacing a few yards behind the boat. Loren was leaning over the transom, pounding a spare diver's lead weight on the stern drive housing. Engrossed in her signaling, she didn't notice him emerge.

'What's wrong?' he shouted.

She looked up, and Pitt saw a desperate fear in her eyes. Lost for words, she simply pointed behind him. He spun his head around – and was engulfed in a massive shadow.

It was a ship, a massive bulk carrier, bearing down on them barely a hundred feet away. The speedboat bobbed in the direct path of the ship's broad, high bow, which pushed an ominous mountain of white foamy water in front of it. Pitt cursed the fools on the bridge, who were either blind or asleep.

Without hesitation, he kicked and stroked furiously to the boat until he could reach an arm over the side.

'Should I start the motor?' Loren's face was drawn. 'I was afraid to try while you were underwater.'

Pitt saw the anchor line was still set, running up into a small locker on the bow. Behind him, he heard the deep rumble of the ship's engines as its towering hulk advanced. It was too close. Any slip in cutting the anchor line or a delay in starting the motor and their boat would be smashed to bits, with them in it.

With the regulator back between his teeth, he shook his head at Loren and waved for her to come closer.

She hurried to the side and reached to help him aboard.

Instead he reached past her hand and hooked his arm around her waist.

Before she could react, she felt herself being jerked over the side. She yelped as her body hit the cold water. Kicking and floundering, she gasped for a last breath of air. The towering mountain of steel was now just yards away.

Then she was snatched like a rag doll and disappeared beneath the rippling surface.

5

The freighter neither slowed nor turned. Its broad steel hull smacked into the speedboat, severing the anchor line before burying the tiny vessel in the bow's wake. The small boat bounced along the ship's hull and then remarkably popped to the surface, where it bobbed in the freighter's receding wake, its port beam only slightly mangled.

Somewhere beneath the surface, Loren found herself clinging to her husband in a desperate plunge to the seafloor. Startled by the cold-water immersion, she nearly panicked when she felt Pitt yank her to the depths without air. Then she felt him force his regulator into her mouth while wedging her arm around his buoyancy compensator harness. Despite the cold, her nerves began to settle. She began to assist their progress by kicking as well, remembering to clear her ears as they descended deeper.

The shimmering light of the surface water grew dark as the black hull passed over them. Loren glanced up, feeling like she could reach out and touch the barnacle-encrusted plates only a few feet away.

Though they had escaped the mass of the hull, Pitt continued driving deeper with frantic kicks of his fins. His lungs felt like they would burst, which only made him push harder until they finally reached the seabed. Seeing a bus-sized rise of coral, he pulled Loren along its curved side. As their knees touched the hard bottom, he grabbed a nodule for leverage.

Loren realized her husband had not taken a breath of air for almost the entire descent. She quickly passed the regulator to his lips. Her pulse racing and her eyes wide, she peered into Pitt's face mask. He gazed back at her calmly and winked, as if cheating death was a daily occurrence.

Pitt gratefully inhaled several deep breaths, then passed the regulator back to Loren and gazed upward. The hull was still sweeping past, while the main source of his fear, its churning bronze propeller, glinted as it drew near. Pitt threw his arms around Loren and gripped the coral mound with his gloved hands as the stern passed overhead. Even from thirty feet away, Pitt felt the suction from the enormous blades as they cut through the water. Sand swirled about them as they were tugged from the bottom. Then the ship passed, and a wash of sediment rained down upon them. Pitt released his grasp on the coral and kicked to the surface with Loren entwined around him. Their heads popped into the bright sunlight, and they eagerly inhaled the warm, fresh air.

'I thought for a second,' Loren said between gasps, 'that you were going to kill me before the ship had the chance.'

'Ducking under seemed the more prudent tack.' Pitt gazed at the stern of the receding freighter noting its name, *Tasmanian Star*.

Loren pivoted in the opposite direction and scanned the sea as she treaded water beside him.

'They ran right over a sailboat,' she said, scanning the

water for survivors. 'It looked like an older couple. I could tell we were next in its path.'

'Quick thinking on your part saved us both, though your Morse code could use a little improvement.' Pitt joined her in searching the nearby waters, but neither spotted any debris.

'We can report it to the police once we get ashore,' Loren said. 'They'll catch up with the crew in Valparaiso.'

Pitt turned toward the coastline and was surprised to see their red speedboat bobbing a short distance away. A section of the port hull hung loose, and the boat sat low in the water, but it was still afloat. Pitt stroked over with Loren close behind. He bellied over the side, then pulled her aboard.

'Our clothes and lunch are gone,' she noted, shivering as the sun began to dry her body.

'My lobster, too,' Pitt said.

He stripped off his tank and wet suit, then stepped to the boat's console. The key was still in the ignition, so he tried pushing the starter. The motor ground over several times, then sputtered to life, as the inboard compartment had remained mostly dry during the boat's immersion. Easing the throttle forward, he glanced ahead at the fleeing freighter.

The *Tasmanian Star* was still proceeding on its same heading and apparent speed. Another mile or two ahead lay the harbor of Valparaiso, which curved to the west in the shape of an open bowl. The commercial port facilities were at the west end, yet the freighter was sailing toward the east. Pitt tensed as he tracked the ship's path, then jammed the throttle to its stops.

With its bilge and cockpit filled with water, the speedboat faltered as it tried to accelerate, but it gradually surged forward, gaining speed.

Loren abandoned her efforts to bail water with a seat cushion and approached her husband. She saw a heightened intensity in his deep green eyes.

'Why aren't we headed to shore?'

Pitt pointed at the freighter. 'Look what's ahead of her.'

Loren peered past the bulk carrier. The large white cruise ship was still anchored in the harbor – and lay exactly perpendicular to the oncoming freighter. If the *Tasmanian Star* didn't change course, she would barrel right into the *Sea Splendour*.

'Dirk, there's probably a thousand people aboard that ship.'

'If there's something more than just a nearsighted helmsman driving the *Tasmanian Star*, hundreds could die.'

Loren grabbed Pitt's shoulder as the speedboat lurched over a wave. The damaged boat surged and wallowed before finding its legs. The bilge pump caught up with the accumulated water, allowing the boat to rise higher as it gained speed. The damage was all above the waterline, so Pitt had no trouble controlling the boat as it bulled its way past twenty knots, quickly gaining on the freighter.

'Can we alert the cruise ship?' Loren yelled to be heard over the straining engine.

Pitt shook his head. 'We have no radio. And the ship is anchored. There's no way they can move in time.'

'At least we could warn the passengers.'

Pitt simply nodded. That would be a tall order in the scant time available.

As they drew near the freighter's stern, he considered his few options. There were no other boats nearby, so a radio warning was impossible. Pitt's immediate thought was to try to board the moving ship. But as he pulled closer, he discarded the notion. There was no easy access, and even if he could somehow find a way aboard, he probably wouldn't make it to the bridge in time. The sparkling white cruise ship lay dead ahead, barely a half mile away.

Pitt held down the button on the speedboat's air horn as they ran past the ship's port flank and shot past its bow. Loren jumped and waved at the forecastle, but there was no response. The *Tasmanian Star* neither slowed nor altered course, simply plodding ahead on its catastrophic heading. Pitt glanced at the bridge, but could see no moving figures behind the glass windows. By all appearances, it was a ghost ship out of control.

Pitt urgently scanned the surrounding waters for assistance, but there was none to be had. A handful of vessels clustered about the commercial port, a mile or so southwest, but the waters ahead were empty all the way to the curling beachfront. Empty but for the towering mass of the anchored *Sea Splendour*.

Crowding together on its upper deck, passengers pointed and waved at the approaching freighter. No doubt the helm watch had reported the approaching vessel, and the liner's captain was furiously hailing the *Tasmanian Star* by radio. But the rogue vessel responded with silence.

On the speedboat, Pitt surveyed the length of the bulk carrier. At its stern it rode strangely high in the water.

A look of determination was etched on his lean, rugged face. In times of crisis, his mind seemed to work in overdrive, processing all facets at play before calmly pursuing a course of action. With few options, Pitt's response came quickly.

Spinning the wheel hard over, he cut across the freighter's bow and held the turn until he was running alongside the ship's starboard side.

'Loren, put on my wet suit.'

'What are we going to do?'

'Try and nudge this behemoth out of the way.'

'In this little boat? That's impossible.'

Pitt squinted at the ship in resolve. 'Not if we hit her where it counts.'

6

Panic had broken out on the *Sea Splendour* as screaming passengers alerted one another of the impending collision. Parents grabbed their children and ran to the opposite side of the ship, while others scrambled up companionways to reach the upper decks. Even the crew joined the passengers in fleeing the anticipated point of impact.

By chance or design, the *Tasmanian Star* was aimed toward the heart of the cruise liner. At roughly the same size, the blunt-nosed freighter churned with sufficient momentum to split the passenger ship in two.

On the *Sea Splendour*'s bridge, Captain Alphonse Franco had few options. He desperately tried to finesse the vessel aside but had only auxiliary power available, as its main engines sat cold. He slipped the anchor line and engaged the ship's side thrusters in hope of pivoting the ship clear.

But staring at the oncoming vessel, Franco knew it was too late. 'Turn away, for God's sake, turn away!' he cried under his breath.

Few on the bridge paid attention to him, as a flurry of distress calls and emergency procedures occupied the panicked crew. The captain stood immobile, fixated on the approaching freighter as if he could stare it down.

His gaze was diverted by a small red speedboat that bounded over the waves toward the stern quarter of the freighter. A tall, lean man with black hair stood at the wheel beside a woman dressed in an oversized wet suit. They were on their own high-speed collision course with the *Tasmanian Star* in what only could be viewed as an attempt at suicide.

'Insanity,' Franco said, shaking his head. 'Pure insanity.'

Pitt pulled back the throttle for an instant, causing the boat to falter, then turned to Loren. 'Jump!'

Loren squeezed his arm, stepped off the seat, and leaped over the side. She was still in midair when Pitt slammed the throttle forward and the speedboat burst away. Bobbing to the surface after a hard splash, Loren watched the boat roar off, praying her husband wouldn't kill himself trying to save others.

Pitt knew he'd have only one chance to pull off a miracle. The freighter was just a quarter of a mile from the *Sea Splendour* – no room for error. Taking aim for the freighter's stern, he braced for impact.

The *Tasmanian Star*'s aft deck hung over the water, its stern hull curving inward to the waterline. That was where Pitt aimed the speedboat. Closing quickly, he spotted the rudder's upper spindle mounting – exposed at the surface. He tweaked the steering wheel to adjust his aim. Inboard of the spindle was the ship's churning propeller. It could easily devour both him and the speedboat.

Had the carrier been fully loaded, his ploy could never have worked. But the ship rode high at the stern, so he had a chance. Aiming a few feet left of the spindle, he braced himself and drove the boat in at top speed.

With a hammering bash, the speedboat's red hull

smacked the freighter's rudder, smashing into the steering plate's outer edge. The small boat's momentum propelled its stern up and out of the water until it was nearly on end. Pitt flew up out of the cockpit but kept his grip on the wheel as the boat fell back. Again the craft slammed into the rudder, this time from above, mangling the spindle and slightly bending the top plate.

Its hull shattered, the little red speedboat slid off the rudder, and its inboard motor gurgled to a halt. The freighter's churning wake swept the boat aside – and the big ship sailed on.

Pitt grabbed a shin that had split open on the windshield, but otherwise he found himself uninjured. A moment later, Loren swam up and pulled herself aboard the slowly sinking boat.

'Are you all right?' she asked. 'That was *some* collision.'

'I'm fine.' He tore off his T-shirt and wrapped it around his bloodied leg. 'I'm just not sure if it did any good.'

He watched the imposing shape of the freighter as it churned closer to the cruise ship. At first, there was no apparent change in its heading. But then, almost imperceptibly, the bow of the *Tasmanian Star* began to inch to port.

When Pitt had rammed her rudder, mashing it twenty degrees over, the ship's automatic pilot had attempted to correct course. But the secondary impact from the speedboat arrived first, mashing the spindle and wedging the rudder in place. Try as they might, the automated bridge controls could not override the damage. Pitt had knocked the freighter off its course. But would it be enough?

On board the *Sea Splendour*, Captain Franco detected

the change. 'She's turning!' Franco's eyes focused on the narrowing gap. 'She's turning.'

Inch by inch, foot by foot, then yard by yard, the freighter's bow began to ease toward shore. Hopeful eyes aboard the *Sea Splendour* prayed that the freighter would pass clear. But the amount of separation between the ships was just too small. There would be no avoiding contact.

A ship's horn bellowed as the crew and passengers braced for impact. The *Tasmanian Star* sped closer, seemingly intent on ramming the liner's starboard quarter. Yet at the last instant, the freighter's high prow swung clear of a crushing blow, easing just beyond the *Sea Splendour*'s stern post. Twenty feet of the cargo ship's bow slipped past before the first grinding squeal of scraping metal.

The freighter shuddered as it ground against an over-hanging section of the *Sea Splendour*'s fantail. The massive ship never slowed, bulling forward as it was sprayed with shredded steel. As suddenly as it struck, the carrier pulled clear, angling off toward shore. Still steaming at better than twelve knots, the cargo ship now carried a twenty-foot section of the *Sea Splendour*'s afterdeck wedged atop its forward hold.

The cruise ship had keeled hard to port at impact but slowly righted itself. Her captain stood in disbelief. The reports being radioed to the bridge cited only minor structural damage. The fantail had been cleared of passengers, and not a single injury was reported. By the barest of margins, they'd avoided disaster.

At the realization his ship had survived and no lives were lost, the captain let relief turn to anger. 'Prepare to lower the officer's launch,' he told a nearby crewman. 'After I survey the damage, I'm going to go deck that clown – the second he steps ashore.'

He had failed to track the *Tasmanian Star*, assuming it would eventually slow and turn toward Valparaiso's commercial port. But the freighter didn't alter course; it sailed on toward a thin sandy beach along the town's waterfront.

A middle-aged Canadian couple, who had consumed a bit too much local Chardonnay at lunch, was dozing on the sand when the *Tasmanian Star* touched bottom a few yards off the surf line. A deep chafing sound, like an enormous coffee grinder, filled the air as its hull scoured the bottom. The prow cut easily through the soft sand before its momentum began to slow. The ship burrowed through the beach, leveling a small ice cream stand whose owner wisely fled.

As the ghost ship groaned to a halt, nearby onlookers stared in disbelief. Only the moan of its engines and still-churning propeller gave sign of any life aboard the stricken vessel.

Hearing the noise and detecting a shadow cross his body, the dosing Canadian, his eyes still closed, nudged his wife. 'Honey, what was that?'

She opened a sleepy eye, then sat upright. Ten feet away rose the towering slab side of the freighter's hull. They had come that close to being crushed.

'Harold –' She blinked and looked again. 'I think our ship has come in.'

7

Captain Franco's face was beet red as he surveyed the *Sea Splendour*'s damaged stern from an enclosed launch. Yet the destruction was much less than he feared; the shredded fantail showed primarily cosmetic damage. Divers would examine below the waterline, but by all accounts, the crew could handle the damage. They would barricade the aft deck, and the ship could continue its voyage with only minimal delay. Franco well knew the wrath he'd receive from the corporate offices if the passengers had to be put ashore and their fares refunded. Thankfully, that was one lesser tragedy averted. But to him the ship was like a family member, and he burned with fury at the disfigurement.

'Take us to the freighter,' he told the launch's young pilot.

A deck officer motioned for the captain's attention.

'Sir, a small boat appears to be in distress off our starboard beam.'

Captain Franco leaned out the open entryway. There was the red speedboat, drifting half submerged. The couple was not only still alive but sitting on the bow and waving at him.

'That's the nut who rammed his boat into the carrier.' He shook his head. 'Go ahead, go pick them up.'

The launch pulled alongside the sinking boat. Pitt

helped Loren onto the launch, then jumped aboard. He turned and watched the battered speedboat a moment before it slipped under the surface.

He turned to face the frowning captain. 'I guess I'm going to have to buy someone a new boat.'

Franco took a long look at Pitt; he wasn't a young fool – or a drunk. He was tall, with a lean, muscular body. Despite the bloody gash to his shin, he stood upright with an easy confidence. His face was rugged, showing years spent outdoors, and he grinned in easy bemusement. Then there were the eyes, a beguiling green that burned with intelligence.

'Thanks for the rescue,' Pitt said, 'you saved us a healthy swim to shore.'

'I watched you destroy your own boat running into the freighter,' Franco said. 'Why did you nearly kill yourself?'

'To knock the rudder over.' Pitt gazed toward the cruise ship's damaged stern. 'Guess I didn't get there quite in time.'

The captain's face turned white. 'My heavens, of course. It was you who changed the freighter's course at the last second.'

He grasped Pitt's hand and shook it until Pitt's arm almost fell off. 'You saved my ship and hundreds of lives. We had no time to maneuver – we would have been mauled by that idiot.'

'He ran over a sailboat, and nearly got us as well.'

'Madmen! They ignored our radio calls and just kept on coming. Look, they've run aground.'

'The bridge crew must be incapacitated,' Pitt said.

'They will be when I'm through with them.'

The launch picked up speed and raced toward the grounded ship, steering well clear of its still-spinning prop. A crowd had gathered on the beach to gawk, while distant sirens signaled the approach of the Valparaiso police.

The ship sat upright, with just a slight list to starboard. Her decks showed no sign of life. A long metal conveyor ramp dangled over the side like a damaged limb, nearly reaching the water. Used to fill and unload the freighter's holds, the conveyor had been knocked ajar during the collision with the *Sea Splendour*. Franco saw it offered a way aboard, and he ordered the launch alongside.

The ramp just about matched the launch's deck height. A seaman was ordered to walk on it to test if it would hold. The man took a few tentative steps, then turned and gave the captain the thumbs-up. He scampered up the heavy conveyor belt, which tilted across the ship's rail, and hopped onto the deck. Captain Franco came next, nervously climbing on the dust-covered belt and making his way up. Too absorbed in keeping his footing, he failed to notice Pitt following a few paces behind.

Franco reached the ship's rail and was helped down by the waiting seaman. He was startled when Pitt jumped off the belt and landed beside him. Franco turned to admonish him for coming aboard, but Pitt beat him to the punch.

'We better get those engines shut down.' Pitt nudged past Franco and headed toward the bridge.

Franco vented at the seaman. 'Search the deck and crew's quarters, then meet me on the bridge.' He turned and hurried to catch up with Pitt.

The bridge sat atop a multistory superstructure near

the stern. Stepping aft, Pitt gazed at the large hatches that covered the ship's five main holds. The last one was partially open. Each hatch had two hinged covers that opened to the side hydraulically. As Pitt approached the hatch just ahead of the superstructure, he peered through the gap. The cavernous hold was empty except for a tiny bulldozer sitting under a layer of silver-colored dust. Pitt guessed the forward holds still contained their cargo, which would account for the high-riding stern. Noticing fragments of silver rock on the deck, he pocketed a large piece in his swim trunks and continued toward the bridge.

'Is there no one aboard this vessel?' Franco reached Pitt as he started up a companionway.

'I haven't seen a welcome committee yet.'

They climbed several flights, then entered the bridge through an open wing door. Like the rest of the ship, the expansive control room was empty of life. The ghostly sense was broken by the ship's radio, which squawked with the voice of a Chilean Coast Guard operator hailing the vessel. Franco shut off the radio, then stepped to a center console and powered down the engines.

Pitt examined the helm. 'The autopilot was set on a course of one hundred and forty-two degrees.'

'Makes no sense that they would abandon a moving ship.'

'Piracy is a more likely answer,' Pitt said. 'The number five hold looks like it was emptied after she left port.'

'Taking the crew for ransom, I could see,' Franco said, rubbing his chin. 'But robbing a bulk carrier of its cargo at sea? That's unheard of.'

The captain noticed a dark splotch on the wall and

similar stains on the floor – and his face turned pale. 'Look at this.'

One glance at the stains told Pitt they were dried blood. When he rubbed a finger across the wall, the dry residue flaked off.

'Doesn't look recent. Can we backtrack the ship's navigation system to see where they came from?'

Franco stepped to the helm, glad to distance himself from the gore. He located a navigation monitor, which showed a tiny representation of the *Tasmanian Star* overlaid on a digital map of Valparaiso Harbor. He tapped on an embedded keyboard and reduced the scale. A yellow line traced the ship's path off the top of the screen as Valparaiso receded into the coastline of Chile, which gradually receded into the continent of South America. The slightly angular line continued north before cutting sharply left off the west coast of Central America. Franco tracked the line across the Pacific, locating its origin in Australia.

'She came from Perth.' Then he zeroed back in on the point where the ship changed heading. He looked up at Pitt and nodded.

'Your assumption of piracy makes sense. She wouldn't be crossing the Pacific with one of her holds empty.'

'Let's see where that course change occurred,' Pitt said.

Franco adjusted the image. 'Looks to be about seventeen hundred miles due west of Costa Rica.'

'A lonely spot in the ocean to stage a holdup.'

Franco shook his head. 'If that's where the crew left the ship, then the *Tasmanian Star* sailed herself over thirty-five hundred miles to Valparaiso.'

'Which means she was hijacked more than a week ago. That leaves a pretty cold trail to follow.'

Franco's crewman suddenly burst through the bridge wing door. His face was flush, and he panted from sprinting up the companionway. Pitt noticed his hand trembled on the doorframe.

'The crew quarters are empty, sir. There doesn't seem to be anyone aboard.' He hesitated. 'I did find one man.'

'Dead?' the captain asked.

The sailor nodded. 'I wouldn't have found him but for the odor. He's on the main deck, near the forward hatch.'

'Take me to him.'

Slowly the seaman turned and led Franco and Pitt down the companionway. They crossed the deck to the port side and marched past the rows of hatch covers. The seaman slowed as they approached the forward hatch, then stopped and pointed.

'He's beneath one of the supporting braces,' the man said, not moving any closer. 'He must have rolled or fallen there.'

Pitt and Franco stepped forward. Then they noticed a blue object wedged in the hatch cover's hydraulics, next to a supporting brace. Inching closer, they could see it was the body of a man dressed in blue coveralls. The odor of decomposing flesh was overpowering, but the sight before them was even worse.

The clothes were unmarked and perfectly clean. Judging by the heavy work boots and a pair of gloves cinched to his waist, Pitt guessed he was an ordinary seaman. But that was the only thing he could determine.

The exposed skin had bloated to grotesque proportions

61

and turned the color of French mustard. Small rivulets of dried blood had pooled around his ears and mouth. A swarm of flies buzzed around the seaman's face and clustered on his open, bulging eyes. Yet it was the body's extremities, marked beyond mere decomposition, that was most grisly. The seaman's ears, nose, and fingertips were charred black, though the skin remained unbroken. Pitt recalled photos of polar explorers who had suffered extreme frostbite, marked by black blisters covering patches of dead skin. Yet the *Tasmanian Star* had sailed nowhere near any polar region.

Franco slowly backed away from the figure.

'*Santa Maria!*' he gasped. 'He's been taken by the devil himself.'

8

A scratched and battered crash helmet sat centered on Pitt's desk when he returned to his office in Washington. A short, typewriten note taped on the visor welcomed him back:

> *Dad,*
> *Really, you need to be more careful!*

Pitt chuckled as he slid the helmet aside, wondering if it came from his son or his daughter. Both children worked for NUMA and had just left for a project off Madagascar involving subsea tectonics.

There was a rap at his office door and in walked a voluptuous woman with perfect hair and makeup. Although Zerri Pochinsky was north of forty, her looks gave no hint of it. Pitt's trusted secretary for many years, she might have become something more in his life if he hadn't met Loren first.

'Welcome back to the lion's den.' She smiled and placed a cup of coffee on his desk. 'I honestly don't know how that helmet got here.'

Pitt returned her smile. 'There's just no sanctity to my inner sanctum.'

'I received a call from the Vice President's secretary,' Pochinsky said, her hazel eyes turning serious. 'You've been asked to attend a meeting in his office today at two-thirty.'

'Any mention of the topic?'

'No, they simply indicated it was a security matter.'

'What in Washington isn't?' He shook his head with annoyance. 'Okay, tell them I'll be there.'

'Also, Hiram is outside. He said you wanted to see him.'

'Send him in.'

Pochinsky slipped out the door and was replaced by a bearded man with shoulder-length hair. Dressed in jeans, cowboy boots, and a black Allman Brothers Band T-shirt, Hiram Yaeger looked like he was headed to a biker bar. Only the intense blue eyes behind a pair of granny glasses revealed a deeper intellectual pursuit. Far from a road-house barfly, Yaeger was in fact a computer genius whose greatest love was writing software code. Managing NUMA's state-of-the-art computer resource center, he had built a sophisticated network that collected detailed oceanographic data from a thousand points around the globe.

'So, the savior of the mighty *Sea Splendour* has returned.' He plopped into a chair opposite Pitt. 'You mean to tell me they didn't whisk you off on a free round-the-world cruise for saving the most expensive ship in their fleet?'

'They were more than willing,' Pitt said. 'But Loren's on a diet, so the ship's buffet would have been wasted. And my shuffleboard game's a bit rusty, so there was really no point.'

'I'd be happy to take the trip for you.'

'And risk the whole agency falling apart without your presence?'

'True, I am rather indispensable around here.' Yaeger lofted his nose in the air. 'Remind me to mention that at my next performance review.'

'Done,' Pitt said with a grin. 'So I take it you found something on the *Tasmanian Star*?'

'The basics. She was built in Korea in 2005. At a length of five hundred and ten feet and a capacity of fifty-four thousand deadweight tons, she's classified as a Handymax dry bulk carrier. She was fitted with five holds, two cranes, and a self-dispensing conveyor system.'

'Which can make for a nice stairwell,' Pitt noted.

'She's owned by a Japanese shipping company named Sendai, and has seen steady service in the Pacific, primarily as an ore carrier. On her last voyage she was under contract with an American petrochemical company. She departed Perth three and a half weeks ago, with a recorded cargo of bauxite, bound for Los Angeles.'

'Bauxite.' Pitt pulled a small plastic bag from his pocket. He retrieved the silver rock he had picked up from the deck of the *Tasmanian Star* and laid it on his desk. 'Any idea of the value of the bauxite she was carrying?'

'I couldn't locate the ship's insured value, but depending on the grade, the stuff sells for around thirty to sixty bucks a ton on the open market.'

'Doesn't make sense someone would hijack a ship over it.'

'Personally, I'd go for a freighter full of iPads.'

'Any theories on where our thieves may have run to?'

'Not really. I took the coordinates you gave me where the ship changed course, but I came up dry. NRO satellite images were a week old. That's a dead part of the

Pacific. It doesn't garner much attention from the spies in the sky.'

'Tapping the National Reconnaissance Office? I hope you didn't leave any footprints.'

An accomplished hacker when circumstances dictated, Yaeger feigned insult. 'Footprints, me? Should anyone even notice the intrusion, I'm afraid the trail leads to my favorite Hollywood celebrity gossip website.'

'A true shame if the government were to shut that down.'

'My sentiments precisely. I do have a theory, though, about the *Tasmanian Star*'s appearance in Valparaiso.'

'I'd love to hear it.'

'The ship made an abrupt southerly turn nine days ago, some seventeen hundred miles west of Costa Rica. One of our free-floating weather buoys bit the dust in that area of the Pacific about the same time. Turns out, a pretty significant tropical storm blew through that area, although it petered out by the time it hit Mexico. We recorded force 9 winds before we lost the buoy.'

'So our pirates may have had to abandon their heist in a hurry.'

'That's what I'm thinking. Maybe that's why they left most of the cargo, and left the engine running.'

Pitt thought for a moment. 'Are there are any islands in the area?'

Yaeger pulled out a tablet computer and called up a map of the area where the ship's course changed.

'There's a small atoll called Clipperton Island. It's only about twenty miles from the position you gave me . . . and dead-on along that same heading.' He looked at Pitt and shook his head. 'Nice deduction.'

'They didn't have time to flood her, so they probably set her on a course toward Clipperton, assuming she'd founder on the reef and disappear.'

'Only the storm blew her clear of the island,' Yaeger said, 'and she kept on sailing for another four thousand miles until arriving in Valparaiso.'

Pitt took a sip of coffee. 'That still doesn't put us any closer to who attacked the ship and disposed of the crew.'

'I've searched for port documents showing recent shipments of bauxite, but nothing's surfaced.'

'And it probably won't. Hiram, see if you can find mention of any other pirate attacks – or lost ships, for that matter – that have occurred recently in the Pacific. And one more favor.' Pitt picked up the silver rock and tossed it to Yaeger. 'I picked this up on the *Tasmanian Star*. On your way back to the computer center, drop this off with the boys in subsea geology and have them tell us what it is.'

'Will do.' Yaeger studied the rock as he headed for the door. 'Not our bauxite?'

Pitt shook his head. 'A pang in my stomach and a large, grounded ghost ship says not.'

9

Pitt jogged up the entry steps to the Eisenhower Executive Office Building, trying to shake his creeping jet lag. Adjacent to the White House, the imposing stone structure was Pitt's favorite federal building. Built in 1888 in the French Second Empire style of architecture, it featured a steep-pitched mansard roof and towering windows, making it look like a transplant from a Victor Hugo story. A monument to the use of granite and slate, almost no wood had been used in its construction, to reduce the risk of fire. Ironically, a fire on the second floor had nearly destroyed Vice President Cheney's office in 2007.

Recent Vice Presidents had maintained only a ceremonial office in the building, preferring to inhabit the West Wing, where they could stay glued to the President. That all changed with the arrival of Admiral James Sandecker. A reluctant appointee when his predecessor had died in office, Sandecker preferred to keep his distance from the spinmasters that infiltrated every administration. Instead he made the vice presidential office in the old Executive Office Building his primary work domain. He gladly hiked the underground tunnel to the White House several times a day, if need be, to the chagrin of his less physically fit aides.

After passing through several layers of security, Pitt

reached the foyer to the Vice President's suite on the second floor and was escorted into the private office. The large room was decorated with the nautical motif befitting a retired admiral, showcasing several antique oil paintings of long-forgotten clipper ships battling the high seas. Though right on time, Pitt walked into a meeting in progress. Two men and a woman sat in wingback chairs around a coffee table, listening to the Vice President, who paced the lush carpet while clenching a large cigar.

'Dirk, there you are.' He zipped across the room to shake Pitt's hand. 'Come, take a seat.'

Though diminutive in stature, Sandecker had the energy of ten men. A fiery intensity burned in his blue eyes, which contrasted with his flaming red hair and matching Van Dyke beard. A Washington veteran who despised politics, he was both respected and feared for bluntness and integrity. For Pitt, he was something of a father figure, having been his boss at NUMA for many years before becoming Vice President.

'Good to see you, Admiral. You're looking fit.'

'One keeps plenty fit in this office just smacking down the gadflies,' he said. 'Dirk, let me introduce you around. Dan Fowler, here, is with DARPA, Tom Cerny is a special aide to the President, and Ann Bennett is from the Naval Criminal Investigative Service.'

Pitt shook hands then took a seat, glancing at his watch.

'You're not late,' Fowler said. 'We just had some earlier business with the Vice President.'

'Fair enough. So how may a humble marine engineer be of service?'

'You're probably not aware,' Sandecker said, 'but there's

been an alarming rash of security breaches in our weapons development programs, stretching back at least three years. Without going into specifics, I can tell you they've been at a high level and are costing us dearly.'

'I take it the Chinese are the primary beneficiaries.'

'Yes,' Fowler said. 'How did you know?'

'I recall them introducing a new fighter jet last year. It looked suspiciously like our F-35.'

'That's only the tip of the iceberg,' Sandecker said. 'Unfortunately, we've had only limited success at plugging the leaks. A multiagency task force has been formed, by request of the President, to investigate the situation.'

'These breaches directly threaten the ability of our military forces,' Cerny said. He had a pasty face and large dark eyes and spoke with the fast delivery of a used-car salesman. 'The President is deeply disturbed by these events and has demanded whatever action is necessary to protect our vital technology.'

Pitt fought off the urge to cry 'Hooray for the President!' Cerny, he pegged, was a typical presidential yes-man who relished the power he wielded while accomplishing nothing with it.

'That's well and fine,' Pitt said, 'but isn't half the government already engaged in hunting spies and chasing terrorists?'

'There's plenty of risk to go around.'

Sandecker lit his cigar as the men engaged, puffing it in defiance of the building's smoking ban. 'The task force has a need for some marine resources. Just a small project I thought you could assist with. Agent Bennett has the particulars.'

'It's a missing person, actually,' Bennett said.

Pitt locked eyes with the thirtyish agent, a pert, attractive woman concealed behind a conservative appearance. Her blond hair, layered short, matched the serious cut of her charcoal business suit. But the effect was softened by her dimpled cheeks and a petite nose that held up a pair of clear-framed reading glasses. She returned Pitt's gaze through lively aqua-colored eyes, then looked down at the folder in her lap.

'An important research scientist with DARPA, Joseph Eberson, disappeared several days ago in San Diego,' she said. 'He was believed to have gone on a fishing excursion aboard a private pleasure craft named *Cuttlefish*. The bodies of the boat owner and his assistant were found a few miles offshore by a passing sailboat. Local search-and-rescue teams combed the area but failed to locate Eberson or the boat.'

'You suspect foul play?'

'We have no specific reason to think so,' Fowler said, 'but Eberson was involved with some of the Navy's most sensitive research programs. We need closure on what happened to him. We have no reason to suspect that he defected, but an abduction has been viewed as a possibility.'

'What you really want is a body,' Pitt said. 'Unfortunately, if the boat sank and he drowned with his buddies, his body could be halfway to Tahiti by now. Or inside the stomach of a great white shark.'

'That's why we'd like you to help us find the boat,' Ann said, a hint of pleading in her eyes.

'Sounds more like a job for the San Diego Police Department.'

'We'd like to recover the boat so our investigators can try to determine if Eberson was aboard,' Fowler said. 'We're told the waters could be rather deep, so that's beyond the police department's capability.'

Pitt turned to Sandecker. 'Where's the Navy in all this?'

'As it happens, the Navy's West Coast salvage fleet is engaged in a training exercise in Alaska. On top of that, the bodies were found in Mexican territorial waters. Things will be a lot less complicated if an oceanographic research ship handled the search and recovery.'

Sandecker walked to his desk and peered at a memo. 'It just so happens that the NUMA survey vessel *Drake* presently is docked in San Diego, awaiting assignment.'

Pitt shook his head. 'I've been done in by my own kind.'

Sandecker's eyes twinkled. 'I've still got a few friends over in your building.'

'Well, then,' Pitt said, giving Ann a sideways glance, 'it would seem that I'm your man.'

'Exactly how will you go about the search?' Cerny asked.

'The *Drake* has several different sonar systems aboard, as well as a small submersible. We'll set up a survey grid and perform a thorough sweep of the area with sonar to try and locate the *Cuttlefish*. Once we find her, we'll investigate with scuba divers or send down the submersible, depending on the depth. If the boat's still intact, we'll see about raising her.'

'Ann will be joining you to observe the operations,' Fowler said. 'We would, of course, appreciate an urgent resolution to this matter. How soon do you think you can get started?'

'About as soon as I can find a flight to San Diego . . . and Agent Bennett can rustle up some boat clothes.'

Pitt was thanked for undertaking the project and departed the meeting. After he left the room, Sandecker turned to Cerny.

'I don't like leaving him in the dark. There's not a man alive I trust more.'

'Presidential orders,' Cerny said. 'It's best that nobody knows what we've potentially lost.'

'Can he do it?' Fowler asked. 'Can he find the boat if it sank?'

'It'll be a piece of cake for Pitt,' Sandecker said, blowing a thick ring of smoke toward the ceiling. 'What I'd worry about is what, exactly, he finds aboard.'

The man strolled across the deck with a pair of scuba tanks under each arm, showing all the strain of carrying a feather comforter. His arms were almost as thick as his legs, while his chest bulged like an overinflated tractor tire. Al Giordino's brown eyes and dark curly hair reflected his Italian heritage, while his sharp brows and upturned mouth hinted at his devilish wit.

He broke stride when he spotted Pitt and Bennett approach and met them at the gangway, still clutching the dive tanks.

'Greetings, Kemosabe,' he said to Pitt, 'welcome back to the salt air. You have a good flight?'

'Quite. The Vice President fixed it so we could hop a Navy Gulfstream that was flying a couple of admirals to Coronado.'

'And I always end up on a Greyhound bus.' Giordino gazed at Bennett and smiled. 'Another attempt to add beauty and sophistication to the crew?'

'Ann Bennett, this is Albert Giordino, NUMA's Director of Technology – and occasional leering deckhand. Miss Bennett is with the NCIS and is joining us on the search.'

'I'm pleased to meet you, Mr Giordino.'

'Please, call me Al.' He rattled the tanks. 'We can shake hands later.'

'I don't think we'll need those on this hunt,' Pitt said. 'The water will likely be too deep.'

'Rudi only said that we had an underwater recovery job. He didn't say what it was.'

'That's because he doesn't know. Is he aboard?'

'Yes. We all just returned from the funeral this morning.'

'Buddy Martin?'

Giordino nodded. Martin, the *Drake*'s captain, had died unexpectedly from a sudden illness.

'I'm sorry I couldn't make it in time,' Pitt said. 'Buddy was a man of true loyalty and a dear pal. He'll be sorely missed.'

'He bled turquoise,' Giordino said, referring to the color all NUMA craft were painted. 'But now Rudi has taken temporary command of the ship. A regular Captain Bligh, if you ask me.'

Pitt turned to Ann. 'I usually try to keep Rudi as close to Washington as possible, in order to safeguard the NUMA budget.'

'You'll find him in the lab,' Al said, 'tending to his flock of deepwater fish.'

Pitt and Ann found a pair of empty cabins and tossed their travel gear in them, then went hunting for Rudi Gunn. The search didn't take long for the *Drake* was compact, both the newest and smallest in the NUMA fleet. Barely over a hundred feet, the research ship was designed for inshore survey work but was also more than capable in blue water. Her cramped deck carried a three-man submersible and an autonomous underwater vehicle. Any enclosed space not devoted to her small crew was configured as research labs.

They entered one of the labs and found it nearly pitch-black. With the lights off and the windows sealed, the only illumination was cast by a few tiny blue bulbs overhead. Pitt figured the lab's air-conditioning unit must have been working nonstop as the temperature felt like the low fifties.

'Keep the door closed, please.'

As their eyes adjusted, they spotted the voice's owner, a thin man in a jacket hunched over a large tank that almost filled the room. He wore a set of night vision goggles and was staring intently into the tank.

'Spying on the mating habits of the grunion again, Rudi?' Pitt asked.

Recognizing the voice, the man bolted upright and spun to greet the intruders.

'Dirk, I didn't know it was you.' Gunn tore off the goggles and replaced them with a pair of horn-rimmed glasses. A brainy ex–Navy commander, Gunn served as NUMA's Deputy Director. Like his boss, he escaped the confines of the Washington headquarters at every opportunity.

Pitt introduced Gunn to Ann.

'Why the cold, dark room?' she asked.

'Come take a look.' Gunn handed her the night vision goggles.

He guided her to the edge of the tank, where she slipped on the goggles and peered inside. A half dozen small fish swam in a lazy circle, glowing blue under the augmented light. But they were unlike any fish Ann had ever seen – flat translucent bodies, giant protruding eyes, and multiple rows of razor-sharp teeth jutting from their open mouths. She took a quick step back from the tank.

'What are those things? They're hideous.'

'Rudi's pet creatures of the deep,' Pitt said.

'*Evermannella normalops* is their scientific name,' Gunn said, 'but we call them sabertooths. They're an unusual species found only in very deep water. We discovered a large school of them thriving around a deepwater thermal vent near Monterey and decided to try and capture a few to study. Took quite a few dives with the submersible, but we brought up twenty of them. These are the last few we haven't moved to shore yet.'

'They look like they'd eat you out of house and home.'

'Despite their appearance, we believe they are non-predatory. They're actually quite docile. They don't seem interested in eating other fish, so we think they may be scavengers.'

She shook her head. 'I'm still not going to stick my hand in the tank.'

'Don't worry,' Pitt said, 'your cabin door has a lock on it, in case they grow legs in the night.'

'They're no worse than a pet goldfish,' Gunn said. 'Albeit, an ugly goldfish that can live a mile deep.'

'We'll leave them in your care,' Pitt said. 'Rudi, how soon can we shove off?'

Gunn tilted his head. 'I think we can make like that pizza delivery outfit. Thirty minutes or less.'

'Then let's get under way,' Pitt said. 'I'm curious to find out where Ann is going to take us.'

True to his word, Gunn had the *Drake* inching away from the dock a half hour later. Ann joined him on the bridge with Pitt and Giordino, watching the green hills of Point

Loma drift past as they exited the harbor. Feeling more secure at sea, she opened up and explained their objective to Gunn and Giordino, then handed Pitt a small piece of paper.

'Here's the coordinates where the two bodies were picked up. Apparently they were within sight of each other.'

'That may be a good indication the currents didn't get too daffy with them,' Giordino said.

Pitt typed the coordinates into the *Drake*'s navigation system, which plotted the position as a triangle on the digital map display. It lay just beyond a small rocky island grouping off the Mexican coast called the Coronados.

'The currents run southerly along the coast,' Pitt said, 'so that would likely define a lower boundary from which to conduct the search.'

'The coroner's report placed their time of death between eight and ten hours earlier,' Ann said.

'That gives us something to work with.' Pitt drew a box on the map with a cursor. 'We'll start with a ten-mile-square grid, working north of the discovery point, and expand beyond that as necessary.'

Ann contemplated the size of the *Drake*, then asked Pitt, 'How are you going to handle the recovery?'

Pitt tilted his head at Gunn. 'Rudi?'

'I found a local barge and crane that's waiting on call. It'll come to the site once we find her. I guess I should have asked, but how big a boat are we looking for?'

Ann glanced at her notes. 'The *Cuttlefish* was registered at forty feet.'

'We'll get her up.' Gunn took over the helm and set the *Drake* on a path to Pitt's grid.

Two hours later, they reached the site where a passing sailboat had found the bodies of Heiland and his assistant Manny. Pitt saw the depth was around four hundred feet. He decided to conduct the search using the vessel's towed array sonar, choosing ease of deployment over the deeper-diving AUV. Crewmen at the stern deployed the bright yellow sonar fish, which was soon relaying electrical pulses to a processing station on the bridge via its tethered cable. Pitt took a seat at the controls and adjusted the cable winch until the fish was skimming a few meters above the bottom.

Ann stood glued to Pitt's shoulder, staring at the monitor that displayed a gold-tinted image of the sandy, undulating seafloor.

'What will the boat look like?'

'We're running a wide swath, so it will appear small in scale but should be readily identifiable.' He pointed to the screen. 'Here, you can see what a fifty-five-gallon drum looks like in comparison.'

Ann peered at a dime-sized object as it scrolled down the screen, easily recognizing it as an old barrel someone had dumped in the ocean.

'The clarity is quite remarkable.'

'The technology's improved to where you can almost see a carbuncle on a clamshell,' Giordino said.

The seas were empty, save a large powerboat flying a Mexican flag a mile or two away, its occupants busy fishing. Gunn piloted the *Drake* in a slow, steady pattern, running wide survey lanes north and south. The sonar registered some tires, a pair of playful dolphins, and what looked to be a toilet – but no sunken boats.

After four hours of surveying, they drew near the Mexican powerboat, which held its position with a pair of unmanned fishing rods protruding over its stern.

'Looks like we'll have to skip a lane to get around those guys,' Gunn said.

Pitt looked out the bridge window at the craft a quarter mile ahead, then turned back to the monitor. He smiled as a triangular object appeared at the top of the screen.

'Won't be necessary, Rudi. I think we just found her.'

Ann leaned over in puzzlement, then saw the shape expand into a boat's bow and grow into the full image of a cabin cruiser, sitting upright on the seafloor. Pitt marked the wreck's position and measured its length against a digital scale.

'Looks to be right at forty feet. I'd say that's our missing boat.'

Gunn looked at the image, then slapped Pitt on the shoulder.

'Nice work, Dirk. I'll call the lift barge and get them headed our way.'

Ann stared at the image until it scrolled off the bottom of the screen. 'Are you sure you can raise it?'

'It looks intact,' Gunn said, 'so that should be no problem for the lift barge.'

'So we're just going to wait here until the barge arrives?'

'Not exactly,' Pitt said, giving Ann a sly grin. 'First, we're going to drag a Washington spook to the bottom of the sea.'

11

The submersible dangled from a suspension crane, rotating lazily in the air before Gunn lowered it into the cool waters of the Pacific. He engaged a hydraulic release clamp, which allowed the submersible to drift free. Inside, Pitt tapped the electric motors, powering the sub away from the *Drake*, while Giordino flooded the ballast tanks from his perch in the copilot's seat. Ann sat behind them in a cramped third seat, watching with all the excitement of a small child.

Giordino glanced over his shoulder and noticed her fascination with the green murk beyond the view ports. 'Ever been diving before?'

'Lots,' Ann said, 'but only in a swimming pool. I was a platform diver in college.'

The submersible settled into a slow descent. Beyond the range of the exterior spotlights, the sea quickly turned black.

'I was never one to voluntarily throw myself off high objects,' Giordino said. 'How'd you go from jumping off diving boards to chasing bad guys?'

'I was a Marine brat growing up, so I joined ROTC in college. Took my commission with the Navy at graduation and finagled them into paying for law school. I worked at a JAG unit in Bahrain, then spent a few months at Guantánamo, where I made a number of Washington contacts. My military marriage failed about that time, so I decided to try something different. A friend referred me to the NCIS two years ago and I landed in their counter-intelligence directorate.'

'You sound like a regular Perry Mason.'

'Used to be. In the JAG's office I enjoyed the investigations but not the prosecutions. That's what I like about my current assignment. Most of my work is strictly investigative, which allows me to spend a lot of time in the field. I was assigned the Eberson case to determine if he or the boat had been a target of espionage.'

'We'll know more shortly,' Pitt said. 'The bottom's coming up.'

Giordino neutralized their ballast as a sandy seabed appeared. Pitt eyed a lobster scurrying across the bottom, which reminded him of his lost meal in Chile. He engaged the thrusters and propelled the submersible forward. They traveled only a short distance before a large white object appeared to their left. Pitt swung the submersible to port and closed on the sunken boat.

In its underwater world, the *Cuttlefish* appeared like a lost alien. Still pristine and gleaming under the submersible's lights, it appeared in stark contrast to the dark, lifeless bottom. Pitt brought the submersible in tight, slowly circling the boat's perimeter. Sitting perfectly upright, she showed no signs of major damage.

'I think she might be breached underneath,' Pitt said, noticing a hairline crack in the hull.

'We'll see when we raise her,' Giordino replied. 'Looks like there'll be no problem sliding under a pair of slings fore and aft. We should be able to get her up in a jiffy.'

Pitt guided the submersible to the *Cuttlefish*'s stern, then ascended to peer over the side.

Ann gasped. Wedged against the transom was the body of a man. His pale skin was bloated and shredded in spots where sea creatures had fed on the flesh. A small school of rockfish floated above his face, nibbling at his features.

'Joe Eberson?' Pitt asked in a low tone.

Ann nodded, then averted her eyes.

Pitt took a closer look. Monofilament line was tangled around Eberson's feet and ankles. The line had looped around a deck cleat, securing the body to the boat when it sank. No wounds or burn marks were readily apparent on the DARPA scientist, but then Pitt saw Eberson's hands.

They were bloated to nearly double their normal size, the skin discolored with charcoal blotches. It was just as Pitt had seen in Chile.

Like the dead crewman on the *Tasmanian Star*, Joe Eberson had died a horrific and unexplained death.

12

It took two more dives for the submersible to remove Eberson's body. A large canvas tarp, hastily sewn into an oversized body bag, was carried to the sunken boat. Using a pair of articulated arms that protruded from the base of the submersible, Pitt slid the bag over Eberson's head and torso. The monofilament line was cut and the bag brought gently to the surface. Ann insisted on remaining aboard the submersible during the gruesome business of removing and transporting Eberson to the *Drake*. Once back on deck, Pitt and Giordino set about laying out the slings they would use to raise the *Cuttlefish*. Soon a decrepit-looking barge with a massive crane arrived at the worksite. Gunn had found the barge in San Diego Harbor, where it was used to support municipal dredging operations. Pitt returned the wave of a friendly-faced man with a gray beard, who was steering the powered barge from a small pilothouse.

Ann joined the two men on deck after she and Gunn briefly examined the body.

'Is that your man?' Giordino asked.

Ann nodded. 'We found a waterlogged wallet in his pocket that confirmed as much. We'll have to leave it to the coroner for a definitive ID and cause of death.'

'A week underwater won't make that an easy job,' Pitt said.

'At least it appears that his death was accidental. Perhaps they had trouble with the boat and simply drowned.'

Pitt kept silent about Eberson's hands as he locked one of the slings into the submersible's steel claws.

Ann observed his work. 'Is there much danger of damaging the boat when it's lifted?'

'We can't really tell the extent of any structural damage, so the answer is yes. There's a chance she could collapse on us – but I suspect she'll pop up without a hitch.'

'Just in case,' Ann said, 'I'd like to examine the deck and interior before you make the attempt.'

'We're about set to make the next dive, so hop aboard.'

The *Cuttlefish* came into view a short time later, somewhat less menacing without Joe Eberson's body aboard. Pitt hovered the submersible just above the rear deck, then slowly rotated it to let the exterior floodlights expose the sunken craft.

'Stop!' Ann cried, pointing out the view port. 'That box, there.'

Pitt froze the controls, allowing them to study an oblong box strapped to the starboard bulwark.

'Something of importance?' Pitt asked.

'Might be, judging by the padlock.' She was angry with herself for not spotting the box earlier. 'Let's take it up.'

'It looks pretty secure where it is,' Giordino said.

She shook her head. 'I don't want to risk damaging it while lifting the boat.'

Pitt shrugged. 'Suits me, but we've got to empty our hands first.'

He rotated the submersible's manipulator arms, showing Ann the sling they contained. He maneuvered away from the boat, dropped the sling in the sand, and stretched it around the vessel's bow. He grabbed one end and pulled it under the hull as far as it would go, then raised the looped end and deposited it on the cabin roof. He then repeated the process with the sling's opposite end. Piloting the submersible above the rear deck, he set about extricating the hardened plastic box. With some effort, he loosened the straps with one of the manipulator claws until the box fell free. Clutching a handle with one claw, he worked the second arm beneath the box as a cradle. Giordino purged seawater from the ballast tanks, and the submersible floated to the surface.

Gunn was waiting for them at the *Drake*'s rail and pulled the submersible aboard. 'How goes the initial lasso?' he asked as they climbed out.

Giordino smiled. 'As easy as roping a baby calf.'

'The stern will be a bit harder,' Pitt said. 'We'll have to dig some to get the sling under her.'

Gunn noticed the long box held by the manipulator arms. 'So, you brought me a present?'

'That would be Miss Bennett's.' Giordino raised his brows to warn Gunn to keep his hands off.

As Giordino removed the box from the steel arms and set it on a protected section of the deck, Ann followed his every move. Gunn helped Pitt secure the second sling, then mounted a thick section of PVC pipe with an attached hose to the forward ballast relief valve.

'How're your battery reserves holding up?' Gunn asked.

'If we can get this second sling on without too much trouble, we should have enough juice for one more dive to attach the lift cable.'

'I'll tell the barge operator to stand by.'

Pitt and Giordino were lowered into the ocean, this time without Ann. Once they reached the seafloor, Pitt proceeded to the boat's stern and set the submersible down adjacent to the port quarter. Using the manipulator arms, he set down the sling and grabbed the PVC pipe, which he inserted into the sand along the boat's seam.

'Ready for suction.'

'At your pleasure.' Giordino released a small stream of compressed air from the forward ballast tank, which fed through the flexible hose and into the lower third of the PVC pipe. Air bubbles sailed up the pipe and out the open end, expanding as they rose and generating suction at the bottom end of the pipe. The soft sand beneath the boat began swirling up the pipe, disgorging in a brown cloud behind the submersible that dissipated with the current. It took just a few minutes to clear a large enough gap beneath the boat's stern quarter to insert the sling.

Giordino killed the air release, and they moved to the opposite side of the boat and repeated the process. Then they pulled the sling under the exposed corners and gathered the free ends above the cabin. As Pitt held them in place, Giordino retrieved a heavy D ring and snapped the four ringed ends of both slings into it. Sweat beaded on his forehead as he worked the manipulator claws to clasp the last ring in place. Now they just needed to attach a lift cable from the barge's crane to the D ring and it could hoist away.

'Performed with the delicate hands of a surgeon,' Giordino said, securing the manipulator arms.

Pitt glanced at his partner's meaty paws and shook his

head. 'A surgeon who moonlights as a butcher, perhaps. Nicely done, all the same.'

Pitt purged the ballast tanks, and the submersible began a lazy ascent. The sun had just slipped beneath the horizon when they broke the surface off the *Drake*'s beam. Gunn stood by the crane as the sub drew alongside. He expertly lowered the jaws and clamped onto the submersible's hoist ring. Gunn lifted the sub out of the water to deck level, then left it dangling.

'Come on, Rudi,' Giordino said, 'bring us on in.'

Pitt stared out the view port, then stiffened. A large man unknown to Pitt stood near Gunn, holding a pistol. The man smiled at Pitt, but there was no warmth in the expression. Gunn eased his hands off the crane controls, then gave Pitt a grim shake of his head before stepping away.

Giordino saw Gunn abandon the controls and asked, 'What's going on?'

Pitt kept his eyes fixed on the gunman aboard the *Drake*.

'I would say that we've been hung out to dry.'

13

They had attacked the *Drake* under the guise of helplessness.

The crew on the Mexican powerboat floating nearby had surreptitiously monitored the NUMA vessel all day – until they spotted their objective. When the sun began to follow the submersible beneath the waves, a Spanish-accented voice hailed the *Drake* over the marine radio, feigning a shortage of fuel. Taking the call on the bridge, Gunn told the boat to come alongside if they were able and he would pass across some gasoline.

The boat made a show of limping over at minimal speed, swinging around the back of the barge before inching toward the NUMA ship. While the boat was temporarily out of view, a lone gunman leaped aboard the barge's stern and sneaked his way to the pilothouse.

Soon a large man stood on the boat's afterdeck, waving at Gunn with a cold smile. He wore black slacks and a loose knit black shirt, odd attire for a fishing trip. The approaching twilight obscured his coffee complexion and flat facial features, more typical of Central American heritage than Mexican. The man tossed a line to a waiting deckhand, then turned to Gunn, who leaned over the rail with a five-gallon container of gas.

'Thank you, señor,' he said in a baritone voice. 'We

stayed too long fishing and feared we would not make it to shore.'

He reached for the can and set it on the deck. Then, moving as quickly as a cat, he grabbed the rail and leaped aboard the *Drake*. A Glock semiautomatic materialized from his back paddle holster – and was leveled at Gunn's chest the instant his feet touched the deck. 'Tell your crewmen to put their hands on the rail and face the sea.'

Gunn relayed the order to a pair of shocked crewmen on the deck, who nodded. They raised their arms, then shuffled to the rail.

Two more gunmen climbed aboard and sprinted up to the *Drake*'s bridge. Gunn winced when he heard gunfire, but then breathed easier a few moments later when he saw the helm watchman marched down to the deck. One gunman had spotted the *Drake*'s rigid inflatable lifeboat and casually pumped several rounds into it, making the rubber boat sag like a limp balloon. When a scientist ducked out of the lab to see what the commotion was about, he was grabbed roughly and herded together with the other crewmen.

Gunn looked to the tall man in black. 'What is it you want?'

The man ignored him as a small radio clipped to his waist chirped.

'The barge is secure,' radioed an unseen voice.

'Bring it alongside and join us aboard the research ship,' the gunman replied. 'We'll be ready shortly.'

The radio sounded again. 'Pablo, the submersible has surfaced.'

The man in black cursed as he looked over the side,

seeing the crown of the submersible. Pocketing the radio, he grabbed Gunn by the collar and marched him to the lift crane. 'Raise your friends out of the water, but don't bring them aboard the ship.' He stepped back, keeping his weapon drawn.

As Gunn reached for the controls, he searched for a way to warn Pitt. The idea was abandoned when he felt the Glock pressed against his spine. Gunn attached the recovery clamp, raised the submersible, and stood by helplessly as he left it suspended in the air.

A few seconds later, the old barge bumped against the *Drake*'s stern. A fourth gunman, also wearing dark clothes and carrying a pistol, raced across the deck and jumped onto the *Drake*. He stepped over to Pablo, breathing heavily. His shirt was ripped, and a trace of blood trickled from his lower lip.

'What happened to you?' Pablo asked.

'The captain gave me some trouble, at first.'

Pablo shook his head and frowned. 'Get the crate aboard. Now!'

The new gunman meekly joined the other two in hoisting the box recovered from the *Cuttlefish* and placing it on their boat. Gunn suddenly thought of Ann and realized she wasn't on deck.

The leader of the assault team turned to Gunn, waving his Glock. 'Do not follow us or call for help or we shall return and kill you all.' Pablo smiled at Gunn, his dark eyes glistening. 'Thank you for your assistance.' He stepped to the rail without looking back and climbed onto his boat.

Pitt and Giordino were forced to watch the drama from

the confines of the submersible. Though they could have exited the sub's hatch, they would have had a precarious leap to get aboard the *Drake*. Before they could act, it was all over.

Watching Pablo step over the rail, Pitt detected a movement at the forward part of the ship. He turned to Al. 'Did you see something go off the side, near the bridge?'

'No,' Giordino said. 'I was keeping tabs on the guy who pulled the gun on Rudi.'

They watched as Pablo boarded the powerboat and it pulled away from the *Drake*. But as it turned and sped toward shore, they caught a glimpse of its opposite deck in the fading light.

Giordino poked a finger at the view port. 'Is that what I think it is?'

Pitt had seen it too and he nodded.

It was the outstretched figure of a drenched blond woman, hiding on the narrow side deck of the boat as it thundered toward Mexico.

14

Gunn wasted no in time hoisting the submersible aboard as Pitt and Giordino waited at the open hatch.

'Is everyone all right?' Pitt asked.

'No one was hurt,' Gunn replied. 'They threatened to kill us if we call for help or pursue them.'

'Who were *they*?' Giordino asked.

Gunn shook his head. 'I have no clue. The leader was called Pablo. They came for that box you guys lifted from the *Cuttlefish*. Any idea what was in it?'

'No,' Pitt said, 'but I think Ann does. How did she get aboard their boat?'

'Ann? I thought she was in her cabin.'

'We saw her hiding beside the wheelhouse of their boat as it stormed away,' Giordino said.

Gunn turned pale. 'They may kill her if they catch her.'

'Call the Coast Guard,' Pitt said. 'Maybe they have a drug interdiction patrol boat nearby. But don't say anything about Ann, in case they're listening in. Al and I will try and track them in the inflatable.'

'Not going to happen,' Gunn said. 'They shot up the bridge radio and the inflatable. We've got some handheld radios I can make the call with, but you're out of luck with the RIB.'

'What about the barge?' Giordino said.

'First we better check out the pilot. I think they may have roughed him up.'

'Rudi, you go make the call,' Pitt said. 'Al and I will check the barge.'

Pitt and Giordino ran to the stern rail. The bow of the barge was pressing alongside just below the deck, the older vessel pushing the research ship at a turtle's pace. They jumped aboard and sprinted the length of its oily deck to the small wheelhouse at the stern. They heard a dog growl as they approached and stepped inside.

A gray-haired man knelt by the helm, holding his palm against a bloody gash along his hairline. A black-and-tan dachshund stood guard in front of him and barked at the intruders.

'Hush, Mauser,' the man said.

'Are you all right, old-timer?' Pitt helped the man to his feet after easing past the dachshund. He nearly matched Pitt's six-foot-three height, but carried a few more pounds.

'That son of a gun walked in out of nowhere and started smashing my radio.' As the old man spoke, clarity returned to his blue eyes. 'I gave him a good lick, but he got me with the butt of his pistol.'

Giordino found a first-aid kit and applied a bandage to the man's wound.

'Thanks, son. Who were those guys, anyway?'

'I don't know,' Pitt said, 'but one of our people is aboard their boat. Do you have a launch we can borrow?'

'There's a small Zodiac out back. Not much for an engine, but help yourself.'

The captain gazed out the windshield – and realized the

94

barge was pushing the *Drake*. 'Deuces! Let me back off your vessel before you boys cut loose.'

He briefly jammed the throttle in reverse, then shifted to neutral. Turning to Pitt, he raised his brows with worry. 'You watch yourself with them.'

'Will do.'

Pitt nodded at the man, then turned to follow Giordino out the door. As he exited the wheelhouse, he noticed the old man's commercial master's license hanging on the bulkhead. Seeing the name Clive Cussler printed on the document, Pitt wrinkled his brow, then hurried onto the deck.

Giordino had already unlashed the small inflatable from the wheelhouse. Rather than take the time to lower it over the side with a winch, the two men manhandled it over the rail, then climbed aboard. Pitt primed the outboard motor, then gave a few tugs on the starter pulley, bringing the engine to life. Easing the throttle to full, he turned away from the barge and headed toward shore.

The Mexican powerboat was still visible in the growing darkness, and Pitt set an angle of pursuit along its path. But they were in a losing race, as the cabin cruiser beat the waves a good ten knots faster than the little Zodiac. All Pitt could do was try to keep them in sight long enough to determine where they would put ashore.

'I hope you remembered to bring our passports,' Giordino shouted. Their southeasterly tack had them on a clear course for the Mexican mainland.

'I wish I had remembered to bring an RPG instead.'

Giordino had already searched the Zodiac; their only potential weapon was a small anchor. But Pitt had no intention of going head-to-head with the armed thieves. His only concern was for Ann's safety.

As the faint shape of the powerboat faded in the distance, he thought about the plucky NCIS agent and wondered what on earth she actually planned to do.

15

Lying soaked as she clutched the rail of the cabin cruiser, Ann was asking herself the same question. She wanted to commandeer the boat and sail it to San Diego, but that was a tall order against four armed men. She felt along her back at the waist, making sure the holster containing a SIG Sauer P239 had survived the plunge into the ocean.

Her decision to sneak aboard the Mexican boat had been driven more by adrenaline than strategy. She was exiting one of the ship's labs while searching for a secure place to store Heiland's crate when she saw Pablo on deck, pulling a pistol on Gunn. She ducked into a companionway, slipped down to her cabin, and retrieved her own weapon. When one of the gunmen drew everyone's attention by blasting the *Drake*'s inflatable, she crept up to the bridge – only to find the ship's radio destroyed. While the crew had been startled by the attack, she knew why the gunmen had appeared. They were after the crate. It, not Eberson's body, was the real reason Ann was aboard.

The gunmen acted quickly and off-loaded the crate before she could devise a counterattack. Just one thought ran through her mind. If it could not be saved, then it must be destroyed.

With her heart pounding, she stepped to the bridge doorway and peeked aft. Pablo was busy with Gunn near the submersible, while the other gunmen were securing the crate aboard the powerboat. She took a deep breath, stepped onto the bridge wing, and dove over the side.

Ann's years of springboard diving kicked in. She stiffened her body as she dove and stretched her hands above her head, reaching for the sea. She hit the water at a vertical angle, the desired rip entry barely producing a splash. The cool Pacific made her body shudder as she dove deep, then turned and swam toward the Mexican boat.

Surfacing off its outer beam, she moved in close alongside to stay concealed. She heard a man jumping aboard, then noticed the boat was drifting clear of the *Drake*. With a swift kick she reached up the side of the hull and grasped a rail stanchion on the deck. Then the engines rumbled, and the boat lurched forward. Ann held firm and let the boat's momentum drag her across the surface as she swung one leg up and caught her foot on the deck. She yanked her torso up and rolled aboard on the narrow deck that ran alongside the enclosed cockpit.

She lay patiently, catching her breath and building her nerve, as the boat raced toward shore. It would be a half-hour journey. With darkness her ally, she waited for the sky to turn black. Salt water sprayed her face, and she bounced like a rodeo rider, battling to hold her position while praying no one looked her way.

Pablo and his men hung on the stern deck rail for several minutes, watching the *Drake* behind them. The barge faced them, obscuring the launch of the small Zodiac from its stern. After several minutes, the party moved into the cabin. Pablo made a phone call, then sat and drank a bottle of Dos Equis.

When a charcoal wash crossed the skies, Ann crept

backward along the rail until she could catch a peek at the open deck. A dark, heavy-set man sat on a side bench, cradling a handgun as he gazed off the stern. He had a high forehead and a long full beard, reminding Ann of a young Fidel Castro. Secured on the deck in front of him was Heiland's crate, which he used as a footrest.

Though the odds were against her in a gunfight with the full crew, this lone man she could subdue, especially with the element of surprise on her side. Her objective was simple: just get the crate over the side by any means she could. Perhaps Pitt and the NUMA ship could find it later. At least it would stay out of foreign hands.

She inched backward along the side rail and dropped quietly to the deck. Voices came from the main cabin, which was several steps below deck and out of clear view. Just above the cabin was the boat's cockpit, where Ann could see the pilot's legs a few feet away. With the boat closing in on the coast, she could only hope the pilot kept his eyes on course.

She slipped the compact SIG Sauer from its holster, reversed her grip, and sprung at Fidel. He never heard her coming. She aimed for his temple but struck high, and the pistol butt skipped over the crown of his head. He grunted and fell on his side, dropping his handgun to the deck.

Ann kicked it aside and knelt to free the case, which had been tied to the bench.

Only stunned by the blow, the man cradled his bleeding head with one hand and groped the deck for his gun. Instead of locating it, he found Ann's ankle. He wrapped an angry fist around it and pulled with all the strength he could muster.

Hunched over the crate, Ann was caught off balance and went sprawling across the deck. But her reflexes were quick, and she quickly rolled to her feet. The gunman still clutched her left ankle, so she let go with her right foot, landing a vicious blow on the side of his head.

He grunted and pulled harder, so she let fly with another kick, connecting with his jaw. His fingers finally went limp, his eyes glazed over, and he sunk to the deck.

Ann scurried back to the crate, untying one strap and then the other. At last it was free. She dragged it to the stern and hoisted one end onto the rail. She bent to lift the other end, then froze. A cold ring of steel touched the back of her neck.

'That will be staying here, my dear,' boomed the deep voice of Pablo as he pressed his Glock pistol into her flesh.

16

Twinkling lights blanketed the shore in a glowing wave of amber, but the serene image only irritated Pitt. The full outline of the Mexican boat had long since disappeared, leaving only its running lights to track its position. As the glow from the fast boat shrank in the distance, it melded with the shore lights until becoming lost from view.

Pitt held the tiller steady, tracking to the boat's last visible position while hoping it didn't dramatically alter course. He didn't realize that the Mexican coast from the border south offered no natural harbor for some thirty-five miles. After running blind for several minutes, they approached the shoreline and the bright hillside lights above it. Around them, the seas appeared empty, so he angled the Zodiac south. Two minutes later, they caught sight of it.

'There!' Giordino shouted, pointing off the bow.

A mile ahead, they could just make out a small rock jetty that fingered into the Pacific. A primitive quay had been constructed over the first fifty feet of rock – and here an illuminated boat sat, idling. As they motored closer, Pitt and Giordino could make out several figures moving along the dock to a waiting four-door pickup truck. Two figures returned to the boat, then carried an oblong crate to the truck and dropped it onto the rear bed.

'That's our box,' Giordino said. 'Do you see Ann?'

'No, but she might be one of the people in the truck. I'll try to get us to shore on the other side of the jetty.'

He kept the boat well out to sea as they approached the jetty and backed off the throttle to lessen the motor's whine. When they had drawn close, the Mexican boat suddenly burst away from the quay. It looped around the end of the jetty, coming within a whisker of flattening the unseen Zodiac as it sped down the coast.

Rocked hard by the wake, the Zodiac's lone fuel can tipped over. Giordino shook the can before setting it upright. 'We don't have the fuel to chase her any distance.'

Pitt spotted the truck's taillights illuminating as its engine started. 'Then we best get to shore.'

He gunned the throttle, ignoring any attempt at stealth while racing the inflatable along the jetty. He could see by the lights of some nearby homes and businesses that the jetty extended from a shallow beach. He ran the boat through the surf and straight up onto the sand just as the pickup began pulling down the street.

Giordino leaped out of the Zodiac and was dragging it past the tide line even before Pitt could kill the motor. Both men sprinted to the dirt road. The truck was just a block ahead. Without a ready alternative, they took off after it.

The truck traveled slowly over the rough road until it came to a paved cross street, brightly illuminated and dotted with traffic. A string of tiny stores in crumbling stucco buildings ran along it, most of them closed for the night. But a handful of cantinas and small restaurants kept a steady stream of people flowing along the sidewalks.

Turning left, the truck picked up speed briefly, then caught up to some slow-moving traffic. Pitt and Giordino reached the intersection a few seconds later.

'I'm not keen to run a midnight marathon without my glow-in-the-dark racing shorts.' Giordino gasped as they watched the truck accelerate ahead.

'And I forgot my lucky headband,' Pitt said between breaths.

They searched for something resembling a taxi, but saw none. Then Pitt motioned toward the next corner. 'I think I see a loaner.'

A pair of electricians in gray coveralls were busy working on the panel box of a two-story industrial building. Moonlighting from their day jobs with Mexico's national electric company, they were also making use of their employer's small utility van. Several yards from the electricians, the van was parked at the curb with both its doors flung open and its radio blaring.

Pitt and Giordino sprinted straight to the vehicle and leaped into the front seats. The keys were dangling from the ignition. Before the electricians knew what was happening, Pitt had the engine started and was laying rubber.

'¡Alto! ¡Alto!' shouted one of the men as he dropped a screwdriver and gave chase. His partner stared for a moment, then retrieved his cell phone and made a frantic call.

Pitt caught a break in the traffic and quickly outdistanced the pursuer. Some tools and wire bounced out the back of the van until Pitt stormed over a speed bump and the rear doors slammed shut.

'Those boys are going to have some explaining to do in the morning,' Giordino said.

'You don't think their supervisor will believe that their truck was stolen by a pair of mad gringos?'

'Perhaps. But I think we should be a little gentle, all the same,' he said, patting the dashboard.

Pitt promptly hit a deep rut, jarring both men out of their seats.

They had lost sight of the four-door pickup, so Pitt drove anything but gently. He kept the pedal glued to the floor, bursting around several slower cars on the narrow road. He braked hard to avoid striking a woman, who had darted across the road with a pair of caged chickens, then narrowly avoided a pack of stray dogs at the edge of town.

The avenue meandered up a hill, leaving behind both traffic and roadside businesses – and also any lighting. Passing a rusty Volkswagen Beetle, Pitt caught sight of the truck a half mile ahead. The utility van's small engine howled in protest as he kept the accelerator floored, while the small tires lapped up the asphalt. The road curved sharply, and Pitt screeched through the turn, spraying a cloud of dust on a blue Dodge Charger parked on the shoulder. The Charger's headlights instantly popped on, and it eased onto the road.

'You still feeling sorry for those utility men?' Pitt said.

'A wee bit. Why do you ask?'

'I think they went and called the *Federales* on us.'

'How do you know?'

Pitt glanced in the rearview mirror as flashing lights exploded on the Charger's roof.

'Because they're right behind us.'

17

The Charger's roof-mounted light bar bathed the parched hillsides in alternating rays of blue and red. A short distance ahead, the pickup truck's driver clenched the steering wheel when he saw the lights behind him.

'Pablo! It's the police. They were waiting at the last bend.'

Sitting in the truck's rear seat, Pablo glanced over his shoulder at the lights, then looked at the speedometer.

'You were not speeding?'

'No more than a kilometer or two over the limit, I swear.'

Pablo showed no signs of concern on his bullish face. 'Lose them before we get close to the airport,' he said without emotion. 'If necessary, we'll ditch our weapons. And the girl.'

Ann tensed, wondering if they would kill her first. Sitting between Pablo and the bearded man named Juan, she didn't know which man to fear more. Shrinking from Pablo, she turned toward her other guard. With a black eye and dried blood on his cheek, Juan sat with a pistol against her ribs and a snarl etched on his face.

Ann's hands had been bound and a gun held on her after Pablo discovered her on the boat. Fear had gripped her since, but now a glimmer of hope surfaced in the form of the Mexican police. Perhaps Pitt had somehow informed them. She silently prayed that she wouldn't get caught in the cross fire of a shoot-out.

The driver accelerated sharply, which caused the four-door pickup to sway and bounce over the rough road. It zipped through several switchbacks before cresting a high coastal ridge. Once over the summit, the road wound down the opposite flank, dropping into the broad valley that housed the border town of Tijuana.

A million lights twinkled through the hazy smog suspended over the city. That view soon vanished as the pickup raced down the slope and entered the city's outskirts. Looking back, the driver saw he had distanced himself from the police car's flashing lights.

The truck approached a busy four-lane freeway that looped around the southern end of Tijuana. Pablo noticed the driver begin to turn onto the highway. 'No, stay off the highway! Go through the city, it will be easier to lose them.'

The driver nodded and headed into the congested confines of Tijuana. He glanced into his mirror once more. Another vehicle was preventing the police car from closing pursuit.

The intervening vehicle was the utility van. Pitt was doing everything he could to keep within reach of the pickup, despite the police car on his tail. He had nearly melted the van's small engine, whipping it up the hill at high revolutions to keep pace. The more powerful police Charger easily caught up to the van, then rode its rear bumper with authority.

Pitt created a slight advantage for himself on the downhill run, driving the van on the very edge. Gravel flew as he rocketed through the turns, more focused on staying with the pickup than eluding the police car. The Charger's driver was more cautious, allowing Pitt to create some separation as they barreled toward the city.

'We're going to have to do something about our companion,' Pitt said, as they entered the city of nearly two million people.

Giordino glanced at the back of the van, which was stockpiled with tools and electrical supplies that had been clanging back and forth.

'I'll see if there's a *Federales* removal device in back.' He carefully climbed out of his seat as they swayed down the road.

The van's walls were lined with spools of wire and bins full of electrical connectors, plus an assortment of tools. Hardly an arsenal of defense, Giordino thought. Then he spotted a short rack of conduit pipe. Used to protect exposed wiring, the thin four-foot sections of galvanized steel were threaded at each end. Giordino's brow arched as he found a binful of couplings. He called up to Pitt. 'I think I've got something.'

A minute later, the van sped past the freeway on-ramp and continued into the city. The pickup turned right at a stoplight two blocks ahead, and Pitt called out to Giordino, 'Coming up!'

He eased off the accelerator, ensuring that the police car hung close behind. When they got within a few car lengths of the stoplight, Pitt yelled, 'Now!'

Giordino kicked open the rear doors and slid out an eight-foot section of conduit he had coupled together. He wedged one end against a chunk of wood braced by the rear wheel wells and secured its lateral movement with pieces of wire he wrapped around the door hinges. Pitt gave him a second to scramble out of the way and then slammed on the brakes.

The police officer had already slowed when he spotted the pipe slide out like some kind of medieval jousting lance and braked heavily when the van's rear lights lit up. Pitt had the advantage with a lighter vehicle and he pressed his case by slamming the van into reverse the instant it lost forward momentum.

The police car rammed into the van's rear bumper moments after being impaled by Giordino's makeshift weapon. The conduit pipe rammed through the Charger's grille and radiator before striking the engine block and crumpling like an accordion. A cloud of steam burst from the engine bay, unseen by the policemen inside whose vision was blocked by exploding air bags.

Pitt threw the van into first gear and stepped on the gas. A grinding sound erupted from the rear as the van struggled to move forward. The bumper finally broke free from the Charger, and the van lurched ahead. Giordino looked back to see the pipe jutting from the grille of the police car like the beak of a hummingbird, steam billowing behind it.

Giordino made his way back to the front seat. 'Now you're really going to cost those utility boys.'

'Just proves those two gringos really were crazy.'

Pitt tightened his grip on the wheel and scoured the road ahead with renewed urgency. Every cop in Tijuana would soon be searching for the battered utility van. Wheeling around the corner, he pressed the accelerator to the floor. They'd have to make a play for Ann – and quickly.

18

'I don't see the police lights anymore.' The pickup's driver flashed Pablo a dirty smile. Years of drug use had left his mouth a cavern of brown gums and decayed teeth. 'I think we lost them.'

'Do not draw attention to your driving,' Pablo said, 'but get us to the airport without delay.'

The driver checked the route on the truck's navigation screen: it angled across the city toward the airport on the northeast side of town. Glancing constantly in the mirror for police lights, he paid little attention to the small utility van that followed a short distance behind.

As they approached the city center, the streets became more congested. The pickup's driver turned east, down a street called Plaza El Toreo, where the dirty sidewalks were swarming with people. As he dodged some jaywalkers, the pickup hit a large pothole, which sent the crate bouncing on the truck bed.

Following close behind, Pitt and Giordino saw the unsecured box move.

Giordino rubbed his chin. 'What do you suppose is in there that's causing all the excitement?'

'I wish I knew.' Pitt had to suppress his anger over leading the crew of the *Drake* into a dangerous situation without any advance warning.

Giordino pointed at the truck. 'If you pull alongside the bed, I might just be able to grab hold of that thing.'

Pitt considered the idea. Driving a wanted vehicle, and with no weapons, they had little chance of overpowering the men in the pickup. Their options were limited, if not suicidal. 'Maybe we could negotiate a swap for Ann,' he said, 'if they don't kill us outright.'

They had the advantage of being in a crowded city, one with a sketchy reputation. Giordino agreed it was worth the risk.

Pitt kept the van close to the pickup's rear bumper, waiting for a break in the oncoming traffic so he could pull alongside. The vehicles reached a stop sign, which Pitt eased past without stopping. He was chagrined to look up and see a police car passing in the opposite direction.

He held his gaze ahead as the car passed, then tracked it in his mirror. The police car rapidly made a three-point turn on the narrow street, nearly flinging a boy off a motorbike.

'I think we've been made,' Pitt said.

Giordino rolled down his window. 'Then let's at least get something for our trouble.'

Pitt edged closer to the truck as lights erupted behind him.

The police car tried to fight its way across the intersection, but a semitrailer truck had turned in front of it, slowly navigating through a tight turn. Pitt looked ahead, waiting for a battered Isuzu to pass in the other lane before catching a gap in the oncoming traffic. Flooring the accelerator, he surged into the other lane and pulled alongside the truck. Giordino leaned out the side window and thrust his arms into the bed, grasping for the crate.

The pickup's driver, alerted by the police lights in his mirror, saw Giordino lunge out of the van. He immediately tapped his brakes. Giordino just managed to duck back inside his window to avoid colliding with the truck's cab. For an instant, the two vehicles traveled alongside.

'Almost got it,' he said to Pitt. 'Give me one more try.'

Giordino sat nearly face-to-face with Juan, who was desperately lowering his window.

Pitt matched the truck's braking, then looked ahead and saw a cement mixer rambling down the road directly in front of him. 'Make it quick!' Pitt stepped harder on the brakes.

The pickup accelerated, and Pitt fought to match it before facing a head-on collision.

As the van again pulled alongside the pickup's bed, Giordino was true to his word. Hanging half out the window, he snared a handle on one end of the box. With a hard pull, he yanked the box out of the bed, letting it dangle alongside the van. 'Got it!'

Pitt had no room to accelerate past the truck, so he braked hard. But the truck also slowed, keeping him hemmed in the opposite lane with the cement mixer just yards away. A narrow side street appeared on his left, and Pitt stomped on the accelerator and turned the wheel hard over.

Inside the truck, Juan finally lowered his window. He climbed halfway out and aimed a Glock 22 at the van. He fired a wild volley of shots – until the pickup driver shouted, 'Look out!'

Too late, Juan turned to see the front fender of the cement mixer a heartbeat before it clipped him just beneath his collar. His clothes caught on the fender and he was plucked out of the truck. Both legs were smashed as he was ripped backward.

Swerving left, Pitt barely escaped a collision of his own. As the van screeched across the cement mixer's path, just missing its front bumper, a spray of bullet holes opened along the side panel and up the passenger door. Only the last bullet did any damage, splintering the crate and nicking Giordino's hand. Nerve reflex caused him to release his grip, and the crate plunged to the pavement.

Panicked, the cement mixer's driver slammed on the brakes. Briefly clutching the fender, Juan slid off and under the left front wheel. The opposite tire found the dropped crate, and the mixer bounced over both. The massive vehicle skidded to a halt, but only after flattening the remains of Juan and the crate under its dual rear wheels.

Stunned by the sight in his rearview mirror, the pickup's driver lost rein of his own vehicle. He drifted right and barreled into a Chevy Cobalt parked at the curb. The four-door pickup rode up onto the little car's trunk before grinding to a halt. A bang filled the air as the pickup's front tire cut into the car's shredded body and burst.

Across the street, the utility van went from careening past the cement mixer to nearly rear-ending an SUV. The side street was clogged with traffic, and Pitt locked the brakes to slide to a halt. Crowds of people filled the sidewalks and street, blocking the traffic ahead. Pitt noticed flashing lights reflecting off the storefront windows; the police car was approaching the scene.

'I think,' Pitt said, 'this would be a good time to kiss our utility van good-bye.'

Giordino shook his head. 'And I was just getting rather attached to her.' He found a roll of electrical tape and began wrapping his bleeding hand.

'You okay?' Pitt asked, just realizing his friend had been injured.

'I may have to give up two-fisted drinking for a spell, but I'll live.'

They jumped out of the van and blended into the crowd that began to surround the cement mixer. Ignoring Juan's flattened body, they moved to examine the smashed box.

There was little to see. A mangled assortment of wires, circuit boards, and metal casings were spread under the truck like a disemboweled robot. Whatever the box had contained, it was well beyond any attempt to resurrect.

They slid away from the mixer as two police officers approached with their sidearms drawn. Pitt and Giordino worked their way toward the pickup truck, using the mass of onlookers to avoid detection. The crowds were thicker on the sidewalk, so they joined the throng moving alongside the mangled sedan and truck. With a sense of dread, Pitt stepped forward and peered inside the pickup.

Both right doors were flung open, but Ann and the other occupants were nowhere to be seen.

19

Pablo had watched the destruction of the crate with disbelief. The death of his fellow gunman registered as little more than a nuisance, but losing the box made his face turn crimson. He vented his rage on Ann.

'What do you know of the device?' He jabbed his pistol against her.

Ann gritted her teeth and said nothing.

'Pablo . . . the police are approaching.' The driver's face was pale, and his fingers shook atop the steering wheel.

Pablo glared at Ann. 'You will talk later. Do as I say or I will kill you here. Now, get out of the car.'

Ann followed him out the passenger-side door as the driver grabbed a light jacket and draped it over her bound hands. She glanced back toward the utility van but failed to see Pitt or Giordino. She had been as shocked as Pablo to see them appear alongside the truck, and she wondered how they had been able to track her.

As they stepped onto the sidewalk, a young man in a black silk shirt accosted the driver.

'That's my car,' he said, pointing to the smashed Chevy. 'Look what you did.'

Pablo stepped over to him and discretely mashed his pistol into the man's stomach. 'Be quiet or die,' he said in a low voice.

The man stumbled backward, nodding profusely. His eyes wide, he turned and fled down the street.

Pablo stepped back and grabbed Ann by the arm, then glanced over his shoulder. He saw the police officers exit their car, and then he studied the crowd. He quickly spotted two Americans in work clothes looking under the cement mixer's right rear wheels. He had recognized them when their van had pulled alongside as the men who piloted the *Drake*'s submersible.

He turned and nudged Ann forward. 'Move.'

'What about Juan?' The driver gazed toward the cement mixer with a look of shock.

Pablo said nothing, ignoring the body of his dead partner as he guided Ann into the center of the busy sidewalk.

Arriving at the pickup a minute later, Pitt and Giordino scanned the crowds for Ann. A small girl sat on the curb, selling fresh-cut flowers out of a cardboard box. She caught Pitt's eye and held out a clump of daisies. Pitt paid for the flowers, then handed them back to the girl with a smile. Blushing, she sniffed the daisies, then raised a hand and pointed down the street.

Pitt winked at the girl and took off in the same direction. 'This way, Al.'

The crowd grew thicker as they made their way down the block. Pitt surveyed the moving mass, trying to spot Ann's blond locks. They moved with the herd to the end of the street, which opened into a large parking lot packed with cars. Finally, Pitt and Giordino saw where all the people were headed.

A newly rebuilt stadium towered over the opposite end of the parking lot. The structure was perfectly round, yet much smaller than a typical American baseball or football stadium. Streams of people headed into the building, following ramps at either end. Pitt looked up to see the top of the stadium capped in electric lights that read PLAZA EL TOREO.

'Soccer?' Giordino asked.

'No. Bullfight.'

'Darn, and I forgot to wear red.' Giordino hadn't noticed that his bloody hand had stained one pant leg crimson.

They hustled up the nearest ramp, jockeying to gain entrance with the other late arrivers. The aroma of roasting corn from a vendor's stand filled the night air. Giordino filled his lungs, trying to mask the odor of burning trash from a nearby slum that was mixed with the sweat- and alcohol-laced crowd entering the arena.

Keeping his eyes on the ramp ahead, Pitt spotted a large man enter the stadium, holding a blond woman beside him. 'I think I see her.'

Giordino made like a bulldozer, pushing his way through the crowd, with Pitt close behind. As they fought their way to the turnstiles, Pitt asked Giordino, 'Do you have any money?'

Giordino fished through his pockets with his good hand, extracting a loose handful of bills. 'The late-night poker games aboard the *Drake* have been kind to me.'

'Thank goodness there's no talent aboard that ship.' Pitt plucked a twenty and handed it to the attendant.

They didn't wait for the change, bursting through the turnstiles and running up into the stadium.

Trumpets blared from a live band as the evening troupe

of matadors and their assistants was introduced, the *cuadrilla* traipsing across the circular dirt arena in a colorful procession. A raucous crowd filled the stadium, standing and cheering. Lost in the mass of bodies, Ann and her abductors were nowhere to be seen.

'They might be making for the exit on the other side,' Pitt said.

Giordino nodded. 'In that case, we better split up.'

They descended a stepped aisle to the lower section of the arena, where Giordino moved right while Pitt cut left. Pitt worked his way across the first section of seats, scanning up and down, with no success. When the fans suddenly cheered, he glanced at the ring and saw a lone matador entering for the first fight. An ornery half-ton bull named Donatello was released to join him. Initially ignoring the matador, the beast stood, pawing the dirt and absorbing the crowd's cheers.

Pitt wormed his way through the next section of spectators, dodging vendors selling cotton candy and cold drinks. Suddenly he caught a glimpse of a woman with blond hair seated by the aisle one section over. It was Ann. The burly figure of Pablo was wedged against her, busily scanning the crowd. He soon noticed Pitt and locked eyes on him. Pablo spoke rapidly to the driver beside him, then stood up, pulling Ann to her feet. She looked at Pitt for an instant, her face a mask of fear and pleading. While the driver stood and tracked Pitt, Pablo jerked Ann away, leading her down the aisle steps to a narrow walkway that circled the ring.

Separated by a full section of cheering fans, Pitt took off at a run down the nearest steps. In the next aisle, the driver hustled to match him. When Pitt reached the low wall that surrounded the bullring, he turned and needled his way toward Ann and Pablo, who were fleeing in the other direction just a few yards ahead. Then the driver leaped off the next set of steps and stood in his path.

He was an inch or two shorter than Pitt but carried broad shoulders on a thick frame. As he shook his head for Pitt to stop, he briefly hitched up his shirt to expose a gun holstered at his waist.

Pitt moved without hesitation, lunging forward and throwing a left cross that struck the driver on his cheekbone. The driver staggered to the wall. Giving him no time to recover, Pitt pressed the barrage with a quick combination to the head.

The driver instinctively tried to block the blows, raising his hands in protection rather than reach for the gun. Then he regained his senses. He charged back at Pitt, swinging with both fists. Pitt ducked the first punch but caught a blow to the ribs that made him gasp.

Pitt countered with more blows to the head as the driver hurtled into him, knocking them both hard against the safety wall. The driver got his left arm hooked around Pitt while grabbing for his gun with his right. But his feet became entangled with Pitt's, causing both men to lose balance as they fell back.

As they teetered against the wall, the driver pulled the gun free but was forced to catch himself with the same hand. As he grasped for the wall, Pitt swung an elbow into his arm. The gun fell free, and both men tumbled over the side.

Nearby spectators gasped as the men dropped six feet

into the ring. At its center, a matador stood with his back to them, not seeing their intrusion, as he flirted with the fresh bull.

Pitt took the brunt of the fall, landing hard on his shoulder, as the two men struck the dirt together, then rolled apart. The driver bounced to his feet first and searched the ground for his lost gun. As he shuffled toward the wall, he bumped into a wooden rack stocked with *banderillas*. Long, razor-sharp darts wrapped in colorful ribbons, they were the tools of the *banderilleros* who assisted the matador. They would fling the *banderillas* into a knotty mass on the bull's back, which would agitate the bull and weaken his neck muscles so he would charge with his head lowered.

Pitt was just regaining his feet when the driver grabbed one of the darts and flung it at him. The throw was high, and Pitt easily ducked the projectile. He backpedaled along the wall as the driver grabbed three more *banderillas*. Pitt spotted a matador's cape hanging on a peg beside him. He grabbed it and wadded it into a makeshift shield.

Across the ring, a pair of *banderilleros* on foot noted the scuffle and began to make their way around the perimeter wall. The matador was still oblivious, his attention focused solely on the bull. Dangling his cape in an orchestrated movement called a *veronica*, the matador lured the bull to charge. The animal brushed by, just inches from his body. Clearing the matador's cape, the bull trotted a few paces – then stopped, seeing Pitt and the driver moving along the wall.

Some bulls are calm in the ring, requiring much prodding and wounding to entice them to charge. Others are naturally aggressive, bolting after anything that moves. The rust-colored beast named Donatello rated at the top of the belligerence scale. Yet to be speared by the *banderilleros*, he was an ornery bull at full strength. He trotted closer to the new targets, carefully eyeing the two men.

Pitt saw the bull draw near but was more concerned with fending off his attacker's *banderillas*. Facing Pitt, the driver didn't see the bull.

The driver stepped forward and began to release his barrage on Pitt, heaving the darts like a lancer. Pitt kept his eyes focused on the projectiles. Still stepping backward, he batted the first dart away with the wadded cape. The second throw went a centimeter wide when Pitt jumped to one side. The driver yanked back his arm with the last *banderilla*, then took a step closer for a better aim. As he flung the dart, the bull charged.

The throw was perfect. The razor tip shot straight at Pitt – and would have struck him in the chest if he hadn't blocked it with the cape. The dart tore through the fabric, losing just enough of its momentum before slicing Pitt's hand. As if touching a scalding pot, Pitt hurled the balled cape and embedded spear back at the driver, then dove to the ground.

Any uncertainty over which figure to target vanished from the galloping bull. The brute animal followed the airborne cape to the driver, who reached out and grabbed the bundle.

The bull lowered his head and accelerated.

The driver was confused by Pitt's sudden dive to the ground, and then he detected movement behind him. He turned, seeing the charging bull just a few feet away, and froze.

Donatello barreled straight into the man. The crowd screamed as the bull's horns punctured the driver's stomach, nearly breaking through to his back. Tossing his head, the bull lifted the impaled man into the air and paraded him for several feet before dumping the limp, bloodied body onto the dirt.

Pitt heard a delayed solitary scream from the crowd and looked behind him. A short distance across the ring, Ann tussled with Pablo. In a quick motion, the big gunman scooped Ann off her feet and tossed her into the ring. Her hands still bound, she landed awkwardly and fell to the ground. She struggled to get up, then felt a burning pain in her ankle. She could stand on only one foot.

Frenzied by his fresh kill, the bull studied Ann for a moment and snorted. Lowering his head, he angled toward the woman and charged.

The two *banderilleros* and the matador sprinted across the ring, yelling, but the bull ignored them. They were too distant to attract the bull's wrath. But Pitt wasn't.

He jumped to his feet, ran and scooped up the shredded cape, then bolted for the bull. Charging hard, the animal was less than twenty feet from Ann.

She tried shuffling to the wall but could barely move from the pain in her ankle. Her heart pounded as she faced the charging animal, then froze like the driver had. Her frightened trance was broken by a sudden shout.

'*¡Toro! ¡Toro!*'

She turned to see Pitt rushing toward her, wildly waving the shredded cape. The bull took one look at the tall, bounding man with the bright magenta cape – and bit.

Ann felt the heat from the beast's breath as it veered away from her at the last second and chased after Pitt.

He skidded in the dirt as the bull overtook him. Extending the cape to his side, he shook the material like a dusty rug, drawing the bull's eye. Donatello followed the movement. He burst into and through the cape, his sharp horns skimming just millimeters past Pitt's body.

Pitt yanked the cape upward as the bull tore through, then spun to face the animal. He was too engrossed in self-preservation to hear the applause and chants of *Olé* that poured from the crowd. He shook the cape, then stepped aside as the bull charged once more.

'Allow me, *señor*,' the matador said, rushing up with an embarrassed look.

With the aid of a *banderillero,* the matador drove the bull to the center of the ring while two other men dragged away the driver's body.

Pitt turned to approach Ann, only to see her hoisted into the stands by Giordino. He stepped closer and grasped Giordino's outstretched left hand. To the thunderous applause of the crowd, Pitt climbed over the wall. A pale and shaken Ann grabbed him by the arm. 'That bull would have mauled me if you hadn't stepped in. It was a crazy thing to do, but thank you.'

Pitt gave her a tired grin. 'You forget that I work in Washington. I'm fighting bull all the time.'

Then his face grew serious, and he gazed around them. 'Your abductor, Pablo?'

Ann shook her head. Giordino was already scanning the crowds, but he too came up empty.

The big man had made himself small in the crowd and disappeared.

20

'I'm thinking we really shouldn't lollygag to chat with the authorities,' Giordino said. He tilted his head toward a bullring official who was making his way across the stadium with two security guards.

'Lead on,' Pitt said, and cinched his arm tight around Ann's waist.

She took a hesitant step with her injured leg, then grasped Pitt's shoulder for support as a burst of pain bolted through her ankle.

'Just put your weight on the good leg, and we'll get there,' Pitt said. He easily supported her one-hundred-and-ten-pound frame.

Giordino charged through the crowd like a snowplow, clearing a path for the hobbling duo following close behind. They found the rear exit ramp and hustled out of the stadium, to the crowd's fading cheers. Unable to draw close, the bullring authorities could only watch in puzzlement as the three Americans jumped into a taxi and roared off into the night.

Ann begged to be taken to the American consulate but was outvoted by the NUMA men, who had already negotiated a supplemental fuel purchase from the taxi driver. As the cab zipped across Tijuana, the exhaustion of the chase caught up with them and the conversation fell silent.

Pitt had plenty of questions for Ann, but now was not the time to ask.

She had kept her emotions bottled up since leaving the ship, refusing to allow her fears to overcome her. Now that she was free from Pablo's death threats and safe in the company of Pitt and Giordino, the fright seeped out. She shivered in the warm night air and fought back her emotions. Pitt gently tucked an arm around her and gave her a light squeeze, which seemed to purge her stressful feelings. Within a few minutes, she had drifted off to sleep.

The drive to the coast took over an hour at legal speeds, pushing the clock to almost ten when they arrived at the small sandy beach. Pitt was relieved to spot the barge's inflatable sitting where they had left it. He dragged it down to the surf and helped Ann climb aboard. Giordino retrieved the inflatable's fuel can and passed it to the cabby, who siphoned a few gallons of gas from his car with an old hose he kept in the trunk.

'*Gracias, amigo,*' Giordino said as he parted with the balance of his poker winnings. Then he hauled the fuel can down to the beach.

Counting his cash windfall, the cabby beamed and shouted, '*¡Buen viaje!*'

Pitt attached the engine's fuel line to the gas can and then with Giordino's assistance shoved the inflatable past the surf line and climbed aboard. The outboard fired up with little trouble, and they were soon racing past the rocky breakwater.

'You sure you can find the *Drake*?' Ann asked, scanning

125

the black horizon. Her eyes were again alert but tinged with apprehension.

Pitt nodded. 'I think Rudi will leave the lights on for us.'

Once clear of the jetty, he turned the inflatable north and followed the coast. After a mile or so, he veered out to sea to retrace their original course. Gazing over his shoulder, he found a bearing, the lights of a lone house high on a hill that lined up vertically with a pale yellow streetlamp near the shoreline. Steering to keep the two lights in alignment, he guided the inflatable offshore until the beacons vanished. They motored on for several minutes in complete darkness, Ann fighting her fears that they would become lost at sea. Just as the waters around them became blackest, a faint glow appeared a few points off the bow. A single white light emerged from the distant sea, gradually morphing into several lights. As they bore closer, they could see they belonged to three vessels grouped together.

The *Drake* and the barge were stationed alongside each other, while a larger ship waited nearby. Pitt observed its white-and-orange-banded hull, signifying a US Coast Guard vessel. A pair of lookouts on its deck monitored the inflatable as Pitt eased it alongside the *Drake* and killed the engine.

When he saw Ann, a visibly relieved Rudi Gunn leaned over the rail above them. 'Thank heavens, you're safe.'

'Careful, she's got a bad wheel,' Giordino said. He lifted her to the rail, where Gunn helped her aboard the ship.

'I'll call for the *Edisto*'s medic to come aboard,' Gunn said.

Ann shook her head. 'All I really need is some ice.'

'Me, too,' Giordino said, pulling himself onto the deck. 'In a glass with a shot of Jack Daniel's.'

Pitt remained in the inflatable, acting as taxi driver to shuttle over the Coast Guard medic. Ann was quickly settled into her cabin with her ankle iced and a dose of painkillers in her stomach. Pitt returned the medic to his ship, tied off the inflatable, and climbed aboard the *Drake*.

When he met up with Gunn and Giordino on the bridge, Al had already explained their chase through Tijuana.

'*El Matador* Pitt, eh?' Gunn smiled.

'I must have some Spanish blood in me.' Pitt sighed and gazed out the bridge window toward the *Edisto*. 'Nice work, getting the Coast Guard out here, but why aren't they pursuing the Mexican boat?'

'Absent a lifesaving emergency, they weren't prepared to encroach on Mexican territorial waters without authorization. They've called in the Mexican Navy, who will take the lead.' Gunn took off his glasses and wiped the lenses. 'Unfortunately, they don't seem to have a vessel in the area, so the outlook isn't good. I thought it best if the *Edisto* stood by until we heard back from you.'

'A prudent call.'

'It seems the thieves were standing by, waiting for us to salvage the *Cuttlefish*,' Gunn said. 'What was in that crate that was so valuable?'

Pitt's eyes narrowed. 'That's a question I'd like an answer for.'

'Whatever it was,' Giordino said, 'nobody's going to be too happy about its demise. Now it's nothing but a worthless bundle of mashed wires.'

'Speaking of which,' Gunn said, 'we replaced the bridge radio with a spare unit from belowdecks. I guess I should let the *Edisto* know we can all head back to San Diego now.'

'Rudi, aren't you forgetting some unfinished business downstairs?' Giordino said, pointing toward the sea.

He looked down his angular nose at Giordino. 'Do you think we've been sitting around playing tiddlywinks while you were gone?'

He stepped to the rear of the bridge and pointed out the window at the barge. Bathed in the glow of a dim deck light sat the *Cuttlefish*, supported on a pair of wooden cradles.

'You landed her without us!' Giordino turned to Pitt. 'Now, how did we miss that?'

'Guess we were too focused on the Coast Guard cutter. Nice work, Rudi. Did she give you any trouble coming up?'

'None at all. We just ran the sling cables from the submersible to the barge crane and hoisted away. She came up clean as a whistle, but I think you'll want to take a look at her hull.'

'Now's as good a time as any,' Pitt said.

Gunn gathered some flashlights, and they motored in the inflatable to the bow of the barge. The vessel was ghostly quiet, its pilot asleep in his bunk with the dachshund curled at his feet.

The *Cuttlefish* stood tall above them. The hull's sides were clean and dry, and the boat's chrome sparkled bright under their lights, showing little indication it had been submerged for nearly a week.

Giordino let out a low whistle as they viewed a gaping hole ripped in the base of the hull. 'She must have sunk in a heartbeat.'

'I guess the DARPA folks had reason to be suspicious,' Gunn said. 'By the looks of it, this was no accident.'

'Our buddies in the cabin cruiser probably attached some explosives to the hull,' Giordino said. 'Must have detonated prematurely, before they could lay their hands on the crate.'

'Actually, they planted the explosives inside the boat.' Pitt studied the damage with his flashlight. 'The blast marks seem to indicate an internal explosion.'

Gunn put his hand on a serrated section next to the hole; it flared outward. 'You're right. The explosives must have been placed inside the cabin.'

Pitt knelt beneath the opening and shined his flashlight into the dark interior. The remnants of the boat's galley were visible above him, with black-stained bulkheads and a crater-sized blast hole through the ceiling. Still, the interior damage was less severe than the breach in the hull.

Examining the damage, Pitt noticed a pair of frayed orange wires trailing from the hole. He traced the wires' path across the galley to an aft corner bulkhead, where they rose through a drilled hole. Squeezing through the blast hole, Pitt climbed into the galley and stepped aft past the cramped dining area to a flight of steps. He followed them up to the wheelhouse, where he stopped and studied the helm. In front of the pilot's seat, he pulled open a kick panel, which contained a rat's maze of colored wires that powered the boat's electronics. He soon found the orange wires. One was spliced to a power lead, while the other ran up to the throttle housing. A minute later, he found its terminus – a hidden toggle switch mounted beneath the helm panel.

Giordino and Gunn had walked around the *Cuttlefish* and climbed up its stern. Finding Pitt standing at the helm, lost in thought, Gunn asked what he had discovered.

'A slight twist in my theory,' Pitt said. 'It wasn't the Mexicans who blew up the *Cuttlefish*. It was Heiland himself.'

21

Stepping into the *Drake*'s mess just after sunup, Pitt was surprised to find Ann seated across from Gunn, finishing her breakfast. Grabbing a cup of coffee, he headed to their table.

'Good morning. Mind if I join you?'

Gunn waved him to a seat next to Ann. 'Always interrupting my fun.'

Pitt looked to Ann. 'Sleep well?'

'Just fine,' she said, softly averting his gaze.

Pitt smiled at her sudden sheepishness. Returning from the barge the night before, he had gone straight to his cabin to go to bed. He'd answered a light knock at his door to find Ann in the doorway, an expectant look on her face. She'd worn a loose-fitting ship's bathrobe that failed to conceal the straps of her lingerie. Barefoot, she stood on her good leg, relieving the pressure on her wrapped and swollen left ankle.

'I was hoping you would stop by to say good night,' she whispered.

Pitt quelled an uneasy desire as he gazed into her needy eyes. 'Negligence on my part,' he said with a smile.

He bent down and plucked her off her feet, holding her tight. She buried her head in his neck as he carried her down the narrow corridor and into her cabin. Setting her gently on the bunk, he leaned over and kissed her forehead.

'Good night, my dear,' he said softly. Before she could respond, he'd backed out of her cabin and closed the door behind him.

'Your cook is excellent,' Ann said to Gunn, now pushing away her empty plate while trying to change the subject.

'Food is a key element of shipboard morale, particularly on long voyages. We insist on highly trained chefs for all our vessels.' Gunn took a bite of toast and turned to Pitt. 'Ann was just telling me how she put her college springboard experience to good use by diving from the bridge wing last evening.'

'I'd give her a 9.0.' Pitt winked. 'Though I might raise my marks if she would dive into what this expedition was really all about.'

Ann gave a nervous cough into her napkin. 'What do you mean?'

'We were searching for much more than just a missing boat, weren't we?'

'It was important that we find the boat, and any equipment that was still aboard.'

'We succeeded on both counts,' Pitt said, 'so how about you tell us something about that equipment?'

'I can't disclose that.'

Pitt's eyes narrowed. 'Aside from nearly getting yourself killed, you also placed this ship and crew in danger. I think we're entitled to some answers.'

Ann looked Pitt in the eye for the first time – and realized she couldn't sidestep the issue. She gazed around the room to ensure no one was eavesdropping.

'As you know, Dr Heiland's company was engaged in a

high-level research-and-development project for DARPA. His work was in support of a secret Navy submarine program called *Sea Arrow*. Heiland was specifically involved in the development of an advanced propulsion system. I really can't tell you more than that except that he was doing some final prototype testing on a breakthrough development when his boat was lost at sea.'

'That was the item in the crate?'

'A scale model,' Ann said. 'While there was a suspicion of foul play in the loss of the *Cuttlefish*, no one anticipated any interference with our search-and-recovery project. I'm truly sorry your crew was placed in danger. It was thought that the fewer people aware of Heiland's research, the better. I know the Vice President wasn't happy about keeping you in the dark, but he was forced to go along at the request of Tom Cerny.'

'So who were those guys who tried to steal it?' Gunn asked.

Ann shrugged. 'A mystery, at the moment. By their looks, I don't believe the men were from Mexico, but possibly Central or South America. I've already spoken to Washington and been assured we'll have the Mexican authorities' assistance in examining the two bodies and tracing the pickup truck.'

'We've provided a pretty good description of their boat to the Mexican Navy,' Gunn said.

'They don't seem like the usual suspects for a defense-related theft,' Pitt noted. 'Did you think they had already absconded with Heiland's magic box?'

'Yes,' Ann said. 'When the bodies of Heiland and his assistant were found, we presumed they had been hijacked at sea and the prototype stolen. That's why I was so shocked to see the crate still secured aboard the *Cuttlefish*.'

'I guess you have Heiland to thank for that,' Pitt said. He described his discovery of the orange wires and hidden toggle switch. 'I'm guessing that Heiland realized he was under attack and blew up his own boat.'

'The two bodies showed severe trauma consistent with a fire or explosion,' Ann said. 'We never considered it was of their own doing, but that may need to be reevaluated now.'

'I think Heiland beat them to the punch,' Pitt said. 'And, to make matters worse for the bad guys, the *Cuttlefish* sank in water too deep for conventional diving. They were probably scrambling to locate their own salvage ship when we showed up. So they let us raise it for them.'

Gunn turned to Ann. 'Your high diving saved the day.'

'No, it was Dirk and Al who recaptured the crate. Though its destruction saved it from falling into the wrong hands, the loss of the model has magnified some other problems.'

'Namely?' Pitt asked.

'I've been told that neither DARPA nor the Navy have any detailed plans or design specs for Heiland's work. Carl Heiland was a highly respected engineer – a genius, really – and because of that he was given free rein. Over the years he's made many brilliant modifications in submarine design and torpedo development. As a result, he wasn't required to submit the usual mountain of documentation demanded by most defense contracts.'

'So no one else knows how to complete the *Sea Arrow*?' Pitt asked.

'Exactly,' Ann replied with a tight-lipped grimace.

'With Heiland dead and his model destroyed,' Gunn said, 'those plans would be extremely valuable.'

'Fowler tells me that is now our top priority.' She looked at her watch and then at Pitt. 'The Vice President's office has arranged a return jet for us to Washington. It leaves San Diego at one o'clock. I'd like to visit Heiland's head-quarters in Del Mar before we go. Could you drive me there on the way to the airport?'

Pitt rose from the table and offered Ann her crutches. 'I never fail to heed the call of small children, little old ladies, or pretty girls with wrenched ankles.' He gave a slight bow. 'Just show me the way.'

An hour later, they pulled into the headquarters of Heiland Research and Associates. The office occupied a shared building on a rise overlooking the beach town of Del Mar, just north of San Diego. The site offered a clear view of the ocean to the west, as well as Del Mar's famed racetrack in the valley below. Ann flashed her credentials at the front desk and signed them in.

'Welcome, Miss Bennett,' the receptionist said. 'Mrs Marsdale is expecting you.'

A minute later, a stylish woman with short dark hair entered the lobby and introduced herself as Carl Heiland's operations manager. As she led them to a nearby confer-ence room, Ann followed awkwardly on her crutches.

'We won't take much of your time, Mrs Marsdale,' Ann said. 'I'm on the team investigating the death of Mr Hei-land, and I am concerned about securing his working papers related to the *Sea Arrow* project.'

'I still can't believe he's gone.' The shock of Heiland's

death still marked her face. 'I assume his death was no accident?'

'Why would you think that?'

'Carl and Manfred were just too competent to die in a boating accident. Carl was a safe and prudent man. I know he always had concerns about maintaining the secrecy of his work.'

'We don't think it was an accident,' Ann said, 'but the investigation is still ongoing. We do believe that someone was trying to acquire his test model.'

Marsdale nodded. 'The FBI were here a few days ago, and we gave them what we could. But as I told them, this is Dr Heiland's business headquarters. We handle the government contracts and related admin support, and that's about it. The entire firm employs only twelve people.'

'Where is your research facility?' Pitt asked.

'We don't really have one. There's a small shop out back, where we employ a few interns for ongoing research topics, but Carl and Manfred seldom worked here. They traveled frequently but actually conducted most of their research in Idaho.'

'Idaho?' Ann asked.

'Yes, there's a Navy research facility in Bayview. Dr Heiland has a cabin nearby, where he and Manfred would escape to problem-solve.'

'That would be Manfred Ortega, Dr Heiland's assistant?'

'Yes. Carl called him Manny. A brilliant engineer in his own right. The two of them together created magical work. They were the brains of the whole company. I don't know what we'll do now.'

There was a long silence as they all realized the deaths of Carl and Manny meant the likely demise of Heiland Research and Associates.

'Did the FBI gather all of the materials here on site?' Ann asked.

'They took all of our admin files – and even our computers, for a time. We had sent the technical files to DARPA headquarters, which was just as well. The FBI agents were like a bull in a china shop, so I didn't let them in Carl's office, but they had the run of the rest of the place.'

'Would you mind if I had a look around his office?' Ann said. 'I'm sure you can understand the national security ramifications of securing all of his work.'

'Sure. He never left much here, but his office is just down the hall.' Marsdale grabbed some keys from her desk and led them to a corner office. Of modest size, Heiland's office looked seldom used. Like the man, it was frugal in décor, sporting a few submarine models and a painting of a mahogany rumrunner under sail. The only incongruous item was a stuffed moose head, with an assortment of fishing caps dangling from its antlers, mounted just above the desk.

Marsdale gave a puzzled look when she saw several desk drawers had been left open. 'That's odd.' She suddenly stiffened. 'Someone's been in here and searched his desk. I remember leaving a contract in his in-box for signature and now it's gone.'

She turned to Ann with a worried expression. 'I'm the only one in the building with keys to his office.'

'Were there any other important documents in here?'

'I can't say for sure, but I don't think so. Like I said, he was seldom here for very long.'

She looked at the desk and then glanced up at the moose. 'There was a picture of his boat and cabin on his desk – it's gone, too. And Carl used to hang the keys to his cabin on the moose antler when he was here and they're also missing.'

'Do you have security cameras in the building?' Pitt asked.

'We do. I'll contact our security firm immediately.' Her voice cracked in distress. 'I'm very sorry.'

'If you don't mind,' Ann said, 'I'd like to call the FBI back in to scour the office. Combined with your security video, that should allow us to develop some potential leads.'

'Yes, of course. Whatever it takes to find out who is behind all this.'

As Ann and Pitt returned to the car, she stopped and stared out at the ocean. 'They were here, weren't they?'

'I'd bet on it,' Pitt said.

'I've got a favor to ask.' She turned and locked eyes with him. 'Would you mind delaying our return to Washington a day? I'd like to redirect our flight to Idaho. If Marsdale is right, all of Heiland's plans may be safe in Bayview without us even knowing it.'

'I'm game,' Pitt said. 'Fact is, I've always been curious to see where all those famous potatoes come from.'

22

The government Gulfstream jet descended out of a sapphire sky and touched down on the main runway of Coeur d'Alene Airport's Pappy Boyington Field. A native son of the scenic Idaho town, Gregory 'Pappy' Boyington had grown up to fly F4U Corsairs in the Pacific, winning the Medal of Honor while commanding the legendary Black Sheep Squadron. The airport that bore his name was now home to tame Piper Cubs and private jets of wealthy tourists. Pitt grabbed Ann's crutches and helped her off the plane at the private jet terminal, where they negotiated the use of a rental car. Pitt took the wheel as they headed north on Route 95.

They were traveling up Idaho's northern panhandle, a region of rich forested hills and pristine blue lakes, far from the potato fields in the state's southern plains. Traffic was light, and Pitt nudged the rental car past the sixty-five-mile-per-hour speed limit. Twenty minutes later they reached the town of Athol, where Pitt turned onto a side road and drove east. A large sign welcomed them onto the grounds of Farragut State Park.

'An Idaho state park named after a Civil War admiral?' Pitt said.

'As a matter of fact, it is.' Ann scanned a travel brochure she picked up at the airport. 'In the early days of World War Two, the Navy established an inland base here after it was feared the Japanese would bomb the West Coast. The Farragut Naval Training Station was indeed named for David Farragut, hero of the Battle of Mobile Bay and the first full admiral in the US Navy. Nearly fifty thousand men were stationed here at one point. After the war, the base closed down, and the land was conveyed to Idaho, which turned it into a state park.'

'There's some trivia to fling at your next Pentagon cocktail hour,' Pitt said.

The road exited the park and corkscrewed down a hill into Bayview. The hamlet was at the tip of a narrow inlet on the large glacial lake of Pend Oreille. Pitt had to squeeze past some road construction equipment before dropping down to the main waterfront drive. Several marinas filled with bass boats, day cruisers, and a large number of houseboats occupied the northern half of the bay. The Navy Acoustic Research Detachment controlled the southern shore.

'There's the lab's entrance,' Ann said, pointing to a gated entry.

Pitt pulled into the visitors' lot and parked next to the guard station. After they signed in with the guard, a uniformed escort arrived and chauffeured them into the facility in a gray sedan. As they drove along the waterfront, Pitt noticed an oddly shaped submarine with the designation *Sea Jet* tied up at dock.

The driver stopped at a towering beige-and-teal metal building built over the water, then escorted Ann and Pitt to the door. An animated man with bright red hair and dancing blue eyes greeted them.

'Chuck Nichols, assistant lab director,' he said in a rapid-fire voice. 'Please, follow me.'

He waved off the driver and led Ann and Pitt to a small office crowded with papers and technical journals. He cleared off a pair of chairs overflowing with binders so they could sit down.

'We were all pretty shocked to hear about Carl and Manny's accident,' Nichols said. 'Have you figured out what happened?'

'Not entirely,' Ann said, 'but we don't believe it was an accident. We have reason to believe they were killed during a failed attempt by a foreign party to obtain the model prototype they were testing.'

Nichols's lips tightened. 'Yeah, *Slippery Mumm*. He was pretty secret about that one. I can't believe anybody would have known about it.'

'*Slippery Mumm?*'

'He always had a pet name for his models. He called his last hull model *Pig Ghost*. He gave us lots of grief over naming our test boat *Sea Jet*.'

'Any significance to the name?' Pitt asked.

'Sure, but probably only to Carl and Manny. He said the *Mumm* was from a champagne he liked. He talked a lot about speed and bubbles in attacking the supercavitation issue, so that must be the connection.'

'Tell us about your facility here,' Ann said.

'Heiland practically built the place. His family had a cabin here on Lake Pend Oreille, so he fell in love with the area.'

Pitt noticed he pronounced the lake's name 'Pond-o-ray.'

'When he headed up acoustics at the Naval Surface Warfare Center,' Nichols continued, 'he convinced the brass in Washington to open an offshoot research lab here, using some remnants from the old Farragut naval base. He pretty much built it all from scratch. About ten or twelve years ago, he grew tired of the day-to-day management and decided to retire. That's when he started his consulting business. Carl was always an engineer first.'

'You're a long way from blue water,' Pitt said.

'Yes, but the lake is an ideal testing ground. It's large, lightly populated, and features depths of over a thousand feet. Our work here focuses on research in advanced hull and propulsion designs – ones that allow for submarines to operate with a minimum acoustic signature. The lake is a nearly perfect controlled environment in which to test new designs and technologies.'

'The *Sea Jet* being a test platform?' Pitt asked.

'Exactly,' Nichols said. 'It's what we call an Advanced Electric Ship Demonstrator. Though it looks a bit like a submarine, it is actually a quarter-scale model of the new DD(X) class of destroyer. We've used it to experiment with some radical new hull designs and propulsion systems. It was originally built with waterjet propulsion, but we've migrated to some other technologies I probably shouldn't talk about. We were scheduled to test Carl's latest tinkering related to the *Sea Arrow* project, but we're at somewhat of a loss there now.'

'The technology in the *Slippery Mumm*?' Ann asked.

'Yes. He was here testing it in the lake just a few weeks ago. I remember him telling the boys that he was really going to be scaring the fish with it. A couple of the fellows were out on the lake at the time and they claimed he was registering some crazy speeds.'

'Didn't he work on it here at the facility?'

'Not much. He'd come in and run things on our computers, but he was always three steps ahead of us. When he was in town, he was usually holed up at his cabin with Manny, tinkering away.'

'It's important that we find and secure all of his research related to the *Slippery Mumm*,' Ann said.

'I already received that request from the folks at DARPA and I'm pulling together what we have,' Nichols said. 'The fact of the matter is, Carl maintained ninety percent of the data. What wasn't in his head is probably still out at his cabin. Here, let me give you the address.'

He checked his Rolodex and jotted down the address for Ann, giving directions as he wrote. 'There's a rusty bell sitting on the patio table in back. Underneath it should be his spare keys to the house and boat.'

Ann gave him a *How did you know that?* look.

'I've downed more than a few beers with Carl on his porch and his boat,' Nichols said with a wink.

Ann thanked him for his time, and they were escorted back to the front gate. Ann felt a sense of optimism for the first time. 'See, I think this little side trip is going to pay off. Let's go check out Heiland's cabin, and then I'll call the FBI to come secure the place.'

'No objection to having dinner first?' Pitt said. 'It'll be getting dark soon.'

'Only if I can buy.'

Their options in the small town were limited. Pitt selected a waterfront restaurant called the Captain's Wheel just down the road. Ann sampled a Greek salad while Pitt polished off a cheeseburger and beer as they watched the marina lights begin flickering on.

Ann noticed a tranquil look cross Pitt's face as he gazed at the lake's still waters. There was something enigmatic about the man, yet she felt entirely safe with him. She had met him just days before and knew almost nothing about him – other than the disappointing discovery that he was married.

'I'm not sure I ever thanked you for saving my life in Tijuana,' she said.

Pitt looked at her and smiled. 'I'm not sure jumping aboard a boat filled with armed thugs was the smartest act of law enforcement I've ever seen, but I'm glad things worked out.'

'I'm occasionally prone to rashness.' She thought of her uninvited visit to his cabin the night before. 'I'm hoping that we can be friends in Washington after this case is resolved.'

'I'd like that.'

With a grin he slid the check across the table to her. 'But for now, how about we go find Heiland's cabin before it gets completely dark.'

Nichols had told them they couldn't get lost and he was right. His directions sent them down a single-lane road that skirted the Acoustic Research Center and continued along the southern edge of the inlet. They passed clusters of cabins that grew fewer in number as the town lights receded behind them. The road tracked toward the bay's entrance, then turned south, following the lake's irregular shore. They drove another few miles before the road ended in a pine-clustered cul-de-sac. A narrow gravel drive led to a red wooden house facing the water.

'That looks like the place,' Ann said, confirming the address on a mailbox.

Pitt drove the rental car down the drive and parked beside an attached garage that looked large enough to house a dozen vehicles. No lights were on in the house, and a desolate silence permeated the grounds.

Ann noticed the first stars visible overhead as she felt a light breeze blow in from the lake. 'I wish we had a flashlight,' she said, poking her crutches at the uneven ground that sloped toward the lake.

'Why don't you just head for the front door and I'll go look for the keys out back,' Pitt said.

He stepped around the side of the garage and followed a footpath to the rear of the house. Just a thin band of tall pines separated the backyard from the water. Pitt could tell the house sat on a prime parcel of land that offered a breathtaking view of the lake. He swatted at a mosquito buzzing in his ear as he stepped onto a wide porch that ran the length of the house. He quickly spotted the old bell centered on a coffee table surrounded by some Adirondack chairs. The keys were indeed there, attached to a floatable chain used by boaters. Retracing his steps, he glanced toward the lake, noticing a private dock at the property line with a dark-colored boat moored alongside.

Ann had made her way to the front door and stood resting on her crutches. 'Any luck?'

Pitt dropped the keys into her hand. 'Just as advertised.'

She unlocked the door and stepped inside, groping for a switch. Pitt followed her in as she flipped on a bank of overhead spotlights that illuminated the interior. The antique cabin had been tastefully updated over the years. The kitchen glimmered with stainless steel appliances and granite countertops, while the living room featured a large flat-panel television. A pair of stuffed trout hung next to an antique fly rod above the rock fireplace, an ode to one of the owner's longtime passions.

Uncomfortable scouring the dead man's refuge, Ann quickly hobbled through the house searching for an office or workshop. All she found were four large bedrooms.

'We better hope there's something in the garage.' She looked toward a door at the end of the hall.

Pitt followed her as she opened the door and flicked on the lights. The sight surprised them both.

Though they expected to find a workshop of some sort, they never anticipated that a top-drawer research lab would be hidden in the Idaho woods. The garage looked like it had been transferred from the heart of Silicon Valley. The bright overhead lights illuminated a spotlessly clean white room filled with stainless steel workbenches. Rack after rack of electronic test equipment lined one wall; another corner was set up as a fabrication area. A long, narrow tank filled with water, used for marine hull and propulsion testing, stretched nearly the length of the building. But the space wasn't entirely devoted to work, Pitt noted. In one corner stood a 1950s-era pinball machine next to an elaborate espresso machine.

'Jackpot,' Pitt said.

Ann limped her way across the room, where a large executive desk was positioned next to two easy chairs. A pair of laptop computers sat open beside several bound journals and stacks of schematic diagrams. Ann picked up a journal and read a few lines of the handwritten notes.

'This is dated just a few days ago,' she said. 'He describes a series of successful tests of "SM" in the lake and his plans for a final saltwater proof run in San Diego.'

'SM. That would be *Slippery Mumm*.'

'Thank goodness. His notes and data look to be all here. The plans haven't been lost.'

The words had barely left her mouth when the lights to the house went off, leaving them in a sea of blackness.

23

The two men had pulled up short of the cabin upon seeing a car parked in the drive. The driver opened the trunk, and each man retrieved a Glock semiautomatic pistol and a pair of night vision goggles. Darkness had enveloped the mountain lake by then, and a moonless night offered little illumination.

With trained stealth, they surveyed the cabin's perimeter and located the electrical panel box. Prying open the cover, one of them found the main breaker and flipped it off.

Inside the windowless lab, it turned as black as a mine shaft at midnight. Ann let out a faint gasp. 'What a place to be when the power goes out,' she said, a nervous uptick in her voice.

'May be just a power surge,' Pitt said. 'Stay still for a moment so you don't trip and fall.'

As they waited, an uneasy apprehension bedeviled Pitt's thoughts. 'Try turning on the laptop computer for light,' he said. 'It should have some battery power.'

'Good idea.' Ann set down the journal and felt on the desk for one of the laptops. She located one and pressed a variety of keys, hoping to locate the power button.

From inside the house, Pitt heard the hall floorboards creak. They weren't alone. He reached toward the workbench beside him and ran his hand across its surface, probing for a weapon. Ignoring some strands of loose wire, he felt a tool – a tiny pair of needle-nose pliers – and he palmed it in his hand.

'There, I think I got it,' Ann said. The computer began to boot up, and she spun the screen toward Pitt, casting the room in a turquoise glow. The faint light reached the house door just as it burst open. Two intruders charged in, then froze as they surveyed the interior.

Pitt saw they were both short but muscular, dressed in dark clothes and wearing night vision goggles. They held Glocks at arm's length and swept the room mechanically until locking sights on Ann and Pitt.

'Do not move!' the lead assailant shouted with a slight Spanish accent.

He produced a flashlight and aimed its beam at them. Ann had to squint when the light lingered on her face.

The gunman strode forward, keeping his weapon trained on Pitt. 'Back against the wall,' he said, illuminating the path with his flashlight.

Ann eased up her crutches and hobbled over to Pitt, then they both stepped to the side wall. A door in the wall led to the backyard, and Pitt gently nudged Ann closer to it as the gunman called to his partner. The second man approached and took up a guard position in front of Ann and Pitt, his gun fixed on them. The other man holstered his weapon, raised his goggles, and used his flashlight to begin searching the lab.

He was thorough, Pitt noted, and he knew what he was looking for. He started by examining the laptops and desk journals Ann had found, then methodically searched the lab itself. It took nearly ten minutes before he returned to the desk and organized the items he wanted. Locating an empty plastic bin, he stuffed it with Heiland's notes and journals.

Ann huddled close to Pitt, stunned that she was staring down the barrel of a gun for the second time in two days. Anger began to push aside her fear as she saw Heiland's work being stolen right in front of her. Emptying the desk drawers, the burglar stuffed the contents into the bin, finishing it off with the two laptops.

'Are you done?' the man standing guard asked.

'Almost.' The other man glanced at Ann and Pitt with annoyance. 'Stay here with them until I get back.'

He hoisted the bin onto his shoulder and crossed the lab, guided by his flashlight.

A few seconds after he left the room, the guard called out to him, but he received no reply.

Pitt could hear the intruder as he lumbered through the house and exited the front door. He didn't have to be a psychic to know nothing good would come from his return.

Without the lights from the flashlight and computer, the garage had again turned inky black. Too black, Pitt realized with a sudden flicker of hope. The guard's night vision goggles required some form of ambient light to function, be it only faint starlight. But the only source of ambient light in the garage was the laptop computer and it had been removed. That's why the guard had called to his partner – because he could no longer see anything.

Pitt's theory was confirmed when he heard a zipper being pulled open on the guard's jacket. He was fishing for his own flashlight. Pitt didn't let him make the catch.

Pulling one of Ann's crutches from her grasp, he spun it into a battering ram and charged forward. He could only hope that the guard remained where he was when his partner had left, five feet directly in front of Pitt.

As he fumbled for his light, the guard had lowered his gun hand and was totally unprepared when the rubberized foot of the crutch slammed into his sternum. The unseen blow thrust him backward, sprawling across Heiland's desk. He whipped his gun around and fired several blind shots, not realizing he was aiming three feet over Pitt's head.

'Ann, get out the back door now!' Pitt shouted.

Ducking low, he spun the crutch around again and started swinging it, trying to make contact with the prone gunman. The muzzle flashes gave him guidance, and he batted the aluminum crutch against the man's wrist with a bone-shattering crack, sending the gun flying.

Ann had dropped to the ground at the first gunfire and felt along the wall until locating the door, then the handle. She twisted the knob of the dead bolt above it and flung open the door. Grabbing her remaining crutch, she crawled out, then hopped away from the building.

Before the door swung shut, she heard the gunman let out a wail from the pain of his fractured wrist. He scrambled off the desk to escape Pitt's onslaught. Pitt could hear him stagger to his feet, but now he was beyond reach and out of sight. Knowing that Ann couldn't move fast with her hurt ankle, Pitt pressed the attack to buy her more time. He dropped the crutch and hurled himself onto the desk, sliding across the spot where the guard had backpedaled seconds before.

Spinning as he slid, Pitt landed on his feet and took a step forward, blindly swinging his fist in an arc in front of him. His knuckles only grazed the jacket of the guard, who had stepped to Pitt's left.

The guard countered with his good hand, striking a solid punch to Pitt's shoulder.

Pitt recoiled and shook off the blow. He knew where his target was and he stepped forward with two quick strikes. He connected with both fists, barreling a left and a right into the guard's chest. The man grunted as he staggered backward, tripping over a chair and clattering to the ground.

Pitt had no time to finish the attack. The hallway door flew open and the other gunman, alerted by the shooting, ran in. He scanned his flashlight across the room, hesitating on the guard's fallen body before focusing on Pitt a few steps away.

Pitt reacted instantly, flinging himself back across the desk. The gunman tried to track his movements with the light while firing a snap shot, but the bullet went high.

Pitt slid off the desk and onto the floor, ducking out of the shooter's sight. He wasted no time lying still, scurrying across the floor to the back wall. He bumped against the discarded crutch and plucked it up.

The gunman bolted after Pitt. The beam from his light bounced across the floor as he moved, gradually zeroing in on his prey.

But the light also illuminated the rear door, just a few feet beyond Pitt. Still crouching, he lunged for it, reaching for the handle a second before his torso slammed against the lower half of the door. He caught the handle and twisted, and his weight blasted the door open.

Halfway across the lab, the gunman raised his arm and fired three quick shots on the run. Pitt felt a sting in his leg as he yanked the crutch after him and slammed the door closed.

Springing to his feet, Pitt wedged the crutch's arm pad beneath the door handle as a makeshift lock. It might give him an extra ten, maybe twenty seconds. But that still wouldn't be enough. Somewhere in the darkness, Ann was hobbling about. He had to find her, and fast. They would both be sitting ducks for the gunmen, with their night vision goggles, once they exited the lab.

He scrambled toward their car, but then heard a motor cranking over nearby. It didn't come from the road but down by the lake. Pitt spun in his tracks and ran for the water, thinking that they might just have a chance after all.

24

The motor rumbled to life, not the tinny whine from a compact rental car but the throaty gurgle of a power-boat. Pitt took off toward the dock, admiring Ann's plan to escape in Heiland's boat. For her part, it was simply easier to navigate downhill on her tender ankle, and the boat represented a closer target. With the keys already in her pocket, she had just prayed that she could get it started.

Inside the lab, the gunman found himself stymied by the back door. The aluminum crutch had pinned it closed, at least momentarily. The angered man shoved violently at it, finally bending the crutch until it slid from beneath the door handle and fell to the ground. Charging out the door, he turned toward the sound of the boat. He spotted the shadowy blur of Pitt running amid the shoreline trees and took off in pursuit.

Pitt was breathing hard, and his left leg ached, as he reached a gravel footpath that led to the lakefront. He could faintly make out the figure of Ann standing in the boat's cockpit, looking in his direction. Having heard the crash of the lab door opening, he didn't have to look behind him to know the gunman had no plans to let them get away.

'Cast off, Ann!' he shouted. 'Don't wait.'

Ann crawled onto the dock and untied the stern line,

then limped over and released the bowline. She was sliding back into the passenger seat when Pitt pounded onto the dock.

As Pitt approached, he was surprised to see the boat was an old dual cockpit runabout, built of mahogany. Had there been sufficient light, he would have recognized it as an early 1940s Chris-Craft.

Not losing a step, Pitt crossed the dock and leaped into the rear cockpit. He bounded off the cushion and vaulted into the front pilot's seat, jamming down the boat's throttle. As he fell into the seat, the old boat charged away from the dock with a bellow from its vintage six-cylinder Chrysler engine.

'This was fast thinking,' he told Ann as he guided the boat away from shore.

'I was afraid you'd never make it out of there.'

He looked back at the dock to see the dark figure of the lead gunman charge onto the platform.

'Better get down!' Pitt yelled, spinning the wheel hard over.

The cockpit floor was spacious enough for both of them and they ducked beneath the cowl as the boat jutted left. Pitt reached up and eased back the wheel, letting the boat run blindly ahead.

His move had turned the boat parallel to shore as it sped across the lake, its occupants hidden from view. The gunman ran to the end of the dock and aimed at the pilotless craft, firing until his clip was empty.

The roar of the engine drowned out the gunshots, but Pitt detected several faint thumps when a few rounds struck the hull. He waited a minute, then popped his head up for a quick look. The dock was lost from view among the trees as the boat skittered toward shore. Pitt slid into the seat and bumped the wheel over to keep them in deep water. Once on course, he pulled Ann up beside him. With all focus on their escape, he had ignored the throbbing pain in his leg, and the sticky wetness that told him he was now bleeding.

'Are you all right?' he asked.

She nodded. 'That was a little too close for comfort.'

'It would have been even closer if I hadn't had your crutch handy. Sorry to leave you off balance.'

'I was so scared, I didn't even think about my ankle. I just saw it was downhill to the dock and remembered I had the house keys in my pocket. Fortunately, the boat keys were also attached.'

She unconsciously rubbed her ankle, now noticing the pain.

'Where to now?' she asked.

The wheels of justice had already been turning in Pitt's mind. 'Simple,' he said. 'We head them off at the pass.'

There was only one road out from Heiland's cabin. Pitt knew the thieves would have to pass through Bayview to escape with the stolen documents. They could be stopped, but only if he and Ann got there first. It was a race that would depend on a seventy-year-old boat.

Though long in the tooth, Heiland's Chris-Craft was no turtle. The Custom Runabout was fitted with the company's Model M engine, which churned out 130 horsepower. The old speedboat was as stylish as she was speedy, featuring a varnished mahogany finish, dual cockpits, and a rakish 'barrelback' stern. A desirable boat when it had left the Algonac, Michigan, factory in 1942, it was now a prized collectible for classic boat lovers.

The elegant boat cut easily through the waves as Pitt kept the throttle down, mustering full speed from its inboard engine. Although they had a healthy head start, Pitt knew the gunmen would be desperate to escape and could travel the road back at nearly twice the boat's speed.

A star-filled sky gave him ample light, and he nudged the boat near the shoreline to trim the distance. After a few minutes of hard running, a wide inlet appeared on Pitt's left, and he angled the boat into it. The lights of Bayview appeared off the bow, twinkling at the far end of the aptly named Scenic Bay. Pitt glanced toward the shore-line road but didn't spot any headlights.

'How do we stop them?' Ann shouted.

Pitt had been ruminating on that question since they had cleared the dock. Sitting weaponless in a seventy-year-old boat with a woman who could barely walk did not give rise to many options. The obvious course of action would be to storm into the Navy facility and request help. But such an assault would more likely get them shot or arrested than gain them immediate assistance. Peering ahead, he spotted a marina dock close to the lab's fenced security entrance. The road from Heiland's cabin inter-sected the town's main street just a short distance away. He pointed out the dock to Ann.

'I'll run us in there,' Pitt said. 'See if you can make it up to the guard hut and convince them to call for some secur-ity to seal the road. I'll see if I can find something to slow them down.'

'Okay, but be careful.' She reached into the rear seat for her lone crutch and braced herself to exit the boat.

The old speedboat roared through a no-wake zone and past the main marina. Angry houseboat residents ran to their windows, staring at the noisy source of their homes' rocking. The shoreline dock was filled with small fishing boats, but Pitt spotted an empty berth and barreled toward it. Cutting power at the last second, he slid in with just a slight bump to the side of the boat. He popped from his seat and leaped to the dock, helping Ann up after him.

'I'm fine,' she said, tucking the crutch under her arm and hobbling down the dock.

Pitt sprinted ahead of her and ran toward the main road, leaving a trail of bloody footprints behind him. Ann cringed when she realized the damp prints weren't created from lake water.

The streets of Bayview were deserted and the town almost silent. In the distance, Pitt detected the sound of a speeding car, and he looked down the inlet. Sure enough, headlights glimmered through the trees on the road from Heiland's cabin.

Pitt scanned the roadway where it entered town, searching for something he could use as a barricade. The road was lined by the Acoustic Lab's tall security fence on one side and a sloping hill on the other. There were no rocks, logs, or even other cars within view that he might use as a blockade. The only vehicles in sight were for construction, parked up the hill, a gravel truck and a yellow earthmover.

He glanced again at the approaching lights; they'd arrive in less than a minute.

'Road crew it is,' he muttered, then ran up the hill as fast as he could.

25

Ann charged into the Acoustic Lab's guard station with all the subtlety of a Kansas tornado.

'The lab's been robbed!' she shouted. 'I need your help out front *now*!'

The duty guard had been seated behind a tall security glass, casually reading the sports page. He flew out of his chair as if stung by a cattle prod.

'Ma'am, I can't leave my station,' he stuttered. 'Now, calm down and tell me who are you and what this is about.'

Ann already had her identification pressed against the glass. 'Call for your backup. I need all the roads out of this town closed off immediately.'

The guard noticed a general resemblance between the wild-eyed woman screaming at him and the neatly groomed female pictured on the NCIS badge. He nodded at Ann and picked up the telephone. He was still dialing when a loud screech resonated outside.

They both turned to see a speeding dark sedan swerve across the lakeshore road. From over the hill, the yellow earthmover suddenly appeared, sliding down the steep incline, apparently out of control. Ann could see it was on a collision course with the car, which the car's driver had realized too late. In the glow from a nearby streetlight, Ann caught sight of a black-haired man in the cab of the earthmover – Pitt.

As he had staggered up the hill with a sharp pain in his left leg, Pitt had seen no other options. The gravel truck had been parked too close to the earthmover to maneuver around it, leaving the yellow mover his only option. The construction workers in this quiet town hadn't bothered to lock either vehicle. Pitt climbed behind the controls, looked down the hill, and saw the headlights of the fleeing car already skirting the naval center. In seconds, it would pass directly below him.

Pitt depressed the clutch and slapped the gearshift lever into neutral, releasing the parking brake with his other hand. The big machine lurched forward downhill, prompting Pitt to tap the unassisted brakes. He gripped the rubberized steering wheel and tested the play. The well-used earthmover didn't have a locking steering column, so Pitt had some maneuverability as long as he could muscle the wheel.

Glancing again down the hill, he saw the car emerge from the trees a short distance away. He had no time to waste.

Releasing the brake pedal, he let the earthmover roll forward a few feet to gain momentum, then bulled the steering wheel sharply to his right. The two front wheels turned easily, slicing through the earth at the foot of the hillside. The big steel blade scraped into the berm, slowing the mover momentarily before lurching ahead.

The ungainly machine nearly jackknifed as it tumbled over the ledge, managing to right itself with a heavy bounce. The steep hill dropped almost fifty feet, causing the mover to accelerate quickly. Pitt straightened the wheels, hoping to keep it upright. The glare of oncoming headlights filled his right windshield.

Had the car's driver not been speeding, he might have been able to brake to a stop ahead of the runaway earthmover. But his rate of speed, combined with the shock of seeing the big piece of construction equipment bounding down the hill, caused him to overreact. Rather than brake first, he instinctively flicked the steering wheel to the side to escape the mover. He then stood on the brakes.

It was the worst choice. The car skidded twenty feet before the right front fender slammed into a telephone pole. Sitting unbuckled in the passenger seat, the man who had played guard in Heiland's house flew into the windshield. His neck snapped, and he died instantly.

The driver suffered only a crushed leg, but his reprieve was temporary. He looked up over a now deflating air bag to see the charging yellow monster only inches away.

The prow of the earthmover struck the driver's door square, knocking the car clear of the telephone pole and driving it sideways. Pitt dropped the mover's steel blade, slowing the mover as a shower of sparks erupted from the asphalt. It was just enough to halt the momentum of both vehicles. When the passenger side of the car smacked against the Navy Lab's fence, both jarred to a halt.

Ann was already hobbling toward the scene, followed by a siren-blaring security car racing through the lab's main gate. She made her way alongside the earthmover as Pitt climbed out of the cab. His left leg was bloody, and he looked pale.

'Your leg,' she said. 'Are you all right?'

'It's not serious,' he said, moving gingerly.

They walked to the mangled car and peered inside. The

body of the driver was flung forward, his eyes locked in a lifeless gaze. His bloodied partner, equally frozen in death, sprawled across the passenger-side dashboard.

'You cut them off, all right,' Ann whispered. She took a closer look at their features, noticing details that had gone unseen in the darkness of Heiland's lab. 'Associates of our friends in Tijuana?'

'They might have accessed Heiland's office in Del Mar and tracked down his cabin here,' Pitt said. He looked again at the gruesome scene in the car as the Navy security car pulled up. 'I hope it was worth it.'

Ann limped to the rear of the car and pried open the crash-damaged trunk. Inside was the bin containing Heiland's documents. She gazed at Pitt with look of grim satisfaction.

'It was.'

PART TWO
Rare Earth

26

The Gulfstream's wheels touched down with a thump, jarring Ann awake. The excitement of the past few days had finally caught up with her, and she had slept since the plane left the ground in Idaho. She yawned and glanced across the aisle at Pitt, who sat engrossed reading a Jeff Edwards novel.

'Home at last,' she said.

Pitt looked up and smiled, then gazed out at the gray gloom hanging over Reagan National Airport as evening fell. 'I was beginning to have my doubts we'd ever make it back.'

He had spent the better part of the morning being interrogated by Navy, FBI, and local Idaho law enforcement authorities about the previous night's fatal accident. Ann redirected the questioning as best she could and ultimately gained his release, along with Heiland's plans salvaged from the wrecked car.

The Gulfstream rolled off the runway, bypassing the commercial terminals for a private hangar reserved for government aircraft. A blue Ford Taurus shot onto the tarmac and pulled alongside as the jet's wheels were chocked. Dan Fowler climbed out of the car and stood by, tapping his foot and checking his watch, until the jet's door opened. He rushed over to Ann, took her hand, and helped her down the steps.

'Ann, are you okay?'

'Dan, I wasn't expecting to see you here. We're both a little tired, but holding up fine.'

'I thought you could use a lift home.'

Pitt followed her out of the plane and handed her a new pair of crutches.

'Good to see you, Dirk.' Fowler reached out to shake Pitt's hand.

'After the last two days, I'm not sure I'm so happy to see you,' Pitt said, returning his handshake.

Fowler noticed Pitt was moving with his own limp. 'Were you hurt, too?'

'A bullet grazed my calf. I got off easier than Ann.'

'I can't tell you how sorry I am,' Fowler said. 'We obviously had no idea of the danger you both were walking into. We had only speculated that someone might be trying to obtain Heiland's research when he disappeared. We certainly had no idea of the seriousness of the threat.'

'You mean threats,' Ann said. 'At least they ended up as failed threats.'

Fowler gave Ann an anxious look. 'Do you have Heiland's plans?'

Pitt ducked into the Gulfstream and returned with the bin containing Heiland's laptops and research journals. 'It's all here,' Pitt said.

Fowler looked relieved. He stepped to the rear of his car and opened the trunk. Pitt followed, shooting the security director a sharp glance as he dropped the bin in.

'You may not know it,' Fowler said, 'but that represents a priceless bit of naval technology.'

'Then why didn't you arrange an armed security escort to keep it safe? Someone is willing to kill for that data.'

'Don't worry. It's headed to a secure room in the bowels of the DARPA headquarters building – just as soon as I take Ann home.'

Pitt retrieved Ann's bag from the Gulfstream and placed it in the trunk beside the bin.

'Can I give you a lift, too?' Fowler asked.

'No, thanks,' Pitt said. 'I actually live within walking distance of here. After being cooped up the last few hours, I could use a good stretch of the legs.' He turned to say good-bye to Ann.

'Good luck with the investigation.'

Ann threw her arms around Pitt and gave him a tight hug and a kiss on the cheek. 'Thanks,' she whispered.

'You take care of that leg.' He helped her into the car, and waved as they drove off into the gloom.

Pitt's left leg ached from the bullet wound, while his right shin was still tender from his boat collision in Chile. He paused and sucked in a deep breath of the night air, cool and crisp from a recent rain shower. Hoisting his duffel bag over his shoulder, he ambled across the tarmac, his tight limbs slowly loosening as he moved.

The whine of engines sounded from across the tarmac as he made his way past a row of private jet hangars toward a little-used section of the airport. He crossed an empty field and approached a lone hangar that looked as if it hadn't been occupied in fifty years. High weeds surrounded the structure, which was coated in equal parts of rust and dust. A bank of windows beneath the roof's eaves showed a continuous web of cracks, with shards of glass scattered on the ground near a battered trash can. Only an expert eye examining the building up close could discern that the derelict appearance was in fact a façade designed to deter attention.

Pitt stepped to a side door illuminated by a dim yellow bulb and reached for an industrial-grade light switch. The switch assembly flipped open on a hinge, revealing a concealed keypad. Pitt entered a code that deactivated the alarm system and opened the door's lock.

He stepped inside, turned on the lights – and was greeted by a fleet of gleaming antique cars parked in rows across the hangar floor, their polished chrome glistening under the overhead illumination. The culmination of a lifelong passion for the fast and the beautiful in automotive design, he had assembled an eclectic collection that spanned the dawn of the twentieth century through the 1950s. The museum-like appearance was augmented by a Ford Trimotor aircraft parked to one side near a beautifully restored Pullman railroad car that his adult kids occasionally used as a temporary apartment.

Pitt drifted across the hangar, patting the fender of a 1930 Packard Speedster 8 Runabout that was parked next to a workbench, the right side of its hood raised. He reached a cast-iron circular staircase and climbed to his second-floor living quarters, which he shared with Loren.

Dropping his duffel on a chair, he pulled a Shiner Bock beer from the refrigerator, then read a note taped to the freezer door.

Dirk,

I'm staying at my Georgetown condo until you get back. Too many automotive ghosts around here! Extended committee hearings will probably keep me on the Hill working late. Missed you.

XXXX,
Loren

Pitt downed the beer and returned to the hangar floor. Something was gnawing at him about the Heiland case, something he couldn't quite put his finger on. Replaying the recent events had failed to spark a clue, so he slipped on a worn mechanic's jumpsuit and made his way over to the old Packard. With a careful devotion, he began disassembling its updraft carburetor. By the time he had the mechanism overhauled an hour or so later, he knew exactly what was troubling him.

27

'I guess it was a good call, enlisting Pitt on the case,' Fowler said as he drove away from the airport.

'He's quite a resourceful man.' Ann stared out the window and considered her impressions of Pitt. 'He saved my life twice.'

'He evidently has quite a track record for averting disaster,' Fowler said. 'I'm sure he can be trusted, but, just for the record, did he become aware of Heiland's work and its capabilities?'

'He has the basic idea, but he didn't press for more. He seemed primarily concerned about the safety of his ship and crew.' Ann reached down and rubbed her ankle. 'We really should have told him all the facts in the beginning.'

'Couldn't be helped. Tom Cerny was firm that discussion of the technology was off-limits. I think we were all surprised by the tenacity of those chasing after it.'

Fowler cleared the gates of the airport and stopped at a red light. 'You live in Alexandria, right?'

'Yes, I'm near Old Town, right off King Street. Just take the Jefferson Davis Highway into town.'

Fowler nodded and turned south.

'Any updates from the FBI while we were in the air?' Ann asked.

'Nothing yet. It will probably be several days before we

learn anything from the Mexican agencies. And you probably know more than me about the two guys in black from Idaho.'

'They were Latin in appearance. If they are in fact connected to the men in Tijuana, I suspect they may be operatives from Central or South America.'

'Venezuelan rogues?'

'Possibly. There is certainly no shortage of world powers that would like to use that technology. China or Russia probably head the list. Maybe they've got a surrogate working for them.'

'Don't forget the Iranians.' Fowler gunned the car to clear a yellow light. He turned onto King Street, a main drag that bisected Alexandria.

'The attackers were pretty brazen,' Ann said, 'and well informed.'

'Yes, it sounds like they were fearless.'

'You thinking what I'm thinking?' Ann asked.

'What's that?' Fowler said, turning down a side street.

'Inside help. There must be a security leak, possibly at a high level.'

'Possibly, but you know how much classified information winds up in the press. It may not have been that difficult for someone to figure out that Heiland was working on something important. Since he wasn't working in a secure environment, he made an easy target.'

'You may be right.' Ann pointed down the street. 'I'm up ahead on the right, just past the big oak.'

Fowler spotted an empty space at the curb and pulled in behind a car that was idling with its lights off. Ann recognized it as a Chrysler 300 sedan.

'Why don't you take the day off tomorrow?' Fowler said. 'You've been through the wringer the last forty-eight hours. You could probably use some rest.'

'Thanks, but I'd go crazy just sitting around. I need to find out who these people are.'

Fowler turned off the car's engine, and Ann climbed out. As she turned to retrieve her crutches, she was grabbed from behind. She just caught a glimpse of her assailant, a tall black male, who wrapped his hands around her and hurled her onto a small patch of lawn. The heavy man was on her instantly, jamming his knee into the small of her back while mashing her face into the grass with a plate-sized hand. She struggled to break free, then relented when she felt a gun barrel press against her temple.

'Don't even breathe,' the big man said.

She heard Fowler cry out, followed by the dull thumping of a body being pummeled. A few seconds later, car keys jingled, and the Ford's trunk was popped open. From the corner of her eye, Ann saw a second man carry something to the backseat of the Chrysler, then jump into the driver's seat. The thug on her back leaned down and whispered into her face with foul breath. 'Now, you lay nice and still for five minutes or else old Clarence will have to come back and hurt you.'

He eased himself off her, loped over to the Chrysler, and climbed casually into the passenger seat. The car shot forward with a chirp of its rear tires and sped down the street. Ann looked up to scan the car's rear license plate, but it had been temporarily covered with a few strips of duct tape. Pros, she thought. They'd rip the tape off a block away, then meld into traffic, driving safely under the speed limit.

Ann jumped up and limped to the far side of the Taurus, where she found Fowler lying facedown next to the front wheel.

'Dan,' she cried, kneeling beside him.

He pried his eyes open and eased himself to a sitting position.

'I'm okay.' He rubbed his jaw. 'Never saw that coming.' His eyes gradually focused on Ann. 'Are you hurt?'

'No, I'm fine. But that was no random stickup.' She tilted her head toward the open trunk.

'Not the files!' blurted Fowler, struggling to his feet. Holding each other for support, they stepped to the rear of the car and peered into the open trunk.

Inside sat Ann's travel bag. And nothing else.

28

The memorial service for Joe Eberson was well attended by his fellow research scientists at DARPA, many of whom stepped to the Annandale Church podium and expressed their esteem for him. Sitting in a middle pew, Ann felt a bit uncomfortable because she'd been assigned to the agency only at his death. But clearly Eberson was a respected man, and that sharpened her resolve to catch his murderer.

Fowler sat at her side, a small bandage on his chin reminding her of the attack the night before. Alexandria paramedics and police had responded quickly to Ann's residence and found no serious injury to either one of them. But the authorities also found no trail to the muggers. Ann alerted federal officials of the theft, and an alert was put out on the assailants' Chrysler for the greater Washington metro area. By morning, it had been found in a grocery store parking lot. Reported as stolen the day before, it also had been scrubbed of any incriminating fingerprints and Heiland's records as well. A special FBI team was assigned to the theft, but they had very little to go on.

'I'd like to pay my respects to Joe's family,' Fowler said as the service ended. 'How about I meet you at the car?'

Ann nodded, thankful that he had offered to drive. When they climbed into Fowler's car a short time later, Ann commented on Eberson's popularity.

'He had a lot of years in the business,' Fowler said. 'Made a lot of friends. And also a few enemies.'

'What kind of enemies?' Ann asked.

'The professional sort. The typical DARPA research project parcels out work to different companies and universities. Then we tie everything together – and garner all the credit. The little guys who make the real breakthroughs often go unnoticed.'

He turned to Ann. 'I don't think that any research scientist knocked off Eberson and Heiland, if that's where you're headed.'

'Just touching all the bases,' Ann said. 'I know we've talked before, but I want to ask again what the prospects are that a leak came from inside DARPA?'

Fowler frowned. 'Anything's possible, but I just don't think that's the case. There's just a relatively small team here running the *Sea Arrow* program. Most of the work is farmed out. That's where I think the real risk is – with our external subcontractors. Of course there are people at the shipyard with knowledge, and that's an obvious focus.'

'Yes, that's why we've already assigned a dedicated NCIS team to Groton.'

'It may not mean anything,' Fowler said, 'but I find it somewhat curious that Heiland and Eberson were killed shortly after the President toured the shipyard. I wasn't there, but I ran the security list.'

'Are you suggesting someone at the White House might be involved?'

'Not directly. But you know the White House is a sieve. Although this administration is better than most, it wouldn't surprise me if details about the *Sea Arrow* were released to the wrong people.'

'Can you give me the security list?' Ann said.

'Sure, it's in my office – if you don't already have enough on your plate.'

'At this point we have to cast a broad net. I'd like to check the history of any recent technology thefts of a similar nature. Have you dealt with any foreign espionage cases?'

'Not since I've been at DARPA,' Fowler said. 'Our issues are mostly lost computer disks and the like. But I've been here only a year. We had a few espionage cases while I was with the Army Research Laboratory, both suspected Chinese and Israeli spies, but we never had enough to prosecute.'

'The bagmen in this case seem a bit out of character for the typical espionage operatives,' Ann said.

'True, but you never know who's footing the bill.'

'I suppose,' Ann said. 'Any idea of the impact to the *Sea Arrow* program?'

'I'm not technically savvy enough to know, but apparently the program hinged on Heiland's supercavitation model, which would totally transform the *Sea Arrow*'s capability. Now that his original research is lost, the program may be set back several years. No one believes they can duplicate Heiland's work easily without his designs.'

'I can't believe they robbed us of them in Alexandria. How could they have known?'

'Hard to say. Perhaps someone was tracking you after the incident in Tijuana. I'd have to think there was a third member of the party in Idaho, monitoring events. Somehow they arranged a jump on us here at short notice.'

He gave her a worried look. 'Maybe you should check into a hotel for a few nights, just to be on the safe side.'

'No, I'm fine,' she said, her own safety not a concern.

'Still, I'll follow up with the Alexandria police to make sure they patrol your town house on a regular basis.' He rubbed his jaw beneath the bandage. 'I'd like to see those guys go down hard.'

Fowler turned into the parking lot of the DARPA headquarters building in downtown Arlington. Ann preferred to work at the DARPA site rather than her NCIS office across the river in Anacostia, having commandeered a small, windowless office next to Fowler. With her laptop computer, she could access nearly the same criminal resources while establishing relationships with the DARPA team working on *Sea Arrow*.

As she returned to her desk, she felt oddly energized. Aside from its importance to national security, the case had become personal. She shrugged off the physical and emotional drain of the past few days, motivated to dig into the evidence and discover who was behind the thefts and murders.

Her first call was to the FBI field office in San Diego. An agent named Wyatt was managing the local investigation.

'Have you heard anything from Mexico yet?' she asked.

'A few things,' Wyatt said. 'The two deceased males, both in their early thirties, were not Mexican nationals. Colombian passports were found on both bodies. I can give you the names, but in all likelihood they're phony. We checked with the State Department in Bogotá, and both names came back negative with the Colombian government.'

'The passports were fake?'

'Yes, high-quality counterfeits. We checked the prints on the deceased and found no matches in either the FBI or Interpol databases. Our best guess is, they were low-level hired muscle. Customs showed that they actually came into the US with three other men a few weeks ago. They crossed the border at Tijuana with temporary visitors' visas.'

'Any of them go by the name of Pablo?'

'No, nothing close to that.'

'How about the pickup truck and the boat?'

'The truck was recently purchased from a used-car dealer in Tijuana. Paid cash, registered to one of the Colombians at a taco stand's address in Rosarito Beach. I'm afraid the Mexicans haven't found anything on the boat.'

'Any record of their activity while in the US?'

'We're still looking. Interesting thing is, five individuals were recorded crossing the border in the truck, but only three returned. We followed up your tip about a possible break-in at Heiland's company office. Surveillance video shows a janitor entering Heiland's office after hours. The individual appears to match the passport photo of one of the Colombians.'

'Wyatt, I suggest you call the Spokane field office when we're finished. Two men were just killed in Bayview, Idaho, after a break-in at Heiland's lake house. I'll wager a month's salary that those are your two missing men.'

'How about a bonus if one is our janitor?' Wyatt asked. 'They seem to be a persistent bunch, that's for sure.'

'Agreed. Do you have anything else?'

'We had an explosives expert examine Heiland's boat. He confirmed that a charge of low-grade plastic explosives was embedded in the boat's interior and mechanically detonated. The wiring looked to have been in place for some time.'

'So Heiland triggered the explosion,' she said – Pitt had been right after all – 'Any idea why?'

'He may have been aware of the threat or maybe just sensitive to the nature of his work. Was it anything worth killing over?'

'It would seem so.'

'There's one more bit of mystery tied in with the event.'

'What's that?'

'The autopsy report on Eberson. Based on the physical evidence and the position of his body at the back of the boat, we believe he was not killed by the explosion.'

'His feet were tangled in fishing line,' Ann said. 'I assume he panicked when he couldn't get clear of the boat and ended up drowning.'

'Actually, the pathologist says he was dead before he hit the water.'

'Was he shot?'

'No –' Wyatt fumbled for the proper description. 'His skin showed signs of severe burns. His death was attributed to trauma related to burn damage.'

Ann had seen his gruesome blackened limbs but assumed it had to do with his body's submersion at such depth. 'Why doesn't the pathologist think he was killed by the explosion?'

'Because his surface burns were atypical of fire damage – and extended beneath the skin. In other words, he cooked from both inside and out.'

Ann shook her head. 'From the inside?'

'The damage is consistent with acute microwave irradiation.'

Ann fell silent, trying to make sense of the report.

'Could it have anything to do with the equipment Heiland was testing?' Wyatt asked.

'I can't imagine. It was still in its case.'

'Understood. It's got everyone here stumped, too. I'll send you the report, and we can talk again.'

'Thanks, Wyatt. And let me know if you hear any more from Mexico.'

Eberson's death was an odd twist that didn't make any sense. If Pablo's crew was going to kill him, why didn't they simply shoot him? And what could have caused the microwave irradiation?

Ann beat Wyatt in phoning the FBI's Spokane field office – and confirmed what she'd already guessed. The two men killed in Bayview had also carried phony Colombian passports. They had arrived in Idaho on a private chartered flight, which accounted for their ability to bring in weapons. The charter operator was being investigated but had no apparent connection to the Colombians.

Ann opened her laptop and began scouring national law enforcement databases, searching for criminal acts in the US by Colombian nationals. In the National Crime Information Center's system, she assembled a list of such felonies prosecuted in the past five years. Aside from a few random murders and a bank robbery, the major crimes were primarily drug related, concentrated in Miami and New York. A search of the FBI's Guardian Threat Tracking System also failed to trigger any obvious links.

Until the FBI completed DNA testing on the bodies in Idaho, she was only chasing ghosts anyway. So she turned her attention to potential internal leaks.

Fowler had given Ann detailed profiles of fifteen DARPA scientists and administrators assigned to the *Sea Arrow* project. She spent the next hour sifting through the reports, keeping an eye out for the three D's of nonideological subversion: debt, drugs, and divorce. She made note for Fowler to check up on a female physicist who was undergoing a bitter divorce, as well as a lower-grade engineer who had recently acquired a new Corvette. But, on the surface, none of the employees fit the profile for a security risk.

'Got a second?'

Fowler appeared at her door, walked in and placed a thick folder on her desk. 'Here are the staff reports on the DARPA subcontractors working on *Sea Arrow*. Groton obviously has their own subs under review, plus the Office of Naval Research has a number on their end.'

'What's the damage locally?'

'Eight private defense contractors, not counting Heiland, plus three university research programs.'

'Enough to keep us busy a while. Thanks, Dan. Can you do me one more favor?'

'Sure, name it.'

'Can you pull the travel history of your DARPA team

assigned to *Sea Arrow*? I want to check for any trips to the major hot spots: East Asia, Russia, and the Middle East.'

'No problem. By the way, here's the security list for the President's shipyard tour at Groton a few weeks ago.' He handed her a sheet, which she placed to the side of her desk.

'Interested in lunch?'

'No, I'm good,' she said, diving into the subcontractor data. 'Thanks for the reports.'

As she dug into the files, Ann soon realized there was only a peripheral connection between the other contractors and Heiland. Most of the subcontracts focused on hull design and electronic systems, with little, if any, interplay with Heiland's supercavitation system. Eberson had been the central conduit for all the systems Heiland was developing.

Ann stood and stretched before picking up the security list from the President's Groton tour. There were only seven names, three from the White House and four from the Pentagon. She immediately noted Tom Cerny's name. With only Fowler's off-the-cuff remark as a basis, she phoned in the names to an NCIS colleague and requested an online background check. While she waited to receive an e-mail with the results, she thought of the rarity of a murder like Heiland's.

The theft of industrial or defense secrets seldom crossed over the line to homicide. Yet Heiland, Eberson, and Manny had been murdered for their work on the *Sea Arrow*, while Ann and Pitt were nearly added victims. Only a handful of rogue nations would risk such provocative measures, but others might if working through a proxy. The Colombian government certainly wasn't competing with the US in defense weaponry, so clearly the thieves were working for someone else. But who?

Ann began examining other domestic espionage cases, searching for a pattern. Ignoring terrorist and computer hacking cases, she found that most spy busts involved diplomatic and policy secrets, from individuals or groups serving the old antagonists of Moscow, Beijing, and Havana. Of greater interest were a handful of cases involving military and commercial technology thefts by Chinese operatives. Though none had the earmarks of Heiland's case, it was clear that China, more than anybody, was aggressively pursuing foreign military technology.

She found that China had a long history of stealing and imitating technology from foreign powers, primarily the Russians. Copycat artillery systems, antiaircraft missiles, and even Navy destroyers had long upset the Kremlin brass. But the Russians weren't the only target. Several items in the Chinese arsenal bore strong similarities to American weapons. Aviation experts found a suspicious resemblance between China's J-20 stealth fighter jet and the American F-22A Raptor. The country had recently announced the deployment of a crowd-control system identical in appearance to a device developed by the US Army. And a new Chinese helicopter that mimicked the US's Apache was said to be imminent.

Engrossed in her work, Ann didn't realize it was nearing six o'clock until her phone rang. She had covered a lot of ground but had little to show for it. She answered the call with a weary voice, becoming alert when she heard a familiar voice.

'Hi, Ann, it's Dirk. Still at the salt mine?'

'Yes, chipping away. How are you?'

'Just fine. Say, I was wondering if you could meet me for dinner tomorrow night? I have something we need to discuss.'

'Tomorrow? Yes, that would be fine. Is it something important?'

'Could be,' Pitt said, hesitating. 'I'd like to know if you'd go on a cruise with me.'

29

Ann caught several men staring at her as she swept through the dining room of the Bombay Club with only a slight limp. Dressed in a saffron linen dress that clung to her curves, she resembled a runway model more than a criminal investigator. She ignored the looks as she stepped through the restaurant onto an elegant patio that over-looked Lafayette Park. She quickly spotted Pitt at a corner table.

He was seated next to a tall, attractive woman who looked vaguely familiar. With a touch of unease, Ann forced a smile as she approached the table.

Pitt rose and greeted her warmly. 'No more crutches?'

'No, the ankle is much better, I'm happy to say.'

'Ann, I'd like you to meet my wife, Loren.'

Loren sprang to her feet and gave Ann a warm hug. 'Dirk's told me all about your ordeals in Mexico and Idaho. Though he apparently forgot to mention how pretty you are,' she added without spite.

Whatever instinctive resentment Ann may have felt toward Loren melted at the unexpected compliment. 'I'm afraid to say that all our troubles went for naught.' Ann gave Pitt a guilty look, and described how she and Fowler had been robbed of Heiland's research.

'That sounds like no coincidence,' Pitt said, concern etched on his face.

'More like blatant espionage,' Loren said. 'We need to get some high-powered resources involved.'

'There's already at least three FBI teams assigned to the case,' Ann said, 'along with DARPA's staff security and several NCIS investigators, besides me.' She looked at Loren, her eyes brightening in recognition. 'You're the congresswoman from Colorado.'

'Careful, you'll blow her cover,' Pitt said with a laugh.

'I thought you looked familiar,' Ann said. 'I remember your efforts to pass legislation to improve benefits and leave for enlisted parents in the military. You're a hero to women in the armed forces.'

Loren shook her head. 'They were just some minor changes that should have been enacted long ago. Seriously, though, if there are any chains that I can rattle at Homeland Security to help your case, just say the word.'

'Thank you. We've got the support of the Vice President as well as the White House, so I think the resources are in place. We just need a break or two so we can find out who these people are.'

A waiter arrived and they each ordered a curry dish for dinner, with Pitt tacking on a bottle of Saint Clair Sauvignon Blanc from New Zealand.

'How long have you two been married?' Ann asked.

'Just a few years,' Loren said. 'With both our travel schedules, it often seems we're two ships passing in the night, but we make it work.'

'The trick,' Pitt said, 'is making sure the ships collide on a regular basis.'

Loren turned to Ann. 'Is there a special person in your life?'

'No, I'm happily unattached at the moment.'

Their entrees arrived, all spicy enough to mandate a second bottle of wine.

'This shrimp curry is withering my tongue, but I can't stop eating it,' Ann said. 'It's really delicious.'

Later Ann excused herself to visit the ladies' room. Once she was out of earshot, Loren leaned over to Pitt. 'That girl is attracted to you.'

'Can I help it if she has good taste in men?' he said with a grin.

'No, but if you get any ideas, I'll cut out your spleen with a rusty butter knife.'

Pitt laughed, then gave Loren a long kiss.

'Not to worry. I'm quite attached to my spleen – and prefer to keep it that way.'

When Ann returned, they nibbled on sorbet for dessert. Then Pitt pulled a silver rock from his pocket and set it on the table.

'One lump and not two?' Loren said.

'It's a souvenir from Chile,' Pitt said. 'I think it may have something to do with the Heiland case.'

'What exactly is it?' Ann asked.

'One of our NUMA geologists identified it as a mineral called monazite. I found it aboard an abandoned freighter that was barreling toward Valparaiso.'

'I heard about that,' Ann said. 'You diverted the freighter from crashing into a crowded cruise ship.'

'More or less,' Pitt said. 'The mystery is, what happened to the ship's crew? And why did the ship end up thousands of miles off course?'

'Was it hijacked?'

'It was a bulk carrier, supposedly loaded with bauxite from a mine in Australia. By all appearances, the cargo was of limited value. We discovered that of the ship's five holds, three contained bauxite, but the two aft were empty.' Pitt picked up the rock. 'I found this chunk of monazite by one of the empty holds.'

'You think the monazite was stolen from the ship?' Ann asked.

'I do.'

'Why would someone steal that and not the bauxite?' Loren asked.

'I had the rock assayed, and the results were quite interesting. This particular monazite contains a high concentration of neodymium and lanthanum.'

Loren smiled. 'Sounds like a disease.'

'They are actually two of the seventeen elements known as rare earth metals, several of which are in very high demand by industry.'

'Of course,' Loren said. 'We held a congressional hearing on the limited supply of rare earth elements. They're used in a large number of high-tech products, including hybrid cars and wind turbines.'

'And a few key defense technologies,' Pitt said.

'As I recall,' Loren said, 'China is the dominant producer of rare earth elements. In fact, there's only a handful of other active mines around the world.'

'Russia, India, Australia, and our own mine in California round out the bulk of global production,' Pitt said.

Ann shook her head. 'I don't see what this rock has to do with the Heiland case.'

'It may have absolutely nothing to do with it,' Pitt said,

'but there are two interesting coincidences. The first is that clump of monazite in your hands. The neodymium it contains happens to be a key material in the *Sea Arrow*'s propulsion motors.'

'How could you possibly know that?' Ann asked.

'My information systems manager at NUMA found that several rare earth elements were critical components in the propulsion system of the new Zumwalt class of Navy destroyer. Some additional digging and guesswork led us to conclude they would be even more important to the *Sea Arrow*'s electric motors.'

'I'd have to verify that, but I don't doubt that's true,' Ann said. 'Still, I don't see a significant connection.'

'Maybe not,' Pitt said, 'yet there is a second curious link – the DARPA scientist killed on the *Cuttlefish*, Joe Eberson. I'll wager that he didn't die by drowning but was killed by an acute dose of electromagnetic radiation.'

Ann dropped the rock, and her jaw followed suit. 'How could you have known that? I just received a copy of his autopsy report this morning. It confirms exactly that.'

'It was on account of Eberson's condition. His extremities were bloated, and his skin was blistered and blackened. The bloating isn't unusual in a drowning victim, but the blackened skin was odd. We found a dead sailor aboard the freighter in Chile who exhibited even more extreme characteristics. Chilean authorities say he died from thermal damage believed to be caused by microwave irradiation.'

'The same cause,' Ann said. 'Eberson's pathologist failed to identify a possible source of the irradiation. How could they have died in that manner?'

'Aside from falling asleep on a microwave antenna dish,

it's hard to say. I asked a number of my scientists and we came up with a weak yet possible theory.'

'I'd like to hear it.'

'There's been a number of crowd-control devices fielded in the past few years that use microwave beams to lightly burn the skin of people in its path. Our Army has deployed one they call the Active Denial System, or ADS, often referred to as the "pain ray". The systems are not meant to be lethal, but we've learned that simple modifications could make them deadly.'

'Could they be used at sea?' Loren asked.

'They are currently truck-mounted, so they could easily be placed on the deck of a ship. The ADS system has a range of up to seven hundred meters. People inside a ship would be immune, but anyone on deck or accessible through a window, such as on the bridge, would be susceptible. A powerful enough design might even damage the communications systems. It's also possible they might simply use it against a larger vessel as cover for an armed boarding party.'

'You think something like that was used on both vessels?' Ann asked.

'They could have used it to stun the crew of the *Tasmanian Star* to steal its monazite,' Pitt said, 'and against the *Cuttlefish* to kill Heiland, Manny, and Eberson in order to steal the *Sea Arrow* test model.'

'They would have obtained the model directly from the *Cuttlefish* if Heiland hadn't blown up the boat,' Ann said. 'Any clue to the attacking vessel?'

'We're searching, but haven't found anything yet.'

'Then we don't seem to be any closer to identifying who these people are.'

Pitt gave her a sly look. 'On the contrary, I intend to find out within the week.'

'But you have no idea where to find them,' Loren said.

'Actually,' Pitt said, 'I intend to let them find me. Just like baiting a trap with cheese to lure the mouse, only our cheese is a rock called monazite.'

He pulled a world map out of his coat pocket and spread it on the table.

'Hiram Yaeger and I were intrigued by the *Tasmanian Star*'s hijacking, so we conducted a search of known shipwrecks and vessel disappearances over the last three years. Insurance records show that more than a dozen commercial vessels sank either with all hands or without a trace. Of those, no less than ten were carrying either rare earth elements or related ore.'

He pointed to the map. 'Seven of the ships were lost in the vicinity of South Africa, while the remaining vessels disappeared in the eastern Pacific.'

Ann could see small shipwreck symbols had been marked on the map, a few near a small atoll marked Clipperton Island. 'Why haven't the insurance companies investigated this?'

'Many of the ships were aged freighters, independently owned and probably underinsured through multiple carriers. I can only guess, but it's likely no single insurer has taken a large enough hit to detect the pattern.'

'Why would someone go to the trouble of sinking or hijacking these ships,' Loren said, 'if they can buy the minerals on the open market?'

Pitt shrugged. 'The global supply is very tight. Perhaps

someone is trying to control the reserves and manipulate the market.'

'So what is your plan to identify these people?' Ann asked.

Pitt pointed to the clump of monazite. 'That bit of ore came from a mine in western Australia called Mount Weld. The mine is being closed temporarily so they can expand production. We discovered that their last scheduled export shipment was loaded on an ore carrier last week bound for Long Beach.'

'You think she's going to be hijacked?' Loren asked.

'She's sailing on the same route where two other ships disappeared and the *Tasmanian Star* was attacked. It's the last scheduled shipment of rare earth from Australia for at least six months. I'm willing to roll the dice and say she's a pretty good target.'

'So that's the cruise you invited me on?' Ann said with a twinkle in her eye.

Pitt nodded. 'The freighter is owned by a shipping line whose CEO happens to be friends with Vice President Sandecker. He's made arrangements for us and a Coast Guard SWAT team to rendezvous with the ship south of Hawaii.'

'Is that enough protection?' Loren's concern for her husband was evident in her violet eyes.

'We're not going up against a warship. Plus, I'll be in constant communications with Rudi at headquarters if we need any extra muscle.' He turned to Ann. 'We'll have to leave for Hawaii in two days. Are you in?'

Ann picked up the rock and turned it around. 'I'd love to, but I'm in the heart of the investigation and I would hate to break things off now. Plus, I wouldn't be much help aboard ship.' She looked in Pitt's eyes. 'But, I tell you what. If you're right, then Loren and I will be waiting for you at the dock in Long Beach.'

Pitt smiled at the two attractive women and raised his wineglass. 'That would be a sight any lonely sailor would welcome.'

30

Viewed from the air, the dense jungle spread across the horizon like a lumpy green carpet. Only the occasional wisp of smoke or a quick glimpse of a shack in a clearing gave any sign that human life existed beneath the foliage.

Though the helicopter had departed Panama City's Tocumen International Airport just a few minutes earlier, the roar of its turbine was already grating on Pablo's nerves. He gazed ahead and spotted the sprawling green waters of Gatun Lake, a massive body of water formed during the construction of the Panama Canal. Their destination was close.

The pilot banked the chopper and followed the eastern shore of the lake, passing several large islands known for their assortment of primates. A narrow peninsula rose up ahead, and he guided the helicopter back over the jungle, gradually reducing speed. As he reached the center of the landmass, the pilot put the craft into a hover.

Pablo gazed at the treetops below – and noticed them move. The trees weren't swaying from the chopper's rotor wash, but instead began to spread apart. A seam appeared in the foliage, and it grew into a large square opening with a helicopter landing pad marked with lights and a reflective white circle.

The pilot centered the helicopter and gently dropped

onto the pad. The moment the pilot cut the power, Pablo tore off his headphones and climbed out.

Once beyond reach of the twirling rotor, he glanced up as the artificially landscaped roof closed overhead. The hydraulically powered cover was a stand-alone structure built on pilings in a jungle clearing. Two armed men in fatigues operated the controls from a panel box at the side.

As the sky disappeared, a golf cart emerged from the surrounding jungle and pulled to a stop in front of Pablo.

'*El Jefe* awaits,' the driver said with the hint of a Swedish accent. Out of place in the Panamanian jungle, he was a husky blond man with pale skin and ice blue eyes. He wore a nondescript Army officer's uniform and a holstered Beretta.

The two men stared at each other with a mix of respect and disdain. Both employed as hired muscle, they observed a cold, formal truce. 'Good day to you, too, Johansson,' Pablo said. 'And, yes, I had a very enjoyable flight, thank you.'

Johansson stomped on the accelerator as Pablo climbed into the golf cart, not waiting until he was fully seated.

The two men rode in silence as Johansson followed a paved path through the jungle. They entered a shaded clearing dotted with more armed men in fatigues. To their right sat a pyramid-shaped pile of gray rocks. A group of ragged men, wearing dirty, sweat-stained clothes, were shoveling the rocks into small carts and pushing them down a carved path.

The golf cart bounded through another stretch of dense jungle, then stopped in front of a large, windowless concrete structure. Its flat reinforced roof, landscaped with vegetation, disguised it from the air even more realistically than the landing pad. Only a row of palm trees on either side of the entrance offered the structure any semblance of warmth.

Pablo jumped out of the cart. 'Thanks for the lift. Don't bother to keep the motor running.'

'I wouldn't plan for a long visit, if I were you,' Johansson said, then drove away.

As Pablo climbed a short flight of steps to the doorway, a breeze from the lake helped stir the muggy air. A guard at the threshold opened the door and escorted him inside.

In marked contrast to the plain walls outside, the building's interior was an exercise in opulence. Built as a personal residence, it was decorated in bright tropical colors, illuminated by a surplus of overhead lighting. As Pablo was led down a white-marbled corridor, he passed a sunken living room decorated with modern art on one side and an indoor, glass-enclosed lap pool on the other. The rear of the house ran along the rim of a low hillside that jutted above the water. Floor-to-ceiling windows showcased an expansive section of Gatun Lake.

Pablo was led to a large open office that overlooked the rocky shoreline below. In the distance, a containership could be seen heading south through the canal on its way to the Pacific.

He stood in the doorway a moment until he gained the attention of the man seated behind an antique mahogany desk. Edward Bolcke peered over a pair of reading glasses and nodded for Pablo to enter.

Beginning with his conservative suit and tie, every detail of Bolcke's appearance testified to his exacting nature. His silver hair was perfectly coiffed, his fingernails precisely trimmed, and his shoes highly polished. His office was almost spartan in décor, his desktop devoid of clutter. Bolcke took off his glasses, leaned back in his chair, crossed his arms, and stared at Pablo through hawk-like brown eyes.

Pablo took a seat across the desk and waited for his employer to speak.

'So what went wrong in Tijuana?' Bolcke asked, the words tinged with a German accent.

'You know that Heiland destroyed his own boat during our initial operation,' Pablo said. 'This, of course, upset our planned extraction. Before we could get an appropriate recovery vessel there, the Americans arrived and raised the test model. They were from their civilian group NUMA, though, so we had no trouble getting the device from them at sea. But two of their men managed to follow us to shore in Mexico. And there was also a female investigator involved.'

'Yes, so I hear.'

Surprised at Bolcke's comment, Pablo cleared his throat. 'There was a traffic incident in the streets of Tijuana as we were making our way to the airport. The device was destroyed, and Juan was killed in the collision. I lost my man Eduardo as we made our way out of the situation.'

'Quite the blown opportunity,' Bolcke said, his eyes narrowing. 'At least there appear to be no repercussions.'

'All the men I work with are trained mercenaries from

Colombia with manufactured identities and no criminal records. There will be no connection to you.'

'A good thing, as the team you sent to Idaho was also killed.'

Pablo stiffened in his chair. 'Alteban and Rivera are dead?'

'Yes. They were killed in a "traffic incident" after departing Heiland's cabin,' Bolcke said, his expression stern. 'The female investigator, one Ann Bennett, and the Director of NUMA, whom you apparently met in Tijuana, were responsible. Fortunately, I was able to arrange the recovery of the research plans in Washington.'

Bolcke reached into a desk drawer, retrieved a thick envelope, and slid it across the desk. 'You shall enjoy a fine payday, my friend. Your own wages, plus those of your four dead comrades.'

'I cannot accept this,' Pablo said as he reached over and grabbed the envelope.

'No, I pay for the job, not the results. In light of the events, however, I have decided to rescind the bonus I had intended to pay for your good work at the Mountain Pass Mine.'

Pablo nodded, grateful to get his hands on the envelope. 'You have always been generous.'

'I will not be so generous should there be any more failings. I presume you are prepared for the next assignment?' He crossed his hands on the desk as he gave Pablo a fixed stare. Pablo avoided the gaze, instead looking at Bolcke's hands. That's what gave the man away, the hands. They were thick, gnarled, and blemished by the sun. They weren't the hands of a man who had spent his life in corporate boardrooms, as Bolcke appeared to be. They were the hands of a man who had spent a lifetime digging rocks.

Born and raised in Austria, Edward Bolcke had spent his youth scouring the Alps for gold and rare minerals. It was his means of escape after his mother had run away with an American GI, leaving him in the care of an alcoholic father prone to violence. The young Bolcke's mountain hikes fostered a love of geology, which led to a degree in mineral resources engineering from Austria's University of Leoben.

He took a job at a copper mine in Poland, and before long was hopscotching the globe, working tin mines in Malaysia, gold mines in Indonesia, and silver mines in South America. With an uncanny ability to locate the richest ore concentrations, he boosted recovery rates and profits everywhere he went.

But in Colombia, life threw him a twisted bone. Bolcke took an ownership interest in a small silver operation in the Tolima district. His astute analysis of the claim revealed a more valuable deposit of platinum alongside his property. He secured the rights and struck a major deposit, making him wealthy in a matter of months. While celebrating his good fortune in Bogotá, he met the vivacious daughter of a Brazilian industrialist and soon married.

He led a storybook life for several years, expanding his riches from the mine – until one day he returned to his home in Bogotá to find his wife in bed with an American consulate worker. With a fury he never knew he possessed, he shattered the man's skull with a rock hammer.

His wife came next, her throat crushed by his thick, burly hands.

A Colombian jury, well greased by his defense attorneys, acquitted him on the grounds of temporary insanity. He walked away a free man.

He was free physically, but not psychologically. The event reopened childhood scars of abandonment, while slashing new wounds. A bloodthirsty anger flooded his soul – and refused to recede. He sought revenge, turning to the easiest victims he could find: helpless young women. Cruising the slums of Bogotá at night, he would hire young prostitutes, then beat them unmercifully to vent his rage. Nearly gunned down one night by a watchful pimp, he finally abandoned that outlet for his rage and left Colombia, selling his remaining interest in the mine.

Bolcke had invested in an underperforming gold mine in Panama and he relocated there. Years earlier, he had studied the mine's operations and knew it had been mismanaged. A privately held American firm with other holdings owned it, and to take control he was forced to purchase the entire company. But to enable the deal, he had to forfeit a portion of the mine's equity to Panama's corrupt government, headed at the time by Manuel Noriega. When the US military ousted Noriega, the succeeding government laid claim to the mine and harassed Bolcke into amassing a mountain of legal bills before he reacquired ownership at a considerable cost. He blamed the Americans for his losses, inflaming an already deep-seated hatred against the country.

As part of the mining conglomerate, he found himself ironically owning a small enterprise in America: a trucking firm, several commercial freighters, and a small security business. What began as a minor annoyance turned into a major opportunity for revenge.

Every night the vision of his wife with the American officer haunted his dreams, replaying his childhood abandonment, and every morning he woke enraged. The perpetrators, though both long dead, remained targets of wrath, and, by association, their country of origin. The anger never left him. But rather than venting it through random violence, he turned down a new path of vengeance. Using the skills and knowledge from a lifetime of mining, he initiated his own economic war of retribution.

Bolcke's joyless dark eyes, set in a lean, hardened face, probed his visitor while his hands flattened on the desk.

Pablo spoke uneasily. 'I am not eager to return to America right away. My understanding was that I would remain in Panama City for several weeks before the next phase.'

'We had an outdated delivery schedule, and now the time line has been moved up. The shipment is being made in four days. You'll need to return at once.'

Pablo didn't balk. The ex–Colombian Special Forces commando never refused an order. He'd worked for the old Austrian for more than a dozen years, since first being hired to help quell a labor unrest at the mine. His unwavering loyalty had been well rewarded over the years, particularly as his boss drifted further over the line.

'I will need to assemble a new support team,' Pablo said.

'There is no time. You will be assisted by two American contractors.'

'Outside help cannot be trusted.'

'We will have to take that chance,' Bolcke snapped. 'You lost your entire team. I can give you some of Johansson's men, but they are untrained in your line of work. My Washington representative assures me these contractors are reliable. And besides,' he said, looking Pablo in the eye, 'they accomplished what your team could not. They recovered the supercavitation data.'

Bolcke slid Pablo a smaller envelope.

'The phone number of our man in Washington. Contact him when you get in and he will arrange a meeting with the contractors. All other arrangements are in place, so you simply need to make the acquisition and delivery.'

'It will be done.'

'The company jet will be standing by tomorrow to take you into the country. Any questions?'

'This female investigator and the people from NUMA – are they a problem?'

'The woman is of no concern.' Bolcke sat back in his chair and further contemplated the question. 'I don't know about the NUMA personnel. Perhaps they are worth monitoring.' He gazed back at Pablo. 'I will take care of it. Proceed with the plan. I will be in Beijing waiting for your confirmation.'

His eyes grew darker as he leaned forward. 'I have been working toward this moment for many years. Everything is in place. Do not fail me, Pablo.'

Pablo puffed out his chest. 'Do not worry, *Jefe*. It will be like taking sweets from a baby.'

31

Ann hit the office running at seven in the morning, inspired to investigate Pitt's potential link with the ship hijacking. Her first stop was Joe Eberson's replacement as the DARPA director of Sea Platforms Technology, Dr Roald Oswald. She had met the scientist a few days earlier and wasn't surprised to find him already at his desk, working on a status report.

She poked her head through the doorway. 'May I intrude on your morning silence?'

'Of course, Miss Bennett. I could use a diversion from the depressing state of our new submarine's delivery schedule.'

'Please, call me Ann. Will there be a launch without the supercavitation device?'

'That's our dilemma. The collective loss of Eberson and Heiland has put us back months – if not years. The vessel's capabilities are cut to the bone without the device. There will still be merit in testing the propulsion system, I suppose, if we can ever complete the final assembly.'

'What's holding you up?'

'Critical material delays, I'm told.'

'Would any of those materials include rare earth elements?'

Oswald took a draw from his coffee and probed Ann with his pale blue eyes. 'I don't have enough information here to answer that. But, yes, certain rare earth elements play a significant part in the *Sea Arrow*'s design – especially in the propulsion system and some of the sonar and electronic systems. Why do you ask?'

'I'm exploring a possible link between Dr Heiland's death and a hijacked shipment of monazite ore containing high concentrations of neodymium and lanthanum. How important are those elements to the *Sea Arrow*?'

'Very. Our propulsion system relies upon a pair of highly advanced electric motors, which in turn power two external jet pumps, as well as the rest of the vessel's operating systems. Both components contain rare earth elements, but especially the motors.' Oswald took another sip of coffee. 'They utilize permanent high-intensity magnets to achieve a multigenerational leap in efficiency and output. These magnets are produced under exacting standards at the Ames National Laboratory, and they contain a mixture of several rare earths, most certainly including neodymium.' He hesitated a moment. 'We believe that Heiland's supercavitation system relies on some rare earth components as well. I suspect you may be onto something.'

'Why do you say that?'

'The *Sea Arrow*'s motors have yet to be installed. The first motor was just completed at the Naval Research Lab at Chesapeake Bay and is ready for shipment to Groton. The second has been delayed due to a disruption in the materials' supply chain. I haven't caught up with all the information, but I understand that a shortage of rare earth elements is holding us up.'

'Could you find out exactly which materials are involved?'

'I'll make some calls and let you know.' He sat back in his chair with a look of introspection. 'Joe Eberson was a friend of mine. We used to go fishing in Canada every summer. He was a good man. Make sure you find his killers.'

Ann nodded solemnly. 'I intend to.'

She had been back at her desk for only a few minutes when Oswald called with an alphabet soup list of elements whose short supplies were delaying the *Sea Arrow*: gadolinium, praseodymium, samarium, and dysprosium. At the top of the list was neodymium, the very element in Pitt's monazite sample from Chile.

A quick online search revealed the market prices for those elements had recently skyrocketed. Commodity analysts cited two factors for the increase. One was a fire that had devastated the facilities at Mountain Pass, California, the site of the only active rare earth mine in the US. The second was something Ann already knew, an announcement by the owners of Australia's Mount Weld Mine that they would temporarily cease production to modernize and expand the mine.

As she digested all this, Ann picked up the sheet Fowler had left on her desk. It was the file of biographies for all the nonmilitary personnel who had toured the *Sea Arrow*. Skipping those who worked at DARPA and ONR, she studied the remaining names. Her eyes widened when she scanned the bio of White House aide Tom Cerny. She reviewed it a second time, jotted down some notes, and printed the entire file.

Fowler appeared at the door and stepped into her office with a donut and coffee. 'You're rustling the leaves early. Where is the hunt taking you today?'

'Would you believe the South Pacific?' She told him of Pitt's suspicions about the ore carrier in Chile and his plans to protect the ship inbound from Australia.

'It's carrying rare earth elements?'

'Yes. I think he said she was called the *Adelaide*, sailing from Perth.'

'You're not going to join him, are you?'

'I considered it, but he's leaving tomorrow. It's probably a wild-goose chase, and frankly, I feel like I'm making some progress here.'

She slid the bio of Tom Cerny across the desk to him. 'I'm not prepared to pronounce a leak in the White House, but look at Cerny's background.'

Fowler read aloud a few of Cerny's biographical entries. 'Ex–Green Beret officer, served as military adviser in Taiwan, later Panama and Colombia. Left Army for a stint at Raytheon as a program manager for directed energy weapons programs. Later moved to Capitol Hill as a defense specialist. Served on the board of directors of three defense contractors before joining the White House. Married to the former Jun Lu Yi, a Taiwanese national. Operates a child education charity in Bogotá.' He set the paper down. 'Interesting range of experiences.'

'He seems to have been in the vicinity of a few defense systems that the Chinese have duplicated,' Ann said. 'The Colombia bit certainly caught my eye.'

'Worth looking into. I suspect you could make some discreet inquiries without raising any red flags.'

'I agree. I'm not ready to throw away my career by barging into the White House, but I'll press the fringes a bit more. How are things going with your internal reviews?'

He shook his head. 'I've double-checked every DARPA employee working on the program. To be honest, I haven't found a single nugget of suspicious behavior. I'll pass the files to you when I finish the interviews.'

'Thanks, but I'll trust your review. Where are you headed next?'

'I figured on making site visits to our three largest sub-contractors. Maybe you should join me? It would make the work go faster.'

'I'm thinking of looking at a few of the smaller sub-contractors. These three caught my eye.'

'Too far down the food chain,' Fowler said. 'They'd likely have only limited access to anything classified.'

'No harm in a little probing,' Ann said. 'You know the saying about the blind pig finding the acorn.'

Fowler smiled. 'Suit yourself. I'll be around the rest of the day if you come up with any nuts to share.'

Late in the day, she got her next break. After more follow-ups with the FBI, she went back to her list of subcontractors. The first two companies were publicly traded, so she readily obtained background information on their businesses. But the third firm was privately held and required more digging. She found an article about it in an engineering periodical and rushed into Fowler's office.

'Dan, take a look at this. One of the subcontractors, a firm called SecureTek, provides secure data lines for engineers in remote locations to share their work. Without having their own security clearance, they could gain access to private engineering work.'

'That's probably harder to pull off than you think.'

'More interesting is this. SecureTek is part of a small conglomerate based in Panama that also owns a transportation company in the US and a gold mine in Panama.'

'Okay, but I don't see where that leads.'

'The company holds a minority interest in Hobart Mining. Hobart owns a mine in Australia called Mount Weld.'

'All right, so they've expanded their mining operations.'

'Mount Weld is one of the largest producers of rare earth elements outside of China. Dr Oswald told me this morning how vital rare earth elements are in the *Sea Arrow*'s development – and how shortages have delayed the program. There could be a connection.'

'Seems a bit tenuous,' Fowler said, shaking his head. 'What's the motivation? The mine owner should be happy we're buying what he produces, not cutting off one of his best customers. I think you're letting Dirk Pitt lead you astray.'

'Maybe you're right,' she said. 'It seems like we're grasping at straws.'

'That happens. Maybe things will look different in the morning. I find exercise helps me in solving problems. Every morning, I take a run along the Potomac, and find it's a great way to relax my mind. You should try it.'

'Maybe I will. Just do me one favor, will you?' she said. 'Add SecureTek to the list of contractors on your site visits.'

'That I'll be happy to do,' he said.

Ann took his advice and stopped at a health club on the way home and ran a few miles on a treadmill before grabbing a chicken salad to go at a café. She thought of Pitt on the way home and called him the second she entered her town house. There was no reply, so she left a lengthy message about her findings and wished him luck on his voyage.

As she hung up, a deep voice grumbled from the hallway.

'I hope you remembered to say good-bye.'

Ann nearly jumped out of her shoes. She wheeled around to see two large black men emerge from her darkened bedroom. She recognized the first man and began to tremble.

Clarence smiled coldly as he walked into the room and leveled a .45 at her head.

32

Zhou Xing had the face of a peasant. His eyes were set close together, his chin was almost nonexistent, and his nose listed to starboard from a long-ago fracture. A pair of jug ears and a pauper's haircut completed the rural simpleton appearance. It was a countenance perfectly suited to the undercover intelligence agent. Aside from allowing Zhou to fit into almost any field situation, it habitually caused his superiors in the Chinese Ministry of State Security to underestimate his guile and ability.

At the moment he was counting on the same effect for a less sophisticated crowd. Wearing the worn and dusty clothes of an unskilled laborer, he looked like most of the inhabitants of Bayan Obo, a company town in Inner Mongolia that was itself worn and dusty. Zhou crossed a paved street bustling with trucks and buses and made his way to a small drinking establishment. Even from the street he could hear the voices inside. He took a deep breath, then pulled open a wooden door emblazoned with a faded red boar.

The scent of cheap tobacco and stale beer filled Zhou's nostrils as he stepped through the door and scanned the confines with a practiced eye. A dozen tables filled the narrow room, occupied by a coarse and rugged assortment of miners off duty from the town's open-pit mine. A fat, one-eyed barkeep poured shots behind an elevated platform lined with hard-drinking locals. The bar's only decoration was its namesake, a stuffed and mounted boar's head that was missing several tufts of fur.

Zhou ordered a *baijiu*, a grain alcohol that was the locals' favorite, and slid onto a corner chair to study the clientele. Cloistered in groups of two or three, most were well on their way to numbing themselves from the day's labor. He scanned from face to hardened face, searching for a suitable target. He found one a few tables away, a brash, loudmouthed young man, talking the ears off his silent, towering partner.

Zhou waited until the talker had nearly drained his shot glass before approaching the table. Pretending to stagger, he flung an elbow against the talker's glass, sending it flying.

'Hey! My drink.'

'A thousand pardons, my friend,' Zhou said, slurring his words. 'Please, come to the bar with me and I shall purchase you another.'

The young miner, realizing he had just scored a free round, rose quickly, if unsteadily, to his feet. 'Yes, another drink.'

With a full ceramic bottle of *baijiu* in hand, Zhou was welcomed back to the table.

'I am Wen,' the man said, 'and my quiet friend here is Yao.'

'I am Tsen,' Zhou replied. 'You both work at the mine?'

'Of course.' Wen flexed his biceps. 'We didn't build this strength by plucking chickens.'

'What is your job at the mine?'

'Why, we are the crushers,' Wen said with a laugh. 'We

feed the mined ore into the primary rockcrushers. They're as big as a house and can mash a boulder the size of a dog down to this.' He balled his fist in front of Zhou.

'I come from Baotou,' Zhou said, 'and am in need of work. Are there any jobs available at the mine?'

Wen reached over and squeezed Zhou's arm. 'A man like you? You are too scrawny to work in the mines.' He laughed, spraying a shower of saliva across the table. Then noting a sad look on Zhou's face, he felt a touch of pity. 'Men get injured, so they occasionally bring on replacements. But there will probably be a long line ahead of you.'

'I understand,' Zhou said. 'More *baijiu*?'

He didn't wait for an answer and refilled their glasses. The silent miner, Yao, peered at him through listless eyes and nodded. Wen raised his glass and downed a shot.

'Tell me,' Zhou said as he sipped at his drink. 'I hear there is a black market mining operation at Bayan Obo.'

Yao tensed and looked at Zhou suspiciously.

'No, it all comes from the same place.' Wen wiped his mouth with a sleeve.

'It is not safe to speak of,' Yao said, breaking his silence with an earthy bellow.

Wen shrugged. 'It all takes place beyond us.'

'What do you mean?' Zhou asked.

'The blasting, the digging, the crushing, that is all performed by the state operation that pays Yao and me,' he said. 'It's only after the crushing that other hands start dipping into the pot.'

'What hands are those?'

Yao slammed his glass down on the table. 'You ask a lot of questions, Tsen.'

Zhou bowed slightly to Yao. 'I'm just trying to find myself a job.'

'Yao's just touchy because his cousin drives a truck for the operation.'

'How do they operate?'

'I guess they're paying off some of the mine's truck drivers,' Wen said. 'At night, some of the trucks that haul the raw diggings to the crusher pick up a load of crushed ore and deposit it at a remote part of the mine. Then Jiang and his private fleet of trucks come in and haul it away. Hey, there he is now.' Wen waved over a squat, grit-faced man who had just stepped into the bar. The man moved with a determined swagger.

'Jiang, I was just telling my friend how you haul hot rocks from the mine.'

Jiang flung an open hand against the side of Wen's head, nearly knocking him out of his chair. 'You need to quit your babbling, Wen, or you'll lose your tongue. You're worse than an old woman.' He sized Zhou up, then regarded his cousin Yao. The big man faintly shook his head.

Jiang eased around the table and stood close to Zhou. He suddenly reached down, grabbed Zhou's collar, and jerked the agent to his feet.

Zhou kept his arms at his sides and smiled harmlessly.

'Who are you?' Jiang said, his face millimeters from Zhou's.

'My name is Tsen. I am a farmer from Baotou. Now, you tell me your name?'

Jiang's eyes flared at his boldness. 'Listen to me, farmer.' He held Zhou's collar tightly. 'If you ever want to tread the soil of Bayan Obo again, then I suggest that you pretend you never came here. You saw no one and talked to no one. Do you understand?'

Jiang's breath reeked of smoke and garlic, but Zhou never flinched. With a pleasant grin, he nodded at Jiang. 'Of course. But if I was never here, then I didn't spend eighty yuan on drinks with your friends.' He held out an open palm as if waiting for reimbursement.

Jiang's face turned red. 'Don't ever enter this bar again. Now, get out.'

He freed his grip on Zhou's collar so he could punctuate the threat with his fist, but he was too close to throw a punch and he took a step back.

Zhou anticipated the move and scissored his foot behind Jiang's, catching the back of the truck driver's ankle. Jiang stumbled, but still unleashed a hard right as he fell back. Zhou moved left, absorbing the punch to his shoulder, then countered by shoving Jiang's torso. Jiang lost his footing and fell backward, out of control.

Zhou kept a grip on him, driving him toward the table, where Jiang's head smashed against the lip. He collapsed to the floor like a felled redwood, knocked out cold.

At the sight of his cousin's takedown, Yao leaped up and tried to grab Zhou in a bear hug.

The smaller and more sober Zhou easily spun away, then launched a sharp kick to Yao's knee. The big man buckled, allowing Zhou to deliver several lightning strikes to the head. A final blow struck his throat. Yao turned and fell to his knees, clutching his throat while overcome by a false sense of suffocation.

The bar fell silent, and all eyes turned to Zhou. Drawing

attention to himself was foolish, but there were times he couldn't help himself.

'No fighting!' the bartender shouted. But he was too busy pouring drinks to bother throwing out any of the culprits.

Zhou nodded at him, then casually picked up his glass of *baijiu* from the table and took a swig. The other patrons returned to their drinks and jokes, ignoring the two men on the floor.

Wen had watched the brief fight in a stupor, not moving from his chair. 'You have quick hands for a farmer,' he stuttered.

'Lots of hoeing.' Zhou swung his hands up and down. 'What do you say our friend Jiang buys us a drink?' he asked.

'Sure,' Wen slurred.

Zhou reached into the unconscious man's pocket and took out his wallet. Finding his resident identity card, he memorized Jiang's full name and address. He replaced the wallet, but not before retrieving a twenty-yuan banknote, which he handed to Wen. 'You drink for me,' Zhou said. 'It is late, and I must go.'

'Yes, my friend Tsen, if you say so.' Wen raised himself in his chair with some difficulty.

'See you at the mine,' Zhou said.

'The mine?' Wen asked. He looked up in puzzlement, but the little farmer from Baotou was already gone.

33

Jiang Xianto, the truck driver, crept out of his apartment complex at half past seven the next morning. A bandage was plastered across his forehead, and he walked with rigid strides to try to minimize the spasms that shot through his skull with each step. Had he been less preoccupied, he might have seen his assailant from the Red Boar, seated in a Chinese-built Toyota parked across the street, reading a *People's Daily*.

Zhou smiled to himself as he watched Jiang hobble down the street. He had felt no joy in flooring Yao the night before, but he felt no empathy toward Jiang. He had recognized Jiang's type instantly, a hotheaded loser who tormented weaker men to make himself feel better.

The black market truck driver walked down the street to a crowded bus stop. True to form, Jiang bullied his way to the front of the line, then took one of the few remaining seats when the bus arrived. Zhou started his car and pulled into traffic, keeping the bus a few car lengths ahead.

By the time the bus stopped in front of a dilapidated apartment building at the southern edge of town, most of the passengers had departed. Zhou wheeled his car around a corner, parked behind a street vendor, and watched Jiang step off the bus. Pulling a brimmed hat low over his eyes, Zhou locked his car and followed on foot.

Jiang walked a little way down a side street, then turned

into a trash-strewn alley. A morning breeze chilled the air, and Jiang zipped up his jacket as he reached a large fenced lot topped with rusty barbed wire. He stepped through a slit in the fence and walked past stacks of empty pallets that towered over the dusty lot. At the rear of the property, beneath a corrugated tin awning, stood five large canvas-covered trucks and a battered pickup. Several rough-looking men stood around the trucks, drinking hot tea from paper cups.

'Jiang,' one of the men said, 'did your wife brush your hair with a wok this morning?'

'I'll brush yours with a tire iron,' Jiang said. 'Where's Xao?'

A tall man wearing a black peacoat stepped from between two of the trucks. 'Jiang, there you are. Late again, I see. Keep this up and you'll be back digging ditches.' He turned to the other men. 'Okay, everyone, we're ready to move.'

The men gathered around him as he pulled a folded paper from his pocket.

'We'll be dropping the load at Dock 27,' Xao said. 'I'll take the lead truck, so follow me, as we'll be entering through an auxiliary gate. We're expected to arrive at eight o'clock, so let's not have any delays.'

'Where will we stop for fuel?' asked a man with a threadbare wool cap.

'The usual truck stop in Changping.' Xao looked about for other questions, then nodded toward the trucks. 'Okay, let's get moving.'

Xao, Jiang, and three other men drifted to the large trucks, and the remaining men piled into the pickup.

Jiang's truck was at the end of the line. He climbed in and started the engine, which kicked to life with a cloud of black smoke. Adjusting the heater, he waited for the other trucks to exit the lot ahead of him. When the truck next to him pulled ahead, he shifted into gear and lurched forward, catching sight of a dark blur in the side-view mirror.

The trucks drove through an open gate attended by a burly bald man who carried a Russian Makarov pistol under his coat. When Jiang got to the gate, he mashed on the truck's brakes. 'Check the back!' he said, reaching out the window and slapping the side door to catch the guard's attention.

The guard nodded and stepped to the rear of the truck. As he peered over the tailgate, he was greeted by Zhou's boot slamming into his jaw. The blow sent him sprawling, yet he yanked out the Makarov even as he fell. He raised the pistol and aimed it toward the truck, but Zhou was already on him. The agent kicked the pistol aside, then dove forward and thrust his elbow into the guard's jaw. The bone-on-bone collision emitted a muted crack, and the guard fell limp.

Zhou popped to his feet and spun around. Jiang was already there, lunging at him with a knife he carried on his belt. Zhou saw the glint as the blade thrust toward his chest. He tried twisting away, but the tip caught his sleeve, and he felt it slice across his right bicep.

He ignored the cut and hurled a left cross into Jiang's temple. Jiang let out a curse, realizing he was battling the man who had crushed his head the night before.

Zhou gave him no time to contemplate that. The Makarov was too far away to retrieve, so he did the unexpected and pressed the attack. He followed his punch with a round-house kick that struck Jiang in the thigh. It was designed less to punish than to incite a response, and it succeeded. Jiang pulled back the knife and recklessly thrust toward his opponent's stomach.

Zhou was ready. He threw his left hand on Jiang's wrist, easily shoving the parry aside. Using Jiang's momentum, he pulled and twisted the knife-wielding wrist, propelling Jiang forward. Zhou continued the spinning motion, driving his opposite shoulder against Jiang's arm with his full weight.

Jiang's arm felt like it was being yanked from its socket, and he stumbled forward in agony. The knife dropped free, and he fell to the ground. In the blink of an eye, the knife was in Zhou's hand, driving toward Jiang's head. Zhou wanted to kill the man, and could have done so easily, but he resisted the impulse. Jiang would suffer more by rotting in a jail cell. He reversed the blade, striking Jiang below the ear with the butt of the knife. Jiang's world turned black as the blow to his carotid artery cut the flow of blood to his brain. Zhou stood over him, catching his breath. A phone call to the People's Armed Police would ensure the bully an unpleasant welcome when he awoke. But first Zhou had to catch the caravan.

The trucks had disappeared down the street. Zhou found the Makarov and stuffed it in his pocket. Then he flipped Jiang on his stomach and stripped off his jacket. With the man's knife, he sliced off a strip of Jiang's shirt for a bandage. Zhou's right arm was wet and sticky, but the bleeding had already stopped. He'd have to mend himself on the fly.

Zhou jumped into the truck and gunned the motor, spraying the two prone men with a blanket of dust as he rumbled out of the lot toward Bayan Obo's main highway. The mine was north of town, so he turned in that direction and mashed the accelerator.

Cutting through traffic and passing wildly, he raised a symphony of honking horns and angry shouts. The traffic lessened as he neared the city's northern limits, and the road began climbing through dry scrub hills. Cresting a ridge, he spotted the caravan a mile ahead, and he soon closed ranks with the last truck.

With Zhou tailing the crowded pickup, the line of cargo trucks drove past the main entrance to the Bayan Obo Mine, then turned onto a rutted dirt road two miles beyond that. Circling back to the south, they crossed a downed section of fence and entered the mine site. A pair of massive open pits appeared ahead. The trucks skirted them and approached the main operational area. The pickup veered away, leading the cargo trucks to a fire-damaged warehouse that looked abandoned. They pulled to a stop in back of the building, where a massive mound of crushed ore was piled high.

The theft operation was simple. On certain night shifts, every third dump truck transporting crushed ore to the extraction plant would get lost along the way and dump its load behind the old warehouse. All it took was a few large bribes to select drivers and administrators, who adjusted the mine's production records, and the ore was there for the taking. Every few days, the truck convoy would haul it away to market.

The men from the pickup opened a back door to the

warehouse, where a portable conveyor was stored. They rolled it to the mound of ore and connected a portable generator. Zhou watched as the lead cargo truck backed up until the end of the conveyor poked over the truck bed. The work crew began shoveling the ore onto the belt, which carried it into the truck. It took less than fifteen minutes to fill the bed, then the next vehicle backed in.

Zhou wiped his arm and rewrapped the makeshift bandage around the knife wound. Feeling light-headed from the loss of blood, he replenished himself with some rice balls he found in a paper sack on the seat. He swapped jackets with the one he'd taken from Jiang and raised the collar. Breathing heavily onto his side window, he fogged up the glass so the others couldn't see him while he waited his turn.

When the fourth truck pulled clear, Xao waved him over and guided him to the conveyor. Zhou kept his hands high on the steering wheel to obscure his face as Xao walked in front of the hood and waved him backward.

The ore spilled into the truck bed with the roar of an avalanche. The minutes trickled by as Zhou held his breath, fearful someone would try to speak with him. Finally, the rumbling ceased, and the conveyor fell silent. Zhou looked in the side-view mirror and saw the crew drag the conveyor back to the warehouse. Xao rapped his knuckles on the fender, then continued to his own vehicle. The convoy leader climbed into the first truck, stuck his arm out the window, and pointed ahead. The rest of the trucks started their engines and followed Xao.

The heavily loaded trucks moved slowly down the rough road until they reached the main highway, then they rolled south through the dusty town that was built by the mining operation. Leaving behind that small bastion of civilization, they drove across the same barren steppes of Inner Mongolia that Genghis Khan had conquered eight centuries earlier. Zhou figured they would off-load their cargo at the nearest railroad depot. When they reached the populous city of Baotou several hours later and turned east, he knew otherwise.

The convoy rolled onto the busy Jingzhang Expressway, which ran to Beijing. Outside of the capital city, they paused at a truck stop in the suburb of Changping as dusk was settling. A light wind had picked up, blowing swirls of sand from the Gobi Desert. Zhou wrapped his face with a scarf he found in Jiang's coat pocket and stretched his legs away from the others while the trucks were refueled.

The trucks moved off slowly, fighting their way through the thickening city traffic. They looped around the west side of Beijing to avoid the worst of the congestion and continued southeast. It took the better part of two hours before they reached the port city of Tianjin. Xao led the trucks through a maze of streets to the center of the large commercial docks.

They reached an old dockside warehouse and pulled down a side alley. Two men appeared from the shadows and accepted a sack filled with yuan that Xao passed out the window. A gate opened at the end of the alley, and the trucks rumbled through, entering a cavernous warehouse that opened to a dock on the far side. The trucks drove through the building and stopped beside a moderate-sized freighter whose lights illuminated the pier.

A large conveyor system stretched from the dock to an open hold on the ship, and Xao backed his truck to the end of it. A work crew appeared with shovels and began emptying the truck's load of ore. As Zhou watched from the end of the line, he realized he'd seen all he needed. He slipped out the passenger door and crept toward the back of the truck.

A deck officer from the freighter, who was standing on the dock checking the ship's lines, glanced over at Zhou. Playing the part of a tired driver, Zhou stretched his arms and yawned as he stepped toward the officer.

'Good evening,' he said with a slight bow. 'A fine ship you have here.'

'The *Graz* is old and tired, but she still plows through the sea like a hefty ox.'

'Where are you headed?'

'We do a cargo swap in Shanghai, then we're off to Singapore.'

He looked at Zhou closely under the lights, noticing a damp streak of red on the sleeve of his jacket.

'Are you okay?'

Zhou glanced at the blood and grinned.

'It's transmission fluid. I spilled it, adding some to the truck.'

Zhou saw Xao's truck was finished unloading and the next truck in line was moving to take its place. He nodded at the officer and smiled. 'Have a safe voyage,' he said, turning his back on the loading operations and walking away.

The officer looked at him oddly. 'What about your truck?'

Zhou ignored the query, sauntering away from the dock until he vanished into the night.

34

The *Sea Arrow*'s propulsion motor looked like a stretch limousine driven through an oversized tire. The limousine part, in fact, was a rectangular induction housing that drew in water and expelled it through a trio of gimbaled exhaust outlets in the back. Just forward of it, at the motor's midpoint, a donut-shaped nacelle contained the sophisticated jet pump that could push the submarine to high speeds. The entire motor was coated in a slippery black substance, which deflected water and gave the entire device a cold, futuristic appearance.

High overhead lights shined starkly on the prototype propulsion motor as a crane lifted it from its floor blocks and placed it on a large flatbed trailer. An army of work-men secured it with steel cables and covered it with canvas tarps. A semi-truck, operated by a company that special-ized in hauling secure freight, was backed in and hitched to the trailer.

It was half past six in the morning when the truck pulled out of the Naval Research Laboratory's facility at Chesapeake Beach, Maryland. As it drove inland from the bay, the surrounding woods and fields were damp with morning dew, while a leaden sky obscured the sunrise.

'What's our ETA to Groton?' the codriver asked, sup-pressing a yawn.

The truck's driver glanced at his watch. 'The GPS says

seven hours. Probably longer if we don't beat the worst of the Beltway traffic.'

In the lightly populated region of southern Maryland, the early-morning traffic leading toward Washington was almost nonexistent. As they rounded a sweeping curve, the two men noticed a wisp of black smoke rising ahead. When it became apparent that the smoke originated from the road, the driver downshifted.

'Is that a car on fire?' his codriver asked.

'I think so. Looks like some old clunker.'

It was in fact a twenty-year-old Toyota Camry that had been severely wrecked at some point in its life. Now it sat in the middle of the road on four bald tires, flames sprouting from beneath its crumpled hood.

The truck driver eased the flatbed to a stop a few yards away and searched the road for victims. A white van was pulled off the road a short distance ahead, but there were no signs of life around it or the burning car.

'We better call this in,' the driver said as his partner reached behind the seat for a fire extinguisher.

A crash jarred them out of their seats as the head of a sledgehammer burst through the passenger-side window. A gloved hand thrust through the shattered glass and dropped a smoking canister of tear gas in the cab.

In an instant, the truck's interior was filled with an acrid white smoke that made the men gag. Their eyes burned as if hot lava had been poured under their lids, and they groped for the door handles to escape the agony.

The driver made it out first, leaping from the cab onto the roadway. A man wearing a ski mask zapped him with a stun gun, sending him to the ground, convulsing. On the other side of the truck, the codriver had managed to pull out his gun as he exited the cab. But with his eyes clenched shut from the gas, he failed to see the second assailant strike him with another stun gun.

A third man, wearing a gas mask, climbed into the cab and hurled the still-smoking canister out into an adjacent field. He slid behind the wheel and jabbed a knife into the cab's headliner. He pulled away the fabric until spotting a wire, which he deftly sliced, disabling the roof-mounted GPS transmitter that allowed the shipping company to track the vehicle. Jamming the truck into gear, he eased it forward until its broad chrome bumper kissed the burning car. Then he floored the accelerator while nudging the steering wheel to the right. The torque-strong truck brushed the Toyota aside like an insect and flipped it into a ditch.

Straightening back onto the small road, the new driver shifted gears and lowered his side window. Within seconds, the last remnants of gas had been flushed out. Pablo pulled off the uncomfortable gas mask and tossed it on the seat beside him.

He glanced at his watch and smiled. In just two minutes he had taken one of America's most secret technologies. He pulled out a cell phone, dialed a long string of numbers, and smiled, thinking about his payoff to come.

35

Pablo drove the long flatbed another mile before maneuvering it off the highway and onto a small dirt road. The narrow, rutted track crossed a large pasture dotted with sleepy-eyed cows. A half mile in, the road passed a large pond, then ended at an abandoned farm just beyond.

The charred remnants of the farmhouse were still visible, scorched by a fire decades earlier. Nearby, a large weathered barn leaned to one side as if the next nor'easter would send it tumbling. Pablo drove to the barn and guided the truck into an opening at one end of it.

Inside he found a high stack of freshly cut bales of hay guarded by a mini forklift. At the opposite end of the barn stood another semi-truck cab. He pulled the flatbed alongside the bales, parked the truck, and climbed out to examine the object under the tarps.

A few minutes later, the white panel van pulled in, and two large black men jumped out.

'You take care of the drivers?' Pablo asked.

The first man nodded. 'Clarence cuffed them together around a big oak off the highway. Some farmer will find them in a day or two.'

'Good. Now, let's get to work. I'm on a tight schedule.'

The two hired thugs pulled away the tarps covering the *Sea Arrow*'s motor. Then they donned heavy gloves and went to work on the bales of hay. Clarence started up the forklift, and using an attached device called a bale squeeze, he began hoisting blocks of multiple bales onto the flat-bed. The second man stood on the bed, guiding the bales into place around the motor.

Meanwhile, Pablo unhitched the truck from the flat-bed. He parked the truck off to the side and returned with the other big rig, a blue Kenworth. In ten minutes he had the new truck hitched to the trailer. He scrutinized the flatbed for a second GPS tracking device. Finding none, he swapped the rear license plate.

The other two men had nearly finished building a wall of hay around the *Sea Arrow*'s power plant. Pablo helped them pull a tarp across the top of the bales and tie it to the sides of the trailer, completing its disguise as a hay truck.

Clarence, the larger of the two men, pulled off his gloves and approached Pablo. 'That concludes our part of the job,' he said in his raspy voice. 'You have our pay?'

'Yes,' Pablo said. 'And you have the plans?'

'In the back of the van. Along with an added present for you,' he said, grinning.

'Bring the documents to the truck. I'll get your money.'

Clarence opened the back of the van and pulled out the plastic bin containing Heiland's supercavitation plans. He followed Pablo to the Kenworth and placed it on the pas-senger seat. Pablo reached behind the seat and handed the hired thug a thick envelope. The big man ripped off one end, revealing several bound stacks of hundred-dollar bills.

'My, that does look pretty.' He folded the envelope closed. 'Now, if you'd be kind enough to retrieve your gift, we'll be on our way.'

Pablo gave him a puzzled look. Clarence jerked his thumb toward the van and led Pablo to the open back doors, where the other man stood, smiling.

As Pablo peered past him into the van's interior, his eyes flared in anger. Coiled on the van's floor was the bound-and-gagged Ann Bennett.

A look of rage seared her face until her eyes met Pablo's, then the shock of recognition hit home. The Colombian terrorist was the last person she expected to see here. Her brazenness evaporated, and she wriggled farther into the confines of the van.

Pablo turned to Clarence. 'What is she doing here?'

'We got a call to pick her up,' Clarence said. 'We were told not to waste her, so here she is.'

Pablo reached under his jacket, pulled out a Glock pistol, and aimed it into the back of the van.

'Yo, man, don't do her in the back of the van,' Clarence said. 'It's a rental.'

'Okay.'

Pablo wheeled around and fired the Glock point-blank in Clarence's face. As he fell back dead, his partner lunged at Pablo. But the Colombian was quicker. He turned and pumped three shots into the man's chest. The dying thug could only grip Pablo's collar and pull him to his knees before collapsing.

Ann screamed, but her cry was muffled by a band of duct tape. Pablo gazed at her a moment, then calmly holstered the Glock. He reached into the van, yanked Ann out, and tossed her onto a leftover bale of hay. 'I'm afraid it won't do to kill you here.'

As she watched in terror, he hoisted the two dead

bodies into the back of the van and closed the doors. Tossing the now bloodied cash envelope toward Ann, he looked at her and said, 'Don't move.'

An instant later, Pablo peeled the van out of the barn, spraying dust and loose hay. He drove just a short distance, then stopped and carefully positioned the van. He lowered the windows, removed all the keys from the fob except for the ignition key, then walked around searching for a large flat rock. Finding one, he placed it on the accelerator pedal and mashed it down flat. Climbing out of the truck, he reached in through the open window and started the engine. Before the revolutions could skyrocket, he pulled the column shift into drive and jumped away.

The rear tires spun in the loose dirt, and the van shot down the road. It traveled less than fifty feet before it angled off the road and careened through a small ditch. Its momentum carried it up the opposite side and over a small embankment, where it lunged into the pond.

A lone goose scattered with an angry honk as the van hurled up a wall of green water. After a few seconds, the van filled with water and disappeared into the deep pond, leaving only a diminishing froth of bubbles.

Pablo didn't wait for it to sink but instead jogged back to the barn. He picked up the envelope and threw it into the truck's cab before coming back for Ann. Without a word, he carried her to the cab and dropped her in a flat compartment behind the front seats.

'You might as well get comfortable,' he said, starting the truck and shifting into gear. 'We have a long trip ahead of us.'

36

The helicopter flew in fast at treetop level, zooming low over the hangars to surprise the waiting dignitaries seated along the runway. It was a military chopper, its fuselage designed with sharp angles and coated with an absorbent material that rendered it nearly invisible to radar. A special composite five-blade main rotor and matching tail assembly added to its stealth qualities by dramatically reducing its noise signature. An aviation expert from *Jane's Defence Weekly* would take one look at the chopper and identify it as a Stealth Hawk, one of the US Army's heavily modified UH-80 Black Hawks, like the one used in the raid to capture Osama bin Laden. But this helicopter was entirely Chinese built.

The craft swooped about the Yangcun Air Base south of Beijing, buzzing the field several times before alighting. The crowd of generals and defense officials stood and applauded the exhibition of the country's latest technological triumph. The cheers became muted when a Party official took to an elevated podium and launched into a tired diatribe touting China's greatness.

Edward Bolcke leaned over to a bullet-eyed man wearing a uniform draped with medals. 'Splendid aircraft, General Jintai.'

'Yes, it is,' Jintai said. 'And we didn't even need your help to build it.'

Bolcke shook off the jab with a grin. Having just received Pablo's call from Maryland, he was brimming with confidence.

The crowd suffered through several more long-winded speeches before being herded into an open hangar with a buffet line. Bolcke trailed the general, a vice-chairman of China's Central Military Commission, as he mingled with other top People's Liberation Army officials. After inquiring about a fellow general's new condominium in Hong Kong, Jintai backtracked to Bolcke.

'My hospitality duties are now complete,' he said to the Austrian. 'We have some business to discuss?'

'If you please,' Bolcke replied.

'Very well. Let me find our chief spymaster, and we'll speak in private.'

Jintai scanned the crowd until locating a slight, bespectacled man drinking a Heineken beer. Tao Liang was a directorate head in the Ministry of State Security, the agency that handled China's intelligence and counterintelligence activities. Tao stood talking with Zhou Xing, the field operative from Bayan Obo, who calmly studied the assembled dignitaries. The peasant-faced man subtly alerted Tao that Jintai was stalking him while the general was still halfway across the room.

'Tao, there you are,' the general said. 'Come, we have a business proposal to evaluate with our old friend Edward Bolcke.'

'Our old friend Bolcke,' Tao said with an acid tone. 'Yes, I am curious to hear his latest offerings.'

With Zhou following, the men crossed the hangar to a small private office. It had been prepared for them with a portable liquor cabinet and a platter of dim sum. Jintai poured himself a whiskey and sat down with the others at a teak conference table.

'May I offer my congratulations, gentlemen, on your latest deployment,' Bolcke said. 'It is an admirable day for China's guardians. In a small way.'

He paused, letting his insult register. 'I would propose that tomorrow, however, may bring a revolutionary day to your country's defense.'

'Are you going to emasculate the Russian and American military for us?' Jintai said, chuckling to himself as he downed the last of his whiskey.

'In a manner of speaking, yes.'

'You are a miner and a petty thief, Bolcke. What are you saying?'

Bolcke peered at the general with narrowed eyes. 'Yes, I am a miner. I know the value of important minerals, such as gold and silver . . . and rare earths.'

'We understand the value of rare earth elements,' Tao said. 'That is why we manipulate the price by using you as a broker to make acquisitions on the open market.'

'It's no secret that China holds a near monopoly on the production of rare earth elements,' Bolcke said. 'But that monopoly has been put at risk by activity at two large mines outside your country. The Americans recently re-opened their Mountain Pass Mine, while Australia's Mount Weld operations are undergoing expansion.'

Jintai puffed out his chest. 'We will always be dominant.'

'Perhaps. But you will no longer control the market.'

Bolcke removed a large photo from his attaché case. It

236

showed an aerial view of some smoldering buildings in a desert setting next to an open-pit mine.

'This is the remains of the American facility at Mountain Pass,' Bolcke said. 'Their processing operations were destroyed by a fire last week. They will be unable to produce an ounce of rare earth elements for the next two years.'

'You know something about the fire?' Tao asked.

Bolcke stared at him in silence, his lips upturned in a smug grin. He placed a second photo on the table. It showed another open-pit mine in a desert setting.

'This is the Mount Weld Mine in western Australia. It's owned by the Hobart Mining Company, in which I have recently become a minority shareholder.'

'I understand the Australians have temporarily halted production while they modernize the facility,' Tao said.

'You are correct.'

'That is all very interesting,' Jintai said, 'but what does this have to do with us?'

Bolcke took a deep breath and looked down his nose at the general. 'It has to do with two actions that you are about to undertake. First, you will underwrite five hundred million dollars so I may purchase outright the Australian mine at Mount Weld. Second, you will institute an immediate ban on Chinese exports of rare earths.'

The room fell silent a moment before Jintai chuckled. 'Anything else you desire?' he said, rising to fetch himself more whiskey. 'Chief Executive of Hong Kong, perhaps?'

Tao stared at Bolcke, intrigued. 'Tell us why we will do these two things.'

'Economics and security,' Bolcke said. 'Together, we

can control the entire market in rare earth elements. As you know, I broker much of the remaining world output – from places like India, Brazil, and South Africa – which I sell to you, bolstering prices. I can easily contract for long-term delivery from these sources before you announce a halt in exports, locking in those supplies. As for Mount Weld, if you fund my purchase, I will repay you in ore, which you can quietly resell to select trading partners at exorbitant profits, if you so desire. With the Americans out of commission, China will control virtually the entire global output of rare earth.'

'We already control the bulk of the market,' Jintai said.

'True, but you can control it *all*. The fire at Mountain Pass didn't happen by accident. Mount Weld didn't suddenly suspend operations of their own volition. It was all due to my influence.'

'You have been a valued trading partner for both minerals and American defense technology,' Tao said. 'So – prices are driven up, and we ultimately profit from the sale of the minerals . . .'

'No,' Bolcke said, 'you can do better than that. With full control of the market, you can force every global company that uses rare earth elements to consign their manufacturing and technology to China. Every smartphone and laptop, every wind turbine, every space satellite, will be yours. And technology's the key. Nearly every cutting-edge technology today makes use of rare earth elements, and that will place you in a dominant position for tomorrow's advances in consumer products and, more importantly, defense weaponry.'

He stared at Jintai. 'Wouldn't you rather introduce the

most advanced attack helicopter yourself rather than copy somebody else's?'

The general simply nodded.

'Instead of playing catch-up with Western technology, China will lead the way. By totally controlling the supply of rare earths, you put an immediate halt to a multitude of Western military advances. New generations of American missiles, lasers, radars – even ship propulsion systems – rely on rare earth elements. By shutting off the supply, you can erase the technology gap. Rather than China copying Western defense technologies, they will be copying you.' Bolcke casually collected the photos and returned them to his briefcase. 'As I said, it's a matter of economics and security. They go hand in hand – and you can dominate the world in both arenas.'

The comments struck a nerve with Jintai, who constantly decried the inferior weapons the People's Liberation Army fielded. 'Perhaps it would be an appropriate time to act,' he said to Tao.

'Perhaps,' Tao said, 'but wouldn't it create havoc with our Western trading partners?'

'It's possible,' Bolcke said, 'but what can they really do? To maintain their own shaky economies, they will have no choice but to partner with you and share in their developments.'

The spymaster casually lit a cigarette with an expensive lighter. 'What is in all this for you, Mr Bolcke?'

'Your actions will increase the profitability of my mineral brokering business. And I trust you will allow me to sell a portion of the Mount Weld output to friendly trading partners at a healthy profit.' He said nothing of his intent to supply the growing black market in rare earth elements from the mine, nor the fact that he could purchase the property for two hundred million dollars less than he demanded.

Tao nodded. 'We will take the matter up with the politburo as an urgent priority,' he promised.

'Thank you. In hope of arriving at a mutually beneficial outcome, I have one other item to offer. In the past, I've been able to pass along a few military technologies from my US security firm, for which you have generously compensated me.'

'Yes,' Jintai said. 'We have already fielded the crowd-control device to quell some incidents of unrest in the western provinces.'

'I have installed units aboard two of my ships, which have been modified to an impressive level of lethality. I will be happy to share these modifications if you are interested. But that technology is inconsequential compared to what I can now offer you.'

He spread two more photos on the table.

'This is an artist's rendering of the *Sea Arrow*.' Bolcke pointed to the first glossy. 'The *Sea Arrow* will be the world's most highly advanced stealth submarine.'

Jintai gave a curious look, and Tao nodded in recognition.

'The *Sea Arrow* will operate at extremely high speed, using a complex propulsion unit in conjunction with a supercavitation system.' Bolcke pointed to the second image. 'It will place the American Navy's submerged fleet several generations ahead of your own.'

Jintai's face simmered red. 'We are always three steps behind.'

'Not this time,' Bolcke said with a shark-toothed grin. 'Less than one hour ago, I came into possession of the initial power plant that was scheduled to be installed on the *Sea Arrow* next week. In addition, I now have the one and only copy of the plans and drawings for the submarine's supercavitation system.'

He leaned over the table in a gloating pose. 'The Americans can duplicate the power plant only with rare earth elements. And without the supercavitation plans, their submarine is worthless.'

The Chinese officials did their best not to appear too eager. 'You are willing to share these items with us?' Tao asked with feigned indifference.

'Sources tell me the Americans have secretly spent over a billion dollars in developing the *Sea Arrow*. If we have a deal on the other items we discussed, I shall be happy to sell you the motor and the plans for an additional fifty million dollars.'

Tao didn't blink. 'When could you deliver it?'

'The motor and plans will arrive by ship in Panama in five days. I'll be happy to make the transfer there.'

'It is an attractive proposal,' Tao said. 'We will afford it appropriate consideration.'

'Excellent.' Bolcke collected the photos and glanced at his watch. 'I'm afraid I have to catch a flight to Sydney. I've opened preliminary discussions for the acquisition of Mount Weld, so I will eagerly await your reply.'

'We will move as quickly as we can,' Jintai said.

The general called for an aide, and Bolcke was escorted out after everyone stood and shook hands. Jintai poured a whiskey for Tao and another for himself.

'Well, Tao, our Austrian friend makes a compelling case. Since our economy is strong, we can afford to muscle the marketplace. And why not try to make the technological leap that will assure our safety for the next century?'

'There could be potential economic repercussions that the General Secretary won't relish,' Tao said, 'but I agree that it is worth the risk.'

'Will he balk at the loan and cash payments?'

'Not when I explain the value of the *Sea Arrow* technology. We've had agents trying to penetrate the program, but with no success. I don't question Bolcke's estimate of their expenditures. In fact, he may be understating their costs.' He studied his glass of whiskey. 'We must do what we can to obtain it.'

Jintai smiled. 'Then it is agreed. We will jointly support the proposal to the General Secretary.'

'But there is one problem with our Austrian friend.' Tao turned to Zhou, who had been sitting silent throughout the meeting. 'Please, tell the general what you have learned.'

Zhou cleared his throat. 'General, I was assigned to investigate thefts of rare earth elements from our primary mine operation in Bayan Obo. There I found an organized crime ring that was systematically stealing crushed ore and transporting it to Tianjin. I tracked an illicit delivery that was loaded aboard a freighter called the *Graz*.' He paused, glancing at Tao for confirmation to keep talking.

'Should the name mean something to me?' Jintai asked.

'The *Graz*,' Tao said, 'is owned by Bolcke's shipping company.'

'Bolcke is orchestrating the theft of our own rare earth?'

'Yes,' Tao said. 'He was brought in as a consultant at the mine some years ago, giving him opportunity to establish the theft ring. But it's worse than that.' He nodded at Zhou.

'I examined a number of port records to track the freighter's path,' Zhou said. 'From Tianjin it sailed to Shanghai, and then to Hong Kong, where it off-loaded thirty metric tons of crushed bastnasite that the Ministry of Commerce had purchased on the open market. The purchase was brokered through Bolcke's firm, Habsburg Industries.'

'Bolcke is selling us our own rare earth?' Jintai nearly popped out of his chair.

Zhou nodded.

'The greedy swine!' Catching his breath, he turned to Tao. 'What do we do now?'

Tao carefully snuffed his cigarette in an ashtray before locking eyes with Jintai.

'The American technology must be obtained at all costs. We will send Zhou to Panama to proceed with its acquisition.'

'What about the rare earths? Do we proceed with the export ban and fund the mine acquisition?'

'We will still push for the export ban. As for the mine funding . . .' His hardened face turned sly. 'We will arrange to pay back Mr Bolcke in a manner that will produce the same ends.'

37

Plumeria blossoms, mixed with the faint aroma of aviation fuel, filled the air as Pitt and Giordino exited the terminal at Honolulu International Airport. The bright sunshine and tropical breeze instantly washed away the fatigue of their twelve-hour flight from Washington. Giordino hailed a cab, and they hopped in for the short ride to Pearl Harbor.

The palm-lined streets brought back a flood of memories to Pitt. He had spent considerable time in the Hawaiian Islands during his first years with NUMA. It was here he had fallen in love with a radiant woman named Summer Moran. Though it had been decades since he had last seen her alive, her delicate face and sparkling eyes remained as clear to him as the sky overhead. The deceased mother of his two grown children, she lay buried in an ocean-view cemetery on the other side of the island.

Pitt shook away his recollections as they reached the entrance to the Navy base. A young ensign was waiting for them at the visitors' gate and politely loaded their bags into a Jeep. He navigated onto the docks and pulled up next to a slab-sided vessel with a slim, round superstructure that looked like it had been lopped off with a sharp knife.

'What is it?' Giordino asked. 'Some sort of car ferry on steroids?'

'You're not far from the mark,' Pitt said. 'The *Fortitude*'s design is based on a high-speed automobile ferry built by an Australian company.'

'Catamaran hull?' Giordino said, noting the ship's rotund bow was supported by twin vertical hulls.

'Yes, and made of aluminum. The *Fortitude* is driven by water-jet propulsion. She's part of the Military Sealift Command, and is designed to transport troops and equipment quickly. The Navy's building a small fleet of them.'

As they retrieved their bags from the Jeep, a lantern-jawed man in fatigues approached them. 'Mr Pitt?'

'Yes, I'm Pitt.'

'Lieutenant Aaron Plugrad, Coast Guard Maritime Safety.' The man reached out and shook Pitt's hand with an iron grip. 'My men are already secured aboard the *Fortitude*. I'm told we can shove off at any time.'

'What's the size of your team, Lieutenant?'

'I lead a squad of eight men, well trained to combat piracy operations. If there's a hijacking attempt, we'll stop it.'

Plugrad and his men came from a little-known command called the Coast Guard Deployable Operations Group. Essentially a SWAT team at sea, they were trained in counterterrorism, high-risk ship boardings, and explosives detection.

'One question for you, sir,' Plugrad said. 'We received a crate from NUMA containing a dozen high-end Hazmat suits. We went ahead and loaded the crate aboard ship.'

'Those are for your men,' Pitt said. 'Be sure each is issued a suit when we board the *Adelaide*. We have a theory that the potential assault may involve the use of a beefed-up microwave system similar to those developed by the Army for crowd control.'

'I'm familiar with that system,' Plugrad said. 'We'll take the necessary precautions.'

Pitt and Giordino boarded the sleek ship, where they were greeted by the *Fortitude*'s captain, a prematurely gray Navy commander named Jarrett. He led the NUMA men to the bridge, where he outlined their proposed course on a navigation monitor.

'We'll be looking to rendezvous with the *Adelaide* here,' Jarrett said, stabbing a finger at an empty expanse of ocean southeast of the Hawaiian Islands. 'It's about eleven hundred miles from Oahu. We'll zero in on the *Adelaide*'s course once we get closer, but we should catch her in less than twenty-four hours.'

'Twenty-four hours?' Giordino shook his head. 'Do you have jet engines on this thing?'

'No, just four big turbocharged diesels. On a good day, we can run close to forty-five knots. Since we are carrying a light load, we should be able to sail close to that speed.'

'Why fly and miss out on a nice sea breeze?' Giordino said.

'That's what the *Fortitude* was designed for. We can transfer a battalion of men across the Atlantic in two days.' Jarrett eyed a nearby chronograph. 'If you gentlemen have no objection, we'll get under way.'

The *Fortitude*'s diesels started with a rumble. The lines were cast, and the 338-foot ship maneuvered out the narrow entrance of Pearl Harbor and turned southeast. It cruised past Waikiki and the towering face of Diamond Head before cranking up speed. The brick-shaped ship accelerated quickly, rising up on its sharp catamaran hulls. The seas were calm, allowing Jarrett to run at nearly full out. Pitt watched the navigation monitor in awe as the vessel easily eclipsed the forty-knot mark.

In a few hours, the last of the Hawaiian Islands disappeared off the stern horizon as they raced into an empty expanse of the Pacific. Pitt and Giordino joined Plugrad and his team on deck, sharing insights on what they might encounter, as they reviewed defensive boarding measures. After dining in the ship's cavernous mess hall, they turned in for the night.

Pitt detected the *Fortitude*'s engines slowing later the next morning while he was exploring the hold with Giordino. The two men climbed to the bridge, where they spotted the *Adelaide* a mile off the bow.

She was a dry bulk carrier, six hundred feet long, sporting a forest green hull and a gold superstructure. A black-stained funnel and rust around her hawsehole indicated a seasoned career, but she otherwise looked well cared for. She cut through the waves low to the surface, her five holds filled to their hatch covers.

'Her captain has acknowledged our arrival and is prepared to take you on board,' Jarrett reported.

'Thanks for the quick run, Captain,' Pitt said. 'You have a gem of a vessel.'

'Sure you boys can't stick around?' Giordino asked Jarrett. 'If the *Adelaide*'s a dry boat, I may need you to make a beer run.'

'Sorry, but we're due stateside in thirty-six hours.' Jarrett shook hands with both men. 'I've ordered our launch deployed for you. Good luck and safe travels.'

Plugrad had his Coast Guard contingent assembled when Pitt and Giordino reached the deck. They climbed into a covered launch and were piloted to the freighter, where an accommodation ladder had been lowered along the *Adelaide*'s flank. Plugrad's men leaped onto the platform and bounded up the ladder, seemingly oblivious to the weapons and sixty-pound packs they carried. Pitt waved to the launch's pilot as he stepped off it and followed Giordino up the ladder.

A dour pair of crewmen in ill-fitting jumpsuits and black boots met them on the deck. 'Your quarters are this way,' one of them said, motioning toward the stern superstructure. 'The captain will meet with you in twenty minutes in the ship's mess.'

The two crewmen led the party aft as the *Adelaide*'s engines rumbled to higher revolutions and the big ship resumed speed. As they were led to their berths on the second level of the superstructure, Giordino glanced back at the *Fortitude* speeding off to the northeast and he suddenly felt thirsty for a beer.

38

The master of the *Adelaide* was nothing like Pitt had expected. Rather than the staid, experienced captains that typically commanded large commercial ships, the *Adelaide*'s master was a young, scrawny man with jittery eyes. He stepped into the mess and regarded Pitt, Giordino, and Plugrad coolly before shaking hands and sitting down with them.

'My name is Gomez. I'm told you are expecting a hijacking attempt.' If he was concerned by the news, it didn't show on his face.

'We've found a pattern of attacks in the Pacific,' Pitt said. 'The ships were all carrying rare earth elements, the same as your cargo.'

'You must be misinformed,' Gomez said. 'This ship is loaded with manganese ore.'

'Manganese?' Giordino asked. 'Didn't you take on a full shipment of monazite in Perth?'

'We shipped from Perth, but our cargo is manganese.'

'Your corporate headquarters,' Pitt said, 'confirmed otherwise.'

Gomez shook his head. 'An honest mistake. The electronic manifest record must have been confused with another of the company's vessels. These things happen. I'll call your supply ship and have them retrieve you.'

'That won't be possible,' Pitt said. 'The *Fortitude* has its own schedule to keep.'

'Plus,' Giordino said, 'we might not be the only ones who are misinformed.'

'That's correct,' Plugrad said. 'I wouldn't want to pull my men off, then find out later that you ran into trouble. We're supposed to remain aboard until you dock in Long Beach, so we'll stick to the plan.'

'Very well,' Gomez said, his words laced with irritation. 'Please confine yourselves to the main deck and the second-level staterooms.'

'Al and I will take shifts on the bridge and act as liaison to the lieutenant should we encounter another vessel.'

Gomez noted Pitt's determined tone and nodded. 'As you wish. But no armed men will be permitted on the bridge.' Gomez stood up from the table. 'I must return to my duties. Welcome to the ship. I'm confident you will enjoy a quiet and routine voyage.'

After Gomez left, Giordino looked at Pitt and Plugrad and shook his head. 'Well, how do you like them apples? No rare earth, and a cranky punk for a captain to entertain us the rest of the way.'

'Not much we can do about it now,' Pitt said. 'And if we're wrong, quiet and routine isn't exactly the worst of outcomes.'

The truth was, Pitt's radar had been on full alert since he stepped aboard the *Adelaide*. Something about the crew and captain wasn't right. He'd been aboard enough merchant ships to know that crews came in a variety of flavors and attitudes, and a salty welcome in itself wasn't anything unusual. But the circumstances made it peculiar. Facing a potentially deadly hazard, the ship's crew should have been happy for the added insurance – or, at the very least, curious. As they settled onto the ship, Pitt and his men were instead treated as a nuisance. Crew members seemed to watch their every move, yet refused to engage in even casual conversation.

On the bridge, Pitt and Giordino were shunted aside and ignored, their requests for information falling on deaf ears. Gomez barely acknowledged their existence and refused even to dine with Pitt, holing up in his cabin when not on duty.

During their second night aboard, Pitt paced the bridge, his presence ignored as usual. Shortly before the shift ended at midnight, a crewman appeared and approached Gomez, glancing at Pitt as he spoke in hushed tones.

Surveying the radar screen, Pitt noticed the image of a vessel appear ahead of them, traveling on a similar heading. He stepped closer to the screen to see the ship's AIS registry. The Automatic Identification System, a satellite-driven program required of all commercial ships over three hundred tons, provided speed and heading data, as well as an identity, for all such ships at sea. But for the ship on the radar now, there was no AIS display.

'She doesn't have her AIS turned on,' Pitt said to Gomez. 'That seems a bit suspicious out here.'

'Sometimes the signal is lost,' Gomez said. 'Or she could be a military vessel. It means nothing.'

The captain stepped close to the helmsman, whispered something in his ear, and then moved to the opposite end of the bridge. Pitt ignored the captain and kept tracking the *Adelaide*'s speed and heading. He wasn't surprised when the mystery vessel slowed a knot or two until it vanished from the radar screen.

Forty minutes of silent tension passed before Giordino entered the bridge to relieve Pitt. 'Are we sailing happy seas tonight?'

'Cruising on waves of hysteria.'

Pitt, preparing to leave, quietly reported the earlier encounter with the ship. A new helmsman arrived to relieve the one on duty, but Gomez remained on watch. As Pitt turned to depart the bridge, he glanced once more at the radar screen. Something caught his eye, and he hesitated, studying the numbers. It was the course heading. The ship had suddenly changed from an east-northeast heading to east-southeast.

'Why are we running southeast?' Pitt asked.

'There is a strong head current at this latitude,' Gomez said. 'We will drop below it for a day or two to maintain speed, then readjust our heading to Long Beach.'

Pitt's recollection was that the north equatorial current ran some distance south of their position, but he didn't argue. He turned and gave Giordino a skeptical look. 'Guess I'll turn in. See you on the next shift.'

Pitt finally exited the bridge and climbed down the companionway. Rather than exit on the second level to go to his stateroom, he continued down to the main deck to get some fresh air. Reaching it, he ran into Plugrad racing up the companionway. The Coast Guard lieutenant had an agitated look.

'You're up early,' Pitt said.

'Trying to find two of my men who didn't report for their watch. You didn't see them up on the bridge?'

'No. I'd suggest the mess. They probably went for some coffee to stay awake.'

Plugrad grumbled an acknowledgment and trodded off toward the mess.

Out on deck, Pitt found the night cool, with a fresh breeze rippling over the port beam. After several hours on the unfriendly bridge, the air felt refreshing. Pitt stretched his legs by hiking across the long, open deck, stopping at the prow and gazing over the rail. A faint light appeared briefly ahead on the horizon, vanishing and reappearing as the *Adelaide* rose and fell with the sea. The mystery ship was still there, directly ahead, at the edge of visibility for both eye and radar.

Pitt watched for several minutes, confirming the other vessel was holding position, then ambled toward the deckhouse. He stopped as he passed the forward hold, noticing some debris on the deck. Part of the cargo of manganese had spilled near the hatch cover during loading. Pitt picked up a fist-sized chunk and held it under a nearby deck light. Silver in color, the ore appeared to be identical to the monazite he had found in Chile on board the *Tasmanian Star*.

Gomez was lying about the manganese, but why? Why also was the crew acting so strange? And what of the ship steaming ahead of them? An uneasy feeling suddenly struck Pitt square in the gut.

Plugrad. He had to alert Plugrad.

Pitt started aft but froze when several figures emerged from the deckhouse. Pitt ducked alongside the nearest hatch cover and watched two men drag a third man between them. They crossed the deck laterally, passing under a bright light. For a second, Pitt could see the two men walking were armed crewmen. The limp body between them was Plugrad, with a splatter of blood glistening on his forehead.

They dragged Plugrad to the port side of the deckhouse, where they unlocked a door and hauled him inside. Once they disappeared from view, Pitt crossed the deck and sprinted aft to the superstructure's opposite side. Racing up the companionway, he exited onto the second level and rushed to the four cabins that housed the Coast Guard team.

He knocked on the first door and flung it open but found no one inside. When he found the second cabin empty, he began to fear the worst. The third and fourth cabins were also empty. The entire Coast Guard team had quietly been neutralized. Pitt was exiting the fourth cabin when he heard whispers in the corridor. He stepped back into the cabin and slipped behind its open door.

Through the crack, he watched as two armed crewmen crept down the hall and stopped in front of Pitt's door. They readied their weapons, then one twisted the handle and both charged in. Finding the cabin empty, they returned to the corridor, speaking quietly to each other in Spanish. One stomped off toward the companionway while his partner lingered. Moving slowly, he stepped to the opposite end of the corridor and cautiously entered Giordino's cabin. Finding no one there, he began working his way back, checking the other cabins.

Pitt held his breath when the gunman approached where he was hiding. The barrel of an assault rifle poked past the door as he took a step into the cabin. Pitt waited a second, then burst from his spot. Shoving the door with all his strength, he crushed the gunman against the bulkhead. Still clutching the chunk of ore, he clubbed the man in the side of the head with it. The man lost consciousness and collapsed to the deck before he could find the trigger on his weapon.

Pitt pulled the gunman all the way inside the cabin and listened for his partner. Hearing nothing, he took the man's AK-47 and stepped into the hall, closing the door behind him. He reached the companionway and was about to move down the steps to release Plugrad when he heard a gunshot.

The shot seemed to come from above. If it had been fired from the bridge, then it meant one thing. Giordino.

Pitt reversed course and raced up the steps as silently as he could. At the bridge, he stopped and peered around the door. The lights had been dimmed for nighttime running, darkening the bridge except for the glow of a few monitors. A nearby console obstructed much of his view, but all seemed quiet. Perhaps the shot had originated elsewhere. Spotting only the helmsman, he quietly advanced into the bay.

'Mr Pitt,' hailed the voice of Gomez. 'I thought you would come for your friend.' The captain rose from a crouched position, firmly holding an outstretched pistol. It wasn't aimed at Pitt, however, but at the floor. Pitt took a step closer to see that Gomez was aiming the weapon at Giordino, who lay on the floor, clutching his leg.

'Put down your weapon,' Gomez said, 'or you both shall die.'

Pitt caught a movement out of the corner of his eye.

The earlier gunman had materialized from behind another console, his AK-47 aimed at Pitt's back.

As Pitt looked from his wounded friend to Gomez, his eyes flared with anger. Without a word, he let the gun fall to the deck.

39

The President rolled an unlit cigar between his thumb and forefinger. 'Why?' he asked in an irritated tone. 'Why would the Chinese suddenly halt all exports of rare earth elements?'

An uncomfortable silence filled the Oval Office.

'I can only suspect it's for leverage,' the Secretary of State said. 'Something they can use as a bargaining chip to counter our pressure on their support of trade with Iran or their refusal to float the yuan.'

'Have they told you as much?'

'No, the Foreign Ministry has only indicated it was done out of "strategic necessity".'

'Sure,' said Vice President Sandecker. 'The necessity to torpedo our economy.' A cigar aficionado himself, he eyed the President's stogie with envy.

'It is quite a bold move,' the Secretary of State said. 'I would have expected some hint of negotiation over the matter, but the Chinese are playing it close to the vest.'

The President turned to his national security advisor, a raven-haired woman named Dietrich. 'How bad is it going to hurt us?'

'Over ninety percent of our rare earth imports come from China,' she said. 'Commercially, it will devastate a number of industries, particularly electronics and the alternative energy fields. Almost every high-tech industry in the country will be affected.'

'Are we just talking higher prices?' asked Tom Cerny.

'Skyrocketing prices will be just the first impact. Until work-arounds can be developed, products will be in short supply – or simply unaffordable. Either way, demand will evaporate, and jobs along with it. It could easily drive the economy back into a serious recession.'

'What about other sources of rare earth?' the President asked. 'I know we've got that mine in California. Tell me the Chinese aren't the only game in town.'

'The Mountain Pass Mine came on line a few years ago and was just ramping up their production,' Dietrich said, 'but a recent fire at the facility destroyed the mine's extraction operations. It's effectively closed for an indeterminate period, probably two years. That was our only domestic source.'

'Has anyone looked into the cause of the fire?' Sandecker asked.

'It was believed to have been accidental, but now the owners have called in the FBI to find out if it might have been arson.'

'How about other foreign sources of rare earth?' the President asked.

'We do source a fraction of our imports beyond China,' Dietrich said. 'Australia has been the primary backup, with additional smaller amounts from Russia, India, and Malaysia. But there's also a problem down under, I'm afraid. The major Australian producer has announced a temporary shutdown due to an expansion program.'

The President shoved his cigar into an ashtray. 'So we're left whistling past the graveyard while our economy sputters to a halt?'

Dietrich nodded bleakly. 'I'm afraid we have little, if any, control over the supply situation.'

'That's only the half of it,' Sandecker said. 'The shortage strikes a pretty nasty blow to several of our key defense technologies.'

'The Vice President is correct,' Dietrich affirmed.

'Where's the damage?' the President asked.

'The Navy gets hit hard,' she said. 'The propulsion system for the Zumwalt class destroyer and the new stealth cruiser relies heavily on rare earth elements, so those programs will come to a crashing halt. I'm waiting for a report from the Air Force, but I've been told there's a significant impact to the new joint fighter and several satellite development programs.'

'We're talking programs that are budgeted in the billions of dollars,' Cerny said.

'Sounds to me,' the President said, 'as if the Chinese might be exploiting their monopoly as an opportunity to catch up militarily.'

The heads in the room nodded.

'What if we tell the Chinese their export ban is unacceptable?'

The Secretary of State squirmed in his seat. 'I don't think that dog will hunt, sir. The Chinese leadership won't take well to any threats. If we get into a trade war, we'll be the bigger loser. And if they stop purchasing our debt securities, that would create even worse problems.'

'So we're facing an economic nosedive when we can least afford it,' the President said. 'On top of that, we're sacrificing our military readiness by delaying the next class of destroyers, fighters, and spy satellites.'

'There's one other casualty,' Sandecker said. He moved close to the President and spoke in a whisper. 'The *Sea Arrow.*'

The President nodded. 'Of course.'

The President walked to his desk and peered out the high windows behind it for several minutes. When he turned back to his audience, he spoke in a soft, defeated voice. 'Find out what the Chinese want,' he said, 'and give it to them.'

40

The hijacking of the *Sea Arrow*'s motor incited an immediate nationwide dragnet. Roadblocks were quickly set up along every major road and highway leading north or south out of Washington. FBI teams were dispatched to all nearby airports and to every East Coast port facility, from where analysts assumed the motor would be smuggled out of the country. Extra security was even called in to the northeast border crossings into Canada.

Yet the stolen motor wouldn't be found in any of those places. It had been driven west, away from the major ports and airports, and across rural Appalachia, hidden in the back of a hay truck. Entering Lexington, Kentucky, Pablo slowed the big rig, keeping a wary eye out for passing police cars.

Ann was relegated to the back of the cab, one wrist cuffed to the frame of the bench seat. She could partially stretch out on the narrow seat but had to lean at an awkward angle to glance out the window. They traveled in silence. After Pablo ignored her initial barrage of probing questions, she'd decided to save her energy. It took a bit of conjecture, but she eventually linked Pablo's theft of the *Sea Arrow* plans with the large device hidden on the flatbed. It had to be the submarine's new propulsion motor.

Pablo was pleased with the time he had made, covering

four hundred miles in seven hours, before pulling onto a quiet side road and letting Ann stretch her legs. A short time later, they pulled into Lexington, where he found a truck stop and parked at a distant fuel pump. After filling the truck's tank, he opened the cab door and peered at Ann.

'Do you want something to eat?'

'Yes, please,' Ann said. 'I'm very hungry.'

'I'll be right back.' He slammed the door and locked it.

Ann watched him stroll past several fuel islands and enter the truck stop's building. She scanned the parking lot, searching for potential help. The hour was late, and she spotted only one person nearby, a bearded truck driver, washing the windshield on his idling rig a dozen yards away.

She waved, and screamed at the top of her lungs. But the sealed cab's tinted windows rendered her nearly invisible, and her muffled cries went unheard over the idling engine. She reached for the truck's air horn but couldn't quite stretch her fingers far enough. The bearded man climbed into his rig and pulled away, oblivious to Ann's plight.

She searched the truck's interior for something to use as a weapon. But the cab's interior, even down to its glove box, was stripped clean except for a map and laptop computer on the front seat. Ann lunged for the computer.

She reached with her free hand and grasped the computer, flipping open its monitor and powering it on. As it booted up, she glanced out the window. Pablo stood at the register, purchasing some items. She'd have very little time to send a plea for help – if the truck stop had Wi-Fi.

She held her breath as the computer screen slowly lit up. After an eternity, a bubble icon asked if she wanted to join the Lexington Diesel & Dine network.

'Yes!' She clicked the icon. A few seconds later, an Internet search page opened.

Her joy was short-lived when she glanced out the window to see Pablo exiting the building. Her pulse raced as she considered what to do. There would be no time to sign on to her e-mail account or relay a message through the NCIS website. A desperate idea popped into her head. She quickly typed in four letters and waited for a response. When a new screen popped up, she scrolled to the bottom and found a query link. Clicking on it, she hurriedly typed a message and looked up. Pablo was just ten feet away.

Her fingers flew over the keypad, stopping to click 'Send' as the door latch clicked. She slammed the monitor closed and tossed the computer onto the front seat as Pablo opened the door.

Her heart beat wildly, and she felt her face turn flush, as he climbed into the driver's seat. He turned and looked at her quizzically as he swung his hands around.

'Ham and cheese or tuna?' He held up a pair of wrapped sandwiches.

'Tuna, please.' She exhaled, and reached for one of the sandwiches.

Pablo pulled back onto the highway, eating as he drove. The break had relaxed him, and he finally turned his head over his shoulder briefly and spoke to Ann. 'You are in love with me,' he said, grinning.

'What?'

'Yes, you must be in love with me. Why else do you keep turning up?'

'I didn't ask to go on this trip,' she said. 'Please, let me go.'

Pablo let out a deep laugh. 'You are too smart to let go . . . and too pretty to kill.'

Ann felt instant revulsion but kept the conversation going. 'Is that the *Sea Arrow*'s motor we're hauling?'

'Perhaps.'

'Why did you kill the men who helped you steal it?'

'They served their usefulness, and they knew more than they needed to. I believe that is enough inquiry for now.' He turned on the radio and turned up the volume after finding a local bluegrass station.

They crossed the hills of western Kentucky, listening to the upbeat strains of Flatt and Scruggs. Four hours later, they pulled into Paducah. Pablo parked at a gas station on the outskirts of town and made a phone call. Within minutes, a rusty pickup appeared, driven by a tattoo-covered man, who then escorted the hay truck to the riverfront. A towboat and a barge loaded with shipping containers were moored at the weathered wooden dock. Pablo eased the truck alongside the darkened barge and stopped.

It was well after midnight, and the facility was eerily quiet. Pablo unhitched the flatbed trailer and drove the truck to an adjacent lot. By the time he returned, the tattooed man had strung lifting cables around the trailer and was hoisting it onto the barge with a dockside crane. Pablo jumped aboard the barge and helped secure the trailer to the deck, before returning to the cab for Ann.

She feigned drowsiness as he freed her from the seat frame and recuffed her hands in front of her. She noticed for the first time that the cuffs had a sensor device built into them. Pablo pulled her from the truck and led her to the dock.

The lights of Paducah twinkled to her right along the bank as the Ohio River slid past like a dark current of molasses. Pablo kept a tight grip on her arm as he led her toward the towboat. The weathered boat was secured to the center stern of the barge, ready to guide it down the river. Access to the towboat was by a thin gangplank that stretched over the water. Ann hesitated crossing until Pablo gave her a gentle nudge.

She actually didn't fear crossing the thin gangplank but what lay ahead. First chained to a truck, next chained to a towboat, then who knows what? Wherever she was taken, it was when the handcuffs were removed that she'd have the most to fear. It was this fear that drove her to act.

She mentally braced herself and took a deep breath as Pablo prodded her a second time. Pretending to stagger, she took two steps onto the gangplank and compressed her knees. Springing forward, she took a leaping step up. The gangplank flexed, giving her extra lift, and she bounded easily over the side handrail.

Pablo reached for her, but could only graze a passing ankle. As she stretched her arms before her, Ann plunged into the river, trailing just a small splash and vanishing into the dark muddy water.

41

The *Adelaide*'s auxiliary storage locker was a dim, steamy oven befitting the devil. Pitt could smell decaying flesh mixed with sweat when the bolted door was flung open and he and Giordino were shoved inside at gunpoint. He had struggled to bear the weight of his wounded friend down to the main deck and tried not to collapse under him. He noticed a canvas tarp in the locker and gently laid Giordino on it as the door was slammed and locked behind them.

'Is there a medic among you?' Pitt said. He glanced toward the Coast Guard team he saw huddled nearby.

A young man stood up and slowly made his way to Pitt's side.

'Simpson, isn't it?' Pitt said.

'Yes, sir. I can help.' He knelt over Giordino, quickly noting the spreading pool of blood beneath his right leg. 'Has he been shot?'

'Yes.' Pitt ripped away a torn section of Giordino's pants. 'He's lost a lot of blood.'

Simpson located the blood-soaked wound on Giordino's outer thigh and applied pressure with his palm. 'I need something for a bandage.'

Pitt removed his shirt and ripped off the sleeves, tearing them into long strips. Someone passed over a bottle of water, which the medic used to clean the wound. He took one of the strips and folded it into a pad. Applying it to the wound, he bound it with the remaining strips.

Giordino opened his eyes and looked up. 'Where we headed?'

'To get some beer,' Pitt said. 'Take a nap, and I'll wake you when it's on ice.'

Giordino gave him a crooked grin, then drifted off a few seconds later.

Simpson pulled a section of tarp over him and motioned Pitt aside. 'He's lucky. There were two wounds, indicating the bullet went clean through. Most likely, it missed the bone. But it must have nicked his femoral artery, hence all the blood. He may go into shock with that much blood loss, so we'll need to keep an eye on him.'

'He's a tough old goat,' Pitt said.

'He should be fine for now. His biggest problem will be avoiding infection in this stink hole.'

Pitt saw in the dim light that Simpson had a bruise on his cheekbone. 'What happened to you?'

'Got jumped in the corridor on my way to watch. Bugger hit me with a chain. I was luckier than some of the guys.'

Pitt looked around the bay, which was lit by a single flickering overhead lamp. The Coast Guard team sat nearby, while another group, members of the *Adelaide*'s real crew, was sprinkled about the rear of the compartment. Two oblong shapes, wrapped in canvas and positioned off to one side, were responsible for the horrible odor.

'The captain and another man,' Simpson said. 'Killed in the assault before we came along.'

Pitt nodded, then turned his attention to the Coast Guard team. They all bore wounds and bruises. Plugrad sat among the men with his back to a bulkhead, a vacant look in his eye.

'How's Plugrad?'

'They knocked the lieutenant upside the head pretty good,' Simpson said. 'He's got a concussion but otherwise appears okay.'

Pitt stepped across the bay to the other group. They appeared weary but unhurt. A broad-shouldered man with a thick gray mustache rose and introduced himself.

'Frank Livingston, executive officer,' he said with a thick Australian accent. 'How's your comrade?'

'Gunshot wound to the leg. Lost some blood, but the medic thinks he'll be okay.'

'Sorry I couldn't help. Our chief bosun was the ship's medic. He's over there with the captain.' He pointed toward the canvas-covered bodies.

'How'd they take the ship?'

'A fast freighter came alongside on the evening watch three nights ago. Pulled right alongside our beam, scaring the dickens out of the helmsman. When they didn't respond on the radio, the captain went on deck with the chief bosun. The vessel fired up some sort of radar device amidships that killed them both.' His mouth tightening into a grimace. 'Never seen anything like it. Almost as if they were cooked alive. The freighter sent over an armed boarding party shortly after. There wasn't much we could do. We've been cooped up in here ever since.'

'I'm sorry we were late to the scene,' Pitt said. 'I guess

they were tipped off to our arrival and came after you early.'

Livingston's tired eyes flared with vengeance. 'Who are *they*?'

Pitt shook his head. 'They're part of a ring we believe has hijacked a number of bulk carriers transporting rare earth elements.'

'We're loaded with something called monazite,' Livingston said. 'Guess they got what they came for. Any idea where we're headed?'

Pitt looked around to make sure none of the other men were listening. 'We think they usually transfer the cargo at sea, then scuttle the ships. At least two other carriers were sunk in these waters.'

Livingston nodded, but not with the look of a man sentenced to die aboard a sinking ship. 'Tell me, Mr Pitt, how large were those other hijacked carriers?'

'Not large. They were older dry bulk carriers, maybe ten thousand tons. Why do you ask?'

'The *Adelaide* is rated at forty thousand tons. I got a good look at the attacking freighter before being tossed in here. She's a runt compared to us, capable of carrying no more than half our cargo.'

'Your entire cargo is monazite?'

'Every last ounce. No, sir, I don't think they'll scuttle the *Adelaide*. Not just yet anyway. What we're carrying is just too valuable.'

Pitt glanced at the hurt and haggard men scattered around the fetid prison bay.

'Mr Livingston, I certainly hope you speak the truth.'

42

It took only a few seconds for Ann to panic.

Striking the water cleanly, she kicked hard, with her hands outstretched in front of her, driving deep into the Ohio River. The water was warmer than she expected, easily in the seventies. Reaching a comfortable culmination point, she arched her torso and tried to stroke with her hands. But with her wrists bound by the cuffs, she couldn't do it.

A momentary flash of terror struck, telling her she was going to drown.

'Relax. Relax. Relax,' a voice repeated in her head.

With her heart pounding, she forced herself to hold still and drift with the current for a few seconds. It calmed her nerves, and she began scooping the water with her bound hands in a doggie paddle that would carry her to the surface. But in the inky black water, she no longer knew which way was up.

The answer came quickly when her shoulder grazed the corroded underside of the barge. She pushed herself away and drifted clear, holding on a few more seconds, before ascending slowly into the cool night air.

The current was swift, and she found herself moving away from the barge and towboat. She looked back and saw Pablo running along the dock, scanning the water. Spotting Ann's head bobbing in the river, he pulled his Glock out of its holster.

Ann instantly took a deep breath and rolled beneath the surface. She couldn't tell whether he fired at her, but there was no sense in giving him a target.

She glided more easily beneath the surface this time, holding her breath for nearly a minute, while kicking and paddling with the current. When she surfaced again, she was more than a hundred yards from the barge – all but invisible in the darkness to anyone on the dock. Still, Pablo had disappeared from her view.

She turned her attention downriver, searching for a place to go ashore and find help. But the dock was on the outskirts of town, and the nearside riverbank was dark and empty. A sprinkling of lights glistened a short distance ahead on the opposite bank, marking the small town of Metropolis, Illinois.

Feeling the lure of safety, Ann began kicking and paddling toward the lights. She struggled for a few minutes, fighting the downstream current. Then she realized her efforts to reach the town would be in vain. The river was almost a mile across, and the current would sweep her well past its lights before she could reach the other side.

The awkwardness of swimming with bound wrists increased her fatigue, so she rolled over and rested by floating on her back. Looking into the sky, she noticed a pair of red flashing lights in the distance. Turning herself over, she studied them as they flashed – airplane warning lights. In their brief stabs of illumination, she could see they were affixed to a pair of tall concrete smokestacks. They could only be part of a riverfront power plant.

As she floated past the lights of Metropolis, she worked her way back toward the near shore. The riverbank went black for a mile, and Ann began feeling cold and alone. But she continued to track the blinking red lights and eventually drew closer. A haze of light at the base of the stacks crystallized into a profusion of bright lights that engulfed the power plant. The lights were set well back from shore, but as Ann passed a shrub-lined bank she spotted a thin inlet that had been cut from the river to the plant.

When she approached the mouth of the inlet, she began kicking hard. The Ohio's current tried to drag her past, but she broke free of its grasp and entered the inlet's calm waters. The cut ran about a third of a mile toward the plant, where the water supplied the coal-fired steam boilers.

Exhausted from her final struggle against the current, Ann made for the nearest bank. She rested in the mud for several minutes, then pulled herself off the bank and climbed up a berm that had been graded on top for vehicle access.

She shivered in her wet clothes as she hiked toward the power plant, smelling the rich odor of burnt coal. As she drew closer, she counted several vehicles parked around the plant. Thankfully, a sizable night shift was on-site. Headlights flickered to her left, and she saw a white pickup truck move slowly from the parking lot, an orange light flashing atop its cab. Ann quickened her pace and began waving her bound arms as soon as she thought the driver might spot her.

The truck sped up and turned onto the berm. It bounced along the narrow track and stopped in front of Ann with a swirl of dust. She raised her cuffed hands and approached the open driver's window. 'Can you please help me?'

Her voice quivered when she saw Pablo stick his head out the window, brandishing a portable GPS unit keyed to her handcuffs and the Glock pistol.

'No, my love,' he said in a cruel voice. 'It is you who can help me.'

PART THREE
Panama Run

43

Summer Pitt looked up from a clipboard in her lap and gazed out the submersible's acrylic dome window. With nothing to see but blackness, it felt like being locked in a closet. 'How about some exterior illumination?' she asked.

Her twin brother, seated at the pilot's controls, flipped on a row of toggle switches. A battery of bright LED lights popped on, putting a glow into the coal-black water. But there was still little to see, aside from particles in the water rushing past the acrylic. At least it gave Summer a visual sense of their rate of descent.

'Still afraid of the dark?' her brother asked.

While Summer had inherited the pearlescent skin and red hair of her mother, Dirk Pitt, Jr., resembled his father. He had the same tall, lean build, the same dark hair, even the same easy smile.

'Down here, what you can't see *can* hurt you,' she said. She checked the depth indicator on an overhead monitor. 'Coming up on the bottom in fifty meters.'

Dirk adjusted the ballast tanks to slow their descent, easing the vessel to neutral buoyancy when the seafloor appeared to rise up beneath them. At their depth of three hundred feet, the seafloor was a walnut-colored desolation, populated only by a few small fish and crustaceans.

'The fault line should be on a bearing of zero-six-five degrees,' Summer said.

Dirk engaged the submersible's electronic thrusters and propelled them on the northeast heading. Through the yoke, he could feel a strong bottom current sideswiping them. 'The Agulhas Current is humming today. Like to take us to Australia.'

The powerful Agulhas flowed down the east coast of Africa. Near the southern tip of Madagascar, where Dirk and Summer were diving, it converged with the East Madagascar Current and streams from the Indian Ocean to create an unpredictable swirl.

'We likely drifted a considerable amount during our descent,' Summer noted, 'but if we hold to the heading, we'll still cross the fault line.' She pressed her nose against the bubble and scanned the lightly undulating seabed passing beneath them. After several minutes, she spotted a slight, but distinct, ridge. 'That's our uplift.'

Dirk ascended slightly and positioned the submersible in a hover ten feet above the ridge. 'Ready for video.'

Summer powered on a pair of external cameras mounted to the submersible's skids, then checked the feed on a monitor. 'Cameras are rolling, marking start,' she said. 'Take us down the line.'

Dirk thrust the submersible forward, following the ridge in the seafloor. They were working in concert with a NUMA research ship that had surveyed the area previously with a multibeam sonar system, examining an active fault line off the Madagascar coast in hope of better predicting how earthquakes create tsunamis. The submersible's video would give the shipboard geologists a baseline reference for the area. The submersible would then be sent back to bury small sensors that would precisely record seismic activity.

The project required an interdisciplinary mix of talents that appealed to both siblings. With Dirk educated in marine engineering, and Summer specializing in oceanography, both twins had inherited their father's love of the sea. They had joined Pitt at NUMA only a few years earlier but soon reveled in the opportunity to travel the globe to solve the sea's mysteries. Their work was made all the better when the three of them could collaborate on a project, as they had recently in Cyprus, where they'd discovered a trove of ancient artifacts related to Jesus.

'Passing kilometer number eight of the subsurface ridge that will never end,' Dirk said two hours into their trolling. The constant bucking of the current was taking a toll, and he could feel his arm muscles begin to tighten.

'You're not getting bored already?' Summer asked.

Dirk stared at the unchanging brown bottom that scrolled beneath them. 'It'd be all right with me if someone imported a whale shark or a giant squid to the neighborhood.'

They tracked the uplift for another hour before Dirk became concerned about their battery reserves.

'Fighting the current has put an extra strain on the motors. I suggest we think about breaking off the run soon.'

Summer checked their distance covered. 'How about another six hundred meters? That will put us at an even twelve thousand.'

'Deal.'

Completing that last remaining stretch, Dirk pulled the submersible to a halt while Summer turned off the video cameras. He began purging the ballast tanks to ascend when Summer motioned out the front bubble window.

'Is that a shipwreck?'

Beyond the effective range of the exterior lights, Dirk saw a faint object. 'Could be.' He released the ballast pump and thrust the submersible forward.

A towering black mass gradually emerged, taking on the distinctive shape of a ship's hull. As they drew closer, the rest of the vessel took form, sitting upright on the bottom and appearing remarkably undisturbed. Maneuvering just a few feet off the seafloor, they approached amidships, inching close to the mystery vessel. The red paint that covered the hull reflected clearly under the submersible's lights, detailing every rivet and seam.

'She looks like she just went under,' Dirk said. He drove the submersible up the side of the hull and above the deck rail. There, they spotted three large open hatches on the forward deck. Dirk piloted the submersible toward the bow, skimming over cargo compartments filled with nothing but seawater. They peered down the sharp prow, detecting no damage around the bow. They turned back and surveyed along the starboard rail to the rear superstructure, where they ascended several levels to the bridge. From just a few feet away, they peeked through the intact windows at an empty control station.

'Looks like the helm was stripped of most of its electronics,' Dirk said. 'That makes a good argument for her being scuttled.'

'Somebody call Lloyd's of London,' Summer said. 'I've never seen such a pristine shipwreck. She must have sunk recently.'

'No more than a few months, judging by the minimal sea growth.'

'Why would somebody scuttle a perfectly good freighter?'

'Hard to say. It's possible she was under tow, headed for a refit, and sank in poor weather.' He checked the status of their battery power. 'It's about time we head topside, but let's see if we can get a ship's name.'

He guided the submersible around the superstructure to the stern and descended past the aft rail. A bent flagpole hung forlornly over the rail, its former colors long since vanished. When they were twenty feet off the ship, he turned the craft to face the freighter's transom and adjusted their height so the lights would shine on the ship's name.

'Well, I'll be,' he said in a low voice. 'She was scuttled after all.'

In front of them stood a blank wall of red bisected by a thick horizontal band of rust where the ship's name and home port had once been posted. But somebody had intentionally ground away the name and covering paint, sending the freighter to the lonely depths in total anonymity.

44

The NUMA research ship *Alexandria* was stationed four miles away when the submersible broke the surface, and Summer radioed for recovery. As the submersible drifted with the current, she and Dirk passed the time studying the dusty brown shores of southern Madagascar, which seemed to rise and fall across the choppy sea.

The *Alexandria* arrived promptly, its turquoise hull, like all the ships in the NUMA fleet, sparkling under a sunny sky. A brawny man with a thick mustache and even thicker Texas accent directed the retrieval of the submersible onto the ship's aft deck. Jack Dahlgren opened the vessel's rear-mounted hatch and welcomed Dirk and Summer to the fresh air. 'Y'all have a good swim?'

'We certainly did,' Summer said, holding up a portable hard drive. 'We obtained excellent footage of the uplift and should be able to identify some prime insertion points for the ground sensors.' She climbed past him, scurrying to locate the ship's marine geologist so they could jointly review the seabed footage.

'I take it that means an immediate prep for another dive?' Dahlgren asked with a long face.

Dirk patted him on the shoulder. 'I'm afraid it does, my friend.'

Dirk assisted Dahlgren in removing several heavy sets of battery packs that powered the submersible, swapping them with freshly charged replacements. While they worked on the aft deck, a large patrol boat appeared from shore. As the boat loosely circled the *Alexandria*, two casually dressed occupants on its open bridge studied the research ship with a look of displeasure. When the *Alexandria* moved off-site, the patrol boat ran back to shore.

'I wonder what those boys are up to,' Dahlgren said.

'They didn't exactly look like government officials.' Dirk gazed toward the receding boat, and shoreline beyond. 'I thought the coast around here was pretty well an empty desert.'

'A small freighter came cruising through while you were down. It appeared headed to shore, so there must be some sort of harbor nearby.'

They finished swapping batteries and completed an extensive predive safety check before tracking down Summer in one of the ship's labs. She had assembled a crate of tiny battery-powered ground sensors that would track tremors and movements in the fault line. Each was contained in a stainless steel canister that sprouted a bright orange metal marker flag.

'We've surveyed in a perfect location,' Summer said. 'What we want to do next is go back and bury ten sensors, five hundred meters apart, along the same track.' She looked to Dahlgren. 'Can you drop us back at the same starting point?'

'Can a boll weevil find a Mississippi cotton field? You just go get yourself comfy in my submersible before I decide to put you over the side without it.' He stormed out of the lab, heading for the bridge to confer with the captain.

'What's he so touchy about?' Summer asked.

'I made the mistake of telling him about the wreck we discovered,' Dirk said. 'He's mad that we found it in his submersible without him.'

She shook her head. 'Boys and their toys.' Summer grabbed the sensors and carried them to a cage basket affixed to the front of the submersible. Once they were secured, she climbed inside and joined Dirk in reviewing the predive checklist.

Dahlgren appeared a few minutes later and ducked his head inside the hatch. 'Good to go when y'all are.'

'We're launch ready,' Dirk said. 'Have a couple of cold ones waiting when we get back.'

'Sure, but they're liable to be empty cold ones. Anything else?'

'Yes. See what the records show in the way of southern Madagascar shipwrecks in the past five years.'

'That I can do. Happy sowing.'

Dahlgren sealed the hatch and hoisted the submersible over the *Alexandria*'s stern. He waited until a radio call from the bridge confirmed they were at the designated drop spot, then lowered the sub. Once the grapple was freed, Dirk was given the okay to flood the ballast tanks, and the yellow submersible slipped under the waves.

The bottom appeared a few minutes later, and Dirk guided the submersible on its earlier northeast heading. This time they traveled less than fifty meters before crossing the familiar uplift.

'Kudos to Jack,' Summer said. 'He played the currents almost perfectly.'

'Shall we drop the first sensor?' Dirk asked.

Summer checked their position, calculated from a dead reckoning program initiated at deployment. 'Actually, we should move about thirty meters east to pick up our first track.'

Dirk made the adjustment. He eased the submersible to a flat section of seabed adjacent to the uplift and powered off the thrusters to settle the whirling clouds of sediment they had stirred up. Summer took over from there, activating a pair of articulated robotic arms. She clawed a vertical pit into the seafloor with one arm, then used the other to grasp a sensor from the basket. She wedged the sensor into the pit and covered up the main body of the sensor, leaving just the bright orange flag protruding from the seafloor.

'That went well,' Dirk said. He powered up the thrusters and shot down the rift at top speed.

'You in a hurry to get someplace?' Summer asked.

'I figured we might take another look at the wreck when we're finished.'

Summer smiled. She'd had the same idea and made sure a backup video hard drive was aboard for them to film the wreck.

They proceeded along the fault, planting the remaining nine sensors along the seven-mile route. When the last sensor was secured, Dirk checked their position relative to the shipwreck. He maneuvered the submersible a short distance until the mass appeared before them. 'Right where we left her.'

'I'll get some video this time,' Summer said, activating the forward cameras.

Dirk ascended the submersible as they approached the

hulk, heading immediately for the main deck. He crossed to the opposite rail, allowing Summer's cameras to film the width of the ship's beam and its open holds, which were missing their hatch covers. He was on a mission of identification, as he turned the submersible and its video cameras toward the high rear superstructure. Its design would offer another clue to the age of the ship and its builder.

Creeping up the front face of the superstructure, he zoomed over the bridge and hovered near the funnel, which protruded from the aft side. Commercial ships often carried the company colors or logo there, but this one was painted black.

'Funny there's no smudge marks,' Summer said. 'Looks like it was freshly painted.'

'Another attempt to conceal her identity.'

'Take us in a little.' Summer leaned forward, peering closely at the funnel's surface.

While Dirk drew them in, Summer activated one of the robotic arms and flexed it toward the funnel. Making contact, she dragged the claw across the surface, leaving a foot-long gouge.

'Please don't carve your initials,' Dirk said. 'I don't want a Lloyd's agent knocking on my door at two in the morning.'

'Just checking what's underneath.'

As the paint flakes swirled away with the current, they could clearly see an ocher line beneath the scratch.

'The funnel was originally gold, or had a gold band,' she said.

'That's one more nugget.'

They filmed the wreck for another thirty minutes, capturing its length, deck configuration, and any other details that could aid in its identification.

'Batteries are approaching reserve power,' Summer said.

'I think we've learned all we can,' Dirk said. 'Besides, Jack won't be too happy if we surface after dark.'

He purged the ballast tanks, and they began a controlled ascent. Several minutes later, they broke the surface amid a choppy sea driven by a gusting westerly. The sun was already dipping beneath a bank of clouds on the horizon, stabbing the fading sky with bolts of pink and orange. As waves splashed over the submersible's acrylic canopy, Dirk saw a nearby boat approaching. It was the same patrol boat he and Dahlgren had seen earlier.

'Looks like someone was waiting for us.' The boat turned directly toward them while increasing speed. 'Might be a good time to call the *Alexandria* to come fetch us.'

'I think I spotted them on the horizon.' Summer strained her neck to peer over the rolling waves. 'They still look to be a few miles off.'

She reached for the transmission button on her radio, then froze. 'Dirk, what are they doing?'

Her brother was already tracking the patrol boat, which approached at an uncomfortably high speed. The steel-hulled vessel was less than a hundred feet away. It should have begun to slow or veer off, but it didn't.

'They mean to ram us!' Summer shouted.

Dirk had the thrusters engaged, but with a top speed of only three knots the submersible couldn't outrun a sea turtle. With no chance to elude the patrol boat, and insufficient time to dive, Dirk reacted the only way he could. He turned the submersible directly toward the oncoming vessel.

Summer looked at him as if he were insane and braced for the collision. Dirk kept his eyes glued on the boat, maneuvering toward its sharp bow as if on a death wish. He waited until the craft was nearly upon them, then turned the joystick hard over while reversing the starboard thrusters.

The submersible responded as if mired in quicksand, and Dirk feared he had reacted too late. But after a brief hesitation, it veered to starboard, narrowly slipping past the boat's charging prow.

As Dirk hoped, the patrol boat's helmsman had locked on course and reacted too late to the last-second maneuver. Instead, the boat struck the submersible with only a light blow.

Dirk and Summer heard a bang and felt their craft shudder as the contact crushed one of the rear thrusters. The impact briefly disrupted the power supply, shutting down the sub's electrical systems. As Dirk frantically repowered the thrusters, he glanced out the spherical window as the patrol craft tore by. A man in green fatigues stood at the rail, pointing an assault rifle at the sub. But the gunman didn't shoot, instead just offering a menacing grin.

Summer fought off the urge to flash him an obscene gesture. 'That was close.' She turned her attention to the radio. 'Can you get us submerged?'

'Trying.' Dirk had started flooding the ballast tanks

even before the collision but had to reactivate the pumps after the power failed. They had only a matter of seconds before the patrol boat would swing around for another pass.

'Still no power to the radio,' Summer said, resetting the breaker switches behind her seat. When that failed, she took a quick peek out the bubble. The ballast tanks had resumed filling, pulling the submersible almost beneath the waves.

'She's already turned. Nearly upon us,' she said matter-of-factly.

She jumped back into her seat and cinched the lap belt tight.

'C'mon, get down.' Dirk pressed the yoke all the way forward. With half their thrusters disabled, it did little to speed their descent.

They could hear the patrol boat's charging engines – and then the boat was upon them. The submersible had made it a few feet underwater, but the boat's pilot had drawn a careful bead. Its sharp prow skimmed over the submersible, but its lower hull hit home.

The crunching impact produced an explosion of bubbles as the acrylic bubble cracked and the ballast tanks were ripped free. The submersible bounced under the hull, battered in a series of punishing blows, until finally getting swept aside.

The mangled shell wavered a moment before tumbling into a lazy death spiral that carried it all the way to the seafloor.

45

The submersible moaned like an angry ghoul as it plunged through the pressured depths. It struck the seabed with its nose, kicking up a thick cloud of brown sediment. The bottom current soon dispersed the plume, revealing the submersible's hulk.

Dirk felt like he had taken a ride in a washing machine. With its ballast tanks crushed, the submersible had flipped too many times to count as it sank. A monitor screen had torn loose during the tumble and struck Dirk in the head. He gently touched the top of his forehead and rubbed the length of a nifty gash. Other than the cut and some assorted bruises, he was unhurt – and thankful to be alive.

The submersible's rear frame had taken the brunt of the collision with the patrol boat, mangling the thrusters, battery compartment, and oxygen tanks. Despite numerous hairline cracks, the cockpit's acrylic bubble had somehow survived intact, sparing the occupants a quick drowning. A dozen tiny leaks were filling the cabin with icy water, but the craft had survived the plunge still filled with air.

'You okay?' Dirk asked across the dark interior. He reached for a penlight clipped to the console, but it had broken free.

'Yeah,' Summer said in a shaky voice, 'I think so.'

Dirk released his harness and fell forward into a foot

of cold water. The craft had landed on its face, creating an odd disorientation. Hissing erupted from several points around the submersible. Dirk couldn't tell if it was water spraying in through tiny fissures or the remnants of one of the oxygen tanks. He climbed over the back of his seat and groped for a side storage panel where another light was kept.

Wading through a cold, black, steadily flooding submersible would have led most people to panic, but Dirk felt an odd calmness. Some of his composure came from having trained for just such an emergency. But there was also a personal component.

He had lost a woman he loved in a terrorist attack in Jerusalem the year before, and that had changed him. Since then, joy had become a harder attitude to embrace, and he had taken to viewing the world in a colder, more cynical manner. More than that, death had become a companion he no longer feared.

'We'll have to wait for the cabin to flood before we can pop the hatch,' he said matter-of-factly. 'The pony bottles should get us to the surface.'

He located the storage compartment and retrieved a small flashlight. He flicked on the beam and aimed it at his sister.

One look at Summer's face told him something was seriously wrong. Her eyes bulged in a look of pain and fear, and her lips were set in a grimace. She released her harness and tried to stand but could only hunch over at an awkward angle.

Dirk aimed the beam toward her right leg, which was pinned against the seat. A small stain of blood marked her pant leg just above the ankle. 'It's no time to get attached to this place,' Dirk said.

Summer tried to move, squeezing her eyes shut as she pulled at her leg, but it was no use. 'My foot is pinned,' she said. 'Tight.'

Dirk crawled over for a better look. The collision had driven forward one of the oxygen tanks, which in turn had mashed the lower floorboard. A plate of reinforced steel had curled up, catching Summer's ankle against the seat's housing.

Water had already risen past her calf when Dirk reached down to examine the buckled plate. 'Can you pull forward?'

She tried, and shook her head. 'No good.'

He maneuvered past her. 'I'll try to move the housing.'

With his back braced against the acrylic bubble, he placed his feet against the housing and pressed with his legs. Because of the awkward angle, he could apply only a fraction of his full strength. The housing rocked slightly, but nowhere near enough to free Summer's leg. Dirk tried a few other angles, attempting to rock the housing, but without success.

'I just can't get enough leverage,' he said.

'It's okay.' Summer spoke calmly, trying to mask her own fear and not place undue pressure on her brother. 'Water's rising. Better get the dive tanks.'

Dirk saw the water was already up to Summer's waist. The leaks had increased, and the cabin was filling quicker. He dropped his legs into the water, which stabbed his skin with an icy bite, and climbed past the seats to the rear of the submersible. He reached for a rack next to the hatch that held emergency evacuation gear – two dive tanks fitted with regulators and masks.

He passed one tank down to Summer and looped the other over his shoulder. Then he rummaged around a compact toolbox, cursing that its wrenches and pliers were designed for small electrical repairs. The largest tool was a ball-peen hammer, which he grabbed, along with a short hacksaw blade. The blade summoned up the image of Aron Ralston, the courageous mountain biker who cut off his own arm after becoming trapped under a boulder near Moab. Amputating Summer's foot with the hacksaw blade might become a gruesome last measure to save her life.

'Any ideas?' Summer asked when he climbed over with the tools.

'I'll try and wedge the seat frame apart so you can slip out.' He passed her the light and hoped she didn't notice the saw blade.

'Okay,' she replied, shivering as the cold water swirled around her chest.

Dirk slipped on his mask and regulator and ducked underwater. Jamming the hammer handle in the gap by Summer's ankle, he could tell right away that it offered too little leverage. Still, he pressed himself horizontal and jammed his weight against the handle. The frame wavered but refused to bend or buckle. Further attempts yielded the same result. To force the heavy plates apart he needed more force, but there was nothing available. In frustration, he flipped the hammer around and banged on the frame, creating a tiny dent.

When he surfaced, he saw the water lapping at her chin.

She had her mask on as she handed him the flashlight with a disappointed look. He turned the light toward the entry hatch. At any moment, it would become flooded. As he swung the light around, its beam played on an object beyond the exterior canopy. He felt Summer grip his arm, and she tilted her head out of the water to speak.

'Go on without me.'

There was no anger or panic in her voice, just resignation. She knew Dirk had tried everything. As twins, they shared a bond unknown by most siblings. They trusted each other implicitly. She knew if the situation dictated, he would readily give up his own life for hers. She was thankful that at least he would survive.

Dirk looked in her eyes and shook his head.

'Then cut it off,' she cried. 'Now!' She had seen the hacksaw blade all along. Dirk could only admire her bravery, particularly as she pulled a bandanna from her jumpsuit pocket, twisted it into a tourniquet, and tied it around her lower calf.

Dirk had to wait for her to stick her head above water before replying. 'I'm not ready to play Dr Kildare just yet,' he said, forcing a grin. 'Wait right here.'

Before she knew it, he had opened the hatch and swum out of the submersible, leaving her trapped and alone in the dark.

46

Summer could not remember when she had felt so terrified. Trapped alone in the blackness of the ocean depths, she felt her heart racing. Once the submersible's interior had flooded, Dirk had opened the hatch and swum away with the waterproof flashlight. She shivered uncontrollably, from the fear and the cold water, as her fingers and ears turned numb.

But the worst was the near silence. Crouched on the overturned seat, she could hear only the pounding of her heart and the sporadic sucking and gurgling of her breath through the regulator. As her mind began inventorying her fears, the act of breathing rose to the top of the list. Her air consumption at the current depth was much higher than near the surface. The cylinder might provide her only a few minutes of air. But what if it hadn't been filled to capacity? A devilish voice in her head asked whether each breath from the tank would be her last.

She squeezed her eyes shut and tried to relax, extending the time between inhalations and forcing a steady breathing rhythm. When she felt her heartbeat slow, she pried open her eyes, but still found herself surrounded by a cloak of blackness. Never prone to claustrophobia, she still couldn't help feeling like she was locked in a very small, very dark closet.

She began to wonder if her brother had changed his

mind and headed for the surface – then she saw a dull glow outside the canopy. The light grew brighter until she could make out the flashlight's beam as it drew closer. Though it seemed he had been gone for hours, it had been only a few minutes.

When Dirk climbed through the hatch a second later, she saw he was wielding a five-foot steel pole with a brass ball affixed to one end: the severed flagpole from the shipwreck. The submersible had struck bottom alongside the wreck, which Dirk had recognized through the bubble.

Dirk crawled forward and wedged the pole between the seat frame and the housing that clamped against Summer's foot. Grabbing the opposite end, he pulled like an Olympic oarsman. The metal supporting the seat buckled immediately, allowing Summer to free her foot. She gave Dirk a hug, then signaled 'Ascend' with an upraised thumb.

Dirk shined the light at the open hatch and gave her a shove. They had spent a dangerous amount of time at a depth close to three hundred feet and knew not to linger.

Summer waited outside the submersible for him, and they linked arms and began their ascent together. They kicked in a slow, measured pace, using their rising exhaust bubbles as a speedometer. Ascending too quickly would be a surefire recipe for the bends, and Dirk made sure they lagged behind the fast-rising bubbles.

It seemed to take forever. Summer was glad for the exertion, which slightly warmed her frozen bones, but her mind still wanted to play tricks on her, telling her they weren't actually ascending or that they were actually falling back to the depths. It was the cold, she told herself, making her senses numb along with her extremities. She clung to Dirk, who moved like a robot, seemingly immune to the cold and dark.

At a depth of one hundred and fifty feet, the waters noticeably lightened as the surface light began to penetrate the deep. At one-twenty, they passed through a thermocline, and the water temperature warmed. And at eighty feet, Dirk ran out of air.

He wasn't surprised. Because of his exerted swim to the wreck and back, he knew his air would fail before Summer's. Drawing his hand across his throat to signal Summer, he jettisoned his tank and regulator. She passed her regulator over, and they began alternating breaths, unconsciously kicking more quickly toward the surface.

Dirk looked up and saw a faint ripple of silver far above their heads. They were now close enough to reach the surface if Summer's air failed. But now they had another problem.

Exposure to the pressurized depths allows tiny nitrogen bubbles to form in the body's tissue. If not allowed to dissipate via a gentle reduction in pressure, the gas bubbles can lodge in the body, creating the agonizing and sometimes fatal malady of the bends.

Dirk estimated they had spent close to fifteen minutes on the seafloor. The Navy Dive Tables called for multiple decompression stops, but they had no such luxury. They ascended to what Dirk guessed was about twenty feet and then held their position. Their natural buoyancy and the swift current made it a challenge, but he kept his eye on the surface and fought to keep them in place.

They milked the tank for another ten minutes before

Summer spat the regulator out of her mouth and pointed up. They both shot to the surface, exhaling as they swam.

Their heads broke the surface amid a choppy sea dotted with whitecaps. The sun had already vanished, leaving the sky a darkening shade of pewter. The combined effects would render them almost invisible to a passing ship, even one that was searching for them. Yet that wasn't first on Summer's mind.

Sucking in a deep breath, Summer turned to her brother. 'A flagpole?'

'Best I could do, under the circumstances. How's the foot?'

'The foot's okay, but I have a painful cramp in my ankle.' She shot him a concerned gaze. 'I don't think we came anywhere close to covering our deco time.'

Dirk shook his head. 'No, we were well short. Do you feel any tingling anywhere?'

'I'm too numb to feel much of anything.'

'We might be sleeping in the *Alexandria*'s decompression chamber tonight.' He scanned the horizon. 'Our next problem.'

They finally spotted the NUMA vessel far to the west. The dark band of the Madagascar shoreline was visible a bit closer, to the north.

'The *Alexandria* is up current,' Dirk said. 'No way we can swim to her.'

'They've probably swept by already and are backtracking with a sonar survey to locate the submersible. We'll have drifted to Australia by the time they get back this way.'

'Then to shore it is,' Dirk said. 'Are you up for the swim?'

'Do I have a choice?'

She eyed the coastline, put her face in the water, and started swimming. They were both excellent swimmers in fit shape. Under normal circumstances, the open-water swim to shore would have been little more than a tiring challenge. But the mental strain of their escape from the submersible, combined with their cold-water exposure, turned it into a life-or-death task. Fatigue struck both swimmers almost immediately. Summer couldn't believe how quickly her arms and legs felt like they had turned to lead.

The turbulent seas didn't help. The waves frequently tossed them about and filled their mouths with salt water. Swimming toward the coastline meant they were working across the current. Each stroke to shore carried them a nearly equal distance to the east, and that much farther from the *Alexandria*.

The pair swam side by side, stopping to rest every ten minutes. While treading water, Dirk would fish the flashlight out of his pocket and waggle its beam at the research ship. On their third rest, the light slipped from his numb fingers, dropping into the depths like a candle down a well. By now, the NUMA ship appeared even farther away, just an occasional dancing light on the horizon.

Dirk turned toward Summer. 'C'mon, less than a mile to go.'

She willed her limbs forward, but they had a mind of their own. A deep pain began burning in her left leg, then gradually vanished, along with all feeling in the limb. She began resting at shorter and shorter intervals, and Dirk could see she was beginning to fade.

'Pretend we're in Hawaii,' he said. 'I'll race you to Wai-kiki.'

'Okay,' was all she could manage. Even under the rapidly fading daylight, Dirk could see her eyes turning listless.

He grabbed her jumpsuit and swam with a sidestroke even as his own strength ebbed. The cold seemed to reach down and chill his bones, and his teeth joined Summer's in chattering nonstop.

He felt her body sag, and he realized she could make no more headway. Through his exhausted mind, he realized hypothermia was setting in. They both had to escape the water, and soon.

Though his breath was nearly spent, he kept a running dialogue with Summer, encouraging her, asking endless questions to which he got no reply. When she began to flounder, he turned her on her back and towed her by the collar. There would be no more stopping for him now.

He pressed on, one painful stroke at a time. He had nothing left in the tank, and his muscles pleaded to cease, but somehow he blocked out the agony and kept clawing through the water. The surf line ahead gradually grew larger until he could hear the waves pounding against the land. The sound inspired him to pull harder, depleting the last of his reserves.

A wave washed over them, and Dirk came up sputtering. Summer coughed out inhaled water as they were propelled by a succeeding wave that broke on top of them. Dirk kept his grasp on Summer as they tumbled through the water and were slammed against the bottom. At last they had reached shore.

With the force of succeeding waves at his back, Dirk staggered up the sandy beach, dragging Summer behind him. He pulled her past the tide line, then collapsed to the sand.

'How are you feeling?' he gasped.

'C-c-cold,' she whispered.

It was a positive sign that she could still speak, but he had to get her dry. The night air was still warm, which would make all the difference.

When he found the strength to stand, Dirk hobbled to his feet and looked around. They had landed on a barren stretch of the southern Madagascan coastline, within the uninhabited parklands of Cape Sainte Marie. The beach and inland area were dark. He had no idea how far the nearest help was, but it didn't matter. He lacked the energy to search.

He glanced seaward but found only a black and empty ocean. The coastline curved outward to the west, obscuring the lights of the *Alexandria*. He turned back inland and hiked up the beach, looking for shelter. The sand underfoot turned to hard scrabble, which led to some rocky hills and mounds. Nowhere was there anything resembling shelter.

He headed back toward Summer – and tripped over a protruding mound at the edge of the beach. It extended about a dozen feet and had created a burrow on its leeward side. The indentation would provide some protection from the sea breeze, likely the best shelter Dirk could find. Finding a ragged tassel of sea grass, he ripped up as much as he could and spread it about the burrow for insulation. He returned to Summer, carried her up the beach, and placed her in the makeshift bed.

The sea grass helped dry her skin, and he hiked down the beach to search for more. There was little, but he gathered what he could and returned to the shelter. He sat on the mound and used the grass to dry Summer's skin before adding it to the bedding. When he stood, he knocked a lump of sand off the edge of the mound, exposing a faded band of material buried within.

He thought nothing of it as he took off his own jumpsuit and stood in the ocean breeze, shivering until his skin dried. He then lay down beside Summer as an additional wind barrier for her. She was murmuring more, and her body no longer felt icy. With a warm evening at hand, Dirk grew confident that she was going to be all right.

The exertion caught up with him, and his eyelids began to droop. A crescent moon appeared from behind a cloud and illumined the beach in a silvery glow. Above his head, Dirk could see the buried object protruding from the mound more clearly. It was washed-out yellow in color, marked with a string of faded black letters. His tired mind formed a name, which rang with a strange tone as he drifted to sleep.

Barbarigo.

47

Summer awoke to a scraping sound near her ear. Prying open her eyes, she spotted a hulking object moving a few feet from her head.

'Dirk!' she cried, nudging her sleeping brother beside her.

He awoke with a start, sat up, and smiled when he saw the object of Summer's fear. It was a sunbaked radiated turtle. 'You thinking of having turtle soup for breakfast?'

The ancient reptile looked down his grainy-beaked snout at Dirk as if indicating he wasn't amused. Turning his head down range, he dug his claws into the sand and continued his lethargic journey across the beach.

Summer grinned at her own fears as she watched the big tortoise move away. 'How could somebody harm such a stately creature?'

'Depends on how hungry you are.' Dirk stood and viewed their surroundings in daylight. The beach was flat and sandy, surrounded by rocky limestone hills rising inland. Vegetation was sparse, as the region seldom collected more than a few inches of rainfall a year.

Summer sat upright. 'Do you see the *Alexandria*?'

As he looked offshore, Dirk saw only an empty blue sea sprinkled with whitecaps. There was no sign of the NUMA ship, or any other vessels. 'I guess we drifted farther east than they suspect. If we hike up the coast far enough, maybe we can wave them down.'

Unknown to them, Jack Dahlgren and two crewmen had scoured the coastline all night in a Zodiac mounted with a searchlight. The searchers had even zipped past the beach twice. But hunkered down behind the mound, Dirk and Summer had slept through their passes, the sound of the ocean drowning out the Zodiac's motor.

'Dirk?'

He could tell by her voice that something was wrong. 'What is it?'

'I can't move my left leg.'

Dirk turned pale. He instantly guessed why: she'd gotten the bends after all. The condition usually showed itself by pain in the joints or limbs, but sometimes by paralysis. And paralysis in the legs typically meant that a gas bubble had lodged in the spinal cord.

He rushed over and knelt beside her. 'Are you certain?'

Summer nodded. 'I've got absolutely no feeling in my left leg. But the right one feels fine.' She looked at him with dread.

'How's the pain?'

'Pretty light, actually, but I'll need some help to get back to the ship.'

They both knew that immediate treatment in a hyperbaric chamber was critical for a successful recovery. Summer was fortunate that the *Alexandria* carried such a chamber, likely the only one within hundreds of miles. But it might as well be on the moon, Dirk thought, if they couldn't get to the ship.

He glanced at a rocky rise that towered over the beach. 'I'm going to take a quick hike up that hill. I'd like to see where the ship is and figure out our options.'

'I'll wait here,' Summer said, forcing a smile.

Dirk quickly crossed the beach and scampered up the barren hill. The rocky ground sliced into his stockinged feet, and he regretted having kicked off his shoes when he swam out of the submersible. The hill rose sharply, and he soon obtained a commanding view of the neighboring coastline.

Looking first to sea, he quickly spotted the *Alexandria*. She was a small dot in the distance, moored, he guessed, over the site of the sunken submersible. Dirk estimated he would have to hike five miles up the coast to reach a position where the crew might spot him. Gazing inland, he observed a barren range of rolling hills, part of the Cape Sainte Marie Special Reserve. The large national park, created as a wildlife sanctuary, had few resources, save for a handful of hiking trails and campsites.

He shifted his gaze to the east and was surprised to spot a ship two or three miles distant, rising from a tiny inlet. A handful of buildings stood alongside the ship, while a small dredge was moored nearby. Dirk thought of the patrol boat that had rammed their submersible, but he scanned the inlet and saw no sign of it.

Spotting no other signs of civilization, he hurried back to the beach.

'Do you want the good news or the bad news?' he asked Summer, who sat probing the sand mound with a flat piece of driftwood.

'I'm a sunny optimist. Give me the good.'

'The *Alexandria* hasn't abandoned us. Unfortunately, they still think we're aboard the submersible. As far as I can figure, they're moored over the site where we went down. Plan B says that I hike five or six miles down the beach and try to attract their attention from shore.'

'I missed Plan A.'

'Less than three miles east of here is an inlet complete with a small dock facility and a freighter.'

'And a patrol boat with a bent nose?'

'No patrol boat. I can hike there in under an hour and call the *Alexandria*. We'll have you napping in the ship's decompression chamber in no time.'

'Plan A it is.'

Dirk placed a hand on her shoulder. 'You sure you'll be okay here?'

'Yes, as long as he doesn't get any ideas about sharing burrows.' She pointed to the old turtle. The big reptile had traveled less than twenty yards since they awoke, lying on the beach, tossing sand with his flippers.

'He'll never make it back here in time.'

Dirk turned and moved off down the beach. The morning sun was already baking the sandy terrain, so he followed the shoreline, where the ocean breeze kept it cooler. The growing heat and a dry throat made him crave a drink of water. He knew he was dehydrated, which only added to his lethargy. But Dirk put the thought out of his mind and focused on walking as quickly as his weak legs and shoeless feet permitted.

The narrow beach ended abruptly at a steep crag of limestone that jutted into the sea. He had to turn inland until the rock face shrank and he could climb up a short incline. The top of the rock was flat, and it melded into a series of low hills that continued to the inlet two miles beyond. The white superstructure of the docked freighter peeked like a mirage above a distant sandy ridge.

Summer's condition gripped Dirk's mind, compelling him to hike fast. It had been less than twelve hours since they had escaped the submersible, so her chances for a full recovery were still good – if she could make it to the chamber soon. His concern kept him moving until he reached a small rise forty minutes later. Just below was the small lagoon, encircled by low hills that neatly concealed the ship and dock facility.

As he descended the western hill, he could see it was a bare-bones complex. There were just two permanent structures. A small dorm-like building rose near the inland side, while a warehouse stood at the opposite end of the dock. Between them was a high metal awning that he'd mistaken for a third building. The awning stretched the length of the dock, providing shade to several large mounds of granular sediment. Dirk first thought it was salt from some nearby flats, then noticed it was gray in color.

The freighter, a midsized bulk carrier, sat opposite, occupying every inch of the dock facing. Dirk couldn't make out the name but noticed its yellow funnel sported the image of a white flower. A handful of men were moving one of the mineral piles onto the ship with front loaders and a conveyor belt.

The heavy equipment, combined with a nearby generator, filled the air with clamor. No one noticed Dirk as he climbed down the hill and approached the open warehouse. Inside, he could see a mechanic overhauling a small motor. Dirk started to walk into the building, then froze in his tracks.

Out of the corner of his eye, he had caught sight of another vessel in the lagoon. With the freighter occupying the length of the dock, the second craft had been forced to tie up on the freighter's outboard side. It had been obscured from view as he descended the hill, but the lagoon's swirling waters had shifted its mooring so its bow was now visible – including the freshly scraped gouge on its prow streaked with yellow paint. The patrol boat.

Inside the warehouse, the mechanic looked up and saw Dirk. He gave him an odd look and let out a shout. From the back of the warehouse, a young man in green fatigues rushed out, carrying an AK-47, which he aimed at Dirk's chest. A flood of words spewed from his mouth in a dialect that Dirk didn't understand, but the intent was clear.

Dirk stared at the gunman in disbelief, then opened his palms and slowly raised his arms into the air.

48

Rather than contemplate her paralyzed leg, Summer focused her thoughts elsewhere. She stared at the radiated turtle plodding across the beach, then gazed wistfully at the empty sea. Finally, she considered the object buried in the mound she had slept against.

The material that Dirk had exposed was thick and rubberized. By daylight, she could see that the mound was in a distinct oblong shape, formed by the object buried within. Summer studied the material, rubbing her hand across the faded letters that had been stenciled in black.

Barbarigo. It sounded Italian, which piqued her curiosity. Using her driftwood shovel, she scraped away the sand above the word, revealing a compressed roll of the rubber material. She could tell it had once been inflated. Digging some more, she saw that it was a rubber raft. It was old, but well preserved by the layers of beach sand built over it.

She dug down on the opposite side of the layered rubber and soon struck a hard, flat object. Scooping away the sand, she saw it was a hardwood bench, presumably one of several in the large raft, offering another hint of its age. She continued digging and exposed another section of rubber, the raft's flooring. A small ribbon of blue material poked through the sand, catching her eye. Using her hands, she carefully brushed away the sand, exposing more of the material. It was round in shape, and she saw it was a sailor's cap. Tugging gently, she freed it from the sand, but then suddenly gasped, dropping it from her fingers.

Underneath the hat, she had exposed the grinning skull of its owner.

The warehouse contained a small machine shop, along with several workbenches stacked with carpenters' stores. Banks of lube oil and diesel fuel lined one wall, near a large humming generator. A small forklift and two all-terrain vehicles were parked near an open tool bin by the door. The bay was dimly lit, but warmed by the sounds of an African percussion band blaring from a CD player.

Dirk absorbed all this as he was marched into the warehouse and ordered to stand against a corrugated tin wall. The mechanic and the gunman conversed for a moment in what Dirk guessed was Malagasy, then the mechanic ran to report the presence of the intruder.

The gunman stood next to the workbench with the disassembled motor, rocking on his heels as he held his weapon on Dirk. He was young, no more than seventeen. His hair was worn long, and he stood with a sulking hunch. It was easy to see he had no formal military training. Grease stains covered his military-style fatigues and his fingers. Dirk guessed he was primarily employed as a mechanic's assistant, with secondary duty as a guard.

In a relaxed manner, Dirk brought an open hand to his mouth and tilted it up as if drinking. 'Water?' he asked in a raspy voice. *'L'eau?'*

The gunman eyed Dirk closely. The NUMA marine

engineer carried no visible weapons, his hair was full of sand, and his jumpsuit was caked with dust. He wore no shoes, only dirty, frayed socks. Emerging from the desert in such a condition, he seemed anything but a threat.

The gunman relaxed slightly and slowly turned to the workbench, where a khaki daypack sat on a stool. He pulled a canteen from the pack's side pocket and tossed it to Dirk.

Dirk unscrewed the cap and gulped down several swallows of the water. It was warm and somewhat foul, but he would have gladly consumed a gallon of the stuff. He smiled at the gunman, then savored a few more gulps.

'Thank you,' he said, and replaced the cap.

He took a cautious step forward and reached out with a long arm to return the canteen. The gunman hesitated before stepping forward and extending his free hand. Dirk waited for the young man's fingers to come within a hair of his own, then let the canteen slip.

The boy lunged forward, but the canteen bobbled from his outstretched hand and fell to the floor. He suddenly caught himself and rose up, only to be struck by a left hook that tagged him on the cheek. He staggered against the workbench but quickly pulled his weapon up.

Dirk didn't give him the opportunity to shoot. He dove into the guard, pinning the assault rifle between their two bodies. The gunman tried to spin and knock Dirk clear, but he didn't have the strength.

Dirk ignored the weapon aimed inches from his face and clutched the young man's fatigues, drawing him tight to keep the gun aimed clear, while with his other hand he groped the top of the workbench. Feeling a hard metallic object, he pulled it up and swung it against the gunman's skull. It took three blows before he fell limp and slumped to the floor.

Dirk looked in his hand and saw he was holding a piston and connecting rod from the disassembled engine. 'Definitely a knocking problem,' he muttered, and tossed it onto the workbench.

He sprinted to one of the all-terrain vehicles parked by the door. Each had a small mesh trailer attached for hauling parts and equipment, but more importantly, each had a key in the ignition. He straddled one of the vehicles and turned the key. The motor spun to life just as three men appeared at the doorway.

Dirk reached over and ripped the ignition cable from the adjacent ATV while twisting his own throttle. The little vehicle lurched forward, heading toward the open door. Ahead of him, Dirk saw that the original mechanic had returned, accompanied by a dockhand and a man in fatigues, brandishing a pistol. Dirk goosed the throttle and headed straight for them.

The mechanic jumped to Dirk's right, while the other two ducked left, around the corner of the building. With the trailer bouncing wildly behind him, Dirk tore out of the warehouse and into the sunlight. He whipped the handlebars left, careening around the corner and after the two men. The dockhand jumped clear at the last second, but the man in fatigues hesitated. The ATV's flared fender creased him in the leg, knocking him to the ground. Dirk had to swerve right to avoid a wall of fuel drums, which sent the empty trailer bounding onto the prone man. The man cried out as the trailer's tires rolled over him, leaving him caked in dust.

Dirk had hoped to turn back and drive past the warehouse toward the beach, but was thwarted when the dockhand emerged from the building with the assault rifle.

Cursing himself for not taking the weapon, he wheeled the ATV sharply left and sped down the front of the dock. He waited for a fusillade of lead, but it never arrived. He quickly saw why.

Directly ahead, a half dozen laborers manned the conveyor system. The dockhand didn't want to fire into his compatriots just beyond. Dirk held his course to increase the distance from the armed dockhand, but ultimately he had nowhere to go. Ahead, the conveyor blocked the width of the dock, while to his left sat towering mounds of gray ore.

He edged close to the dock as the workers at the conveyor began pointing and yelling. Barreling toward the heavy conveyor, he seemed bent on suicide. He wondered that himself, but he had no other choice. Building speed down the quay, he held steady until just a few yards from the conveyor. As the workers ducked behind the ramp for cover, Dirk jammed the ATV to his left.

The all-terrain vehicle's knobby off-road tires slid on the sandy dock as he threw it into the turn while holding the throttle to its stops. All four wheels began to bite, and the ATV shot forward toward the mound of ore being loaded onto the ship. Dirk was nearly jolted off his seat when the front wheels met the base of the pile, but the ATV proved its mettle by blasting straight up the mound. It shot past an idling front-end loader and climbed past the feeder end of the conveyor. It was twenty feet up the side of the steep pile when its momentum began to waver, and Dirk eased the front wheels to his right. He came dangerously close to flipping the vehicle, but the trailer acted as an anchor and helped him to pivot the ATV around.

One of the laborers ran, yelling, as Dirk sped back down the hill, angling past the far side of the conveyor. A small avalanche of ore crashed to the dock after him and sent the remaining workers scrambling for cover. As it slammed onto the dock at high speed, the ATV bounced high into the air before landing on all four wheels. The trailer was less artistic, breaking free of the ATV's hitch and smacking into the freighter, then dropping into the water.

Dirk had to throw the ATV into a hard left to avoid the same fate. Braking and skidding, he barely clung to the wheel as the ATV danced and slid. One of the rear wheels struck a bollard, which jolted the vehicle back on track, and Dirk accelerated hard down the dock.

Ahead, he could see the freedom of the open desert, in a gap between the dock and the dormitory. But as he sped ahead, another ATV appeared from around the building's corner. Dirk slowed and waved as he passed the other rider, who he realized was the smirking gunman in green fatigues from the patrol boat. The gunman gave Dirk an empty stare, and then the light of recognition flipped on. By then Dirk had opened his throttle and was tearing past the building.

Across the dock, scores of men were running toward them, shouting and pointing. The gunman whipped his ATV around and gave chase.

A sharp, rocky cliff backed the lagoon, forcing Dirk to ascend a lesser hill that ran parallel to the dock. Shots rang out from below, peppering the hillside around him. He zigzagged up the hill, generating a billow of dust that obscured his path. Ducking low, he urged the ATV on until cresting the rise and disappearing from view below.

As he turned and angled toward the beach, he ventured a glance over his shoulder. Green Fatigues was hot on his trail, less than fifty yards away.

Dirk squeezed harder on the throttle as the ATV wallowed through a dry wash. Passing the other ATV earlier, he had seen a holster on the driver's belt. Once again, he found himself weaponless against an armed man. But at least he had the ATV, and he knew where he was going.

Green Fatigues indeed had a holster with a loaded pistol, which he removed with one hand when the vehicles hit a stretch of sandy flats. Steering and accelerating with his right hand, he used his left to fire a handful of potshots, all of which missed by a wide margin.

Over his shoulder, Dirk caught sight of the gun and threw his ATV into a shallow serpentine course. Already kicking up a large cloud of dust, it now sprayed wide walls of brown that offered sporadic cover.

But that maneuver also allowed the pursuer to draw closer until he was choking on Dirk's dust just twenty yards away. Dirk veered left along a flat rise above the beach, briefly losing his companion in the haze. When Green Fatigues broke free of the dust, he had a clear view of Dirk and fired two shots. One of them hit home.

Dirk heard a loud pop as one of the rear tires burst.

The ruptured tire thumped loudly, and Dirk muscled the handlebars to maintain control.

He was as good as finished. Green Fatigues could speed ahead or alongside and finish him off with an easy shot. Weighing his options, Dirk prepared to swing the ATV around and force a collision. But ahead, in the sand, he saw footprints that angled sharply inland. They were his own footprints from earlier in the day and they signaled a possible riposte – one that just might give him a fighting chance.

49

The sandy surface gave way to dust-covered rock, which rose in an undulating fashion. The gradual inclination concealed the approaching precipice, the one Dirk had climbed that morning. And the one Dirk hoped to use to his advantage.

Over the rocky surface, the ATV's trailing dust grew lighter, forcing Dirk into a dangerous maneuver. Rather than dodge his pursuer, he angled ahead of him, desperate to obscure his vision.

As Dirk crossed his earlier footprints, he eased off the throttle. The lip of the precipice appeared a second later. He hesitated, drawing the gunman in close, before downshifting and jamming on the brakes. The ATV wavered as its knobby tires skidded across the rock. Dirk swung his leg over the seat, let go of the handlebars, and leaped.

Barely ten feet from the ledge, Dirk's ATV regained momentum and soared over the side. Green Fatigues's hard-charging ATV arrived a few seconds later. Too late, he saw the abrupt drop-off. He mashed on the brakes and flung the handlebars over with white knuckles, but to no avail. The ATV skidded off the edge and plunged over the cliff, Green Fatigues flying up and over it, screaming as he fell.

Dirk had missed the sight. After jumping from his own ATV, he had pulled himself into a tuck before hitting the ground hard and rolling several times. Sliding feetfirst toward the cliff, he clawed at the ground as his legs went over the ledge. He stopped just short, legs dangling midair. With his head pounding, he pulled his lower body back over the ledge and lay on his back, recovering.

He felt scrapes and bruises, but he'd managed not to break any bones. After a minute, he rose to his feet and peered over the side.

Forty feet below, his ATV stood on end, its nose augured into the ground and its body telescoped. A few yards away, the other ATV lay upside down, its wheels still spinning. Dirk didn't see Green Fatigues at first, then spotted a motionless leg protruding from beneath the vehicle.

Dirk walked along the cliff, moving gingerly until his limbs loosened. Glancing back toward the dock facility, he saw some movement, a small foot patrol heading his way. Just beyond, at the mouth of the lagoon, he saw the patrol boat heading to sea. They were taking the theft of the ATV rather seriously, Dirk thought.

He retraced his morning footsteps until he reached a shallow face in the ridge where he could slide down. At the crash scene, he found the inverted ATV battered but mostly intact. He dug his feet into the sand, positioned a shoulder against its side, and shoved, rolling the vehicle back onto its wheels. The mangled body of its rider lay embedded in the sand, his back and head unnaturally twisted.

Dirk pocketed the man's pistol and climbed onto the ATV. The seat and handlebars were bent and two fenders torn off, but the drivetrain looked undamaged. He hit the ignition button and heard the starter grind and grind. Gasoline had drained from the fuel line while the vehicle sat inverted, and it took several tries before the engine caught. Dirk gunned it, and the ATV took off, the exposed tires sending sand flying.

At the far end of the beach, Dirk pulled up alongside the small berm. Summer appeared from a large hole in the center and waved. After pulling herself inside, she had excavated nearly a third of the rubber raft.

He hopped off the idling ATV and ran to her. 'You all right?'

'Fine, except for my dead leg.' She noticed his bruised appearance, and the even more battered ATV.

'I thought I heard a crash. What happened?'

'I had a falling-out with an acquaintance.' He motioned his thumb over his shoulder. 'The crowd at the port facility is the same bunch that rammed us. I borrowed one of their ATVs, and they aren't too happy about it.'

Summer saw the urgency in his eyes. 'We need to go?'

'I think that would be a good idea.'

He scooped her off the ground and carried her to the ATV.

'Wait,' she said. 'The *Barbarigo*'s logbook.'

Dirk gave her a quizzical look.

'That's a rubber raft buried in the sand. It's from a vessel called the *Barbarigo*. I found a book wrapped in oilskin under the bench,' she said, pointing at the mound. 'I can't read it because it's written in Italian, but it looks like a logbook.'

Dirk stepped to the partially buried raft and reached in. He froze when he saw a fully exposed skeleton, which he

319

had somehow missed seconds earlier. The torso lay near a bench seat, on which sat the oilskin-wrapped logbook. He snatched it, climbed onto the ATV behind Summer, and handed it to her. 'You didn't mention its scribe was still hanging around.'

'There's at least two other bodies. We need to have the ship's archaeologist examine the site.'

Dirk reached around his sister and twisted the throttle. 'Perhaps another day.'

Leaving the bones and beach behind, they rode up a rocky ridge that fingered into the sea. From its peak, they could view the opposite coastline curve before them in a broad expanse of sandy flats. The turquoise hull of the *Alexandria* bobbed in the swells several miles distant. Dirk focused his eyes on the ground, driving down the rocky hill as fast as he dared, aware of Summer's impaired ability to stay seated.

Summer was the first to notice the vessel, a small Zodiac, skimming parallel to the beach ahead. When the ATV's tires reached the flat sands, Dirk accelerated to top speed. The Zodiac was traveling away from them, but he quickly closed the gap. Honking the ATV's high-pitched horn, he caught the attention of Jack Dahlgren, who was piloting the Zodiac with a NUMA crewman. The parties converged, Dirk driving his ATV into the waves as Dahlgren drew the Zodiac near.

'Enjoying the local tourist sights in comfort, Ah see,' Dahlgren said by way of greeting. The Texan's relief at finding them alive was evident in his eyes.

'More than we really cared to,' Dirk said. 'Permission to come aboard?'

Dahlgren nodded and inched the Zodiac alongside the ATV.

'Summer's lost feeling in her left leg,' Dirk said. 'We think she's bent.'

Dahlgren plucked Summer, still clutching the *Barbarigo*'s logbook, off the ATV and set her in the inflatable boat.

'Everyone aboard *Alexandria* will be anxious to hear what happened. Had us plenty worried when we found the sub downstairs without you in it. Guess you'll have plenty of time in the chamber to fill us in.'

He had to sit down and goose the motor to keep the Zodiac from swamping under a wave. As Dahlgren pivoted back to the ATV so Dirk could jump aboard, he noticed the shredded jumpsuit and multiple bruises. 'If you don't mind me saying, you look like you went square dancing with a rototiller.'

'If it's any consolation, I feel like it,' Dirk said.

'You don't want to park that ATV on dry land?'

'No, the owner was rather troublesome about me borrowing it. I suggest we get to the *Alexandria* as soon as possible.'

Dahlgren gunned the outboard motor and steered toward the research ship. Dirk gazed across the horizon, spotting the patrol boat speeding in their direction. A moment later, a deep rumble drowned out the whine of the outboard, and a shadow darted over the Zodiac. Dirk looked up to see a low-flying C-130 lumber over. It was painted gray, with the multicolored flag of South Africa displayed on its tail. Dahlgren waved at the plane, slowing the Zodiac to be heard over its motor.

'Search-and-rescue plane we dialed up out of Pretoria. About time they showed up. I guess we better let them know you're safe.' He retrieved a handheld radio and informed the *Alexandria* of Dirk and Summer's appearance.

While they waited for the message to be relayed to the airplane, Dirk tapped Dahlgren's shoulder and pointed to the approaching patrol boat. 'Call back and ask the plane if they would buzz those guys. Tell them we suspect they're part of a local piracy ring.'

'I reckon the FAA doesn't extend to these waters,' Dahlgren said, and relayed the message.

The C-130 had already receded to a speck on the horizon. Then it turned and grew larger. The pilot brought it down low, barely fifty feet above the waves. Approaching the patrol craft off its stern, it caught the crew by surprise. Several gunmen threw themselves to the deck as the roar of the four 4,200-horsepower turboprop motors engulfed the patrol boat.

The plane flew past, made a lazy turn, and came back for a second run across the patrol boat's beam. This time, a few of the braver crewmen waved their weapons, but nobody fired a round. Undaunted, the C-130's pilot made three more passes, each one lower than the last. The patrol boat accepted the message, reluctantly veering off and motoring back to shore. Tracking it for good measure, the C-130 hung around at low altitude for almost an hour, before dipping its wings and heading home.

Dirk looked to Dahlgren. 'Remind me to send a case of beer to the South African Air Force.'

'Those boys don't mess around, do they?'

A few minutes later, they pulled alongside the *Alexandria*. Dirk and Summer were surprised to see their mangled submersible on the stern deck as they were hoisted aboard.

'We found her promptly with the sonar and were able to rig her for lifting with an ROV,' Dahlgren said. 'We renewed our shore search when we didn't find you inside.'

The siblings were greeted warmly as they boarded, but Summer sensed a nervousness, even from Dahlgren, as she was helped onto a gurney. The ship's doctor rushed them to the decompression chamber, which was already prepped with food and medical supplies.

Dirk tried to duck out, but the doctor ordered him in as a precaution. Before the hatch closed, Dahlgren poked his head inside to ensure they were comfortable.

'Might not be a good idea to linger around the area,' Dirk said. 'We were able to plant all the seismic sensors before our run-in with the patrol boat. We can deal with the thugs another time.'

'The captain's already winding us up for a run to Durban at flank speed.' Dahlgren's face was taught and serious.

'Why Durban? I thought we were headed up to Mozambique from here?'

The doctor yelled from behind the chamber to seal the hatch.

'Bad news, I'm afraid,' Dahlgren said. 'Your dad and Al have gone missing in the Pacific.'

Before the words could sink in, the heavy metal hatch closed, and the chamber's occupants were pressurized back into the depths.

50

Pitt felt like he was in a chamber of his own, only his was a chamber of horrors.

By the hour, the dank prison he shared on the *Adelaide* felt more and more claustrophobic. A daily rise in the outside temperature had turned the bay into a stifling-hot oven. Making matters worse, the heat intensified the foul odors generated by the confined men and two dead bodies.

Pitt felt constant hunger, but was thankful they were given plenty of drinking water. Periodically the hatch door would be thrown open, and two armed men would toss in boxes of bread and other dried stores from the galley. The prisoners valued the brief gusts of fresh air nearly as much as the food.

Pitt and the SWAT team had tried formulating an escape plan, but their options were nonexistent. The storage bay had been stripped of any tools or equipment to force another exit. The locked hatch, they found, was guarded around the clock. Multiple attempts at testing the handle or hinges were instantly met by a rapping from a gun barrel on the opposite side. Whenever the hatch was opened to deliver food and water, at least two men stood ready with assault rifles.

Noticing the stale rolls they had been given to eat had hardened to the consistency of granite, Giordino suggested using those to attack the guards.

Pitt's friend rebounded swiftly from his wound, which somehow showed no signs of infection. After sleeping nearly three straight days, Giordino had awoken with an irritable vigor, and he quickly regained his strength despite the sparse diet.

While most of the men grew resigned to their captivity, a few began losing control. Fights broke out among the crew of the *Adelaide*, while another man gave in to fits of hysterical yelling. Pitt felt an uneasy gratitude when he noticed a reduction in the ship's engine revolutions, signaling their arrival in protected waters.

Pitt had counted the number of hours passed since he was thrown into confinement. Traveling at sixteen knots, he calculated the *Adelaide* could have covered almost four thousand miles, placing them anywhere between Alaska and Peru. But the warm temperatures suggested something equatorial. If the ship had held its southeasterly heading, Pitt figured they could be somewhere off southern Mexico or Central America.

Confirmation came soon, after the ship had stopped and started several times, accompanied by the sound of dock activity. The ship got under way and sailed another three hours before stopping for good. A short time later, the prisoners were roused from their compartment.

The men stepped from the hot and humid storage bay to an equally hot and humid deck. The ship was berthed at a dock, stern first, surrounded on three sides by dense jungle. Only a small patch of blue off the bow showed they had sailed from a larger body of water and backed into a narrow inlet barely large enough for the freighter to fit.

The brightness of early morning stung their eyes, yet Pitt noted the sun was nowhere in sight.

'Someone really likes their jungle around here,' Giordino said, pointing a finger skyward.

Shading his eyes, Pitt saw a jungle canopy overhead. It took him several seconds to realize it was a huge swath of camouflage netting that was strung over the entire dock complex.

'Maybe just privacy nuts,' Pitt said. He looked at the *Adelaide*, confirming his suspicions. The ship's name had been repainted *Labrador*, while the funnel and deck railing had been painted new colors. The hijackers were well versed at theft and concealment on a grand scale.

The prisoners were herded to a gangway and marched off the ship, where they were greeted by a line of armed men in fatigues, several of them partnered with guard dogs. The captives were left standing along the dock for several minutes, which allowed time for Pitt and Giordino to study the facilities. The dock operation was modest, consisting of two small cranes and a conveyor system. Behind it were several large concrete pads, dusted with gray sediment – transfer stations for the raw ore and processed rare earth elements that were transferred in and out of the facility. Beyond the dock area, several low-slung buildings poked through the foliage. Pitt suspected they were separation-and-extraction plants, used to refine the stolen rare earth ores.

The putt-putt of a small motor preceded the appearance of a golf cart bearing a muscular blond man wearing a fitted uniform with a holstered pistol on his hip. A coiled bullwhip dangled from a belt hook on the opposite side. Pitt noticed the guards tense at his arrival.

'Looks like a lion tamer,' Giordino whispered.

'For a circus I want no part of,' Pitt said.

The overseer, Johansson, crossed the dock and spoke to Gomez, who had followed the prisoners off the ship. The Swede examined the freighter with a satisfied gleam.

'She's carrying a full load of crushed monazite,' Gomez said. 'Testing confirmed high concentrates of neodymium, cerium, and dysprosium.'

'Excellent. The extraction facilities have been waiting for new material. We will engage the new prisoners in off-loading the ore.'

'What about the ship?'

'She would make a nice addition to the fleet. Determine what reconfigurations are required to erase her identity, and we'll discuss it with Bolcke after she's unloaded.'

Johansson turned his back on Gomez to examine the new captives. He reviewed the men with a caustic eye, paying particular attention to the SWAT team.

'Welcome to Puertas del Infierno,' he said, 'the Gates of Hell. You now belong to me.'

He waved his arm across the dock toward the buildings beyond. 'This is an ore-refining center. We take raw ore and process it into various minerals of high value. You will be workers in the process. If you work hard, you will live. If you do not complain, you will live. And if you do not attempt escape, you will live.' He stared down the line of weakened men. 'Are there any questions?'

A crewman from the *Adelaide*, one who'd had a difficult time in captivity, cleared his throat. 'When will we be released?' he asked.

Johansson approached the man and smiled at him.

Then he casually pulled his sidearm and shot the man in the forehead. A swarm of nearby jungle birds screeched at the sound as the man tumbled backward, falling into the water dead.

The other assembled captives gaped in stunned silence.

Johansson grinned. 'Are there any more questions?'

Met by barely a heartbeat, he holstered his weapon. 'Good. Again, I welcome you to Puerta del Infierno. Now, let's get to work.'

51

The deep throb of the towboat's engine fell silent, revealing the lesser sound of waves lapping against her hull. Awakened by the absent growl and vibration, Ann arose from her bunk and stretched her arms. She rubbed her wrists, where the handcuffs irritated her skin, and stepped to a tiny porthole on the starboard bulkhead.

It was still dark. Scattered lights dotted the shore a mile or so across the river, indicating they had docked on its eastern bank. The river, she was certain, was the Mississippi. From their starting point in Paducah, there was only one way to go downriver, taking the Ohio to its confluence with the Mississippi near Cairo, Illinois. The night before, she had peered out to see the glowing lights of a large city, wondering if they shined from Memphis. As she watched the silhouette of a large freighter pass upriver, she guessed they were somewhere near New Orleans.

She rinsed her face in a basin and again searched the cramped cabin for a potential weapon. It was a hopeless exercise she had performed at least twenty times before, but at least it kept her mind working. She got only as far as an empty bureau when she heard the lock jiggle and the cabin door open. Pablo stood in the doorway, a bemused look in his eyes and a baseball bat in his hands.

'Come along,' he said, 'we are changing vessels.'

He led her onto the towboat's deck, where he slipped

the bat across her back, wedging it into the crooks of her elbows.

'There will be no swimming exhibition this time.' Keeping one hand firmly grasping the bat, he led her off the towboat.

The contortion made Ann's shoulders ache as they stepped onto a dimly lit dock. Pablo guided her past the barge, where a mobile dock crane had hoisted the flatbed trailer from the deck. Stray wisps of hay fluttered through the air as Pablo and Ann followed the crane, which crept down an embedded rail track toward a small freighter. In the faint light, she could make out the ship's name on the transom. *Salzburg*. Though the dock was deserted save for the crane operator, several armed men wearing fatigues lined the freighter's rail.

'Please let me go,' Ann said with exaggerated fear.

Pablo laughed. 'Not before we make our delivery. Then, perhaps, you can win your freedom,' he added with a leer.

He marched her up the freighter's forward gangway and across the deck. A large rectangular dish mounted to a wheeled platform blocked their path. Next to it, a crewman was checking cables at a control station mounted with power generators and computer displays. As they passed, the man looked up, briefly locking eyes with Ann.

She gave him a submissive look, pleading with her eyes for help.

He smiled as they passed. 'Don't get cooked,' he said.

Pablo pushed Ann ahead, guiding her to the superstructure at the stern and up two flights to the crew's quarters. Her new cabin was slightly larger than the last but featured a similarly minuscule porthole.

'I hope you are pleased with the accommodations,' Pablo said, removing the baseball bat from her arms. 'Perhaps later in the voyage we can spend some time together.' He stepped from the cabin and locked the door from the outside.

Ann sat on the hard bunk and glared at the door. Despite her act with Pablo, most of her fears had been replaced by anger. Clearly the freighter was leaving the country, taking both the *Sea Arrow*'s motor and its plans. She would be trapped in the cabin for days, or even weeks. Rather than lament, she contemplated how it had all been pulled off.

Her analytical mind went to work, stewing over the thefts. Acquiring the *Sea Arrow*'s plans and motor had been all too easy for Pablo. He must have had inside help. The involvement of the two men who had abducted her, and then were killed, indicated as much. And what about her? Why had she been abducted?

She could draw only one conclusion, that she must have been getting close to identifying the source. She racked her brains, reviewing the contractors and persons of interest. She kept returning to Tom Cerny. Could the White House aide have been alerted to her inquiry?

She paced the small cabin, noticing several cigarette burns on the corner desk. The marks made her think of the crewman and his odd greeting.

'Don't get cooked,' she repeated. The words nagged at her until suddenly their meaning struck like a bolt of lightning.

'Of course!' she said, disgusted that it hadn't come to her sooner. 'Don't get cooked indeed.'

52

A late-night commercial flight from Durban via Johannesburg proved the quickest way back to Washington for Dirk and Summer. They were bleary-eyed when they staggered off the plane early the next morning at Reagan National Airport. Remarkably, Summer walked freely through the terminal, showing stiffness from the flight but no lingering paralysis from her decompression sickness.

Timely immersion in the *Alexandria*'s deco chamber had proved her salvation. While the NUMA ship rushed from the tip of Madagascar to Durban, Summer and Dirk had been pressurized to an equivalent depth of four hundred feet. The paralysis in Summer's leg promptly disappeared. The ship's medical team slowly relieved the pressure in the chamber, allowing the nitrogen bubbles in their tissues to dissipate. When they were released from the chamber almost two days later, Summer found she could walk with only a faint lingering ache.

Since flying could aggravate the symptoms, the ship's doctor insisted they not board an airplane for twenty-four hours. Fortunately, their steaming time to Durban occupied the full duration. Free of the chamber, they had time to brief the others on their work in the submersible, inspect its damage, and book their flight home, before racing to Durban's King Shaka International Airport the moment the *Alexandria* touched the dock.

After collecting their bags at Reagan, they took a cab across the tarmac to their father's hangar. Letting themselves in, they stored their bags and cleaned themselves up in the loft apartment.

'You think Dad would mind if we borrowed one of his cars to run to the office?' Summer asked.

'He's always given us a standing offer to drive what we like,' Dirk said. He pointed to a silver-and-burgundy roadster parked near a workbench. 'He said in an e-mail before he left for the Pacific that he just got that Packard running strong. Why don't we take it?'

He checked to see that it had plenty of gas while Summer opened a garage door. Sliding into the driver's seat, he pulled the choke and adjusted the throttle lever mounted on the steering wheel and hit the starter button. The big straight-eight engine murmured to life. Letting it warm up for a moment, he pulled the car outside and waited for Summer to lock the hangar.

She jumped into the passenger seat with a travel bag in tow, not noticing a white van parked across an adjacent field. 'What's with the funky seats?' she asked.

The Packard roadster's tight cockpit held two rigid seats. Summer's passenger seat was permanently offset a few inches farther from the dash than Dirk's driver's seat.

'More room for the driver to turn and shift at high speed,' Dirk explained, pointing to the floor-mounted gear lever.

'I'll gladly take the extra legroom.'

Built in 1930, the Model 734 Packard chassis carried one of the factory's rarest bodies, a sleek boattail speedster. The trunk line tapered to an angular point, giving the car a highly streamlined appearance. Sporting dual side-mounted spare tires, the body gleamed with metallic pewter paint, contrasted by burgundy fenders and a matching body-length stripe. Narrow Woodlite headlights on the prow, combined with an angled windshield, added to the sensation that the car was in motion even while parked.

Dirk drove north onto the George Washington Parkway, finding that the Packard loped along easily with the highway traffic. It was only a ten-minute drive to the NUMA headquarters, a tall glass structure that bordered the Potomac. Dirk parked in the underground garage, and they took an employee elevator to the top floor and Rudi Gunn's office. His secretary directed them to the computer resource center, so they dropped down three flights to the high-tech lair of Hiram Yaeger.

They found Gunn and Yaeger parked in front of a wall-sized video screen, examining satellite photos of an empty sea. With bedraggled hair and circles under their eyes, both looked as if they hadn't slept in days. But the men perked up at the sight of Pitt's children. 'Glad to have you back,' Gunn said. 'You gave us quite a scare when your submersible went missing.'

Summer smiled. 'Us, too.'

'I thought we were going to have to sedate Rudi,' Yaeger said. 'Your leg okay, Summer?'

'Just fine. I think the coach seat from Johannesburg was more painful than the bends.' She eyed a collection of dirty coffee cups on the table before breaking the mood. 'What's the latest on Dad and Al?'

Both men turned grim. 'Unfortunately, there's not

much to report,' Gunn said. He described Pitt's mission of protecting the ore carrier, while Yaeger dialed up a map of the eastern Pacific.

'They boarded the *Adelaide* about a thousand miles southeast of Hawaii,' Yaeger said. 'A Navy frigate on exercise out of San Diego was scheduled to meet them when they neared the coast and escort them to Long Beach. The *Adelaide* never appeared.'

'Any sign of debris?' Dirk asked.

'No,' Gunn said. 'We've had search-and-rescue craft from Hawaii and the mainland overflying the area for days. The Navy has dispatched two vessels to the scene, and the Air Force has even sent in some long-range reconnaissance drones. They've all come up empty.'

Dirk noted a white horizontal line beginning at the left edge of the screen that ended when it intersected a red line from Hawaii. 'Is that the *Adelaide*'s track?'

'Her AIS beacon provided her track to that point shortly after your dad and the SWAT team went aboard,' Yaeger said. 'After that, the AIS signal went dead.'

'So she sank?' Summer asked, her voice breaking.

'Not necessarily,' Gunn said. 'She could have simply disengaged the tracking system, which would be an obvious move after a hijacking.'

'We've drawn a couple of big circles around her last reported position to see where she could have gone.' Yaeger replaced the ocean map with a split screen of two satellite ocean photos. At the bottom was overlaid a stock photo of a large green bulk carrier labeled *Adelaide*. 'We're looking at coastal satellite photos to see if she might have popped up somewhere.'

'Hiram has accessed every public and not-so-public source of satellite reconnaissance. Unfortunately, the point of disappearance is smack in the middle of a large dead zone in satellite coverage, so we're jumping to the coastlines.'

'North, South, and Central America, for starters.' Yaeger stifled a yawn. 'Should keep us busy till Christmas.'

'How can we help?' Summer asked.

'We've got satellite images for most of the major West Coast ports from the past four days. I'll divvy them up and see if anyone can spot a ship resembling the *Adelaide*.'

Yaeger set up two laptops and downloaded the images. Everyone went to work, scouring the photos for a large green cargo ship. They worked all through the day, studying image after image, until their eyes burned. Yet hopes were raised as they pegged eleven ships from the sometimes fuzzy and obscured photos that appeared to fit the *Adelaide*'s profile.

'Three in Long Beach, two in Manzanillo, four to the Panama Canal, and one each to San Antonio, Chile, and Puerto Caldera, Costa Rica,' Yaeger said.

'I can't imagine any of the Long Beach vessels would be ours,' Dirk said, 'unless they ran to another port to off-load first.'

Gunn looked at his watch. 'It's still early out west. How about we break for dinner? When we reconvene, we can begin calling the port authorities at each location. They should be able to confirm if the *Adelaide* cleared their local facilities.'

'Good thought,' Dirk said, standing and stretching. 'I've run out of gas on a diet of airline food and coffee.'

'Just a second,' Summer said. 'Before we break, I need a quick favor from Hiram, and then I'll need your help in making a delivery.' She picked up her travel pack, which clinked with the sound of bottles inside.

'I'm pretty hungry. Can we grab a bite on the way?'

'Where we're headed,' she said, 'I can positively guarantee there will be something good to eat.'

53

The Packard roared out of the parking garage and skirted past a white van at the edge of the outside lot before merging into the evening rush-hour traffic. Dirk crossed into Georgetown as an evening breeze tousled Summer's hair in the open car. Turning down a shady residential street filled with elegant homes, Dirk stopped in front of a former carriage house that ages ago had been transformed into a courtly freestanding residence.

They had barely rung the bell when the front door was thrown open by a gargantuan man sporting an overflowing gray beard. St Julien Perlmutter's eyes twinkled as he greeted Dirk and Summer and invited them inside.

'I nearly ate without you,' he said.

'You were expecting us?' Dirk asked.

'Of course. Summer e-mailed me with the particulars of your Madagascar mystery. I insisted you both come by for dinner the instant you returned. Don't you two talk to each other?'

Summer smiled sheepishly at her brother, then followed Perlmutter through a book-infested living room and into a formal dining area, where an antique cherrywood table sat overloaded with food. Perlmutter was a marine historian, one of the best on the planet, but he had a second love as a gourmand. His eyes lit up when Summer opened her bag and offered him three bottles of wine from South Africa.

'A Vergelegen Chardonnay and a pair of red varietals from De Toren.' He examined the labels with delight. 'Outstanding selections. Shall we?'

He wasted no time in finding a corkscrew and pouring the Chardonnay.

'I am, of course, distressed to hear of your father's absence. May he be in safe port,' he said, raising his glass.

While discussing Pitt's disappearance, they dined on pork loin in chipotle sauce, fingerling potatoes, and baked asparagus. Fresh Georgia peaches in a cream-and-brandy sauce were devoured for dessert. The host's French cook and housekeeper had the night off, so Summer and Dirk helped Perlmutter clear the table and wash the dishes before sitting back down at the table.

'The wine was delicious, Summer, but don't toy with me,' Perlmutter said. 'You know what I really want to get my hands on.'

'I thought you'd never ask.' She opened her travel bag and pulled out the carefully wrapped journal from the beached life raft. 'The log of the *Barbarigo*,' she said.

'So that's what this is all about,' Dirk said. 'And here I thought you were just happy to see us.'

Perlmutter laughed with a roar that echoed through the house. A longtime friend of their father, he had readily taken to Pitt's twin children as a sort of kindly uncle.

'My boy, your company is welcome anytime.' He opened and poured another of Summer's bottles. 'But a good nautical mystery is sweeter than wine.'

Perlmutter took the package and carefully unwrapped its oilskin covering. The leather-bound journal showed signs of wear, but was otherwise undamaged. He gently opened the cover and read the title page, written by hand in bold lettering.

'*Viaggio di Sommergibile* Barbarigo, *Giugno 1943. Capitano di corvetta Umberto de Julio.*' Perlmutter looked up at Summer and smiled. 'That's our submarine.'

'Submarine?' Dirk asked.

'The raft on the beach,' Summer said. 'It contained the remains of crewmen from a World War Two Italian submarine.'

'The *Barbarigo*, a large boat of the Marcello class,' Perlmutter said. 'She had an illustrious record in the Atlantic early in the war, sinking six vessels and downing an aircraft. But she lost her teeth in 1943 when she was assigned to a project with the code name of Aquila.'

'Latin for "eagle",' Dirk said.

Summer gave her brother a suspicious look.

'Astronomy,' he explained. 'I remember it from a constellation near Aquarius.'

'Mule would have been a more befitting name,' Perlmutter said. 'The Germans were concerned over their high loss of surface ships while trading war materials with Japan, so they convinced the Italians to convert eight of their largest, and somewhat outdated, submarines to transport duty. The interiors were gutted and most of their armaments removed so they could carry a maximum amount of cargo.'

'Sounds like dangerous duty,' Dirk said.

'It was. Four of the vessels were sunk outright, one was scuttled, and the other three captured in Asia before completing a round-trip. Or at least that's what the history books say.' Perlmutter began scanning the pages, examining the dates.

'So what happened to the *Barbarigo*?' Summer asked.

'Designated Aquila Five, she departed Bordeaux on June 16, 1943, bound for Singapore with a cargo of mercury, steel, and aluminum bars. Radio contact was lost a few days later, and it was presumed she was sunk somewhere near the Azores.'

He skipped ahead to the last page. 'My Italian is deplorable, but I read the last entry as November 12, 1943.'

'Nearly five months later,' Dirk said. 'Something doesn't figure.'

'I have the answer, I hope, right here.' Summer pulled out a sheaf of printed pages. 'I had Hiram scan the logbook into his computer system. He claimed it was child's play to translate it into English and gave me the output right before we left.'

She began passing the pages around the table, letting Dirk and Perlmutter devour them like a pair of hungry coyotes.

'Here we go,' Dirk said. 'It says here that they were spotted and attacked by two aircraft in the Bay of Biscayne shortly after leaving port but safely eluded them. Their radio mast was damaged, which prevented them from communicating with central command.'

Via the journal, they followed the *Barbarigo*'s voyage around the Cape of Good Hope and across the Indian Ocean. The submarine off-loaded its cargo in Singapore and then was diverted to a small Malaysian port near Kuala Lumpur.

'"On 23 September, we took on 130 tons of oxidized ore called Red Death by the locals,"' Summer read. '"A German scientist named Steiner oversaw the loading and joined the crew for the return voyage."'

'The first officer later wrote that Steiner stayed holed up in his cabin with a stack of physics books for the rest of the trip,' Dirk said.

'Red Death?' Perlmutter said. 'I wonder if it is something like Edgar Allan Poe's plague of the same name. I'll have to take a look at that – and this fellow Steiner. Certainly a curious cargo.'

The trio flipped through several weeks of entries describing the submarine's return across the Indian Ocean. On the ninth of November, the handwriting turned hurried, and the pages showed saltwater stains.

'This is where they got into trouble, while off the coast of South Africa,' Perlmutter said. He read aloud a terse description of the *Barbarigo* diving to avoid a nighttime air attack. After eluding several bombing runs, the crew believed they had escaped the attack – only to discover that the sub's propeller had been disabled or blown off entirely.

Dirk and Summer sat silently as Perlmutter read of the resulting tragedy. With no propulsion, the sub remained submerged for twelve hours, fearing that additional aircraft had been called to the scene. Surfacing at midday, they found themselves in an empty sea, drifting to the southeast. Carried past the shipping lanes and without a long-range radio, the officers feared they might drift to their deaths in the Antarctica. Captain De Julio ordered the crew to abandon ship, and they took to the four life rafts stowed beneath the forward deck, saluting their beloved vessel as they left her side. In a mix-up of orders, the last officer off failed to prime the scuttle charges and sealed the main hatch. Rather than sinking before them, the *Barbarigo* drifted off toward the horizon.

Perlmutter stopped reading and raised his eyebrows like a pair of drawbridges. 'My word,' he said quietly. 'That is most curious.'

'What happened to the other three boats?' Summer asked.

'The log entries become spottier at this point,' Perlmutter said. 'They attempted to reach South Africa and were within sight of land when a storm struck. The boats were dispersed in the rough seas, and Captain De Julio said the men in his boat never again saw the other three. During the ordeal they lost five men, all their food and water, and their sail and oars. The raft was carried east, drifting away from shore with the coastal current. Eventually the weather turned hot and dry. With no fresh water, they lost two more crewmen, leaving only the captain, the first officer, and two engineers.

'Ravaged by thirst, they eventually spotted land again and were able to paddle closer. High winds and huge swells carried them ashore and tossed them onto the beach,' Perlmutter said. 'They found themselves in a hot desert, desperate for water. The last entry states the captain went off alone in search of water, as the others were too weak to walk. The journal ends, "God bless the *Barbarigo* and her crew."'

'We can attest to the barrenness of the region,' Summer said after a time. 'What a tragedy that they nearly made it safely to South Africa and ended up a thousand miles away in Madagascar.'

'They fared slightly better than the crewmen in the other three boats,' Dirk said.

Perlmutter nodded, though he appeared lost in thought.

He rose from his seat and padded into the living room, then returned a few minutes later with an armful of books and an inquisitive look. 'Congratulations, Summer. It would appear as if you have solved two enduring mysteries of the sea.'

'Two?' she asked.

'Yes, the fate of the *Barbarigo* and the identity of the South Atlantic Wraith.'

'I'll buy the former,' Dirk said, 'but what's this Wraith?'

Perlmutter opened the first book and flipped through its pages. 'From the logbook of the merchant ship *Manchester*, off the Falkland Islands, February 14, 1946. "Light seas, winds out of the southwest three or four. At 1100, the first officer reported an object off our starboard beam. Appeared at first to be a whale carcass, but believe it is a man-made vessel."'

He closed the book and opened another. 'The freighter *Southern Star*, April 3, 1948, near Santa Cruz, Argentina. "Unknown object, possible sailing vessel, spotted adrift two miles distant. Black hull, small superstructure amidships. Appears abandoned."'

Perlmutter picked up a third book. 'Accounts of a South Georgia Whaling Station. In February of 1951, the whaler *Paulita* arrived with a kill of three mature gray whales. Captain reports spotting a ghost ship, low black hull, small sail amidships, drifting one hundred miles north. Crew called it the South Atlantic Wraith.'

'You think the *Barbarigo* is this Atlantic Wraith?' Summer asked.

'It's entirely possible. For a period of twenty-two years, there were sightings of a supposed ghost ship adrift in the

South Atlantic. For one reason or another, no one seemed to get a close view, but the descriptions are all similar. It seems to me that a bottled-up submarine could drift about an empty sea for quite a while.'

'At those southerly latitudes, the sub's conning tower could easily ice over,' Dirk said, 'so from a distance it resembled a sail.'

'That might be confirmed in the last recorded sighting.' Perlmutter opened the final book. 'It was in 1964. An endurance sailor named Leigh Hunt was making a solo round-the-world voyage when he saw something unusual. Ah, here it is,' he said, and began reading aloud the passage,

'"While approaching the Magellan Straits, I encountered a horrific storm, brutal even for these waters. For thirty hours, I battled twenty-foot seas and raging winds that tried with all their fury to drive me onto the rocks around Cape Horn. It was in the midst of this duel that I caught glimpse of the South Atlantic Wraith. I thought it a berg at first, for it was encrusted in ice, but I could see the dark, sharp edges of steel beneath. She washed by me quickly, carried with the winds and waves, toward a sure death on the shores of Tierra del Fuego."'

'Wow,' Summer said, 'still afloat in 1964.'

'But apparently not for long, if Hunt's account is accurate,' Perlmutter said.

'Is Hunt still alive?' she asked. 'Perhaps we could talk to him.'

'I'm afraid he was lost at sea a few years ago. But his family might still possess his logbooks.'

Dirk finished his glass of wine and looked at his sister.

'Well, Summer, I guess you are still leaving us with two enduring mysteries to solve.'

'Yes,' Summer said, finishing his thought. 'Where the *Barbarigo* sank and what she was carrying.'

54

Dirk and Summer left Perlmutter's house satiated with good food and wine and piqued by the *Barbarigo*'s strange fate. The dinner had been a welcome respite from their worries about their father, which returned the minute they said their good-byes.

'We best get back and see if Rudi and Hiram have had any luck with the port authorities,' Dirk said.

'I've been thinking we should re-examine the possibility that the *Adelaide* traveled west.'

As they walked to the street, they heard a car door shut, and Dirk noticed two men sitting in a white van a few spaces behind the Packard. Dirk fired up the Packard with the first press of the starter and flipped on the headlamps. While the Woodlites looked great by daylight, their night-time performance didn't match the rest of the car. Easing away from the curb, he drove slowly down the street, watching in the rearview mirror as the van's lights flicked on when they reached the end of the street.

Dirk turned right and mashed down the accelerator, speeding down a tree-lined street. A few seconds later, the van screeched around the same corner.

Summer noticed Dirk's focus on the mirror and glanced over her shoulder. 'I don't want to sound paranoid,' she said, 'but that same van may have been parked in the NUMA lot when we left the building.'

'One better,' Dirk said. 'I think it was also parked next to Dad's hangar this morning.' He meandered through the wealthy Georgetown neighborhood, turning down O Street and heading west. The van followed his every move, staying a dozen lengths behind.

'Who would be following us?' Summer asked. 'Someone related to the people in Madagascar?'

'I can't imagine. It might be someone interested in Dad. Maybe we should just ask them?'

He slowed the car as they approached a cross street. Just beyond was a pillared and gated pedestrian entrance to Georgetown University. Portable barricades were normally in place to prevent vehicles from entering the gateway, but they had been removed for a delivery truck exiting the campus. As the truck pulled clear, Dirk hit the gas and skirted around it through the open gate.

A security guard gaped as the antique Packard zipped by. A few seconds later, he had to jump back as the white van barreled through in pursuit. Dirk followed the road across the grounds a short distance to a circular drive. A statue of the university's founder, John Carroll, sat at its center, facing the entrance gate. Footlights illumined the statue in a yellow haze, lending a lifelike aura to the long-dead bishop.

Dirk wheeled the Packard around the back of the statue and slowed, double-clutching and dropping into first gear. He watched for the lights of the van as it hurried onto campus and turned onto the circular drive. Dirk turned off the Packard's Woodlites and gunned the engine. The old car leaped forward as he turned the wheel hard, shifting into second while keeping the accelerator pinned to the floorboard.

While the van was slowing, the roadster shot around the circle. Rather than exit back toward the gate, Dirk held the wheel tight, curving around the loop. The van's tail-lights appeared in front of them, and Dirk had to brake to avoid rear-ending it. Summer reached over and turned the Woodlites back on, signaling to the pursuers that the game was up.

The van's driver hesitated, unsure what had happened until he recognized the pale yellow beams of the Packard behind him. Not prepared for a confrontation, he stomped on the gas. The van's tires chirped as it shot forward, turning off the circular drive. He took the first road he could, a straight lane that ran behind a stately structure called Healy Hall and into the center of campus.

'Go after him,' Summer said. 'I didn't get his plate number.'

Dirk shoved the Packard into gear and took off. A fast car in its day, the Packard was powered by a straight-eight engine that boasted 150 horsepower. The van might have left the old car behind on an open highway but not in the tight confines of the college campus.

The van sped past the large stone building. Only a few students were about, and those in the street quickly cleared way for the speeding van. The lane abruptly turned left into a side building complex, but it was blocked by a campus policeman in a patrol car who had stopped to chat with a student.

Unable to turn, the van's driver continued straight, bounding up and onto a concrete walkway that bisected a grass courtyard. A girl on a bicycle screamed as she narrowly missed getting flattened. The Packard followed a few yards behind, inciting an eruption of flashing lights from the patrol car.

'I think we're out of danger and into trouble,' Summer said, noting the lights behind.

Dirk tightened his grip on the wheel as the roadster bounded over the uneven surface. He followed the van along the walkway until it dropped off a curb into the parking lot of a student dormitory. Just ahead, two freshmen were smuggling a beer keg into the building when the van charged at them. The students dove for safety as the van sped by, just clipping the keg.

The aluminum keg skittered across the parking lot and bounced off a retaining wall. A short distance behind, Dirk braked hard but couldn't avoid the keg. The front bumper caught it first, gouging a hole in the aluminum before the right fender knocked the keg aside. The shaken beer exploded in a foamy fountain that doused the side of the car – and Summer inside.

'Dad's not going to like that,' Dirk said.

She wiped the suds from her face. 'You're right, he won't. It's light beer.'

The van and the Packard accelerated through the parking lot, pushed faster by the pursuing patrol car. The van skidded out of the parking lot and onto a cross street. Unable to decide which way to turn, the driver went straight, bouncing onto a sloping gravel road that stretched ahead. The road dipped down a small hill and turned onto the university's football field. In the middle of a practice, the men's lacrosse team was forced to scatter as the van bounded across the artificial turf.

Seeing the old Packard and the police in pursuit, several

players fired lacrosse balls at the van, ringing its side with dents. A few took aim at the Packard until they were disarmed by a wave and smile from the beer-drenched Summer.

The van opened a sizable gap on the Packard as it sped off the opposite side of the field and passed through an open gate. The driver turned left on the facing street, following a sign that directed them toward the university's exit on Canal Road. 'C'mon, we can lose them,' the van's passenger said.

Fifty yards behind, Dirk heard a similar appeal from Summer. 'Don't lose them, I still haven't gotten the full plate number.'

Dirk turned onto the road in pursuit, but had to slow for a trio of coeds crossing the street to a tennis court. Behind him, the campus police had nearly caught up.

The road curved past another residence hall before descending a landscaped hill out of campus. Dirk saw the van accelerate sharply down the hill and he tried to keep pace. At the bottom of the hill, a stoplight marked the intersection with Canal Road, a busy thoroughfare that fed into suburban Maryland.

The light was green, and Dirk feared it would change before he drew close. Then it flashed to yellow, and he knew the van would have to stop.

Only it didn't.

With the van's passenger urging him on, the driver floored the gas when the light turned yellow. The van was still fifty feet from the intersection when the light turned red. Remarkably, the stopped cross traffic hesitated, perhaps detecting the bouncing rays of the van's headlights as it roared down the hill.

Charging into the intersection at better than seventy miles an hour, the van crossed the near lanes of traffic and attempted to turn left into the far lanes. But its speed was far too great, and the panicked driver slammed on the brakes, sending the van into a skid. It slid across the asphalt until its right front tire kissed the curb. The tire burst, but the van kept moving, hopping the curb and plowing into a low retaining wall, the front fender buckling as the rear wheels bounded into and over the curb. The combined forces flipped the van onto its side atop the retaining wall. It slid a few feet, then tumbled over the wall, splashing roof first into the road's namesake, the Chesapeake and Ohio Canal, flowing just beyond.

Dirk skidded the Packard to a halt before the stoplight and raced across the street, with Summer running a step behind. They reached the retaining wall and peered over. The canal had swallowed most of the van, leaving only a portion of its still-spinning tires protruding. A dull glow brightened the murky water at one end, where the van's headlights had yet to short out.

Dirk slipped off his jacket and kicked off his shoes. 'I'll try and get them out,' he said. 'See if you can get the campus police to help.'

He jumped into the canal and swam to the van, diving along the passenger door. The glowing headlights turned the water's visibility from zero to next to nothing, and he had to find the open window frame by touch. The frame height was barely a foot high, telling him the roof had collapsed at impact. It didn't bode well for the occupants.

Reaching inside the open window, he felt a lifeless body

strapped in the seat. Groping blindly, he found the buckle release and freed the seat belt. The body dropped loosely, and he pulled on the victim's shoulders, dragging him through the narrow window.

Dirk shot to the surface, gasping for air, as he pulled the head and torso free of the water. A bright flashlight beam, aimed by the campus policeman, shined on the victim, and Dirk knew he had wasted his time. The passenger's head tilted at a grotesque angle, his neck broken.

Dirk pulled the body to the bank and called up to the policeman. 'Give me your light.'

He passed Dirk the light as he reached out to help pull the body ashore. Dirk swam to the van's other side and dove once more. With the flashlight, he could now see the driver was also dead, his torso pinned between the crushed roof and the steering wheel. Unlike his partner, he hadn't been wearing a seat belt.

Though running short of breath, Dirk shined the light past the driver and into the rear compartment. A row of electronic processing devices was mounted on a shelf. Sitting nearby was a large acrylic parabolic dish used for eavesdropping.

Pushing off from the door, he swam to the back of the van and checked its license plate before popping to the surface. He stroked to the bank, where Summer helped him up the incline.

'No luck with the other one?'

'No, he's dead, too.'

'I've got paramedics on the way,' the policeman said. His inexperience with fatalities was betrayed by a pale face. He regained his composure but spoke with a forced tone of authority. 'Who are those people? And why were you chasing them?'

'I don't know who they are, but they stole something from us.'

'They get your money? Or was it jewelry or electronics?'

'No,' Dirk replied, looking at the dead man. 'It was our words.'

55

It was after midnight when Dirk and Summer staggered back into the NUMA computer center. Gunn and Yaeger were still examining images on the large viewing screen.

'I didn't realize you were taking time for a seven-course meal,' Gunn said. Then he noticed their appearance. Dirk's hair was disheveled and his clothes damp, while Summer's outfit sported a large stain, and she reeked of stale beer. 'What on earth happened to you two?'

Summer related the series of events, including a two-hour interrogation by the District of Columbia police.

'Any idea who would have tailed you?' Yaeger asked.

'None,' Dirk said. 'I suspect it may have something to do with Dad.'

'Could be,' Gunn said, 'especially if they saw you leave his hangar this morning. From a distance, there is a strong resemblance between the two of you.'

Summer handed Yaeger a slip of paper. 'Here's the van's license number. The police wouldn't tell us, but maybe you can identify the owner.'

'With ease,' Yaeger said.

'How're things progressing with the *Adelaide*?' Dirk asked.

'Not well,' Gunn said. 'We've been in contact with every major port authority along the coast of North, South, and Central America. No one has a record of the *Adelaide* making an appearance in the past week.'

'Guess that leaves two options,' Dirk said. 'They either off-loaded at a private facility or they headed in another direction.' He neglected to mention a third option, that the ship had sunk.

'We've been talking about those scenarios,' Yaeger said, 'and we don't believe they headed west. First, it doesn't make a lot of sense to hijack a ship out of Australia in the eastern Pacific if you plan to take the cargo someplace in the western Pacific. The second problem is fuel. Fully loaded, the *Adelaide* would be stretching it to make a double crossing of the Pacific without refueling.'

'Makes sense. That only leaves about a thousand other places she could have ducked into along the coast.'

Gunn and Yaeger nodded. They were searching for a transparent needle in a very large haystack. Gunn described the details of their port searches and the latest surveillance images while Yaeger grabbed the keyboard and began typing. A few minutes later, he called to the others.

'Got something on your van,' he said, as a Virginia Department of Motor Vehicles registration form appeared on the screen. 'The owner is SecureTek of Tysons Corner, Virginia.'

Yaeger brought up another site on his screen. 'The state corporate commission describes their business as providing data encryption links for closed network computer systems. They have eight employees, and their primary customer is the US government.'

'Doesn't sound like the type of security company that would be eavesdropping on people,' Summer said.

'Unless,' Dirk said, 'their declared business is a front.'

'It doesn't appear to be,' Yaeger said after some additional research. 'They have a number of valid contracts with the Army and Navy for data line installations.'

Returning to the corporate commission's site, he noted that SecureTek was a wholly owned subsidiary of Habsburg Industries. 'It's a privately held firm, so information is rather limited, but they're based in Panama and have interests in mining and shipping.'

Yaeger performed several searches but found only brief mention of the firm. A shipping periodical displayed a photo of one of the firm's bulk carriers, the *Graz*, dockside in Singapore.

Dirk glanced at the photo and sat up in his chair. 'Hiram, can you enlarge that photo?'

Yaeger nodded, blowing up the image until it filled the entire screen.

'What is it?' Summer asked.

'The logo on the funnel.'

Everyone peered at the image of a white flower centered on the ship's squat gold funnel.

'I think that's an edelweiss,' Summer said. 'In keeping with the ship's Austrian name, I imagine.'

'I saw that same flower on the freighter docked in Madagascar,' Dirk said.

The computer room fell silent. Then Gunn asked, 'Hiram, can you determine what kind of mining this Habsburg Industries is actually involved in?'

'They operate a small gold mine in Panama near the Colombian border. The firm also has an active brokerage business in specialty ores, including samarium, lanthanum, and dysprosium.'

'Rare earth elements?' Summer asked.

Gunn nodded. 'Rare earth elements. Habsburg Industries suddenly looks very interesting.'

'I'd wager the operation in Madagascar was stealing rare earth minerals,' Dirk said. 'The reason they attacked our submersible was because we were working around the spot where they sank a hijacked ore ship.'

'We found a pristine wreck in the area that had recently been sunk,' Summer said. 'There was no apparent damage, and the ship's name was intentionally obscured.'

'Jack Dahlgren did some digging and thinks it was a bulk carrier called the *Norseman*,' Dirk said. 'She was lost in the Indian Ocean four months ago, carrying bastnasite ore from Malaysia. In case you hadn't guessed, bastnasite contains rare earth elements.'

'Could the Habsburg ship in Madagascar have been hijacked, too?' Summer asked.

Yaeger checked the Panamanian ship registry. 'Habsburg owns four ships, all dry bulk carriers, named *Graz*, *Innsbruck*, *Linz*, and *Salzburg*.'

'What's the Austrian connection?' Dirk asked.

'The company is owned by Edward Bolcke, a mining engineer originally from Austria,' Yaeger said. 'I can't find mention of any of the four ships reported missing.'

'Then that makes Habsburg a likely suspect in the disappearance of the *Adelaide*,' Summer said.

'The key,' Gunn said, 'will be their four ships.'

Yaeger flexed his fingers over the keyboard. 'Let's see what we can find.'

Summer found coffee for everyone while Yaeger taxed his mainframe's circuitry, pursuing inquiries on the four ships and their recent whereabouts. It took the better part of an hour before he could narrow their locations. He displayed a map of the world on which a multitude of colored dots shone, signifying the ships' recent ports of call.

'The blue lights represent the *Graz*,' Yaeger said. 'She is currently believed to be in or about Malaysia. Over the last three weeks, she was seen in Tianjin, Shanghai, and Hong Kong.'

'So she's not in play,' Gunn said.

'The yellow lights represent the *Innsbruck*. She made a transit through the Panama Canal three weeks ago and was seen in Cape Town, South Africa, eight days ago.'

'Dollars to donuts, that's the ship I saw in Madagascar,' Dirk said.

'Likely so. That leaves the *Linz* and *Salzburg*. The *Linz* was reported in a Jakarta dry dock ten days ago, and is believed to still be there for repairs.'

'So the green lights are the *Salzburg*?' Summer asked.

'Yes. She appeared in Manila a month ago, then in the Panama Canal, making a northerly crossing, four days ago. Homeland Security port surveillance indicates she was docked in New Orleans just yesterday.'

Yaeger drew a line on the map across the Pacific from Manila to Panama. Then he inserted a red triangle at a spot in the eastern part of the ocean. 'The red mark is our last known position of the *Adelaide*, about six days ago.'

The track of the *Salzburg* passed within two hundred miles of the *Adelaide*'s mark.

'Wouldn't have needed much of a course deviation to cross paths,' Dirk said.

'The timing is about right,' Gunn said. 'The *Salzburg*

would have been in that area five or six days before reaching the canal, which is when the *Adelaide* went quiet.'

Yaeger returned to an earlier database. 'Panama Canal Authority records show she made the transit last Friday, entering the Pacific locks at three in the afternoon. I might be able to find archival video of her.'

A few minutes later, he projected a clip from one of the locks. It showed, in grainy black-and-white footage, a midsized freighter waiting for the lock to flood. An edelweiss flower clearly showed on its funnel.

Dirk looked at the image with a sense of hope. 'Look at her Plimsoll mark. She's riding high in the water. Her holds must be empty.'

'You're right,' Gunn said. 'If she hijacked the *Adelaide*, she didn't transfer the cargo aboard.'

Yaeger pulled up a profile of the *Salzburg*. 'The *Adelaide* is a hundred feet longer. They'd have to leave a large chunk of her cargo behind if they ransacked and sank her.'

'The rare earth ore she was carrying was too valuable for that,' Gunn said. 'No, she must still be afloat. I'm starting to believe she was taken to a place where her cargo could be off-loaded.'

'But where?' Summer asked. 'You checked all the major ports.'

'She could easily slip into a private facility without our knowledge.'

'There's another possibility,' Dirk said, rising from his chair. 'The wreck we ran across in Madagascar, the *Norseman*. She had had her identity scrubbed from the hull. What if they did the same with the *Adelaide*, only they passed her off for another vessel?'

Yaeger and Gunn both nodded, and Dirk began gathering up his things. When he began moving toward the door, Summer called out to him. 'Where do you think you're going?'

'Panama. And you're coming with me.'

'Panama?'

'Sure. If the *Salzburg* is behind the *Adelaide*'s disappearance, then someone at Habsburg Industries has to know something about it.'

'Maybe, but we don't know anything about Habsburg Industries or even where they're located.'

'That's true,' Dirk replied, shooting Gunn and Yaeger an expectant look. 'But we will by the time we get there.'

56

The bullwhip cracked, and every man within earshot flinched, fearing the lick of its knotted tip. Occasionally Johansson would show compassion and simply snap it in the air for effect. But most of the time he directed the whip to the bare skin of a forced laborer, eliciting an agonized cry.

There were nearly seventy of them, slaves culled from the hijacked ships carrying rare earth. Now they were the ones carrying the rare earth, hauling the stolen ore to various extraction centers hidden in the jungle. Weakened by a regimen of hard labor and a subsistence diet, the men were quickly reduced to haggard zombies. The arriving captives from the *Adelaide* were shocked at the sight of them, in their ragged, soiled clothes, staring impassively at the new arrivals.

Pitt and Giordino took one look at the men and knew there would be no benefit in delaying an escape.

'I'm not impressed by the long-term medical coverage offered here,' Giordino muttered as they were divided into work teams to off-load the *Adelaide*'s cargo.

'I agree,' Pitt said. 'I think we should look for employment elsewhere.'

'What's with the dog collars?'

Pitt had also seen that the laborers all wore tubular steel collars. The men wearing them carefully heeded the edge of the dock, not venturing beyond their immediate work area.

Johansson cracked his whip, and the *Adelaide* captives were marched into a clearing. A table was set up with a box containing the collars, and one by one the men were fitted with the devices, which were locked with a key. Giordino's bull-sized neck barely accommodated his collar, which clung tightly to his skin.

'Do we get a cattle brand, too?' he asked of the armed man fitting the device. His reply was a cold sneer.

When all the men had been fitted, Johansson paced in front of them.

'In case you are wondering, the neck bands you are wearing are a protective device. They protect from escape.' He gave a malicious smile. 'If you look to the dock, you will see a pair of white lines on the ground.'

Pitt saw two parallel faded lines, painted several feet apart. The lines looped away from the dock and disappeared into the jungle.

'The white lines encircle a five-acre area, encompassing the ore depot, the millhouse, and your living quarters. It is your little island of life. Beneath the lines are electrified cables that will emit a fifty-thousand-volt shock to your steel collars should you attempt to cross them. In other words, you will die. Would you like a demonstration?'

The men stood silent, not wishing to witness another sacrifice.

Johansson laughed. 'I'm glad that we understand each other. Now, it is time to get to work.'

Gomez's crew from the ship deployed the dock conveyor to the *Adelaide*'s first hold and began off-loading the crushed monazite. The ore was dumped onto a concrete pad inside the white lines, where it quickly grew to a small mountain. Shovels and rubber-tired ore carts were delivered by a weary group of captives and the new slaves went to work. Plugrad and his Coast Guard team were assigned as shovelers while Pitt, Giordino, and the others were given the less arduous task of pushing the loaded carts to the nearby millhouse and unloading them.

The equatorial heat and humidity quickly took a toll on the men, wringing the strength out of them. Pitt and Giordino worked as slowly as they could, trying to conserve energy, while sweat dripped down their faces. But always they heard the sound of the bullwhip, keeping the pace moving.

The loaded carts were difficult to push for Giordino with his injured leg. He moved unsteadily, shoving his cart with short hops. Pitt was following close behind when Johansson stepped out of the jungle. His whip cracked a second later, the leather tip striking Giordino on the forearm. Despite the eruption of a red welt, Giordino reacted as if a gnat had landed on him, turning to Johansson with an ungracious smile.

'Why is your cart only half full?' the Swede shouted as a pair of guards rushed to his side.

Pitt could see the look in Giordino's eyes and knew his friend was ready to pounce. The two guards would make it a hopeless act. Pitt shoved his cart forward, bumping into Giordino as a signal to stay calm. Giordino turned to Johansson and exposed the bloody bandage on his thigh.

'Playing on an injury?' Johansson said. 'Fill the cart full

next time or I'll do the same to your other leg.' He turned to Pitt and let his bullwhip fly. 'That goes for you, too.'

The lash snapped against Pitt's leg. Like Giordino, he ignored the stinging pain and stared at Johansson with malice. Giordino nudged him this time, and the two men moved off with their carts while Johansson turned his attention to the next group of laborers.

'Woe is me and my goldbricking ways,' Giordino said under his breath.

'I've got some ideas on what I'd like to do with that bullwhip,' Pitt said.

'You and me both, brother.'

They dumped their carts at the side of the millhouse and made their way back to the dock, trying to survey the camp's layout. Four long, low-roofed buildings off the back of the millhouse contained the extraction and separation operations. Beyond them, faintly visible through the brush, a two-story building housed the living quarters for the guards and facility workers. The captives' housing was located on the opposite end of the millhouse. It was an open-walled structure, with a dining area at one end, surrounded by a ten-foot-high wall capped with barbed wire. Hidden farther into the jungle, and well beyond the white lines, a small power-generating station provided electricity for the compound.

The captives worked until dusk, by which time they were ready to collapse. As he returned his empty ore cart, Pitt heard a sharp cry from the dock. One of Plugrad's men had tripped while storing a shovel and had fallen close to the white line. A surge of high voltage had coursed through his body before he could roll clear. He trembled as his heart pounded wildly, but he survived the shock as a living warning to the others.

Pitt and Giordino shuffled into the camp mess area as it began to rain, the palm-covered roof leaking everywhere. They were given bread and watery soup, which they took to a nearby table. Two emaciated men joined them.

'Name's Maguire, and my friend's Brown,' one said in a Kiwi accent. He was a dusty-haired figure with a stringy beard. 'Formerly of the *Gretchen*. You just get off the *Labrador*?'

'Yes. She was called the *Adelaide* when we went aboard.' Pitt introduced himself and Giordino.

'First time I've seen a hijacked ship here,' Maguire said. 'They usually steal the cargo at sea and scuttle the ship. That's what they did to the *Gretchen*, right off Tahiti. Zapped us with their microwave device and took control before we knew what hit us.'

'Was it mounted on a big square dish?' Pitt asked.

'Yes. Know what it is?'

'We think it's an offshoot of an Army crowd-control device called the Active Denial System or ADS.'

'It's bloody nasty, whatever you call it.'

'How long have you been here?' Giordino asked.

'About two months. You're the second crew I've seen come in. Our numbers have been down as the attrition rate's a little high,' he said in a low voice. 'Just drink plenty of water and you'll be okay. At least they don't short us that.' He swabbed up the remains of his soup with a hard crust of bread.

'Pardon the ignorance,' Pitt said, 'but where exactly are we?'

Maguire laughed. 'Always the first question. You're in the hot, rainy, wretched jungles of Panama. Exactly where in Panama, I can't say.'

'Maguire here has befriended one of the guards,' Brown said. 'They apparently take periodic leave by boat in Colón, so we must be near the Atlantic side.'

Maguire nodded. 'Some of the boys think we're in the Canal Zone, but it's hard to know for sure as we never get off our little five-acre island of joy. The boss comes and goes by helicopter, so true civilization must be a bit farther away.'

'Anybody ever make it out of here?' Giordino asked. 'Seems like the prisoners heavily outnumber the guards.'

Both men shook their heads. 'Seen a few try,' Brown said. 'Even if you get past the death stripes, they'll come after you with the dogs.' He noted the welt on Giordino's arm. 'You get kissed by Johnny the Whip today?'

'Something more than a peck,' Giordino said.

'He's a sick one, no doubt about it. Best to steer clear of him whenever possible.'

'Who ultimately does run this place?' Pitt asked.

'A guy named Edward Bolcke. Some sort of genius mining engineer. He's got his own residence just up the way.' Maguire pointed toward the dock. 'He built this entire complex to extract and refine rare earth elements. From what we've learned, he's a major player in the world market, and is particularly tight with the Chinese. One of the extraction workers claims a quarter of a billion dollars' worth of rare earth elements are processed here a year, much of it stolen.'

Giordino whistled. 'Makes for a tidy profit.'

'The extraction facilities,' Pitt said, thinking escape. 'I'm guessing they must use a large amount of chemicals in the process.'

'Some deadly, I hope,' Giordino said.

'Yes, but it's out of reach,' Maguire said. 'All the serious stuff is performed in the buildings beyond our access. We're just the grunts. We load and off-load the ships and run the millhouse. You hoping to play with matches?'

'Something on that order.'

'You might as well forget about it. Brown and I considered it for weeks, but we've seen too many good men die in the attempt. Somebody will blow the whistle on this place one of these days. We just need to hang on until it happens.'

A string of lights above their heads flashed briefly.

'Lights out in five minutes,' Maguire said. 'You boys best find a place to bunk.'

He led them to a large screened room filled with rattan sleeping mats. Pitt and Giordino picked two and lay down as the room filled with men and the lights went out. Pitt ignored the discomfort of the steamy room and the hard mat as he lay in the darkness, contemplating a way out of the death camp. He drifted to sleep without an answer, not knowing his opportunity would come much sooner than he thought.

57

The laborers froze when they heard the thumping whine of a helicopter landing. Johansson's whip immediately prompted the men back to work, purging any hopes that an armed force had arrived to set them free.

Instead it was Bolcke himself, arriving fresh from Australia, where he had set in motion the final stages for his takeover of the Mount Weld mining operation. Climbing out of the helicopter, he bypassed a waiting golf cart and strode to the dock, a pair of armed guards in tow.

A ragged group of laborers, including Pitt and Giordino, were transferring the *Adelaide*'s final hold of ore when Bolcke stepped onto the dock. He glanced at the slaves with disdain, briefly locking eyes with Pitt. In that instant, Pitt seemed to read into the Austrian's psyche. He saw a joyless man, one scrubbed clean of compassion, ethics, and even a soul.

Bolcke coldly eyed the piled ore before examining the ship. He waited briefly for Gomez, who was summoned from the ship and scurried down the gangplank.

'The cargo was what we anticipated?' Bolcke asked.

'Yes, thirty thousand tons of crushed monazite ore. That's the last of it there.' Gomez pointed at the final mound.

'Any trouble with the acquisition?'

'The shipping line sent out an added security team. We subdued them without issue.'

'Someone was expecting an attack?'

Gomez nodded. 'Fortunately, they arrived after we had already seized the ship.'

A troubled look crossed Bolcke's face. 'Then we must dispose of the vessel.'

'After changing identities at sea, we entered the canal without question,' Gomez said.

'I can't afford the risk. I have an important transaction pending with the Chinese. Wait three days and dispose of the ship.'

'There's a salvage yard in São Paulo I can take her to. They'll pay top dollar.'

Bolcke thought a moment. 'No, it's not worth the risk. Strip what's valuable, and dispose of her in the Atlantic.'

'Yes, sir.'

Pitt lingered near the ore pile, straining to overhear the conversation while his cart was filled. He watched as Bolcke turned his back on Gomez and walked toward his residence and Gomez returned to the ship.

'The *Adelaide*'s headed out in a few days,' he said to Giordino. 'I think we need to be aboard when they shove off.'

'Fine by me. I just don't want to go as a piece of toast.' He tapped his steel collar.

'I have a theory about our dog collars,' Pitt said. He fell silent when Johansson emerged from the bush, cracking his whip.

'Pick up the pace,' he yelled. 'You're falling behind the mill.'

The laborers quickened their movements, none making eye contact with him. Johansson paced the dock area until he spotted Giordino, pushing a fully loaded cart and limping. The bullwhip snapped, striking Giordino in the back of the thigh. 'You, there. Get a move on.'

Giordino turned and gave him a look that could blister paint. His knuckles turning white as he pushed, Giordino propelled the ore carrier ahead as if it were an empty grocery cart. Johansson smiled at the display of strength, then wandered off to berate another group of laborers.

Pitt followed Giordino along the path to the millhouse. It ran parallel to the twin white lines alongside the dock, and Pitt gradually eased the cart toward the nearest line. When he approached within three feet, he began feeling a tingling in the collar. He took a quick step and pulled himself onto the cart for a moment as it rolled along. The tingling immediately ceased. He veered the cart back onto the path, catching a brief shock as he pushed off with his foot. When he caught up to Giordino, Pitt was smiling.

After a brief lunch of cold fish stew, the two men were led into the millhouse, where they were assigned to feed the ball mill – a huge metal cylinder mounted horizontally on rotating gears. Crushed ore was fed into one end, where it would collide with hardened steel balls housed inside as the cylinder rotated. The balls pulverized the ore into a near powder, which was filtered out the opposite end. The mill rumbled like an overgrown washing machine loaded with marbles.

The raw ore that had been transferred from the dock was piled in large mounds along the open side of the building. A short conveyor carried the ore to a raised platform built over the ball mill, where it was manually fed into the device through a large funnel. A guard ordered Pitt onto the platform to feed the mill, while Giordino joined another man shoveling ore onto the conveyor.

The work was less strenuous than the hauling. The ball mill took time to digest the ore, which allowed frequent rests for the laborers. During one of these intervals, Johansson made an appearance. The overseer entered the far side of the building, lingering at the back end of the ball mill, where workers collected the powder in more carts and transferred them to the next staging area. The mill guard stepped over and joined him in a brief discussion of the output.

A few minutes later, Johansson walked the length of the ball mill. For once, his hands were empty, the rawhide lash coiled to his belt. As he approached the feed piles, he spotted Giordino and the other worker seated on one of the mounds. Johansson's face flushed, and his eyes bulged with rage.

'On your feet!' he screamed. 'Why aren't you working?'

'The ball mill is full up,' Giordino said, casually pointing to the spinning cylinder. He remained seated while his companion jumped upright.

'I said, on your feet.'

Giordino tried rising, but his injured leg lost its footing, and he buckled to his knee. Johansson lunged forward, catching Giordino before he could recover. Grabbing a shovel wedged in the ore, the Swede swung it hard, aiming for the bum leg.

The blade connected with a whack, striking just above the wound on Giordino's thigh. He collapsed as blood began seeping from the reopened wound.

Standing on the platform, Pitt had seen it coming but could not react in time. His own shovel in hand, he took a quick step across the platform and leaped off the edge. He fell toward Johansson but was too far away to land on him. Instead, he swung the shovel in a chopping motion as he fell, stretching his arms and aiming at Johansson's head.

The shovel missed the overseer's head but struck his left shoulder hard. Johansson winced and spun around as the shovel bounced away and Pitt landed hard at his feet. Still gripping his own shovel, Johansson took a swipe at Pitt. Trying to rise, Pitt was forced to fling himself backward, and he caught a glancing blow on his side as he rolled toward the ball mill.

Pursuing like a rabid animal, Johansson was above Pitt instantly, raising the shovel for a vertical blow to the head. Pitt rolled beneath the spinning gears of the ball mill as the shovel head smacked the ground beside him. Pitt reacted in turn, grabbing the shovel's wooden handle to prevent another blow. Johansson tried to jerk it away, but his left arm was numb from the earlier blow and he didn't have the strength. Changing tack, he pushed the handle down while diving onto Pitt.

The big Swede weighed seventy-five pounds more than Pitt and landed like a rock. The impact knocked the breath from Pitt's lungs. Johansson managed to wedge the shovel handle beneath Pitt's throat as he landed and applied his full strength to choke him.

Pitt struggled to push the handle clear, but he was pinned in an awkward position. As the handle pressed tighter against his throat, he noticed a large gear of the ball mill's drive system whirring above his head. Pitt bucked and twisted, trying to throw Johansson against the gear – or at least to break his grip on the shovel.

It was no use. Johansson didn't budge, and he focused all of his energies on choking the life out of Pitt.

A pounding sensation exploded in his head as Pitt began gasping for air. A wave of desperation fell over him, and he let go of the handle with his right hand and reached up toward Johansson's waist, groping for his sidearm.

But Johansson's pistol was holstered on his opposite hip. Instead, Pitt felt the coiled bullwhip hooked to his belt. He grasped the whip, pulling it free, but he began to sag as spots blurred his vision.

Then a loud whack filled his ears, and the choking eased, if only for a moment.

Giordino had crawled within throwing range and was pelting Johansson with clumps of ore. A hard chunk, driven by Giordino with the velocity of a major league fastball, struck Johansson behind the ear. The Swede grunted and turned toward Giordino, ducking as another rock came flying by.

The distraction gave Pitt time to catch a breath of air, which cleared his vision. Seizing the moment, he whipped up his free arm and looped the bullwhip around Johansson's head.

Johansson retaliated by releasing the shovel and throwing a right fist at Pitt's head.

Pitt could do nothing to deflect the blow, as he was reaching up with the handle of the whip. As the blow struck his face, he jammed a lanyard ring on the handle into the gear teeth spinning just above him.

The punch nearly knocked Pitt out, but he remained alert enough to see the coiled whip tighten around Johansson's neck and jerk him upward. As he flailed to break free, the huge toothed wheel carried the Swede up onto its rotating surface. A hoarse scream passed from Johansson's lips as he was dragged by the neck to the machine's opposite side.

At its base, the external gear engaged with the flywheel from the ball mill's 800-horsepower motor. Johansson fought to escape, but was pulled into the rotating gears. The meshing metal teeth chewing through the leather whip and then into the flesh of the overseer's neck. His screaming ended, and the rotating gear spit a thin line of red across the room. The machine bucked and slowed a moment, then revved back up to speed. Beneath the gears, a pool of blood spread across the floor from Johansson's decapitated body.

Pitt climbed to his feet. The guard at the other end of the mill had finally taken notice and began running toward him.

'You really gunked up the works this time,' Giordino said, grinning despite his pain.

'Thanks for the assist.' Pitt moved quickly toward him. 'You okay?'

'Yeah, but the leg's leaking again. You better take a solo run.'

The guard was now yelling at Pitt while attempting to draw his weapon.

Pitt nodded at his friend. 'I'll be back.' He dove under the conveyor belt as a burst of gunfire echoed through the building. Giordino casually tossed some crushed ore across the floor when the guard rushed after Pitt. His eyes focused on his quarry, the guard slipped on the ore and fell halfway to the floor.

Pitt used the opportunity to spring from the opposite side of the conveyor and dash out the end of the building.

A late spray of gunfire followed him as he cut around the corner and ducked into some nearby foliage. Trapped on the five-acre island, he had no illusion about being able to remain concealed for long. The gunfire had already attracted the attention of several nearby guards.

Pitt needled his way through the brush, using its cover to move well clear of the millhouse. The pursuing guard exited the building too late to see him and was forced to sweep the area slowly as he called in support.

Pitt angled through the brush until he reached the cart path. Then he sprinted toward the dock as fast as his weakened legs would carry him. The path soon opened onto the dock and the remaining pile of ore. Plugrad and a few of his men were shoveling their way through the pile.

As he came off the path, Pitt held his breath, knowing he had only one means of escape. As he caught sight of the men, he saw what he was looking for. With renewed urgency, he stepped up his pace, pushing aside the thought that if his assumption was wrong, he would soon be dead.

58

Plugrad looked up from a shovelful of ore in his hands when Pitt came charging down the path, pointing past him.

'I need one of those,' Pitt yelled.

Plugrad looked behind him and saw a trio of ore carts. The men around him stepped out of the way as Pitt approached. Without slowing, he ran to a lightly filled cart and shoved it toward the dock.

'The white lines!' Plugrad said, but Pitt shook him off, driving the cart forward with all the force he could muster.

On the dock, a lone guard assigned to Plugrad's work detail had been on his radio and didn't react until he saw Pitt thrusting the cart toward the electric lines. He swung his AK-47 toward Pitt and fired a burst.

The poorly aimed shot chewed up the dust by Pitt's feet, inciting him to push harder. The cart's front tires crossed the first white line, and he began to feel a tingle in his neck. The cart was now rolling freely. As the pain began to amplify around his throat, he leaped and dove inside.

He tumbled onto a small mound of ore as the cart's rear tires crossed the line. Fifty thousand volts should have surged through his collar, killing him instantly. But the electrical charge had to find a path from the buried line to the collar. The fat rubber tires of the ore cart failed to conduct the charge, and the shocking sensation vanished from Pitt's neck.

Fortunately for Pitt, the ground was level and the cart continued rolling, crossing the second white line onto the dock. Another burst of gunfire sounded, and Pitt burrowed into the ore at the bottom of the cart. A spray of holes punctured the sides just above his head as the guard took better aim. Pitt caught some shrapnel from an exploding chunk of ore but otherwise escaped injury.

The cart bounded across the dock, then smashed into the raised lip at the water's edge. Pitt looked up to see the *Adelaide* moored above him. Ejecting himself like a jack-in-the-box, he dove out of the cart and over the side of the dock, splashing into the water below.

Caught by surprise, the dock guard didn't fire until after Pitt disappeared. He ran to the edge and aimed his rifle at the concentric circles created by Pitt's splash – and waited for him to surface.

Pitt struck the water near the aft end of the *Adelaide*, which had been backed into the inlet. He dove deep before turning and swimming hard toward the stern. The murky water offered a few feet of visibility, and he easily followed the hull's dark contour until it tapered back and a large bronze propeller appeared.

An expert diver, Pitt was comfortable in the water and could easily hold his breath for more than a minute. He took a few more strokes past the ship and angled away from the dock. Though he was good for some additional strokes, he stopped and eased toward the surface, giving a sudden kick just before he broke for air.

His head burst from the water, and he took an easy stroke toward the far shore before grabbing another fresh breath of air, then pulled himself under. He spun and kicked down as fast as he could, swimming back toward the ship, as a spray of bullets struck the water above him.

While Pitt was in fact backtracking, the guard had bought his feigned motion to shore and aimed his shots accordingly. The gunman stopped firing long enough to yell to two approaching guards. 'Cover the far shore. He's headed over there.'

The two men ran to the head of the inlet, scanning the water for Pitt to surface.

But Pitt had already returned to the *Adelaide* and was swimming along her outboard hull. It was a demanding swim down the length of the big ship, which Pitt conducted underwater, surfacing quickly a few times for air. When he reached the relative concealment of the bow, he scanned both sides of the ship.

Teams of guards with dogs were beating through the jungle on the far side of the inlet. On the dock, the guard who had fired at him was speaking with another gunman while pointing at the water. Pitt saw few safe places to hide, and his position off the *Adelaide* was too exposed for him to remain there long.

A short distance ahead of the freighter, a small crew boat had been docked. The boat was secured with a thick chain, however, which was locked to a dock cleat. Between the two vessels a rusty ladder led up to the dock. That gave Pitt an idea. Ducking underwater, he swam to the base of the ladder in one breath. Pulling himself up a few rungs at a time, he peered over the edge of the dock – and saw the two guards running toward him.

He dropped down the ladder, surprised he'd been detected. As he was about to dive underwater, he hesitated at the sound of boots clanging on metal. He looked up and saw the men race up the *Adelaide*'s gangway and head to the stern. They'd not seen him after all.

The dock was now empty, and Pitt made his move, jumping up and sprinting across its width. He eyed a storage shed near the crew boat and reconsidered escaping by water. There would be tools inside the shed, something he could use to free the boat. But to get there without being seen, he'd have to loop his way through the brush.

He made it to the jungle fringe and cut across a small footpath. Following the path around a thick cedar tree, Pitt suddenly ran smack into another man rushing from the other direction. The men bounced off each other and fell hard to the ground. Pitt reacted first. He sprang to his feet, then paused when he recognized the other man.

It was Bolcke, wearing pressed slacks and a polo shirt. The Austrian was slow to get up but wasted no time in ripping a handheld radio from his belt and pressing it to his lips. 'Johansson, the escaped slave is near the northern dock.'

Pitt shook his head. 'I'm afraid Johnny the Whip won't be making any more house calls.'

Bolcke stared at Pitt as his radio call was met by a long silence. Another voice came on and spoke to Bolcke in hurried Spanish. The Austrian ignored it as he stared at Pitt.

'Just stay where you are.'

'Sorry,' Pitt replied, 'but I've decided to check out of your sadistic hotel.' He could hear voices coming from the dock and movement farther up the path, which Pitt now realized ran from Bolcke's residence.

'You'll be hunted down and shot.'

'No, Edward Bolcke,' Pitt said, staring at the old miner with contempt. 'I fully intend to come back for you.'

He turned and dove into the jungle, scrambling from view seconds before a contingent of guards appeared. Seeing Bolcke, they sprinted up to him.

'You reported seeing the escaped slave?' one of them asked.

Bolcke nodded and pointed at Pitt's trail, then tossed his radio at the man. 'Have all available guards converge here right away,' he said. 'I want that slave brought back to me within the hour. Dead.'

59

Twigs snapped and branches swayed as Pitt bulled through the thick brush. He didn't know how many men were on his trail, and since he couldn't move both quickly and quietly, he abandoned caution and simply advanced as fast as he could.

He kept to the strip of natural vegetation that was contained by the dock on one side and the road to Bolcke's residence on the other. When the brush narrowed and a pair of white lines appeared to his left, he knew he had to change course. He wound his way to the edge of the road, ducking under a fern and holding his breath as a golf cart with several guards careened by. The instant it was out of view, he bolted across the road and into the opposite thicket, heading deep into its cover.

After only a few dozen yards he came to a stop. Beneath a rocky ledge, the lake appeared in his path. Pitt now realized Bolcke's compound had been built on a narrow peninsula. His only hope of escape was to travel the length of the peninsula without being detected and flee into the expanse of landscape that lay beyond.

Breathing heavily, he pressed forward, slowing when one of the extraction facilities blocked his way. As he crept to one end, he saw a guard circling the building. He threw himself to the ground and snaked his way around the end of the building, then rose and sprinted into the jungle. At the base of a small mahogany tree, he sank to the ground and rested.

But his respite was ended by a sound that shocked him back onto the run. It was the shrill bark of attack dogs, making their way in his direction.

Pitt had seen guards patrol with Dobermans, and once with a German shepherd, but he had put them out of his mind. Now clear of the compound, they would be his most dangerous challenge.

The volume of their barking told Pitt they were no closer than the extraction facility, giving him hope that he had a safe head start. He could only trust that they didn't have a specific scent to follow.

But his wet footprints from the dock had given the dogs a faint starting point, and they had picked up just enough scent to track him. The handlers released two of the animals to pursue him on their own, but they kept three others leashed, carefully sweeping his trail to ensure it wasn't lost.

Dragging himself off the ground, Pitt ran. Prickly leaves and sharp branches tore at his face and clothes as he threaded his way ahead. The dogs' constant barking pushed him forward, pushing the aches from his mind. The minimal diet he had endured the past few days quickly showed as his strength waned, producing a weariness he shouldn't have felt so soon. But Pitt's mental strength was a fortress, and he willed himself forward, ignoring the pain and fatigue.

Willpower or not, there would be no outrunning the pursuit dogs, they were simply too fast. Their incessant barking grew louder, reminding Pitt of a locomotive approaching a train station. He stopped and picked up a pointed stick, then headed to an open bluff to his left where he would make his stand. He barely had time to turn when two large Dobermans, running head to tail, emerged from the brush and leaped at him.

Pitt was too late in wielding his stick to spear the first dog. Instead, he had to use it defensively, ramming it across the dog's throat as its jaws tried to snap off one of his ears. He tossed the animal aside, only to have the second dog leap onto his turned shoulder from behind. Pitt ducked his head as a cascade of sharp teeth lunged for his neck.

Pitt waited for his flesh to be shredded, but felt only a weak bite against the top of his shoulder – and then the dog fell limp. Flinging it off his shoulder, he saw a lifeless look in its eye as it fell motionless. But the first dog quickly regained its footing and sprang again for Pitt's jugular. As it leaped, Pitt heard two soft thumps and saw a pair of red dots appear on the dog's chest. The beast's open jaws went slack as Pitt fended it aside with his stick, and the dog joined its partner dead on the ground.

Pitt knew the act was no divine intervention and he spun around to determine its source. Just over the rise, he saw some movement in the grass and stepped closer to investigate. A short, thin man stood up from the brush and moved to meet him.

Zhou Xing was wearing jungle fatigues and combat boots, with a bush hat pulled low over his face. He carried an AK-47, a wisp of smoke still curling from its silencer. He gazed at Pitt with a stony expression, then stepped past him to one of the dogs. 'Quickly, to the ravine,' he said in imperfect English.

He grabbed the Doberman by its collar and dragged it over the rise. On the other side, the hill descended sharply, falling into a narrow ravine. A small creek trickled through the floor of the ravine, surrounded by dense ferns. Zhou dragged the dog to the edge of the precipice and flung it over. The carcass tumbled to the bottom, where it was quickly swallowed up by the ferns.

After catching his breath, Pitt arrived with the second Doberman and duplicated Zhou's disappearing act. He then followed the Chinese agent to a makeshift camp hidden in the side of the hill.

'What are you doing here?' Pitt asked, still listening for the barks of the remaining dogs.

'Call it business,' Zhou replied, picking a laptop computer off a stump, closing its screen, and shoving it into a backpack. But before the screen went dark, Pitt noticed the images displayed: a checkerboard of video feeds showing sections of Bolcke's compound. The agent had planted tiny wireless surveillance cameras around the facility to track activity and guard movements.

'You must keep running,' Zhou said. He scrambled to clean up his makeshift camp, rolling up his bed and stuffing its mosquito netting into his pack.

A second large backpack, its flap open, sat near Pitt's feet. Inside he could see several packets of electronic detonator caps next to clear-wrapped packages of reddish clay-like material. Pitt had been involved with enough underwater demolition projects to recognize it as a cache of Semtex plastic explosives.

Zhou tossed Pitt a protein bar and a canteen from his pack before slipping it on. He then scattered leaves around the compressed grass where he had slept the night before. Finally, he hoisted the second pack, looking warily at Pitt when he noticed the flap was open.

'Go,' he said to Pitt. 'They are less than ten minutes behind.'

'When are you going to blow up the compound?' Pitt asked.

Zhou stared at Pitt, his face an empty slate. The Americans had always been considered an unspoken enemy. But he found admiration for this man, having observed the better part of his escape on his hidden video cameras. Though he had seen labor camps in China, he was repulsed by Bolcke's hidden slave operation.

'Twenty-two hours from now,' he said.

'And the captives?'

Zhou shrugged, then casually aimed his assault rifle at Pitt.

'It is time to go. You travel west, as I am going east.' He pointed into the jungle. 'Do not follow me.'

Pitt looked past the expressionless face into Zhou's black eyes, where a hidden intelligence and compassion were barely revealed.

'Thank you,' Pitt said.

Zhou nodded and turned, disappearing into the bush.

60

Yaeger was still parked in front of his mammoth video display when Gunn popped by for an update. In contrast to Yaeger's casual attire, the NUMA Deputy Director was wearing a sport coat and tie.

'What's up with the fine threads?' Yaeger asked.

'I got called over to a meeting with the Vice President. He'll want to know the latest on the search for Pitt and Giordino.'

Yaeger shook his head. 'Search-and-rescue ops continue to come up empty. The Navy has in fact informed us they will be calling off their search efforts at the end of the day.'

'Anything more on the *Adelaide*?'

'Nothing concrete. Our formal requests to Interpol and every Coast Guard organization between Alaska and Chile have produced nothing.'

'If she's afloat, someone has to have seen her,' Gunn said. 'Have Dirk and Summer arrived in Panama?'

'They were rushing to catch a red-eye to Panama City.' He glanced at the video board, whose numerous displays included a digital clock in the lower corner. 'Presuming they made their flight, they should be landing about now.'

Gunn had followed Yaeger's gaze to the screen and noticed an e-mail notice with Pitt's name on it. 'Mind if I ask what that is?'

'Not at all. In fact, I was just going to ask if it made any sense to you. It's an e-mail that was sent to the NUMA website a few days ago. One of the girls in public relations forwarded it to me when she didn't know how to respond. Probably somebody's four-year-old playing on a keyboard.'

He enlarged the e-mail until its brief message was clearly displayed:

To Pitt. Abduc wsearr haytk lexkyann

'Looks like gibberish,' Gunn said, 'except for the last word. Must have been penned by someone named Ann from Lexington, Kentucky.'

'That's all I made out of it.'

'I'd stick to your four-year-old theory.' He patted Yaeger on the shoulder. 'Give me a shout if anything new on the ship comes in.'

'Will do. Give my regards to the admiral.'

Gunn took the Metro to downtown Washington, exiting at the Farragut West Station and walking the three blocks to Sandecker's office in the Eisenhower Building. The Vice President welcomed him to a meeting table built from old ship timbers, where he introduced him to the DARPA security director, Dan Fowler, and a female FBI division director named Elizabeth Meyers.

Sandecker could see by Gunn's weary face that Pitt's disappearance weighed heavily on him. 'What's the latest on Pitt and Giordino?'

'Search-and-rescue teams still haven't found a thing. The Navy's calling off their efforts today.' He looked at Sandecker and waited for him to react.

He wasn't disappointed. The Vice President's face turned red, and he marched to his desk and buzzed his secretary. 'Martha. Get me the Chief of Naval Operations on the line.'

A few seconds later, he was chewing out an admiral who had previously outranked him. He slammed down the receiver and returned to the table. 'The Navy's search has been extended three more days.'

'Thank you, Mr Vice President.'

'What about that ship you told me about?' Sandecker asked.

'The *Salzburg*?' Gunn said. 'She was last reported in New Orleans. Homeland Security's checking with the local port authority to see if she's still there.'

'What's the connection?' Fowler asked.

'Mostly circumstantial,' Gunn said. 'The *Salzburg* appears to have been in the vicinity of the *Adelaide* when she disappeared with Pitt aboard. Just one of the straws we're grasping at in a mystery with few clues.'

'We know the feeling,' Meyers said.

'Sorry?' Gunn said.

'Rudi,' Sandecker explained, 'before Pitt disappeared, he was involved in the recovery of some highly classified plans related to a submarine project called *Sea Arrow*.'

'The *Sea Arrow*. Isn't that a concept for a high-speed attack sub?'

'There is nothing conceptual about it. At least there wasn't until now.'

'I'm guessing,' Gunn said, 'that this relates to the recovery of that boat off San Diego, the *Cuttlefish*?'

'Exactly,' Sandecker said. 'Only things have escalated

into a full-blown national security disaster. Elizabeth, why don't you fill him in?'

The FBI woman cleared her throat. 'I should caution you this is classified information. Four days ago, an advanced propulsion motor built for the *Sea Arrow* was hijacked during transport from the Navy's research lab at Chesapeake, Maryland.'

'Is that why a recent Homeland Security alert was issued?' Gunn asked.

'It was,' Meyers said. 'Our agency has been working around the clock, examining every airport, shipping terminal, and truck stop in the country. I can't begin to tell you the amount of resources assigned to the case.'

'And still no leads?' Sandecker asked.

'Plenty that have been false or dead ends. The best we have is a description of a Latino male who purchased a derelict Toyota, which was later involved in the hijacking. Beyond that, we're still grasping for clues.'

'Do you think it's still in the country?' Gunn asked.

'We'd like to think so,' Meyers said, uncertainty evident in her voice.

'That's part of the reason you're here, Rudi,' Sandecker said. 'The FBI's looking at all available resources and would like the NUMA fleet to help. Since your ships are often stationed in out-of-the-way places, they want to be made aware of any unusual behavior that might be seen concerning domestic shipping.'

'We've made the same request to the Navy, Coast Guard, and some of the major port operators,' Meyers added.

'Absolutely,' Gunn said. 'I'll pass the word immediately.'

Sandecker turned to Fowler. 'Dan, do you have anything to add?'

'No, sir. Just that we've confirmed that Ann went missing shortly before the hijacking. We, along with the FBI, suspect that she was either killed or abducted by the same perpetrators.'

'Ann Bennett?' Gunn asked. 'She was abducted?'

'Yes, and we fear the worst,' Meyers said. 'She's been missing for five days now.'

Gunn nearly fell off his chair. The garbled e-mail Yaeger had shown him clicked in his head. 'Ann's alive,' he said, 'and I know where she is. Or, rather, where she was a few days ago. Lexington, Kentucky.'

'She's still alive?' Fowler asked.

'Yes. It was a cryptic e-mail we received at NUMA. It must have been a warning or a plea for help. We don't understand the full text, but I think part of it indicates she was abducted with the *Sea Arrow* motor.'

Meyers stiffened in her chair. 'I'll get the local field office mobilized.'

Fowler looked blankly at the Vice President. 'Why Lexington, Kentucky?'

'Perhaps a local airfield that's friendly to the thieves.'

'They could still be in transit,' Meyers said. 'Perhaps they were on their way to the West Coast or Mexico.'

'Looks like you have your work cut out for you, Elizabeth,' Sandecker said. 'All right, let's get after it. I'll want an update, same time tomorrow.'

The Vice President's visitors rose to leave. As they

walked to the door, Meyers approached Gunn. 'I'd like to see that e-mail as soon as possible.'

'Of course,' Gunn said. But not, he thought, until he and Yaeger had deciphered the full meaning of the message.

61

The cabin door burst open with a bang. Ann was sitting atop a corner writing desk, peering out a small porthole at the sea rushing by. She had spent most of the journey perched there. Aside from an early bout of seasickness after leaving the Mississippi Delta, the trip had been a voyage of tedium. Her only excitement was the two meals a day brought by an ugly bald man who she presumed was the ship's cook.

From her hours of staring out the starboard port, she had determined they were sailing south. Guessing their speed was somewhere between fifteen and twenty knots, she figured that put them roughly a thousand miles south of New Orleans by the second day. Her southern geography wasn't that great, but she figured they weren't far off Mexico's Yucatán Peninsula.

She hadn't seen Pablo since coming aboard but had braced herself for his appearance. When the door sprang open, she knew it was him. He plodded into the cabin and slammed the door behind him. He appeared more relaxed than Ann had seen him before, and when he stepped closer, she could tell why. He reeked of cheap rum.

'Miss me?' he asked, grinning like a shark.

Ann retreated farther into her desktop corner, pulling her knees beneath her chin.

'Where are we headed?' she replied, hoping to redirect his thoughts.

'Somewhere hot and steamy.'

'Colombia?'

Pablo cocked his head, surprised that she knew – or guessed – his nationality.

'No, but perhaps after we make our delivery the two of us can fly to Bogotá for a long romantic weekend.'

He moved closer to the edge of the desk.

'When will the delivery occur?'

'Always the questions.' He leaned over to plant a slobbery kiss on her face.

Ann raised the soles of her feet to his chest and pushed with her legs. To her surprise, the big man stumbled backward, falling onto her bunk.

Ann shuddered. Would he kill her for refusing him? But the alcohol had mellowed him and he rose from the bed, laughing.

'I knew you were a wildcat underneath,' he said.

'I don't like being caged like one.' She held up her cuffed wrists. 'Why don't you take these off first?'

'Both wild and smart,' he said. 'No, I think that will be the one thing I let you leave on.'

He began unbuttoning his shirt, staring at her with an unfocused leer.

She trembled in the corner, still atop the desk, and contemplated a break for the door.

Sensing her thoughts, Pablo stepped over and blocked the way, then began inching closer.

Ann was about to scream when another sound blared through the cabin.

It was audio static, emanating from a ceiling speaker wired to the shipboard intercom. Then a voice roared through the cabin, as well as the rest of the ship. 'Señor Pablo, please report to the bridge. Señor Pablo, to the bridge.'

Pablo shook his head and gazed at the speaker with disgust. Fumbling to button his shirt, he stared at Ann with hungry eyes. 'We shall resume our visit later.' He eased out of the cabin and locked the door behind him.

Ann wilted in her corner, tears of relief wetting her cheeks for the reprieve she feared was only temporary.

Leaving her cabin, Pablo climbed to the bridge and approached the captain with irritation. 'What is it?'

'An urgent call for you on the sat phone.' The captain motioned toward a waiting handset.

Pablo shook off his alcoholic stupor and spoke into the receiver. The conversation was one-sided. Pablo remained quiet until ending the call by saying, 'Yes, sir.' Then he turned to the captain. 'How far are we from the canal?'

The captain adjusted the scale on a navigation screen. 'Just over six hundred miles.'

Pablo looked at the digital map and studied the nearby coastline.

'We need to make an emergency trip into Puerto Cortés, Honduras, to pick up some paint and cargo.'

'A delivery to the estate?'

'No, a requirement on board.'

'But we have only a skeleton crew aboard the *Salzburg*.'

'Then I'll need every man's full effort,' Pablo said, 'or skeletons they will become.'

62

Pitt honored Zhou's request and headed west through the jungle. He thought about circling back and trying to locate the boat that Zhou had most certainly arrived in but ultimately figured it would be well concealed. As he pushed through the brush, Pitt wondered who the man was and why he'd been sent to destroy Bolcke's operations. Not that Pitt didn't harbor similar feelings, but he presumed the motive had more to do with the trade in rare earth elements than for humanitarian reasons.

Soon after they had parted, the sun had dropped from the sky, and the canopied jungle turned dark. Pitt stumbled through clouds of mosquitoes that appeared at dusk to feast on his exposed skin. The going became treacherous as the dense world around him gradually faded to black. He found himself walking into sharp branches or tripping over unseen logs, but there was nothing he could do about it.

The dogs continued their pursuit, slow and methodical. Pitt had hoped the trackers would follow Zhou's trail, but they still tracked his scent. Pitt could tell by the sporadic barking that they were perhaps just a few hundred yards behind. He stopped and listened every few minutes, trying to gauge their position.

As the jungle enveloped him, he lost any reference for finding direction. The sound of the dogs became his only clue. Fearful of accidentally backtracking into the teeth of the searchers, he kept a careful ear out for their barking.

The jungle came alive at night with a concert of strange hoots, calls, and cries. Pitt kept his sharp stick in one hand in case the cries came not from a bird or frog but from a jaguar or caiman.

The noises helped take Pitt's mind off his fatigue. Without Zhou's water and protein bar, he might have collapsed, but the minimal nourishment kept him going. Fatigue oozed from his bones, making every step painful. Being unused to the hot, steamy environment only added to his lethargy. Tempted to stop and lie down, he thought of Giordino and the other prisoners, and his feet kept moving.

Though his clothes had dried after his earlier swim, now they were soaked from endless sweat. He prayed for rain, knowing it would help him elude the trackers. But the normally reliable Panamanian skies failed to cooperate, offering nothing more than an occasional drizzle.

He slipped on a patch of mud, then pulled himself onto a tree stump and rested. The darkness also seemed to have slowed the trackers. A distant barking told him he still held a comfortable lead, but he soon spied a faint glow through the foliage from the searchers' lights.

Pitt dragged himself to his feet and pressed on into the gauntlet of unseen branches. Hour by hour, the night wore on in a cycle of plodding, tripping, and stumbling through the jungle. Always, the din of dogs overshadowed the jungle's other sounds.

Moving like a zombie, Pitt staggered through a grove of bamboo – then took a step and felt only air. He collapsed over the lip of a narrow ravine, tumbling headfirst down a grassy hill and into a small stream. He sat there for several minutes, the cool water washing away the pain of his bruises and lacerations. Overhead, a seam of twinkling stars provided a faint but welcome light.

The water would give him the chance to escape the pursuing dogs. After refilling Zhou's canteen, he shuffled down the center of the creek. The water seldom came past his knees, but it was deep enough to mask his tracks. With the starlight, he found the going easier, even as he slipped and fell in the streambed. He followed it for what felt like miles but was in fact only a few hundred yards.

Reaching a low bank, he hobbled up the stream's opposite bank and entered a grove of kapok trees. A low branch beckoned, and he shimmied onto it and rested.

The jungle had quietened, and he heard few noises except the stream. He no longer detected the chase dogs, giving him hope that he had finally given them the slip. As he leaned against the trunk, he realized the pursuit had been almost as taxing mentally as it was physically.

He was fighting the urge to sleep when he heard a rustling in the bushes across the stream. He looked over his shoulder as a yellow glow bounced through the foliage. He froze as the silhouette of a large dog materialized above the far stream bank, sniffing the ground.

Pitt cursed his bad luck. Following the streambed, he had inadvertently reversed his track and traveled toward his pursuers.

The German shepherd gave no indication it saw or smelled Pitt. He held perfectly still in the tree, not even breathing. The yellow glow grew brighter until a gunman with a flashlight emerged from a thicket and called to the dog. It turned to its trainer and began to follow, but not before letting out a growl.

Ten feet from Pitt, a roar erupted like a lion in an electric chair. Pitt nearly flew off the branch but caught himself as the gunman's flashlight scanned the tree. The light found a furry black-and-brown creature perched a little above Pitt. It was a howler monkey, and it let out a second raucous cry before hopping onto another branch and scurrying away from the light.

Pitt sat frozen at the edge of the flashlight's beam as the dog barked wildly. The beam wavered, then bounced back to capture Pitt dead center. Pitt dropped from the branch and hustled through the grove of trees. A second later, a burst of gunfire chewed up the kapok tree's now empty branch.

The jungle fell still as the echo from the gunfire receded. Then the landscape erupted in squawks and cries as a thousand animals fled the scene. Pitt headed the pack, scrambling through the maze of foliage with his hands outstretched. The first rays of dawn were creasing the sky, aiding his run. And run he did.

The German shepherd had been sent to follow but hesitated at crossing the stream, giving Pitt an extra head start. But the dog found a narrow place to cross the stream and resumed pursuit. Its incessant barking allowed Pitt to gauge the dog's steady approach. Although tired itself from the nightlong chase, the dog kept coming.

Pitt had little energy left for an extended sprint. He knew he couldn't outrun the dog, but if he could separate it from its handler, he might have a chance. The question was whether he had enough left in him to fight the dog.

The barking grew closer, and Pitt decided it was time to turn and fight. He realized he'd left his sharp stick by the tree when he fled. As he scoured the ground for a new weapon, he overlooked a low tree branch and ran face-first into it. The blow knocked him flat to the ground. As he lay there dazed, he heard the barking approach. But he also heard a metallic clacking that seemed to vibrate through the earth.

On instinct alone, he crawled forward, past the tree and up a small mound. The sound grew louder. He fought his pain and peeked over the mound.

In the dim light he saw a train – not twenty feet away. He shook off the thought it was a mirage and staggered to his feet. The train was real, all right, crawling through a narrow cut in the jungle, pulling flatbed cars loaded with shipping container after shipping container.

Pitt stumbled toward the tracks as the German shepherd crested the mound and sighted him. With a renewed fury, the dog sprinted after Pitt as he staggered on rubber legs for the train.

A half-loaded flatcar was passing by, and Pitt dove for it. His torso hit the bed, and he clawed forward as the dog attacked. The German shepherd leaped and clamped its jaws onto his dangling right foot.

Pitt rolled onto the flatbed as the dog hung from his foot in midair. Pulling Zhou's canteen from his neck, he flung it at the dog. The canteen struck its snout, and the dog whimpered and let go. But a moment after falling to the gravel beside the rails, the dog regained its senses and chased after Pitt's flatbed. For a quarter mile, the dog ran alongside it, snarling and leaping but unable to jump aboard. Then the train crossed a ravine over a narrow trestle, and the dog was forced to give up. Pitt waved farewell to it as it barked and howled in frustration at the vanishing train. Crawling across the flatbed car, Pitt then curled up next to a rusty container, closed his eyes, and promptly fell asleep.

63

The slow-moving freight train jolted to a stop, awakening its lone passenger. Stretched out on one of its flatbeds, Pitt pried open his eyes under a bright morning sun.

The Panama Railway train had reached its terminus at a rail yard in the port of Balboa. Near the Pacific entrance to the Panama Canal, and just a few miles south of Panama City, Balboa was the key transit point for shipping across the isthmus. Pitt jumped off the flatbed car and found himself surrounded by a steel jungle. Mountains of multicolored shipping containers were stacked in every direction. He looked down a long line of rail cars to see a gantry crane positioned over the tracks and workers beginning to off-load the ubiquitous containers.

Standing near the end of the train, Pitt followed the tracks out of the rail yard, figuring the odds were high that the local rail authorities would treat him as a vagrant. Exiting the yard, he climbed a rusty chain-link fence and found himself in a neighborhood of aged warehouses. A half block away, he noticed a small building with a handful of cars parked out front. It was a run-down bar that catered to the local dockhands. A faded sign proclaimed it *El Gato Negro*, complemented by a painting of a black cat with crossed-out eyes.

Pitt walked into the dim bar, garnering stares from the few early-morning customers already warming the barstools. Pitt approached the bartender, then caught a glimpse of himself in a large mirror behind the bar. The sight nearly frightened him.

It was the image of a tired, emaciated man with a bruised and bloodied face, wearing soiled, shredded, and equally bloodied clothes. He looked like a man returned from the dead.

'*El teléfono?*' Pitt asked.

The bartender looked at Pitt as if he'd landed from Mars, then pointed to a corner next to the restroom. Pitt ambled over and was relieved to find a battered pay phone. Though all but extinct in America, the venerable pay phone lived on around the world, sometimes in the most unlikely of places.

Reaching an English-speaking operator who balked only momentarily at his request to make a collect call to Washington DC, Pitt soon heard the line ringing. Rudi Gunn's voice jumped an octave after hearing Pitt say hello.

'You and Al are safe?'

'Not exactly.' Pitt quickly explained the *Adelaide*'s hijacking, their arrival at the Panama facility, and his escape.

'Panama,' Gunn said. 'We had calls into the Panama Canal Authority to look out for the *Adelaide*.'

'They changed her name at sea. Probably had phony papers already prepared. Bolcke's facility is somewhere in the middle of the Canal Zone, so he probably has inside support at the locks.'

'Did you say Bolcke?'

'Yes, Edward Bolcke. An old Austrian mining engineer who runs the camp of horrors. I was told he's a major player in the market for rare earth elements.'

'He was one of our few leads in your abduction,' Gunn said. 'He owns a ship called the *Salzburg* that was sighted near the *Adelaide* around the time of her disappearance.'

'Probably the same ship that bumped off the *Tasmanian Star* before it made an appearance in Chile. And maybe the *Cuttlefish*, too. Apparently she's armed with some sort of microwave device that proves lethal.'

'Bolcke may have an operation in Madagascar as well,' Gunn said. 'I'll get the ball rolling with the Pentagon to go after Al and the others. It sounds like a joint military operation with Panama security forces is in order.'

'Listen, Rudi, we've got a really narrow window.' Pitt described his encounter with the Chinese agent Zhou and his plan to destroy the facility. Glancing at his Doxa dive watch, he said, 'We've got less than five hours to get Al and the others out of there before the fireworks go off.'

'That's a tall order.'

'Call Sandecker and pull out all the stops.'

'I'll do what I can. Where are you now?'

'A bar called the Black Cat, somewhere near the Pacific rail terminus.'

'Stay put. I'll have someone you know pick you up within the hour.'

'Thanks, Rudi.'

Pitt felt the fatigue of his escape fade away, replaced with a renewed energy for the task still at hand. Saving Giordino and the others was all that mattered. He walked back to the bar, and the bartender waved him to an empty stool. He slid onto the seat to find, served up in front of him, a full shot glass containing a clear liquor. Beside the glass was a pair of long-handled bolt cutters.

Pitt put his hands to his neck and felt the steel collar. He had forgotten it was still there. He looked at the bartender, who returned his gaze and nodded.

'*Muchas gracias, amigo,*' Pitt said, reaching for the shot glass and firing back the contents. A popular local spirit called Seco Herrerano, it burned with the sweet taste of rum. He set the glass down, reached for the bolt cutters, and smiled at the bartender.

'Who says a black cat brings bad luck?'

64

'Are you sure we're in the right place?'

Dirk shot his sister an annoyed look. 'Since they aren't fond of posting street signs around here, the answer would be no.'

He swerved around a stalled truck filled with plantains and accelerated the rental car along the congested road. Since landing at Tocumen International Airport that morning, they had been crisscrossing Panama City, first checking into their hotel, then visiting the mineral brokerage headquarters of Habsburg Industries. It was a tiny, rented storefront office that was closed and appeared little used. The owner of a bakery next door confirmed it was seldom open. Dirk and Summer were beginning to think their trip to Panama was wasted when they received a call from Gunn that their father was alive and waiting at the edge of town.

They passed a sign welcoming them to the district of Balboa, and Dirk knew they were on the right track. He followed a pair of semi-trucks that he assumed were headed to the port facility, then turned down a dirt side road when the port entry gates appeared.

Three blocks down the road, Summer spotted the sign with the black cat.

Dirk barely had the car in park when Summer leaped out and ran inside the bar, ignoring its unsavory appearance. She almost didn't recognize her father, seated at the bar in ragged clothes eating an *empanada*. He was equally shocked to see both his children.

'Dad, let's get you to a hospital,' Summer said.

Pitt shook his head. 'No time. We'll need to coordinate with the Panamanian military to rescue Al and the others.'

Dirk looked at the assorted bar patrons, who all stared at the out-of-place Americans. 'Dad, how about we discuss this in the car?'

'Fair enough,' Pitt said. He looked at the empty shot glass and plate of food. 'Do you have any local currency?'

Dirk opened his wallet. 'I'm told our greenbacks are the preferred currency in Panama.'

Pitt pulled a hundred-dollar bill from his son's wallet and gave it to the bartender, then shook hands with him.

'That was two days' worth of per diem,' Dirk said as they walked out of the bar.

Pitt gave him a wink. 'Put it on your expense report.'

Dirk studied a road map before they took off down the rut-filled road.

'What has Rudi arranged with the Panamanians to get into Bolcke's facility?' Pitt asked.

'Rudi's pulling his hair out,' Summer said. 'He called us three times on the way over. As you probably know, Panama has no standing army in the wake of Manuel Noriega's removal. Paramilitary groups within the Panamanian Public Forces are willing to conduct a joint raid with a US team, but only after they review the evidence and make adequate preparations for a tactical assault. Nobody expects a task force to be assembled within forty-eight hours.'

Dirk looked to his father. 'You think Al and the others may be at risk sooner?'

Pitt explained his encounter with Zhou. 'Once those charges go off, I expect Bolcke's forces to execute all the prisoners and hide their remains. Do we have any US forces that can go in solo?'

Dirk shook his head. 'Special Ops forces out of the Southern Command are our best bet. They've been put on alert but are still ten hours away. Rudi said the only presence nearby he's been able to find is a Navy ship out in the Pacific headed for the canal.'

After traveling just a short distance across Balboa, Dirk drove up a hill to a large, ornate building that overlooked the port district and the canal. A sign on the manicured lawn proclaiming it the PANAMA CANAL AUTHORITY ADMINISTRATION BUILDING.

'The Authority is responsible for the security of the canal and the adjacent Canal Zone,' Summer said. 'Rudi says they are our only hope for an immediate response.'

Inside the building, Pitt's appearance drew stares from the staff and visitors. A receptionist escorted them to the office of the director of Canal Security, a poised man named Madrid who wore a thin mustache. He gave Pitt second and third looks as he introduced himself. 'I have been advised of the urgent nature of your visit. Your Vice President is a very persuasive gentleman,' he said, shocked to have received a personal call.

'Lives are at stake, and time is short,' Pitt said.

'I'll call our nurse, and get you some fresh clothes, while we talk.'

Madrid led them into his office, which had an oversized map of the canal on one wall. A man in fatigues was studying some aerial photographs at a table.

'May I introduce Commander Alvarez. He heads our field security operations and will be leading your rescue operation.'

They joined him at the table, where Pitt described his abduction and the operation at Bolcke's hidden facility.

'We've pulled the Habsburg's company transit records and have found an odd pattern of canal crossings,' Madrid said.

'Their ships enter at one end,' Pitt said, 'and don't exit the other until days later.'

'Exactly correct.'

'They are delivering purchased or stolen raw ore at the facility and then shipping out the refined product.'

Madrid nodded with a pained look. 'The passage of commercial ships through the canal is a tightly controlled operation. They apparently have assistance from the pilots, and perhaps our own locks personnel, to make such transits without attracting attention.'

'There's a lot of money involved with their product,' Pitt said. 'They can afford substantial bribes.'

'Mr Pitt, can you show us where the facility is located?' Alvarez asked.

Pitt walked to the map and tracked the Panama Canal Railway line that ran near the canal's eastern edge.

'I can only guess that I caught the rail line somewhere in this area.' He pointed to a remote area off Gatun Lake, about thirty miles from Panama City. 'The facility would be somewhere between the canal and the rail line.'

Alvarez rifled through a folder and pulled out a packet of color aerial photographs.

'This would be the approximate region.' He examined

each photo closely before passing it around the table. The photos showed swaths of dense jungle that occasionally bordered Gatun Lake. A few pictures showed the Panama Railway line cutting through the jungle, but none gave any sign of Bolcke's facility. They pored through forty photos as skepticism grew on Madrid's face.

'Wait a second,' Summer said. 'Pass that last photo back.'

Dirk handed her the photograph and she lined it up against another on the table. 'Take a look at the jungle in these two pictures.'

The four men craned their necks, seeing a uniform blanket of green jungle flowing across both photos.

Nobody said anything until Pitt slid over a third photograph. 'It's the color,' he said. 'It changes.'

'Exactly.' Summer pointed to one of the photos. 'There's a linear seam here where the jungle color seems to turn a bit gray.'

'I see it,' Madrid said.

'It's the artificial canopies over the facility,' Pitt said. 'They've faded with age and no longer match the surrounding jungle.'

Alvarez pieced the images together with several contiguous photos until the composite showed a distinct peninsula that fingered into Gatun Lake. He took a marker and highlighted the discolored areas, revealing a large rectangle adjacent to a patchwork of smaller squares.

'The large rectangle would cover the dock and inlet,' Pitt said. 'Some artificial mangroves block the entrance and are pulled aside when a ship enters or leaves.'

'What are the other squares?' Summer said.

'The other buildings in the compound.' He took Alvarez's marker and noted Bolcke's residence, the millhouse, the slave housing, and the multiple extraction buildings. He described the facility's security forces to the extent he knew them, leaving out no detail.

'How many prisoners?' Madrid asked.

'Eighty.'

'Amazing,' Madrid said. 'A slave camp hiding right under our noses.' He turned to Alvarez. 'You've got it pinpointed?'

'Yes, sir. It's right here.' He located the peninsula on the large wall map and marked it with a pushpin.

'Clearly within our jurisdiction. Suggested entry?'

'Short notice will dictate an approach from Gatun Lake. We can bring up the *Coletta* from Miraflores as our command ship and run three of our patrol boats off her as assault craft.'

He studied Pitt's markings on the photos. 'If we can enter past the barricade, we'll send one boat into the inlet and land the other two outside, with those forces sweeping in. Once the facility is secure, we can bring the *Coletta* to the dock to evacuate the prisoners.'

'You'd best assemble the men and equipment at once,' Madrid said. 'We'll reconvene aboard the *Coletta* in two hours, and brief the assault team in transit.'

'Yes, sir.' Alvarez stood and scurried out of the office.

'You are welcome to join me on the *Coletta* during the operation,' Madrid said to Pitt and his children.

'We'll be there,' Pitt replied. 'I have an injured friend I was forced to leave behind.'

'I understand. As to the matter of the *Salzburg*, I have

heeded your Vice President's plea and ordered extra security at the Gatun Locks. If the ship should appear for a canal transit, we will be prepared to seize her.'

Pitt shrugged. 'I suppose seizing Bolcke's ship might answer a few more questions.'

Summer could see her father didn't know the full picture. 'Dad, didn't Rudi tell you about your friend Ann Bennett?'

Pitt shook his head.

'She went missing about a week ago – about the same time some sort of propulsion motor was stolen from a Navy research lab truck. Rudi said there was a connection between the two.'

'The *Sea Arrow*,' Pitt muttered.

'Rudi thinks Ann was abducted with the motor. He and Hiram found a cryptic e-mail she sent you over the NUMA website indicating she was in Kentucky.'

'Then she's still alive.'

'Rudi thinks so. They believe she was telling them the motor was hidden on a hay truck. Rudi speculated they were trying to avoid the eastern seaboard in their attempt to get it out of the country. He believes they shipped it down the Mississippi, and Hiram actually found video from the Horace Wilkinson Bridge in Baton Rouge that shows a barge passing by with a hay truck aboard.'

'Seems a bit tenuous,' Pitt said.

'Less so when it was discovered that Bolcke's ship, the *Salzburg*, was in New Orleans at the same time – and departed a day later.'

'The *Salzburg*,' Pitt said. 'So Bolcke has been behind the *Sea Arrow* thefts from the beginning.'

'But what does he plan to do with it?' Summer asked.

Pitt thought back to his encounter with Zhou and the response he gave when asked why he was there.

'Business,' Pitt said. 'He plans to sell it to the Chinese, perhaps as part of a deal related to their combined rare earth holdings.' He looked at Summer. 'How long ago did you say the *Salzburg* left New Orleans?'

'About four days.'

'Recon showed it heading south at the Mississippi Delta,' Dirk said.

'Why hasn't the Coast Guard or Navy tracked her down and boarded her?' Pitt asked.

'They would have but for one thing,' Dirk said. 'The ship has vanished.'

65

Within clear sight of the Canal Authority Administration Building, a rust-covered grain ship sat at anchor, absorbing the gentle waves of the Pacific. Named the *Santa Rita*, she was flagged in Guam, though the government of Guam would have been surprised to learn as much. Aside from never filing papers there, the *Santa Rita* had never once carried an ounce of grain.

She was in fact an aging resource of China's Ministry of State Security. Originally configured as a spy ship to monitor the Taiwan Strait, she later carried missiles to Iran in her grain-hauling configuration. Retired to less clandestine duty, she had been under contract to haul a shipment of Mexican pharmaceuticals to Shanghai when Zhou took her over off Costa Rica.

The tired agent was resting on the bridge, just a short time after returning from his nighttime foray into Bolcke's camp, when his cell phone rang. As he checked the number, his stoic face registered a hint of surprise.

'Zhou,' he answered bluntly.

'Zhou, this is Edward Bolcke. I have to inform you we will be making a slight change in the rendezvous plans.'

'I was expecting the transfer to occur within the hour.'

'There's been a minor security delay, but there's no cause for alarm. The shipment is safe. We will, however, need to postpone the rendezvous for another six hours.'

Zhou grew silent. His explosives would detonate at Bolcke's compound in approximately four hours. He had timed them to go off after he received the *Sea Arrow*'s motor and plans. The entire transfer was now in jeopardy.

'That is unacceptable,' Zhou said calmly. 'I have a strict timetable to adhere to.'

'My apologies, but you can understand the sensitivities at play. My vessel is nearing the Gatun Locks and will still require the complete canal passage. If you wish, you might consider entering the canal at your end. If you head north through the Miraflores Locks, we could make the transfer in Miraflores Lake. That would reduce the time of our delivery by an hour or two. I can make a call and move you up for immediate passage through the lock.'

The last place Zhou wanted to be was trapped in the middle of the Panama Canal. But if that was the only opportunity to acquire the *Sea Arrow*'s secrets, so be it. With luck, Bolcke might not know his facility was a smoldering ruin when he passed over the technology.

'Very well,' Zhou said. 'Make the transit arrangements, and I will proceed to Miraflores Lake. Please expedite your vessel, as we will be waiting.'

Hanging up, he stared out the bridge window, feeling like he was about to dance on the edge of a razor.

66

Nearly forty ships were moored in Limon Bay, congesting like a swarm of bees around a hive. Each awaited its turn to be funneled from the Atlantic Ocean into the Panama Canal. A small containership arrived and cut past the long line of freighters, tankers, and other carriers to take its place at the front of the line.

The century-old Big Ditch was handling more ships than ever, but its capacity was soon to swell. A major expansion was under way, adding two new sets of locks capable of handling the world's largest containerships. While expensive to cross, the Panama Canal shaved thousands of miles off the alternative of traveling around Cape Horn.

Watching the containership sail past, the captains waiting their turn in Limon Bay knew that jumping to the head of the line required paying a steep premium.

The containership slowed as a pilot boat drew alongside, delivering a Panama Canal Authority boarding officer and a canal pilot. The ship's captain escorted them to the bridge, where he relinquished command to the pilot, a requirement of all ships transiting the canal. The boarding officer confirmed the ship's tonnage and dimensions to determine the vessel's fare.

'Manifest, please,' he asked the captain.

The officer thumbed through the document, noting a short list of equipment parts.

'Most of those containers empty?' he asked.

'Yes, taking them to Balboa,' the captain said.

'I noticed you were riding high in the water.' He computed the fee, with a steep kicker for moving up in line. 'Your account will be charged accordingly.' Then he turned to the pilot. 'The *Portobelo* is cleared to proceed.' He left the bridge and reboarded the pilot boat, which whisked him to the next ship waiting in line.

The pilot sailed the *Portobelo* down a long channel to the Gatun Locks, the canal's Atlantic entry point. The locks consisted of a parallel set of three huge sequential chambers, which enabled southbound vessels to be lifted eighty-five feet above sea level to begin crossing the isthmus.

The Panama Canal itself was built like a liquid wedding cake. Its highest point was at its center, the large, manmade reservoir of Gatun Lake. The lake cascaded down three levels at either end. Due to a geographic quirk, the canal's fresh water flowed to the Atlantic Ocean in the north and to the Pacific in the south. The elevated lake allowed for gravity to fill and drain the locks, raising or lowering ships, depending on their direction of travel.

But the Panama Canal was an uneven wedding cake, due to a separation between locks on the Pacific side. While the three chambers of the Atlantic's Gatun were sequential, the Pacific's were far apart, with a single-chamber lock called Pedro Miguel at the lake and a dual-chamber lock called Miraflores a mile beyond. It took a typical ship about eight hours to complete the fifty-mile journey from ocean to ocean.

The pilot inched the *Portobelo* close to the first chamber

at Gatun, stopping just short of its huge open doors, which were called gates. Messenger lines attached to steel tow cables were hoisted aboard and secured, their opposite ends attached to tiny locomotives, called mules, which ran along the lock's edge. Under the pilot's guidance, the mules gently towed the freighter into the chamber and held it in place as the gates astern were closed. Once sealed, additional water was released into the mammoth chamber until the ship had been raised nearly thirty feet.

Armed guards, not usually seen around the locks, patrolled the area, giving the ship a careful once-over. When the water level matched the next chamber's, the front gates were opened and the ship was pulled forward by the mules. The process was repeated twice more, until the *Portobelo* motored out of the last chamber and into Gatun Lake – eighty-five feet higher than when she started. Clearing the locks, the pilot ordered the helm to increase speed.

'Helm, belay that order,' the captain said. 'All stop.'

The pilot's face turned red. 'I command the vessel through the canal!' His demeanor softened when he detected another presence on the bridge. He turned to find Pablo approaching him. 'Pablo! I thought this tub was eerily familiar to the old *Salzburg*. When did you boys get into the container business?'

'About thirty-six hours ago,' Pablo said. 'We'll be taking her from here.'

'Sure, sure.' The pilot spotted the bag in Pablo's hand that contained the usual cash bribe and a bottle of Chivas Regal.

'There's an extra thousand for you,' Pablo said, handing him the bag. 'No more mention of the *Salzburg*.'

'Whatever you say. The monkeys on the dock were looking for you, but I guess you fooled them. See you on the next run.'

The ship's crew lowered a rubber boat and ran the pilot to shore, where he could hop in a taxi to the nearest bar. When the inflatable returned, the disguised *Salzburg* got under way.

'You sure he can be trusted?' the captain asked.

Pablo nodded. 'We'll have completed the transfer before he's halfway through that bottle of scotch.'

Pablo allowed himself his own notion of relief. Since receiving the warning call from Bolcke two days earlier, he had feared every call on the radio and every passing ship. But the rush transformation of the *Salzburg* into the *Portobelo*, aided by a paint respray of the bridge and funnel, and a large load of empty containers, had fooled the canal authorities at the Gatun Locks. That meant one thing.

They were home free.

67

The *Coletta* screamed through the Panama Canal, passing the speed-restricted commercial ships like they were standing still. An Italian-built patrol boat of some forty meters, she sported a 20mm turreted cannon on her bow for muscle.

Below deck, thirty armed commandos were crammed into the wardroom, receiving a final briefing from Alvarez. They were well trained, having conducted numerous joint exercises with international forces in mock defense of the canal. Pitt tried to quell their obvious enthusiasm for the mission by detailing the strength of Bolcke's forces.

Yet Pitt felt his own impatience. Showered, bandaged, and wearing a fresh set of borrowed fatigues, he was anxious to get into the facility and free Giordino. But a daylight raid was risky, and everything hinged on his brief encounter with Zhou. Pitt just hoped that his instincts were right.

Alvarez handed him a holstered SIG Sauer P228 automatic. 'You know how to use it?'

Pitt nodded.

'We should arrive at the deployment zone in ten minutes. I'll be leading boat 1 into the cove. We'll secure the dock, knock out the generator, and release the prisoners. Boat 2 will land on the peninsula and secure the residence, hopefully with Bolcke inside. Boat 3 will follow as a reserve. You can join boat 3, but I must request that you act as an observer only.'

'I'll help where I can. Good luck, Alvarez.'

Pitt looked for Dirk and Summer but didn't see them in the emptying wardroom. He could hear the patrol boat's motor slow, and he followed the others onto the deck.

The *Coletta* had followed the canal's transit route around the eastern shore of Barro Colorado Island, a large nature preserve in the middle of Gatun Lake. The canal's narrow channel was marked with lights and signs to prevent ships from running aground in the nearby shallows. The lightly drafted *Coletta* had no such concerns as she raced across the path of an approaching containership. She traveled east for a mile until she approached a narrow landmass covered with dense vegetation.

The *Coletta* drifted under the hot sun as three inflatable assault craft were lowered over the side, each loaded with ten commandos. Pitt sensed his boat had some extra passengers as he squeezed between two unarmed commandos with bush hats pulled low over their faces.

'A little room for the old man?' he said.

Dirk looked up from beneath his hat. 'We wanted to be here to help.'

'I'd rather you both stayed on the boat.' Pitt unhooked his holster and passed the SIG Sauer to Dirk. 'Keep an eye on your sister.'

'No worries,' Summer whispered beside him.

A commando had already engaged the outboard motor, propelling the inflatable toward shore behind the first two assault craft. The first boat veered left for the cove, while the other two eased right toward a small protected bluff. The boats had been in the water less than five minutes when their entire plan of attack fell apart.

A ring of moored buoys containing sensors and video cameras had detected their approach. Alarms sounded around the compound, alerting Bolcke's security forces. Most deployed to the dock after securing the prisoners, while another force took to the roof of Bolcke's residence.

Boat 1, with Alvarez leading his team, took the first hit. Maneuvering past a fake mangrove swamp, they approached the dock – only to be met with a fusillade from shore. Alvarez and his men gamely fired back, suppressing some of the gunfire, until a battery of rocket-propelled grenades came blasting at them. One landed in the boat, skidding to the rear transom before detonating. Two men were killed instantly as the stern blew apart, sending the rest of the men into the water.

Boats 2 and 3 had a moment's warning before gunfire erupted from the rooftop of Bolcke's concealed residence. Closest to the shore, boat 2 took the brunt of the fire, incurring several casualties, as they maneuvered and returned fire. The pilot managed to run the boat ashore, the commandos finding marginal protection behind a low rock berm. But the team was effectively pinned down by the shooters on the roof.

'Run to the right!' Pitt yelled to boat 3's pilot as the battle ignited in front of them.

He had foreseen boat 2's predicament and motioned for the pilot to sweep hard right and put ashore out of view of the residence. The panicked pilot turned up the outboard's throttle and jammed the rudder to the side. They nearly made it unscathed as the team leader, a burly man named Jorge, organized return fire. But as the rooftop shooters focused on the third boat, Jorge was shot twice in the stomach.

Pitt saw the scared look in the eyes of the other commandos, none of whom had ever witnessed actual combat. He immediately stepped forward.

'We need to suppress the rooftop fire to get the men from boat 2 off the beach. Follow me to the house.'

When their hull touched bottom, Pitt leaped over the side and sprinted into the jungle. Inspired by his show of fearlessness, the commandos tore after him.

'I'll stay here and look after Jorge,' Summer said to Dirk as she rummaged for a medical kit. 'Go help Dad.'

Dirk nodded, thumbing off the safety of his pistol, and leaping from the boat. He quickly caught up with the others as they snaked their way through the jungle. Pitt stopped them at the fringe of a clearing that surrounded the house. Several gunmen were visible on the roof, waiting for them to emerge from the brush.

Pitt studied the residence, noticing an exterior side stairwell that led to the roof. He turned to a young man crouched next to him. 'Do you have any grenades?'

'Only smoke grenades.'

'Give me what you have.'

After collecting four smoke grenades, Pitt lined the men in a picket.

'On my signal, spray the rooftop to give me cover. When I get to the stairs, I'll lob the grenades onto the roof. Move in quickly and secure it.'

Pitt slithered to a position closer to the house and then yelled, 'Now!' The jungle exploded with gunfire, targeting the rooftop guards. Pitt took off running as the guards ducked for cover. But they regrouped quickly and returned fire. Sprinting to the house, Pitt saw the rooftop gunners were obscured by the residence's front porch, and he angled toward the entry. He was nearing the porch steps when the front door burst open and two guards charged out. In their wake followed Bolcke, like a running back behind his blockers. The trio dashed down the first steps, then froze at the sight of Pitt a few feet away.

Bolcke's eyes flared in shock. But there was no hesitation in his voice as he spoke over the background gunfire.

'Kill him!'

68

Bolcke's guards swung their rifles toward Pitt and readied to fire. But Pitt was a step ahead. He popped the pin on one of the smoke grenades and tossed it on the steps. The grenade skidded across the carved stone and stopped at Bolcke's feet.

The guards dropped their weapons, grabbed Bolcke, and heaved him over the far balustrade. One guard dove after him, but the other hesitated. He'd heard the grenade hissing and noticed a first wisp of smoke spurting from it. Realizing it was not an explosive, he kicked it off the steps, and a gray cloud erupted over the lawn. He turned back to Pitt, who stood, exposed, at the corner wall a few feet away.

The guard raised his rifle and took a bead on Pitt. But before he found the trigger, two red splotches appeared on his chest, and he staggered back on his heels. The guard teetered, then collapsed on the steps and rolled to the ground.

Pitt saw his son kneeling on the lawn, the SIG Sauer held outstretched in his hands. Dirk jumped up and ran to the side of the house as a salvo of bullets stitched the ground beside him.

'Thanks for the backup,' Pitt said.

Dirk smiled. 'Smoke is no match for lead.'

Pitt motioned toward the porch steps. 'Bolcke.'

Dirk took the lead as they crept across the porch, but Bolcke and the other guard had already vanished down a jungle path. Reversing course, Pitt led his son up the side stairwell, halting a few feet from the top. He heaved the remaining grenades onto the rooftop, engulfing it in a thick cloud of smoke. Ground fire ceased as the boat 3 commandos streamed out of the jungle and raced up the stairs. A few seconds later, the remaining boat 2 commandos broke from the shore and joined the assault. The combined forces quickly overran the guards, sweeping the roof as the smoke cleared.

As the residence fell silent, they could still hear sporadic gunfire from the dock area.

'Has anyone heard from Alvarez?' Pitt asked, as the commandos reassembled on the roof.

'I've had no response,' said the leader of boat 2. 'We better move to the dock.'

'I'll show you the way,' Pitt said.

The commandos rushed back down the stairs. A small contingent peeled off to secure the interior of the house while the rest followed Pitt down the same path Bolcke had taken. When the commandos arrived at the dock, a half dozen security guards were scattered about it, firing into the water. They had been joined by two armed crewmen on the bow of the *Adelaide*, firing from above.

The Canal Authority commandos opened fire, catching several guards without cover and dropping them quickly. The rest of the dock guards fell back, retreating into the jungle for cover. But the crewmen on the ship held their position and returned fire. An extended firefight ensued, until the better-trained commandos picked off both men.

Over the clatter of gunfire, Pitt had detected a revving motor. He caught a quick glimpse of a small crew boat exiting the mouth of the inlet, the white-haired figure of Bolcke visible next to the pilot.

Pitt turned to the boat 2 commander, who was kneeling behind a rubber tree, reloading his rifle. 'Bolcke has escaped in a small boat. Call Madrid on the *Coletta* and have them pick him up.'

The commando nodded. Snapping a magazine into place, he hit the transmit button on his radio and called the support boat.

Aboard the *Coletta*, Madrid had been using binoculars to watch a small containership approach when he received the call. He turned to see Bolcke's crew boat surging out of the inlet and he brought his patrol boat to bear. 'Gunner, prepare for a warning shot ahead of the approaching boat,' he said. 'Fire!'

A man let loose a blast from the 20mm deck gun, ripping a fountain of water ahead of the crew boat. The fleeing boat reduced speed but held its course across the *Coletta*'s bow. Focused on stopping Bolcke's boat, Madrid had ignored the containership, which was approaching off his stern quarter.

'Gunner, prepare for a burst into the motor. Fire!'

The gunner took aim, but before he could fire he fell to the deck and began flailing his arms as if attacked by a swarm of bees. Screaming, he rolled to the rail and hurled himself over the side to find relief in the lake's waters.

Inside the wheelhouse, Madrid suddenly found his skin inflamed with a searing pain. He danced away from the helm, unable to grip the controls. Screaming in pain, he looked out the window to see the containership bearing down on him.

The ship plowed into the *Coletta* at slow speed, its lumbering mass easily crushing the patrol boat's bow. The smaller boat was kicked backward, as its interior filled with water. In seconds, its stern rose, and the boat plunged underwater.

Bolcke watched the patrol boat disappear as his own boat tied up alongside the containership. He sprinted up the ship's accommodation ladder with his guard in tow, crossed the deck, and climbed to the bridge. Panting, he staggered to the helm, where Pablo stood admiring the modified Active Denial System on the ship's bow.

'We seem to have made a timely arrival,' Pablo said.

'They've . . . attacked . . . the facility,' Bolcke said.

'Who has?'

'One of the prisoners. He escaped yesterday.'

'They would have to be from the Canal Authority. I thought that was their boat. I'm sure Johansson will take good care of them ashore.'

'No, Johansson was killed. By the man who escaped.'

'Can they know of the deal?'

Bolcke shook his head.

'Five hundred million will buy you plenty of new facilities,' Pablo said.

'The plans and motor are safe aboard?' Bolcke eyed the changed appearance of the *Salzburg*.

'Yes.'

'The Chinese are waiting for us in Miraflores Lake.'

Pablo looked at him like a child awaiting a birthday present. 'Then I see no reason to delay our payment a minute longer.' He ordered the ship into the canal's main channel, and the *Salzburg* was swiftly on its way.

69

The Canal Authority commandos fished out Alvarez and the remnants of his team that had been scattered across the inlet or huddled among the dock pilings. The operations leader looked like a drowned rat, but he shook off the loss of half his team to take command of the combined forces.

He pointed to a wide trail off the far end of the dock that meandered into the jungle. 'The prisoners are down there?'

'Yes,' Pitt said. 'The trail leads to a millhouse. The prison housing is just beyond.'

Alvarez split his men into two groups and set off down the trail with the lead force, Pitt and Dirk following. They moved cautiously, fearing an ambush, but the remaining guards were nowhere to be seen. The trail widened as they approached the millhouse, a high-roofed, open building. Alvarez sent three men to scout the side entrance, but they never made it.

Gunmen opened fire from every door and window in the structure. Bolcke's remaining security forces, a dozen strong, had gathered in the millhouse to mount a final defense and counterassault. Their sudden barrage inflicted casualties on nearly half of Alvarez's men.

Alvarez himself was hit in the leg, and Pitt dragged him to cover. The operations leader quickly called in his reserve force, which had followed on the flank. Under a blanket of return fire, he retrieved his wounded men to the cover of the jungle, but the battle regressed into a stalemate. Alvarez radioed the *Coletta* for assistance but heard only static in reply. 'There's no response,' he said to Pitt. 'Without additional support, we'll have to pull back.'

'Not without the prisoners.' Pitt grabbed an assault rifle from a wounded commando who had fallen unconscious. 'Keep them occupied. We'll try to get around to the housing complex.' He motioned to Dirk.

The two men took off through the jungle, skirting wide left around the millhouse. Pitt led them on a partial loop, then cut back toward the tall structure. Peering from behind a gnarled cedar, they eyed the end of the millhouse and the prisoners' housing just beyond.

The housing stood in the center of a wide clearing, fully exposed to the gunmen in the millhouse. Pitt could see several prisoners peering through the housing's lone gate, trying to watch the gun battle.

He noticed an ore cart parked on the grass midway between their position and the gate. 'I'm going to make a run for that cart. If I can get there undetected, I should be able to make it to the gate.'

Dirk gauged the distance between them and the millhouse. 'Tough range to cover you from here. I'll go with you.'

Before Pitt could protest, Dirk sprinted for the cart. Pitt followed on his heels, though his weakened legs couldn't keep pace for long.

They were seen by a gunman on the second floor of the millhouse. Bullets tore into the ground alongside the ore cart as Dirk ducked behind it. A couple steps behind, Pitt had to dive for cover, rolling hard into his son as the bullets struck close by.

Dirk stuck out the SIG Sauer and fired twice, but that only attracted more gunmen from the millhouse. The cart clanked as it absorbed cross fire from several shooters.

'Not the stealth approach I hoped for,' Pitt said.

'They must have gunmen all over that building.' Dirk peeked over the top of the cart, fired another two shots, and ducked back down. 'There's a guy on the second floor with an RPG.'

Pitt stuck his assault rifle around the side of the cart and sprayed a short burst at an open window. The bullets chewed up its frame and shattered the glass. As he pulled his gun away, Pitt saw a guard emerge from the shadows with a bulbous green device on his shoulder. He knew that a successful shot from the RPG would vaporize them both.

He swung his rifle atop the cart and was preparing to fire again when an explosion rang out like a thunderclap. Shooting ceased as all eyes watched a black cloud rise from beyond the prisoners' housing complex.

Pitt looked at his watch and grinned. Zhou had come through after all. 'You're ten minutes late,' Pitt muttered.

A second later, the entire millhouse erupted in a fire-ball. A half dozen additional explosions rang out, leveling the separation-and-extraction buildings that were spread throughout the compound. The entire jungle belched smoke and flames as Bolcke's hidden facility was methodically destroyed. Zhou had spared only the prisoners' housing, Bolcke's own residence, and a staff hall where a dozen research workers were huddling during the fight.

Chunks of the millhouse roof rained down around Pitt and his son as they crowded behind the ore cart. The blast unleashed the ball mill, sending the giant cylinder tumbling out a side wall and rolling into the jungle. Most of the guards inside were killed instantly, but a few were hurled out the windows and landed on the grass unscathed. Canal Authority commandos cut them down on the spot.

Pitt and his son moved quickly to the prisoners' housing. Pitt shot the lock off with his rifle and kicked open the gate. The crowd of captives inside surged forward.

'Boy, are we glad to see you,' Plugrad said, pushing through to pat Pitt on the shoulder.

Maguire and the other men rushed up and shook his hand. Pitt worked his way through the crowd, anxiously counting each man while searching for his friend. Reaching the last man standing, Pitt found himself a head short. Giordino's.

With an uneasy feeling, Pitt stepped through the mess and the living quarters. Both were empty. Turning back toward the gate, he noticed a hammock strung between two grills in the open kitchen. The still figure of Giordino lay on it. Pitt moved closer, staring at his friend with apprehension. Then a familiar snore gurgled from Giordino's throat.

Pitt grinned from ear to ear. 'Rise and shine, big boy.'

Giordino cocked open a sleepy eye. 'You got back pretty quick.'

'I knew you'd miss me.'

Giordino yawned and sat up. 'Quite the fireworks show. Did you get Bolcke?'

'No, he slipped out when the fun started.' He handed Giordino a nearby crutch that had been crudely carved from a stick of zebrawood. 'How are you feeling?'

'Like a contender for the national hopscotch championships.' Giordino hopped up on one foot and planted the crutch under his arm. His wounded leg was bandaged so thickly, it resembled a tree stump. Pitt helped him hobble to the gate, where the other captives were milling about, afraid to leave.

A commando came running past the smoldering millhouse and approached Pitt. 'Alvarez sent me. Are these all the captives?'

'Yes, every man is accounted for.'

'Where did those explosions come from?'

'Planted here ahead of time. They really saved our bacon.'

'They sure did,' the man said. 'Alvarez says to get everyone to the dock.' He turned and started jogging back the way he came. 'We've got a lot of wounded to attend to.'

Pitt began herding the captives out of the compound when Giordino grabbed his arm and pointed to the sky.

'Someone leaving without us?'

Pitt looked up to see a wisp of black smoke rising from the dock area – the sooty exhaust from a large diesel engine.

'It's the *Adelaide*,' Pitt said with resolve. Their fight wasn't over yet.

70

'Al, keep the men moving,' Pitt shouted, already on the run. 'Dirk, come with me.'

In the rush to free the captives, Alvarez had failed to send anyone aboard to secure the *Adelaide*. Hiding on the bridge, Gomez had fired up the ship's engines at the beginning of the assault. After seeing Bolcke escape and the subsequent explosions in the jungle, he had no reason to linger.

Pitt and Dirk emerged from the jungle to find the *Adelaide* still at the dock. The stern mooring line had been released, and Pitt glimpsed Gomez yank the line onto the deck, then disappear into the ship's superstructure. Ahead of the ship, a crewman on the dock moved to release the bowline.

Pitt and his son kept on running. The forward gangway was still in place, so they still had a chance to get aboard, if not hold its bowline. That possibility evaporated when the crewman slipped the line off its bollard, then gazed toward the mouth of the inlet. A small outboard motor could be heard over the drone of the *Adelaide*'s warming engines. As Pitt and Dirk hustled along the length of the big ship, they saw the source.

It was Summer, piloting boat 3. With her were four or five bedraggled men, lying in the bottom of the boat.

The crewman on the dock watched a moment, then

kicked the bowline into the water. As the boat neared the dock, he calmly removed a holstered pistol and took aim at Summer.

A rapid peal of gunshots rang out as a half dozen bullets tore into the crewman's back. At least two shots had come from Dirk's SIG Sauer, the rest from Pitt's assault rifle. The crewman spun and squeezed off a stray shot at his attackers, then collapsed dead.

A second later, a screech and a loud crash filled the air. 'She's under way!' Dirk shouted.

Gomez had engaged the engines and was pulling away from the dock. The noise had come from the gangway, which skidded off the edge of the dock and slammed against the hull, dangling from its deck mountings.

Summer drove the inflatable alongside the dock as the ship pulled away. 'A containership came in and rammed the *Coletta*,' she yelled to Pitt and Dirk. She had sped over in the inflatable and fished out the survivors as the containership sailed away. 'I'm pretty sure they picked up Bolcke. It might have been the *Salzburg*.'

A flood of thoughts filled Pitt's mind. If Summer was right, the *Sea Arrow*'s plans and motor would be aboard. And possibly Ann as well. The ship would have to be stopped before it could escape the canal.

He spoke quickly to his kids as he watched the moving *Adelaide*. 'Dirk, run down to the end of the dock. Summer, keep the engine running, I'm coming aboard.'

He strapped the assault rifle over his back and dove off the dock. He hit the water a few feet from the inflatable but stroked toward the ship. He couldn't match speed with the fleeing vessel, but he had a second target in mind:

the ship's bowline, dangling through its scupper and dragging through the water. He snagged the thick line, then slid along its length until he reached a heavy looped end. A smaller messenger line was attached to it, and he tossed that line to one of the men in the inflatable.

'Stay with the ship,' he yelled to Summer, grabbing the side of the inflatable as she wielded it around and chased after the vessel.

A weakened Madrid leaned over the side and helped Pitt aboard. Together, they reeled in the heavy bowline. Pitt had his daughter push ahead of the ship, dragging the line like an anchor. On shore, Dirk had sprinted to the end of the dock, where a final mooring bitt was mounted. As the inflatable struggled closer, Gomez guessed what they were attempting and turned the *Adelaide* as far across the inlet as he could.

Dirk could see the ship pulling away and urged Summer to hurry. Pitt's and Madrid's arms ached from pulling the heavy line as Summer buried the throttle and took a bead on her brother. Dirk got on his belly and leaned over the side of the dock as the inflatable pulled alongside and Summer cut the motor. Pitt heaved the loop at the end of the line up and Dirk grabbed it just as the line went taut. Muscling it with all his might, he rolled the loop to his side, barely slipping it over the end of the bitt.

'Get clear in case it snaps,' Pitt yelled.

Dirk got to his feet and sprinted down the dock as Summer turned the inflatable around and followed. Suddenly the inflatable veered toward the *Adelaide*, and Dirk quickly saw why. Summer brought the boat alongside the dangling gangway and Pitt jumped up and grabbed it.

Climbing hand over hand, he pulled himself up and boarded the ship.

The bowline was pulled taut, grabbing the ship by its nose and holding it in place. With its propeller still churning, the stern began swinging to starboard, threatening to lodge the ship crossways in the inlet. On the dock, the mooring bitt's mounts strained under the pressure, fighting to hold the ship in place.

As the tug-of-war played out, Summer brought the inflatable alongside a dock ladder, where Dirk helped Madrid and the other injured men ashore. When Jorge, the last man, was transferred to the dock, Dirk jumped into the inflatable. 'Run me over. I'll back him up,' he shouted.

Summer gunned the throttle and shot to the side of the *Adelaide*, allowing Dirk to jump onto the dangling gangway.

'Be careful,' she shouted.

Dirk nodded. 'Just get away from that line.'

Summer hurried back to the dock as a twang arose from the straining rope. Gomez had turned the rudder over and was applying full power against the line. Something had to give and finally it did.

The bowline's threaded loop snapped at the mooring bitt, sending the line whipsawing toward the *Adelaide*. Clinging to the gangway, Dirk ducked as the line slapped against the hull, nearly taking his head off. As the loose line began to fall over him, he scrambled up the gangway and pulled himself onto the deck.

Free of its leash, the ship surged forward, angling out of the narrow inlet. Dirk scanned the deck for his father, but aside from the bodies of the two gunmen on the bow, the ship appeared empty. He eyed the bridge atop the rear superstructure and took off at a run across the long, open deck. He made it to a side door and was on the first steps of the companionway when gunfire erupted overhead.

Repeated bursts of gunfire sounded for nearly half a minute as Dirk raced up the stairs. When he reached the fourth level, the shooting fell silent, and he proceeded cautiously from there up to the bridge deck. He clutched the SIG Sauer at the ready as he crept onto the bridge.

He'd taken only a few steps past the door when a warm muzzle was jammed into the back of his neck. He froze in his tracks, but the barrel was quickly removed.

'I don't remember giving you permission to come aboard.'

Dirk turned his head to find it was his father holding the gun, relief plastered on his face.

'I wasn't aware you were the captain of this tub,' Dirk said.

'Apparently, I am now.' Pitt pointed across the bridge.

There was nothing but carnage around them. The bridge windows were shot out and the radar and navigation monitors shattered. Smoke from the decimated electronics filled the air with an acrid odor. In the far corner lay the bloodied body of Gomez.

'Gave him a chance, but he refused to take it.'

Dirk nodded, then glanced out the broken forward window of the pilotless ship. The *Adelaide* had nearly cleared the inlet, but a wall of rocks and mangroves blocked its path.

'There're rocks ahead!' he said, jumping to the helm.

'They're not real,' Pitt replied. 'Part of the fake scenery to disguise the inlet.'

A few seconds later, the ship charged into the decoys. There was no jarring collision. Instead the *Adelaide* sailed smoothly through. Out the side window, Dirk saw an overturned Styrofoam rock gently float away.

Clear of the inlet, the *Adelaide* charged into the open waters of Gatun Lake. A large crane ship was crossing the canal to the north, while a pair of tankers and a containership were headed around a bend to the south. Pitt stepped to the helm and dialed up the ship's throttle controls to full.

'Not going back for the others?' Dirk asked.

Pitt gave a steely gaze toward the containership vanishing around the channel ahead.

'No,' he said. 'We have a ship to catch.'

71

Bolcke stood peering out the rear bridge window. Billows of black smoke from the site of his hidden facility painted the horizon. It was destroyed, he knew, because of the escaped prisoner, the one who had tossed the smoke grenade onto his front steps.

But Pablo was right. The money he would receive from selling the *Sea Arrow*'s technology would leave plenty for a new rare earth extraction facility. He had already done work at a site on Madagascar; he could safely expand his operations there. But he would lose precious months of trading activity at a critical time in the minerals market. Once he was safely in Colombia, he vowed, he would have Pablo hunt down the prisoner and bring him his head on a platter.

He faced forward as the *Salzburg* entered a narrow stretch of Gatun Lake called Gamboa Reach. 'How much farther to the lock?'

Pablo turned from the helm. 'It's about twelve miles to Pedro Miguel.' He noted the angst on Bolcke's face. 'I've radioed ahead. The lock's transit chief is expecting our passage. There will be no problems.'

The bridge radio blared with the voice of a tanker pilot castigating another ship for passing it on the lake. Bolcke and Pablo ignored the chatter as they eyed the *Sea Arrow*'s motor on the deck below, covered on the flatbed truck and concealed by stacked containers.

Two miles behind them, the tanker's pilot still spouted venom at the large bulk carrier that had cut in front of him. 'The maximum speed in this section of the canal is eight knots, jerk,' he radioed.

On the bridge of the *Adelaide*, Pitt couldn't hear a word the man said, since the ship's radio had been destroyed in his gun battle with Gomez. He didn't even know his speed, as the navigation instruments were also demolished. But he had little doubt the ship was traveling well over eight knots.

Empty of all cargo and most of her fuel, the *Adelaide* sailed light on her feet. Pitt coaxed every ounce of speed he could from the ship, and soon had her approaching twenty knots. She left the tanker and its angry pilot in her wake as Pitt set his sights on the next vessel ahead. It was a large Dutch Panamax tanker, built to the original specs of the canal's locks at nearly a thousand feet long.

The canal channel had narrowed even more as Pitt caught up to the Dutch ship and pulled up to its port flank to pass. The *Adelaide* had just edged alongside the tanker when a large blue containership appeared, sailing in the opposite direction.

Dirk gauged the distance needed to pass the tanker and shook his head. 'No way we can get past her ahead of that containership.'

He expected his father to slow the ship and duck back behind the tanker until there was room to pass. Instead, Pitt stood calmly at the helm. He had no intention of slowing down.

Dirk grinned at his father and shook his head. 'Those boys in that containership aren't going to be happy.'

The pilot of the oncoming ship had already noticed the *Adelaide* in his lane and was making furious demands over the radio for the bulk carrier to back down. But the increasingly frantic calls went unanswered as the vessels converged.

Pitt continued to gain on the tanker, but its monstrous length made passing it an interminable task. Ahead, the tanker and containership had already passed bow to bow, so there was no escape for anyone. Pitt had estimated the canal cut was wide enough for the three ships to pass side by side, but he didn't know if it was deep enough for all three. Positioned in the middle, where the channel would be deepest, he didn't really care.

The tanker's pilot did what he could to slow his vessel and steer it to the right-hand side of the marked channel. But because his ship had the deepest draft, he refused to push it any closer to the bank. That left the game of chicken in the hands of the containership's pilot.

Pitt helped the cause by pulling tight alongside the tanker, close enough that a man could jump from one vessel to the other. But, by all appearances, a collision looked inevitable.

As the containership bore down from the other direction, Pitt and Dirk braced for impact. The approaching ship, stacked to the sky with containers, filled their vision as its bow cut toward them. But the pilot wisely decided that grounding on the bank would be safer than a collision and he guided the ship aside to make way for Pitt.

The ships passed within a few feet of each other as the containership's hull scraped bottom and its propeller churned through mud. The pilot and deck officers hurled a mountain of insults as the bridges of the two ships passed. Pitt merely smiled and waved.

'They're going to want your pilot's license for that,' Dirk said.

'Think how mad they'll be,' Pitt replied, 'when they find out I don't have one.'

The channel turned and narrowed ahead, partially obscuring the outline of the *Salzburg*. Aboard her bridge, Bolcke and Pablo came alert at the latest burst of ire from the radio. When the blue containership had passed the *Adelaide* and the pilot saw the repainted name on her stern, he made further threats over the radio. *'Labrador,'* he said, 'I will be filing a formal complaint with the canal authorities in Colón.'

Bolcke stiffened at mention of the ship's name. *'Labrador.* That's the name given to the hijacked vessel at our dock.' He grabbed a pair of binoculars and sprinted to the rear window. There was no mistaking the large bulk carrier a mile behind them, spurting past the Dutch tanker. It was the *Adelaide*.

His face turned pale. 'They are chasing after us,' he said to Pablo.

Pablo calmly surveyed the navigation screen. 'We should be able to pass safely into the locks ahead. If not,' he added, his eyes turning cold, 'we'll make them regret coming after us.'

72

The two ships had entered the Gaillard Cut, the canal's most dangerous section. Nine miles long, it sliced through the continental divide and had presented the most difficult challenge for the engineers who built the canal. A herculean excavation effort gouged out a trench more than two hundred fifty feet deep in some places, using manual labor and finicky steam shovels. Untold thousands lost their lives, some due to accidents and mudslides, but most from yellow fever and pneumonia.

The magnitude of the feat was obscured when the canal waters were released in 1914, flooding the deep cut. A tranquil appearance belied its tricky currents that made the narrow passage a challenge to navigate.

Pitt stormed into the cut, ignoring a channel marker that indicated a speed limit of six knots for large vessels. He occasionally felt the effects of the currents, as the stern drifted one way or another. But he refused to slow his pursuit. He had a clear bead on the *Salzburg*, having closed to within a half mile.

Though Pablo had ordered the captain to increase speed, it took precious time for the *Salzburg* to increase its pace. Peering back at the faster *Adelaide*, he realized he would have to take the offensive.

When Pitt noticed a few men congregating on the *Salzburg*'s forward deck, he passed the helm to Dirk.

'Just for the record,' Dirk said, 'I've never piloted a vessel this size before.'

'She's easier to handle than a Duesenberg,' Pitt said. 'Just keep her off the bank. I'll be right back.'

As they drew closer to the *Salzburg*, Dirk could see three men on her bow manipulating a tall object that looked like a large radar dish. The men rolled the dish alongside some shipping containers on the portside rail and positioned it so it aimed rearward – at the *Adelaide*.

Pitt appeared on the bridge a moment later. Dirk did a double take at seeing his father dressed in the reflective silver coating of a Level A hazardous materials protective suit. 'What's with the Buck Rogers outfit?'

'We brought them along for protection when we came aboard,' Pitt said. 'Bolcke's ships are outfitted with a microwave device called ADS that's used for crowd control, only theirs is lethal. They likely have one aboard the *Salzburg*.'

Dirk pointed forward. 'You mean that dish on their bow?'

Pitt saw the Active Denial System aimed directly at them and tossed Dirk an extra suit. 'Quick, get this on.'

Dirk was starting to slip on the Hazmat suit when he felt a burning sensation on his back. 'They must have it cranked up,' he said, quickly zipping the suit up.

Pitt felt the same sensation on his face and pulled on the matching hood with faceplate, and stepped to the helm.

'Stay behind the bulkhead,' he said to Dirk, his voice muffled by the hood.

He jammed the helm control to starboard, feeling a hot

sensation on his chest and arms. Standing before the shattered bridge window, he was in the device's direct line of fire. The Hazmat suit provided some protection but didn't block the full effect.

Positioned on the *Salzburg*'s bow, the system had to fire along the ship's port side to strike the *Adelaide*. Pitt could avoid the weapon's beam by sailing to the far right of the channel and tucking in behind the leading ship. Within a few minutes, he did exactly that.

Bolcke watched as the *Adelaide* suddenly altered course. 'She's veering to the bank. I think you got her.'

'The operator reports he had a clear strike on the bridge,' Pablo said.

Then they saw the *Adelaide* straighten its heading. The pursuer still maintained a slight speed advantage and continued to creep closer to the *Salzburg*'s stern.

'I think they might try and ram us,' Bolcke said.

Pablo looked at the navigation monitor and saw they would soon be approaching the first set of locks at Pedro Miguel. 'We need to dispose of them before we are in sight of the locks.' He had a few words with the captain, then departed the bridge.

Bolcke remained where he was, glued to the rear window, watching the pursuing vessel.

Pitt maintained a safe buffer with the ship ahead. He had hoped to pull alongside the *Salzburg* and force her into the bank, but the appearance of the ADS on the port rail had nixed that plan. He was contemplating his next move when the *Salzburg* heeled over in front of him.

At Pablo's command, the captain had turned the *Salzburg* hard to port. The ADS operators immediately aimed the beam at the *Adelaide*'s bridge. Pitt felt the familiar tingle on his skin, but it was what he saw next to the weapon that made his hair stand on end. It was Pablo and another man at the rail, shouldering rocket-propelled grenade launchers. An instant later, they fired the weapons.

'Off the bridge!' Pitt yelled as the grenades flew toward them.

With no time to flee, he dove to the floor, kicking the rudder to port as he fell.

Standing across the bridge, Dirk jumped into the side companionway.

The first grenade struck the steel face of the *Adelaide*'s superstructure just beneath the bridge. It fell to the deck and discharged harmlessly atop a hatch cover.

Pablo had fired the second RPG, and his aim was on the mark. The grenade burst through the shattered window just above Pitt's head. Its high angle of entry sent it careening off the ceiling to the rear bulkhead, where it detonated. The entire structure shook from the explosion, which incinerated the bridge in a fiery cloud of smoke and flame.

Watching from the deck of the *Salzburg*, Pablo smiled to himself. No man could have survived the inferno.

73

Two things saved Pitt's life. First was the bounce of the grenade, which ricocheted off the rear bulkhead and detonated in front of an engineering console. The shrapnel blew up, around, and into the console – but not through it. Lying on the other side, Pitt was spared the lethal spray of exploding steel fragments.

His second salvation was the Hazmat suit. It shielded him from the flash fire that accompanied the explosion and engulfed the bridge. The blast rattled his senses, and he struggled to breathe, but he easily climbed to his feet once Dirk returned and dragged him clear of the carnage.

'Are you okay?' Dirk asked.

His ears ringing, Pitt barely heard the words. 'Yes, thanks to Buck Rogers.'

Shaking off the effects of the blast, he staggered to a nearby window. 'We should be about on her.' He had to yell to hear himself.

The words barely cleared his lips when a bang arose from the bow. Pitt and Dirk grabbed at the bulkhead as the ship shuddered to a halt.

Kicking the rudder to port when he fell had turned the *Adelaide* on an intercept course with the crossing *Salzburg*. Caught in the narrow channel, the *Salzburg* had to hold to its attempted U-turn and hope it could slip by the *Adelaide*. Pitt's action had ensured it couldn't.

Bolcke looked on in disbelief as the *Adelaide*, its bridge a charred ruin, turned toward them as if guided by an invisible hand. The *Salzburg* was halfway through her port turn when the *Adelaide*'s prow struck her amidships. Accompanied by the screech of steel grinding against steel, the charging bulk carrier cut nearly twenty feet into the *Salzburg*'s beam. Had the *Salzburg* been fully loaded, the pressure on her frame would have broken her in two. Still, the collision buckled hull plates all along her sides, allowing a rush of water to penetrate her interior.

On deck, the stacked cargo containers scattered like falling blocks. Several tumbled into the canal after smashing through the starboard rail. On the port rail side, a pair of the empty containers fell onto the ADS, flattening the dish and crushing its two operators. Pablo watched as another container rolled onto its side, pinning the leg of his fellow RPG launcher. The man screamed for Pablo to help, but there was nothing he could do, so he silently walked away.

Both ships were mortally wounded, but the *Salzburg* was clearly in the worse condition. The ship quickly listed to port, sending more containers tumbling over the side. She settled lower as the canal waters washed over her main deck. She was sinking fast.

Pablo raced to the bridge, where Bolcke stared at the damage like a zombie. Pablo ran past him to a locked cabinet, which he kicked open. Inside was the plastic bin with Heiland's design plans for the *Sea Arrow*. 'Where's the captain?' he asked. 'We must get off the ship.'

'He went to check on the chief engineer.'

'There's no time to waste, we've got to get to the crew boat. Follow me.' He picked up the bin and left the bridge.

Bolcke following a step behind. On reaching the main deck, they rushed to the elevated starboard rail, where Bolcke's crew boat dangled. Pablo threw the bin aboard, then snapped at Bolcke, 'Get in. I'll lower you to the water and jump in.'

Bolcke did as he was told. Pablo took the winch controls and had started lowering the boat when Bolcke stopped him.

'Look out, on the other ship.'

At the base of the *Adelaide*'s superstructure, two figures appeared in silver Hazmat suits, one of them coated with black soot. Pablo saw that the other man brandished a gun.

'I know how to delay them.' He dropped the crew boat hard to the water, then tied off its bowline as Bolcke released the winch cable. Pablo sprinted up to the accommodations level and unlocked Ann's cabin.

For once, she was glad to see him. While she wasn't sure what had happened, she could tell the ship was sinking and feared being left to drown in her cabin.

'Let's go!' Pablo grabbed the handcuffs between her wrists and led her down the corridor.

Reaching the main deck, she was shocked to see the towering hulk of the *Adelaide* enmeshed in the *Salzburg*'s side. The entanglement hadn't slowed the degree of the *Salzburg*'s list, which was approaching a sharp angle.

Pablo led Ann down the sloping deck to the port rail, sloshing through ankle-deep water. He stopped in front of a lone container that had slid to the side, smashing partway through the side rail. It stood out from the other containers, and Pablo made sure it stood out even more.

He fished for a key in his pocket and removed one of the handcuffs.

Ann relaxed, feigning submission, as he pulled her close to the container. Taking a step, she sprang her knee into Pablo, just missing his groin.

He fired back in the blink of an eye, backhanding her head and sending her sprawling against the container. He grabbed her cuffed wrist and pulled it to the deck, where he latched the cuff's free end to a loop at the base of the container. 'I'm sorry things didn't work out,' he said. 'Be sure and wave to your friends.'

He turned and moved along the deck, ducking when there was a loud plink on the container behind him. He increased his pace and looked back to see a man at the rail of the *Adelaide*, firing a pistol at him. Pablo sidestepped down a row of containers and out of sight as two more shots followed.

Dirk lowered the SIG Sauer with disgust as his father caught up with him at the rail. They had shed the cumbersome Hazmat suits, which had left them both drenched in sweat.

'There's a woman tied to that shipping container,' Dirk said. 'I took a shot at the guy who put her there but missed.'

Pitt spotted a woman with short blond hair lying at the base of a container. 'That's Ann.'

Any relief at finding Ann alive was dispelled by observing the *Salzburg*'s precarious state. The ship was sinking quickly. The gash from the *Adelaide* was taking her down by the beam, and Pitt could see that the ship would capsize before she went under.

'Let's see if we can get to her.' He took off running for the *Adelaide*'s bow. The whole section was mashed flat but still locked in the jagged grip of the *Salzburg*. The tangled beams of the sinking containership groaned as they tore against the *Adelaide*'s bow.

Pitt threaded his way through the shredded steel until he could drop onto the *Salzburg*'s deck. He ran aft across the ship, snaking around the scattered containers, until he reached Ann.

She looked at him in disbelief as he waded up to her. 'What are you doing here?'

He grinned at her. 'I heard you were trying to take a cruise without me.'

She was too frightened to smile. 'Can you free me?'

He sloshed through the water to take a closer look. She was seated on the deck with her hand pinned low. Water already swirled above her elbow. Then the container creaked and slid a few inches over the port rail, dragging her with it.

'It's a handcuff?' Pitt asked.

She nodded.

Dirk approached, and together they looked for something to free her with. Somewhere on the ship would be tools, but they had no time to search. The ship was already half underwater. And so was the container.

'It's going to go over the side any minute,' Dirk whispered. 'I don't see how we can get her free of it.'

Pitt nodded and gazed up briefly at the *Adelaide*. 'You're right,' he said, a glimmer in his eye. 'I reckon we'll have to save them both.'

74

The *Adelaide*, like the *Tasmanian Star* in Chile, was equipped with its own conveyor for loading and off-loading cargo. The *Adelaide*'s system was mounted on its starboard beam, right above where Pitt stood.

Climbing up the ore carrier's shattered bow, he raced to a control station next to the conveyor. The collision hadn't damaged the ship's auxiliary power, and a generator below deck hummed when Pitt tested the hydraulic controls. The conveyor consisted of a sliding belt that could be moved alongside each hatch. Hopper cranes were fitted on the opposite side of the deck, which would pull the ore from the hold and deposit it onto the conveyor.

Pitt engaged the belt and moved it forward to the number 1 hold. He experimented with the controls until he figured out how to pivot the conveyor. Rotating it out from the *Salzburg*, he aimed it at Ann's container. A separate vertical control allowed him to lower the far end of the belt, which he dropped beneath the rail.

Standing next to Ann's container, Dirk was signaling him closer when a deep bellow sounded from the depths of the *Salzburg*. Containers everywhere shifted as the ship began to founder. In a slow, steady motion, the portside deck dipped toward the canal while the starboard side rose, sending the containers in a mad tumble into the water.

Pitt jammed the end of the belt ahead and below as far

as it would go and engaged it. Looking out, all he could see was a mountain of containers spilling into the water. At the stern, he saw the captain and a handful of crewmen leap for their lives.

As the ship rotated, equipment, stores, and remaining cargo tumbled and crashed. With a sudden rush, the ship broke free of the *Adelaide* and capsized. The inverted *Salzburg* drifted for a minute or two, then let out a gurgle and slipped beneath the waters of the canal.

The tip of the *Adelaide*'s conveyor belt dropped below water level, and Pitt thought he had failed. But the belt stammered and shook, and a beige slab appeared beneath the surface. A moment later, a shipping container emerged, riding unevenly up the belt. Pitt looked over the side to see Ann and Dirk clinging to its base, their feet dangling over the waves.

As water sloshed off the belt it pulled the container up to the side rail, where Pitt powered the conveyor off.

'Nice catch,' Dirk said, 'though I wasn't expecting a dip in the bargain.' He dropped to the deck as Ann touched her feet down beside him.

'You okay?' Pitt asked Ann.

'I thought my arm was going to leave its socket, but, yes, I'm all right.' She shook the water from her hair.

'Hand me the gun,' Pitt told his son.

Dirk pulled the SIG Sauer from his waist and handed it to his father. Pitt shook it to clear the water and held the muzzle to Ann's handcuffs. The shot split the chain that linked the cuffs and freed Ann from the container.

'Would have tried that earlier, but you were too far underwater when we found you.'

'But then I would have missed the ride.' Ann smiled for the first time in days. She got to her feet and looked into the canal where the *Salzburg* had vanished. 'The *Sea Arrow*'s motor was aboard.'

'They're not going to get it now,' Pitt said.

'But they still have the plans,' she said. 'I saw them in the boat with Pablo.'

Pitt nodded. He had seen Bolcke and Pablo flee in the boat while he tried to save Ann. 'There's only one place they can go.' Having examined a map of the canal on the *Adelaide*'s bridge, he knew the next lock was only a short distance away.

Dirk was already crossing the deck to an inflatable secured beneath a tarp. In minutes, he had it winched over the side and lowered into the water with Pitt and Ann aboard. Already drenched, he dove over the side of the *Adelaide* and swam to the side of the boat, where he was helped aboard. Pitt started its small outboard, and they were soon zipping up the canal.

The canal curved past Gold Hill, a small bluff that marked the continental divide and its deepest area of excavation. Just beyond it, the canal straightened, and the Pedro Miguel Locks appeared two miles away. Bolcke and Pablo had already reached the lock and sailed into the north chamber, whose gates had been opened in preparation for the *Salzburg*.

Pablo docked the boat against the center island, which bisected the lock's two chambers. He assisted a pair of canal workers in attaching fore and aft mooring lines to the crew boat before he jumped off. With Bolcke still aboard, the workers walked the boat to the far end of the chamber and tied it off, forgoing the tiny locomotives used to maneuver larger vessels.

Pablo strode toward the control house, a multistory white structure in the middle of the island that managed the water flow for the chambers.

A gruff transit supervisor with a clipboard met Pablo. 'That's no four-hundred-foot bulk carrier.'

'We had an accident with the ship and need to make passage at once. Mr Bolcke will pay triple your usual fee if you don't book it.'

'Is that him in the boat?'

Pablo nodded.

'Haven't seen him for a while.' He pulled a radio off his hip and called the control house. A minute later, the chamber's massive gates began to close. Soon the waters in the chamber would drain out the bottom, lowering the boat for the next section of the canal.

'We'll have you out of here in ten minutes,' the supervisor said.

Pablo glanced at the closing gates, then hesitated. A small inflatable boat was approaching at high speed with three people aboard. There were two men and a woman with short blond hair. Ann Bennett.

'Just one minute.' He pointed to the inflatable. 'Those three attacked and sank our ship. Treat them as terrorist suspects and detain them for at least an hour.'

The man looked at the approaching boat. 'They don't look like terrorists.'

'There's an extra ten thousand in it for you.'

457

The supervisor beamed. 'You know, I might just be wrong about that,' he said. 'Give my regards to Mr Bolcke.'

All he got in reply was Pablo's turned back as the Colombian walked briskly to the waiting boat.

75

As the gates of the northern chamber closed to accommodate Bolcke's boat, the southern chamber's gates were opened to release a large freighter traveling in the other direction. Pitt slipped the inflatable around the wide freighter and motored into the chamber. He angled toward the control house and pulled alongside the dock, where the transit supervisor stood with two armed guards. The water level in the opposite chamber had already dropped several feet, obscuring his view of the crew boat.

Dirk jumped onto the dock with the inflatable's bow-line in hand and held the boat close while Ann stepped off. Dirk turned to the supervisor.

'The crew boat with two men aboard.' He pointed to the boat in the other chamber. 'You must stop its passage.'

'I'm afraid it is you who must be stopped,' the supervisor said. 'Guards, arrest these people.'

Pitt had gazed past the control house and spotted Pablo walking along the dock. Hearing the guards grab Dirk and Ann, he goosed the outboard's throttle. Dirk let the bowline slip, and the small boat took off down the chamber.

It was five hundred feet from the control house to the forward gates, and Pablo was nearly to the end when he heard the inflatable approach. He turned and was shocked to see Pitt at the helm, holding the SIG Sauer.

Unarmed, Pablo looked back to the control house

guards. They were occupied holding Ann and Dirk and made no effort to chase Pitt. Their paid loyalty would go only so far.

The crew boat was still a few yards ahead of Pablo, but Pitt angled to cut him off. On the dock, Pablo saw that a maintenance crew had been repairing a locomotive track and left behind a damaged rail. He scooped up the rail – a slim, forged steel rod about six feet long – and stepped forward.

Pitt motored past Pablo and turned the inflatable toward the dock. He didn't notice Pablo's makeshift weapon as he leaped from the boat and turned his gun on him.

Pitt's reflexes were dulled by fatigue, and when Pablo swung the rail, he reacted too late. He aimed and squeezed the trigger, but the rail arrived first, slamming into his out-stretched hand. The gun fired harmlessly into the sky before being knocked from Pitt's hand and splashing into the water.

Pitt recoiled as Pablo reversed his swing, but he was still tagged in the ribs with a sharp whack that sent him reeling. He managed to stay on his feet and backpedaled as Pablo came after him again.

The rail cut the air with a whistling sound as Pablo swung it like a scythe. 'You've come a long way to die here.'

'Not far enough,' Pitt replied.

Staggering backward to avoid the swinging rail, Pitt had almost reached the gates and the crew boat tied at the end of the dock. The chamber was draining quickly, and the crew boat had already dropped more than twenty feet. He glanced at the boat but saw it was too far to jump.

Sensing Pitt's vulnerability, Pablo closed in for the kill, swinging the rail even harder.

Pitt saw that the weight of the rail was beginning to slow Pablo's backswings and he decided to take the offensive. He stepped back as Pablo whipped the bar at him, but rather than keep retreating, he planted his feet and sprang forward.

Pablo reacted by pulling the rail to his chest in defense as Pitt barreled into him. Pitt managed to catch Pablo slightly off balance and he staggered to the side. Pitt pressed the charge, grabbing the rail alongside Pablo's hands and bulling into him as hard as he could.

Pablo had no choice but to step back and try to regain his leverage. But he had been turned sideways to the dock, and when he tried to plant a foot behind him, he found only air. He tumbled backward off the edge of the dock, taking Pitt with him.

From the base of the control house, Dirk and Ann had watched the battle while the guards held them at gunpoint. Dirk saw the two men fall into the chamber with a large splash and waited for them to surface. As the water settled, he began counting the seconds – and felt a cold chill.

After more than a minute, neither man had returned to the surface.

76

Pablo took the brunt of the fall into the lock chamber, landing on his back as Pitt drove him into the water. From the height of the dock, it felt like he had hit a concrete pad. The impact knocked the breath out of him while his back erupted in pain. His body tensed, shocked to inactivity.

Pitt, however, stayed in control when he hit the water. He kicked his legs hard, driving his opponent deep. With his diving experience, he figured he could outlast Pablo in the water, and pressed on the rail to drive him as far down as possible.

Focused on his attack, Pitt didn't notice the pull of the swirling water. He was surprised, though, to quickly feel pressure in his ears, and he waggled his jaw to clear them.

Slowly recovering from the shock of impact, Pablo's first instinct was to wrestle away the steel rail. But Pitt clung tight, using it to press Pablo deeper. Pablo finally came to his senses and realized he needed air. He pushed himself away from the rail, kicking to the side to escape Pitt.

But a strange thing happened. Instead of ascending, he was drawn deeper by an unseen force. Unnerved, he reached back and grabbed the rail while kicking furiously.

On the opposite side of the rail, Pitt stopped kicking,

but another ache in his ears told him they were being sucked to the bottom.

The two men had fallen into the lock chamber directly over one of the drainage wells that dotted its floor. When valves in the wells were opened, the chamber's water would drain through them into a lateral culvert, which fed an even larger culvert built into the wall. At over eighteen feet in diameter, this huge pipe emptied into Miraflores Lake.

Near the surface, the swirling of the draining water was barely noticeable. But at the bottom of the chamber, it became an inescapable whirlpool. Like Pablo, Pitt briefly let go of the rail and tried to kick to the surface. But the suction of the water refused to release its grip. Pitt brushed against Pablo in the turbulence and regripped the rail, positioning himself parallel to the bottom.

The draw of the water accelerated, pulling them forcefully to the well's four-foot-wide mouth. Pablo fought the downforce, but his legs and torso were sucked into the pipe. The rail would have been swallowed also, but at the last second Pitt muscled it sideways. It clanged atop the circular concrete well, jerking both men to a halt. Neither realized how hard the water had been pulling them and both nearly lost their grip.

The impact threw Pitt off balance, and his legs were sucked into the well. The rest of his body followed, and he found himself hanging side by side with Pablo, clinging to the steel rail overhead, as thousands of gallons of water rushed past them. No longer concerned with battling each other, each man fought for his life.

Their descent had taken only half a minute, but because

of their exertions both men were out of air. Pablo had fought to maintain his breath since hitting the water and now he began to struggle. His heart raced and his head ached. The fear of drowning flooded his thoughts, and he panicked.

Hanging just inches away, Pitt could see Pablo's eyes bulge and his face shudder.

Desperation took hold, and Pablo gave in to his instincts. Letting go of the rail, he kicked and clawed, trying to swim to the surface.

He had no chance.

Instead he whisked past Pitt, disappearing into the depths of the well.

Pablo's surrender only served to give Pitt more resolve. He focused on maintaining his grip on the rail and tried not to think about the pounding in his brain or the overwhelming urge to inhale. He knew the locks could be filled or drained quickly. And the water level had already dropped by more than twenty feet since they had fallen into the chamber. Pitt told himself the draining would have to end soon.

As his fingers went numb, he detected a deep rumble beneath him. For a moment, he felt the draining water pull even harder. It was the valves inside the drainage wells turning to close. Then he heard a bang, and the water ceased its deadly pull.

Unbelieving at first, Pitt pulled on the rail and found himself ascending. He let go and kicked hard, exhaling, long and slow, his reserve of air as he rose. It was still thirty feet to the surface, but he reached it quickly, gasping in the humid air that greeted him.

As he regained his senses, he heard shouts from the dock high above and an engine revving nearby. The lock gates had opened, and Bolcke was engaging the boat to leave the chamber. Two canal workers tossing down the mooring lines spotted Pitt in the water and called to one of the guards.

Bolcke spotted Pitt, too, and gunned the engine, ignoring the tossed lines. The crew boat leaped forward toward the open gates, spilling the stern line in the water.

Pitt reacted at once, swimming a few short strokes and grabbing the floating line. It went taut, yanking him through the water, as the guard arrived and shouted at Bolcke to stop. Bolcke ignored the request, pushing down on the throttle.

Pitt felt like his arms were being yanked out of their sockets, but he hung on as the boat zipped ahead.

Clearing the lock, Bolcke looked back and cursed at seeing Pitt in tow. Leaving the boat's controls, he stepped to the stern line and released the secured end from its deck cleat.

The line bounded over the stern, freeing the boat and Bolcke from the relentless man who refused to let go.

77

'Rudi, you better get down here right away.'

'Okay, Hiram, on my way.' Gunn hung up the phone and bolted from his office. Rather than wait for an elevator, he ran down a stairwell and emerged in the NUMA computer center seconds later.

Yaeger sat in his command chair in front of the massive video screen. It showed a freighter moving slowly into a narrow compartment.

'What do you have?' Gunn looked at the screen.

'Panama Canal. This is the Pedro Miguel Locks, viewed through one of the Canal Authority's live video feeds. I've been monitoring their cameras while waiting to hear from Dirk and Summer about the raid.'

'Yes, I've been waiting for their call.'

'Check this out. I recorded it just a few minutes ago.'

Yaeger keyed up earlier footage of the same view, which showed a small boat come into one of the chambers. A few minutes later, an inflatable boat entered the parallel chamber and landed by the control house.

Gunn stared at the figures who stepped out of the boat. 'That looks like Ann and Dirk.'

'So that is Ann,' Yaeger said. 'I wasn't sure what she looked like. But I pegged Dirk.'

They watched the rest of the events unfold, including

Pitt's battle with Pablo and his watery ride out of the lock. The two could only stare in disbelief.

'Could that be Bolcke in the boat?' Yaeger asked.

'Yes,' Gunn said. 'He must still have the plans or Pitt wouldn't be after him.'

'What do we do?'

Gunn shook his head with a dazed look.

'Sandecker,' he said finally. 'We better call Sandecker.'

78

The line went slack in Pitt's hand after his short aquatic sled ride. Catching his breath, he watched Bolcke speed across the lake.

He'd been pulled just a short distance into Miraflores Lake. At the shoreline a few yards away was a landing with a moored boat. Pitt swam toward the boat and reached it in short order. It was a small auxiliary tugboat used by the Canal Authority to supplement the operating tugs used to maneuver large ships.

Pitt pulled himself aboard and quietly untied the mooring lines, then made his way to the wheelhouse. He started the engine and pulled away from shore, oblivious to the standby crew who were busy assisting with the lock operations. As he turned into the lake, he pushed the tug to top speed as it passed a large object floating in the water. It was the body of Pablo, crushed and mangled from his death ride through the drainage culverts.

The tug was no match for Bolcke's crew boat, but it didn't have to be. Miraflores Lake was small, just over a mile long. Bolcke couldn't escape from view, and if he wished to flee on the crew boat, he would have to pass through another series of locks. Following a half mile behind, Pitt soon realized that wasn't Bolcke's plan.

The crew boat pulled alongside a large freighter idling on the lake and waited for its accommodation ladder to be lowered. Two armed men with Asian features descended the ladder and pulled the boat alongside. Bolcke handed one of the men the bin containing the *Sea Arrow*'s plans, then stepped off the boat.

Approaching from its stern, Pitt saw that the black-hulled freighter was named the *Santa Rita*, ported out of Guam. The men were halfway up the ladder when Pitt barreled alongside in the tug.

Spotting Pitt in the wheelhouse, Bolcke stared at him as if he were a ghost. He spoke quickly to the gunmen.

The man carrying the bin raced to the top of the ladder, but the second gunman stopped and aimed his weapon. He studied the tugboat with a cautious eye and fired a warning burst ahead of it. Then he swung the gun toward Pitt in the wheelhouse. Pitt heeded the message, turning away from the side of the freighter and motoring on ahead.

Zhou approached the deck rail as Bolcke climbed aboard. 'Welcome,' Zhou said with faint emotion.

Bolcke stood wild-eyed, catching his breath after climbing the steps. 'My ship was rammed and sunk, my facility attacked and destroyed. We have lost the motor, and my assistant Pablo was killed. But I escaped with the supercavitation plans. They are worth more than the motor.'

Zhou stared at the Austrian, relieved that he was not a suspect in the destruction of his complex. But the loss of the *Sea Arrow*'s motor was a failure, even with receipt of the plans. 'This changes our agreement.'

'Of course. But we can discuss it later. We need to clear the Miraflores Locks at once.'

Zhou nodded. 'We are next in line to make the transit. Who was that in the tugboat?'

Bolcke looked at the tugboat receding in the distance. 'Just a nuisance. He can't stop us now.'

79

The nuisance named Pitt had plowed ahead of the *Santa Rita*, searching for a way to stop the ship and recover the plans. Alone in the tugboat, he had few options. He studied the lake ahead, seeing that at its far end the slim waterway split. A southerly fork led to a narrow dam and spillway that controlled the water level of the lake. To the north was the twin set of locks also named Miraflores. One of the chambers had just opened its gates, releasing a large white cruise ship.

The locks, he knew, would be a dead end. Bolcke no doubt had the same paid influence at Miraflores as he did at Pedro Miguel. Any plea to halt the freighter's passage through the locks would result in Pitt being arrested, just like Dirk and Ann, until the *Santa Rita* was safely at sea. He had to find another way.

Chugging along the shoreline, he noted an old barge filled with mud that was moored near the dam. He continued on, circling in front of the locks and passing near the cruise ship, which he noted had a familiar look. He dropped back to confirm the name beneath her slightly damaged stern deck, then smiled as a plan came to mind.

'Splendid,' he muttered to himself. 'Simply splendid.'

'Captain, you have a radio call from the canal tug off our port beam.'

Captain Franco stepped across the cruise ship's bridge and grabbed a handset from the deck officer.

'This is *Sea Splendour*, Captain Franco speaking.'

'Good morning, Captain. This is Dirk Pitt.' He stuck his head out of the tug's wheelhouse and waved toward the cruise ship.

'My friend Pitt!' the captain said. 'It is a small world. What are you doing here? Working for the Canal Authority?'

'Not exactly. There's a critical situation at hand, and I need your help.'

'Of course. I owe my ship and my career to you. What do you require?' He spoke for a few minutes, then hung up the phone with a sullen look. He stepped over to his assigned canal pilot, who stood at the helm, monitoring their track.

'Roberto,' the captain said with a forced smile, 'you look hungry. Why don't you go down to the galley for a quick meal? We'll call you to the bridge when we approach the locks at Pedro Miguel.'

The grizzled pilot, who was fighting a rum hangover, perked up at the offer. 'Thank you, Captain. The channel is wide through the lake, so you'll have no problems.' He departed the bridge.

The first officer looked at Franco. 'This is most unusual, Captain. What are you doing?'

Franco stepped to the helm and stared out the window with a vacant gaze. 'Completing the career that should have ended in Valparaiso,' he said quietly, then ordered the ship to turn about.

Pitt maneuvered the tug away from the cruise ship and drove hard toward the shoreline. His target was the rusty barge used in the canal's ongoing dredging operations. Nearly full of thick mud, it rode low in the water, awaiting a tow to be dumped in the Pacific.

Pitt pulled inshore of the barge, tied the tug to its rail, and sprinted across her deck walkway. Near the bow, he found the barge's mooring line, a thick rope that he wrestled to free from a massive cleat. Dropping the line over the side, Pitt raced back to the tug and put it to work.

He turned parallel to the side of the barge and nudged the barge into deeper water. It drifted close to the main channel, so Pitt backed away and took up a new position on its flat stern, shoving the barge toward the locks.

A few hundred yards away, the Chinese ship *Santa Rita* had inched in front of the locks, waiting for a gate to open. Glancing over his shoulder, Pitt saw the *Sea Splendour* sweep up behind him, having used its bow thrusters to quickly turn around.

When Pitt had first spotted the *Sea Splendour*, the cruise ship he had saved in Chile, he thought he might use her to block the entrance to the locks. But the *Santa Rita* was already positioned there, leaving no room for the cruise ship to intrude. His backup plan was much more audacious, if not foolhardy. If he couldn't block the *Santa Rita* from entering the locks, then he'd prevent her from leaving them. From the confines of Miraflores Lake, there was only one way to do that.

Shoving the barge ahead, he guided it toward the locks, then veered south, following the fork in the waterway. Rather than aiming for the locks, the tug and barge were now headed for the adjacent dam. Pitt noticed the shadow of the massive cruise ship as it thundered alongside him.

'*Sea Splendour* ready when you are,' the radio crackled.

'Roger, *Sea Splendour*. I'll guide you in.'

He eased the tug away from the barge and then directed the cruise ship into his place. Matching speed, the cruise ship, its high bow brushing against the barge's stern, maintained headway.

'Looking good, *Splendour*,' Pitt said. 'Give it all you've got.'

Nudging against the barge, the cruise ship briefly applied full power. It was a short burst, but enough to send the barge racing through the water.

Pitt tried to keep pace in the tug, watching the dam loom closer until it was barely a hundred yards away. 'Reverse engines,' Pitt radioed. 'Thanks, *Sea Splendour*, I'll take it from here.'

'Good luck to you, Mr Pitt,' Franco said.

Pressing the tug to full power, he caught up to the barge's stern as the cruise ship dug in to reverse course.

The loaded barge was like a runaway freight train, with the tug simply maintaining its momentum. Pitt bumped its stern quarter, keeping it aligned as it raced toward the middle of the concrete dam. The barge closed quickly, charging dead center into the spillway.

Pitt braced himself for the impact, which came harder than he anticipated. The flat prow of the barge slammed into the spillway with a metallic thud – and stopped cold. The tug bounced off the barge's stern, and Pitt went flying over the helm. Staggering back to the wheel, he turned the tug away, and considered his failed attempt to burst open a dam that had stood since 1914. He had succeeded in only wedging a barge into its century-old spillway.

Then a deep rumble sounded from below. Several feet beneath the waterline, the barge had fractured the dam facing. The fracture grew as the pressure of the lake's water forced its way into the fissure. With a sudden buckle and roar, a fifty-foot section of the dam wall disintegrated, leading the way for the collapse of the entire dam.

Pitt looked in awe as the barge slid forward and disappeared over the edge, crashing with an audible impact as it struck the waterway forty feet below. The tug felt an immediate draw from the escaping water, and Pitt had to quickly steer clear to elude the suction. The *Sea Splendour* had already backed well clear as Captain Franco hurried to take the cruise ship to the deepest part of the lake, near Pedro Miguel. Pitt turned his attention to the *Santa Rita*. The freighter was still stationed in front of the locks, awaiting its passage to the Pacific.

As Pitt turned the tug away from the shattered dam, he saw the gates of the north chamber slowly swing open. He'd done what he could, he told himself. Now it was simply a matter of time and physics.

81

Bolcke was the first to realize what Pitt was attempting. Watching the barge tumble through the break in the dam, he turned to Zhou on the bridge of the *Santa Rita*. 'He's trying to lower the water level to pin us in. We need to enter the locks right away.'

Zhou said nothing. He had no control over the gates and was surprised when a moment later they opened as if by command. The Chinese freighter crept forward, entering the chamber as lines were affixed to the small locomotives on the dock.

A frequent traveler through the locks, Bolcke noted right away that something was askew. The freighter's main deck sat well below the topside of the dock. That shouldn't have happened until the chamber was drained. Already the water level was several feet lower than normal.

He rushed to the ship's radio and screamed into the transmitter. 'Transit Central, this is *Santa Rita*. Close the gates behind us at once. I repeat, close the gates behind us.'

Inside the Miraflores Locks control house, Bolcke's call was readily ignored. The staff was busy trying to determine what was happening at the spillway. Someone had seen the *Sea Splendour* and a tugboat in the area, but nobody had noticed anything until the barge went over the side. The lock's security force was immediately mobilized, and boats were sent to investigate both sides of the dam.

A black-and-white speedboat intercepted Pitt as he made his way to the locks.

Before the security men could hail him, Pitt stopped the tug and shouted, 'A small ship lost control and crashed through the dam. There were many people aboard. You need to look for survivors. I'm going to the lock for more help.'

The security leader bought Pitt's tale and ordered the speedboat to go investigate. Only later would he question the presence of Pitt on a Canal Authority tugboat.

Pitt pushed the tug ahead, spotting a distant gray vessel waiting to enter the south chamber from the opposite end. He headed for the north chamber, following after the *Santa Rita*, noticing that the narrow lake was draining faster than he expected. A large inlet pipe, which fed the lake water into the chambers, was growing more and more visible above the surface.

Pitt was thankful to find the gates to the *Santa Rita*'s chamber still open and he eased the prow of the tugboat inside. There it became even more evident how much water had receded. The *Santa Rita* sat low in the chamber, her main deck easily twenty feet below the dock.

But it wasn't quite enough. The *Santa Rita* was on a Pacific-bound transit and would be lowered twenty-seven feet before passing through the chamber. The water level would have to drop well below that to prevent her from continuing on.

'Transit Central to Auxiliary Tug 16, please state your business,' a voice on the radio called.

Pitt picked up the transmitter. 'Transit Central, this is security. Checking for possible damage to the north chamber gates.'

It didn't take long for Bolcke to intercede. 'Transit Central, that tug operator is an impostor. He is responsible for the damage to the dam. Apprehend him at once.'

Pitt turned off the radio, knowing his play was over. All he could do now was to keep the tug blocking the gates open – to the extent it wouldn't get him killed. Ahead, a handful of armed men appeared on the deck of *Santa Rita* and took up positions along the side and stern rails. Beyond Pitt's field of vision, a contingent of Canal Authority security men exited the control house and ran toward the tug.

A few hundred yards away, the last vestiges of the Miraflores Dam gave way, releasing an expanded flood downstream. Along the lake's shoreline, the water had dramatically receded, leaving muddy flats nearly to the dredged shipping channel. The remaining water's draw became stronger, and Pitt felt the tug drift back when he eased off the throttle. Slipping out the gates momentarily, he saw the outside culvert was now fully visible. The level had dropped almost a dozen feet since Pitt had entered the chamber and continued to drain out the open gates.

He saw the gates begin to close and he bulled into the chamber once more. The lock operator no longer heeded the tug's safety and ordered the gates closed despite him. Pitt considered blocking the gates but realized the small tug would be crushed by the six-hundred-ton gates. Glancing again at the *Santa Rita*, he realized it no longer mattered.

The ship showed a slight list to starboard, where it leaned against the side of the chamber. The water level in the chamber had dropped enough to set the *Santa Rita* on her keel.

Pitt gunned the tugboat past the closing gates and motored alongside the *Santa Rita*, bumping to a stop off its forward port deck. Gunmen appeared at once, aiming their weapons at Pitt as he lashed the tug to the ship. With his hands raised, he stepped to the rail and boarded the freighter. One of the gunmen jabbed an AK-47 against his throat and threatened him in Mandarin.

Pitt looked at him with a hard smile. 'Where's your boss?'

He didn't have to wait for a translator. Bolcke and Zhou appeared a moment later, having watched Pitt pull alongside. Zhou looked at him with curiosity, surprised to see him again after their jungle encounter. Bolcke, on the other hand, glared at Pitt with unadulterated rage.

'You have something, I believe, that belongs to my country,' Pitt said.

'Are you insane?' Bolcke shouted.

'Not at all. The game is over, Bolcke. You've lost. Give me the plans.'

'You are a fool. We will be leaving the lock shortly – and sailing over your dead body.'

'You're not going anywhere,' Pitt said. 'Your ship is grounded, and there's no water in the culvert to refill this chamber.'

In the control house, the lock operator had come to the same conclusion. The water level where the *Santa Rita* sat was now considerably lower than in the next chamber.

There was no way the exit gates would be opened with an uneven level on the opposite side.

'They will simply release additional water from Gatun Lake, and we shall be on our way,' Bolcke said.

'Not with the plans.'

'Kill him, Zhou.' Bolcke turned to the agent. 'Kill him now.'

Zhou stood, weighing his options.

'I didn't expect you to be lending him a free ride,' Pitt said to Zhou. 'I take it you haven't told him who blew up his facility? I guess you two have a few things to talk about.'

A cloud of suspicion crossed Bolcke's face. 'Lies,' he said. 'Pure lies.' But his eyes revealed the desperate realization that his world was crashing down around him. There was nothing left for him to do but silence the messenger.

He spun to a gunman beside him and ripped the AK-47 from his hands. Aiming the weapon at Pitt, he was fumbling for the trigger when a shot rang out. A crisp red circle appeared on Bolcke's temple, and his rage-filled eyes rolled back in his head. The Austrian miner collapsed to the deck, the automatic rifle clattering out of his hands.

Pitt saw Zhou with a Chinese 9mm pistol held at arm's length, smoke rising from the barrel. The man slowly wheeled until he held the gun pointed at Pitt's chest. 'What if I do as Bolcke asked and kill you here?'

Pitt caught a shadow out of the corner of his eye and gave the Chinese agent a sly grin. 'Then you will join me in death a second later.'

Zhou sensed, more than saw, the movement overhead. Then he looked up and saw the chamber dock lined with a dozen armed men, aiming M4 carbines at him and his crew. They were Navy sailors, deployed from the destroyer *Spruance* in the adjacent lock.

Zhou's face expressed no alarm. 'This is liable to create an awkward incident between our two countries,' he said.

'Would it?' Pitt asked. 'Armed Chinese insurgents aboard a Guam-flagged ship apprehended while smuggling a murderous slave trader to safety? Yes, I suppose you are right. It would prove awkward to at least one of our countries.'

Zhou replied in a halting voice. 'And if we return the plans?'

'Then I should think we shake hands and all go on our merry way.'

Zhou looked into Pitt's green eyes, studying the friendly foe who had somehow gained the upper hand. He turned and spoke to one of his gunmen. The man slowly lowered his weapon and walked to the bridge. He returned a moment later with the sealed bin containing the *Sea Arrow*'s plans, which he reluctantly handed to Pitt.

Taking the bin, Pitt walked to the side rail and stopped. He returned to Zhou and stuck out his hand. Zhou stared at Pitt a moment before grasping his hand and shaking it vigorously.

'Thanks for saving my life,' Pitt said. 'Twice.'

Zhou nodded. 'I may come to regret the first instance,' he said with the faint hint of a smile.

Pitt returned to the rail and climbed up a ladder on the side of the chamber, carefully holding the bin. When he reached the top, he waved his thanks to the Navy sailors across the dock – and then was promptly arrested by the Canal Authority security force.

EPILOGUE
Red Death

82

'Looks like we've got company, boss.'

Seated in a lounge chair under an umbrella, Al Giordino kicked open a cooler and tossed an empty beer bottle inside. He closed the lid, placed his bandaged leg atop the cooler for support, and eyed the approaching speedboat. He was dressed for a day at the beach in shorts and a Hawaiian shirt, although he was sitting on a barge in the middle of the Panama Canal.

'I hope it's not another representative from the Canal Authority.' Pitt was kneeling on the deck nearby, checking an assortment of dive equipment.

'Actually, it looks to be our man from Washington.'

The speedboat pulled alongside, and Rudi Gunn hopped aboard the barge. With a travel bag hanging over his shoulder, he wore khaki pants and an oxford shirt and was drenched in sweat. 'Greetings, canal wreckers,' he said. He embraced his old friends. 'Nobody told me this place would be more miserable than Washington in August.'

'It's not that bad,' Giordino said, fishing a cold beer out of the cooler for him. 'The alligators are smaller here.'

'You didn't really have to fly down and check on us,' Pitt said.

'Believe me, I'm only too happy to get out of that town. You created a public relations nightmare with the demolished dam and sunken ships all over the place.'

Gunn peered down the waterway at a large green ship that was aground on the canal bank. A crew of workers milled about her mangled bow, making repairs so she could be floated down the waterway. 'Is that the *Adelaide*?'

'Yes,' Pitt said. 'And we're parked over the *Salzburg*.'

Gunn shook his head. 'The Panamanians are crying bloody murder. Between fixing the dam, raising the *Salzburg*, and compensating for lost traffic through the canal, Uncle Sam is going to be writing the country a pretty large check.'

'It's still a bargain, considering what we almost lost.'

'I can't disagree. Sandecker's pleased as Punch, and the President is extremely grateful. However, for security reasons, he can't divulge what was at stake. He's taking lots of heat for what Panama is calling reckless American adventurism.'

Giordino yanked another beer from the cooler and popped its cap. 'Reckless American adventurism? I'll drink to that.'

'Of course,' Gunn said, 'the President will be much happier if we return the *Sea Arrow*'s motor.'

'I have my best team working on it as we speak,' Pitt said.

Gunn looked up the canal in the other direction, eyeing a gray Navy destroyer moored a short distance away.

'The *Spruance*,' Pitt said. 'Our security escort and lift vessel, if we're fortunate.' Pitt looked Gunn in the eye. 'It was a lucky thing you sent her into the locks when you did. I probably wouldn't be here but for the armed detail they deployed.'

'Hiram and I saw the events unfolding on the canal's

video system. The *Spruance* happened to be heading in for a canal transit, so we accelerated her passage. Or Vice President Sandecker did, I should say.'

He looked over the side rail and saw air bubbles popping on the surface from the divers below. 'How did the cruise ship make out?'

'The *Sea Splendour*? Her captain figured he was history, but a funny thing happened. The Italian media made him out as a hero for his role in stopping Bolcke and exposing the slave camp. Once the cruise line realized our government was footing the bill for all the damage, they gave him a medal and a promotion. The canal pilot aboard at the time didn't fare so well, losing his job. But I understand Captain Franco got him an assignment with the cruise line.'

Gunn smiled. 'Maybe he can get me a new job, too.'

The bubbles beneath him grew larger until the two divers appeared. Gunn recognized Dirk and Summer as they swam to a dive ladder and climbed aboard.

'Hi, Rudi,' Dirk said. 'Come to dive with us? The water's warm.'

'No, thanks.' Gunn looked askance at the turbid water. 'Any sign of the motor?'

'We found it sitting intact, still strapped to the flatbed truck,' Summer said. 'It was somehow tossed clear of the other containers, and the *Salzburg* as well.'

'The flatbed's pretty mangled, but I didn't see any damage to the motor itself,' Dirk said. 'The *Spruance* should easily be able to hoist it up.'

Gunn let out a sigh. 'That's great news. NUMA won't have to pay for a new dam now,' he said, giving Pitt a sideways look.

'Not our area of expertise,' Pitt replied with a laugh. 'The Canal Authority did agree to let us supervise the removal of the *Salzburg* from the ditch, so it looks like we'll be enjoying the balmy local weather for some time.'

Gunn wiped his brow with a sleeve. 'Count me out. But I would like to drag Dirk and Summer back with me to help report on the events that took place.' Gunn reached for his travel bag. 'That reminds me, I have a package for you two that I was asked to deliver.'

He rummaged in his bag and retrieved a thin box, which he handed to Summer. She opened it and removed a lengthy handwritten letter clipped to a leather-bound journal.

As she skimmed the letter, Dirk eyed the box and noted the return address. 'It's from Perlmutter. What does St Julien have to say?'

'He says we're not going back to Washington with Rudi,' Summer said, looking at her father with persuasive eyes. 'Instead, we're to take a trip to Tierra del Fuego.'

83

The Mount Vernon Trail was a picture of tranquillity south of Alexandria, with only the muted whir of light highway traffic nearby intruding its peacefulness. Just a few early-morning joggers and bikers were scattered along its riverfront route, pushing to complete their daily workouts before the business day began.

Dan Fowler pushed himself to sprint the last few steps of his three-mile run, crossing an imaginary finish line before slowing to a walk. He ambled to a nearby drinking fountain, where he lapped up a stream of cool water.

'Good morning, Dan. How was your run?'

Fowler choked, whirling around as water dribbled down his chin. His shock at hearing the familiar voice was evident as he turned to find Ann Bennett standing before him, dressed in her usual business attire.

'Ann . . . how are you?' he stammered.

'Just fine.'

'Where have you been? We've all been worried sick.'

'I had to take a little trip.'

'But you didn't tell anyone. We've had the police searching for you. Is everything all right?'

'Yes. A personal matter came up rather unexpectedly.'

Fowler glanced around nervously, spotting only a few joggers and a man repairing a flat tire on his bicycle. 'Are you alone? I feared you were in danger.'

'I'm fine. I just wanted to talk to you in private.'

'Sure.' Fowler eyed a grove of trees near the Potomac River that offered some seclusion. 'Why don't we walk?' He gently guided her off the trail.

'I had a lot of time to think about the case while I was away,' she said.

'You probably aren't aware of the latest developments,' Fowler said, testing her. 'Somebody hijacked one of the *Sea Arrow*'s propulsion motors on its way to Groton.'

'Yes, I was aware of that. Are there any suspects?'

'No, the FBI hit a wall on the case.'

'I'm not surprised. Tell me, Dan, what do you know about the ADS system?'

'ADS? Isn't that some sort of crowd-control device that the Army cooked up? I really don't know much about it.'

'Cooked up is right.' Ann thought back to her first encounter with the device in New Orleans. 'Didn't you tell me you were with the Army Research Lab?'

'Yes, I did a short stint there. Why do you ask?'

'According to their personnel director, you managed the security for the Active Denial System program. In that capacity, you would have had access to all its plans. Perhaps you'd find it interesting to know that the Army is not alone in possessing the technology. As a matter of fact, Edward Bolcke has a unit on one of his ships.'

'What are you driving at, Ann?'

'Dan, how long have you been on Bolcke's payroll?'

They were almost to the trees. Fowler smiled at Ann. 'That's preposterous. We both know that Tom Cerny at the White House is your likely turncoat. Ann, you really shouldn't jump into the water if you don't know how to swim.'

Ann ignored the insult. 'Cerny was a good red herring. I bought into him for a while, until I reviewed his detailed security clearance. Despite your allusions, he has had no involvement with any military technologies that have been compromised. He also hasn't set foot in Central America in over twenty years. He's clean.'

Fowler said nothing as they reached the edge of the grove.

'On the other hand,' Ann said, 'I just discovered that you were a founding partner of SecureTek, the security subcontractor that was later sold to Edward Bolcke.'

'You're reaching now.'

'Am I? We've tracked financial payments that were wired from Bolcke's company to a bank account in your name here in Washington.' This time she was bluffing, but she was confident that further investigation would prove as much.

Fowler kept walking, guiding her deeper into the trees. After a long pause, he said, 'Suppose you're right. Now what?'

'You'll be tried for espionage and spend the rest of your life in jail.'

Safely obscured from view, Fowler lunged at Ann, cuffing her around the neck and slamming her against a large red oak.

'No,' Fowler said. 'I think it ends here.'

Ann stood frozen against the tree as Fowler yanked a bandanna from his pocket and rolled it thin. Wrapping it around her throat, he pulled on the ends to strangle her.

She pushed against him, but he was too strong, pinning her against the tree with his legs. Her head spun, and she began to choke – then she heard a gruff voice from behind Fowler.

'Let her go!'

Fowler turned to see two men dressed as joggers aiming Glock pistols at his head.

The man he had seen fixing a bike came running up wielding an H&K submachine gun. 'FBI,' he shouted. 'You're under arrest.'

Fowler slowly released his grip on Ann, letting the bandanna fall to the ground. One of the FBI agents yanked him away as another cuffed his hands behind his back.

Before he was dragged to a waiting car, Ann stepped close and looked him in the eye. 'Dan, trust me on this one. I do know how to swim.'

84

The seas off Tierra del Fuego were living up to their latitudinal nickname of the Furious Fifties. A strong westerly blew thick, heaving waves that broke with a boisterous flourish. Rifling currents added to the fury, shoving about the occasional stray iceberg that had drifted in from Antarctica. Over the centuries, these combined forces had carried many a ship to her grave in the frigid waters surrounding Cape Horn. All that was missing was a good williwaw – the sudden violent gusts that pounded the cape without warning.

A small trawler plowed gamely through the maelstrom, giving its occupants a roller-coaster ride. Inside the wheelhouse, Summer grabbed hold of the chart table as the boat slid down a fifteen-foot wave. 'You couldn't have found a bigger boat?' she asked with lament.

Dirk smiled and shook his head. The nautical offerings were slim on short notice in the nearby Argentinean town of Ushuaia. He felt lucky to have chartered the trawler. From Ushuaia, their trek down the Beagle Channel had been relatively calm, but on reaching the open ocean the ride had changed dramatically.

'That's Isla Nueva straight ahead,' said the captain, a stocky man with white hair.

Summer peered out the wheelhouse window at a hilly green island a mile ahead. 'Kind of scenic, in a remote sort of way. How big is it?'

'About eight miles across,' Dirk said. 'We should be able to scan the full perimeter in four or five hours.'

'She sure ended up a long way from home.'

'She' was the *Barbarigo*. Their impromptu search was guided by the package Perlmutter had sent to them in Panama. Inside they had found a logbook from the sailor Leigh Hunt, recording his round-the-world voyage. Intrigued by what Summer had discovered on Madagascar, Perlmutter had tracked down Hunt's family. One of Hunt's children had located the logbook after an extended search in the attic of the family's home. The log provided a detailed accounting of the sailor's position when he sighted the South Atlantic Wraith.

Summer picked up the log and re-examined Hunt's entries, as they rolled through the waves. 'He says he was sailing north of Nueva and Lennox islands when he saw the Wraith drifting toward Nueva. That means it was likely drifting toward the island's west coast.'

The trawler was approaching Nueva's eastern shore, which was faced with high dark cliffs. Waves pounded against the rocky shoreline, spraying billows of white foam.

'Hope the coast is milder on the other side,' Dirk said. 'If she hit the rocks around here, we won't find her on this trip.'

Dirk had the captain bring the trawler as close to shore as possible, and they began a counterclockwise survey of the island. Their search was purely for any visible signs of the submarine, had she run aground. If that failed, a sonar survey of the surrounding waters would follow with the arrival of a NUMA research vessel.

They had scanned dozens of satellite images sent by Yaeger, identifying a handful of coastal anomalies that could be the remains of the *Barbarigo*. The only way to find out was to inspect the sites, regardless of the angry seas.

They reached the north side of the island, passing towering rocks that could have crushed an approaching vessel. Two sites marked on the satellite photos proved to be rock formations that bore only faint resemblance to a submarine.

As they worked their way west, the coastal terrain flattened, revealing a mixed shoreline of coarse beaches and jagged boulders.

'Coming up on our third site,' Dirk said, comparing a satellite photo with the trawler's navigation screen.

Summer held a pair of binoculars to her eyes, struggling to hold focus as the deck rolled. 'Tell me when we're directly offshore.'

Dirk plotted the boat's progress. 'Sometime now.'

Summer studied the shoreline, scanning a small gravel beach between two rocky outcroppings. She caught sight of a smooth shape, then was knocked against the bulkhead by a large wave. 'Take us in closer.'

She searched for the object again – and spotted a smooth, rounded band tucked against the rocks.

'Something's there, though it doesn't look very big.' She passed the binoculars to her brother. 'Take a look.'

'Yes, it's some kind of man-made object.' He lowered the binoculars and looked at his sister. 'Let's go see what's there.'

The captain had to sail another mile down the coast

before he found a small cove that afforded protection from the waves. A small rubber boat was launched, and Dirk and Summer paddled the short distance to land. As they pulled the boat onto the beach, a squall blew in, dousing them with rain.

'Last time we were on an island,' Dirk said, 'I would have killed for this kind of storm.'

They trudged up the coast in the downpour, fighting the stiff offshore breeze that pelted their faces with stinging drops. Despite the dismal conditions, Summer noted the rugged beauty of this island at the tip of South America. But the coastal terrain became monotonous in the pouring rain, and after a half hour of hiking, they became unsure about where they had spotted the anomaly.

Standing at the water's edge studying the surrounding rocks, Summer finally spotted the object farther up the beach. It was a rusty curved plate of steel about six feet long, wedged firmly in the rocks.

'I'll go out on a limb,' Dirk said. 'It could be part of a submarine conning tower.'

Summer nodded and looked out to sea. 'She probably struck those rocks and sank offshore. Or drifted out to sea again.'

'No,' Dirk said, his voice registering surprise. 'I think that we've been looking in the wrong direction.' He tapped Summer's arm and pointed inland. She saw only a narrow gravel beach. Beyond was a shrub-covered hollow at the base of a rocky knoll. The beach was barren, so she gazed at the hollow – and her jaw dropped.

Poking through the shrubs, another fifty feet inland, was the rest of the conning tower.

They scrambled across the beach and into the thicket, where the entire hull of a submarine was concealed in the brush. The vessel was three-quarters buried, but Dirk could tell they had approached it from the stern. Where there once was a drive propeller he saw only a mangled shaft. They hiked along the hull until they reached the exposed conning tower, which rose like an abandoned castle. Summer pulled a black-and-white photo from her pocket and compared it to the rusting steel hulk. It was a perfect match.

She smiled at her brother. 'It's the *Barbarigo*.'

They climbed up the battered remnants of the conning tower, where they could make out the imposing hulk of the entire boat through the underbrush.

'How could it have landed way up here?' Summer asked.

'Probably a rogue wave. The area around Cape Horn is notorious for them. It must have been a real monster to throw her this far inland.'

Summer gazed at the bow. 'Do you think her cargo is still aboard?'

It was the sixty-four-thousand-dollar question – and the reason they had rushed down to Tierra del Fuego. For Perlmutter had uncovered much more than just the sailor's logbook. He had pieced together the mystery of the *Barbarigo*'s last voyage.

It all started with the German scientist Oswald Steiner, who had boarded the sub in Malaysia. Steiner, Perlmutter found, was a highly regarded physicist known for his research in advanced electromagnetics. Pressed into military research by the Nazis, he dabbled in their atomic program before focusing on a secret project of his own: a magnetic rail gun.

Steiner advanced the theory that a projectile launched at extreme velocities could travel up to fifty miles, allowing the Germans to bombard the southeast coast of England from Normandy. For the system to work, he needed the most powerful magnets in the world, and those came from one source. Rare earths.

In 1942 there was little demand for any of the rare earth elements, which were difficult to extract and refine. Germany and her conquests had few of the minerals, but Steiner found a lone source that could meet his needs. A small garnet mine in Malaysia, under Japanese control, extracted samarskite as a by-product. The samarskite contained high concentrations of the rare earth samarium, a key element in producing high-performance magnets.

Traveling to Malaysia, Steiner was stunned to discover a large stockpile of the mineral, amassed over years from mining operations. The local workers referred to it as Red Death due to its deep russet color, but it was Steiner who determined it was lightly radioactive, which in time had produced illness in some of the miners.

Thrilled with his discovery, Steiner requested transport of the samarskite back to Germany. An Italian submarine called the *Tazzoli* was assigned the task but was sunk in transit. When the *Barbarigo* arrived in Singapore, scheduled to pick up a supply of rubber and zinc, Steiner had her orders changed and stuffed her with samarskite. Accompanying the shipment home, he died with the Italian crew after they had to abandon the damaged sub.

Dirk looked down the *Barbarigo*'s forward deck at an

exposed patch of steel near the bow. He descended the conning tower and hiked across the forward deck, which was covered with mud and rocks from the hill above. Summer followed him to an indented section near the bow. Kicking away the built-up soil, he exposed the rusted deck. He eventually uncovered a looped bar welded on horizontally. It was a handgrip for the forward hatch cover. Summer joined in scraping away the overburden until they cleared the cover, complete with its locking wheel latch.

'Think it'll budge?' Summer asked.

Dirk gave the wheel latch a few firm kicks to break the seal. 'Give me a hand and we'll find out.'

They both gripped the wheel and threw their weight against it. After several tries, the latch broke its decades-long grip and spun freely. Dirk gave his sister a hopeful wink and heaved open the hatch.

A dank and musty odor rose from the opening. There was little to see as the dark interior was filled almost to the ceiling with sediment. Sand, mud, or mineral, they couldn't tell. Dirk reached inside and groped around until he grabbed a clump of the material. He held it up for Summer to see.

It was a rock, dark yet shiny and lustrous. In the gray light of the rain squall, Summer could make out a reddish tint. 'Is it Red Death?'

Dirk looked at the rock and grinned. 'No. I think it would be Crimson Gold.'

85

Six months later

A throng of dignitaries and Navy veterans, nearly three thousand strong, poured through the gates of the New London Navy Base under a cool and cloudy sky. The visitors were guided to a dock where row upon row of folding chairs faced Connecticut's Thames River.

Filling the view was the Navy's latest fast attack submarine, the USS *North Dakota*. Having completed her sea trials, she was now awaiting the last formal act of commissioning before taking to the seas in service of her country.

Pitt and Loren threaded their way through the crowd to take their seats in the second row, behind a herd of fleet admirals in full-dress uniform. Eyeing the Navy brass, Pitt wondered if their prime seating was on account of his efforts to save the *Sea Arrow* or Loren's clout on Capitol Hill. When the Chief of Naval Operations stopped by and fawned over his wife, he decided it was the latter.

A short time later, Vice President Sandecker arrived, led by a blockade of Pentagon officials. A trademark stogie dangled from his lips as he was ushered to a seat near the podium. Spotting Pitt and Loren, he slipped from his escorts and made his way to the couple.

'You're looking ravishing as always, Loren,' he said, 'despite the riffraff clinging to your arm.'

Loren laughed. 'He still cleans up well. Good to see you again, Mr Vice President.'

'Where are Summer and Dirk? I thought they'd be here.' Loren raised her brow in curiosity.

'They're both in Rome,' Pitt said. 'The Italian government is holding a memorial for the *Barbarigo*'s crewmen recovered in Madagascar. The kids were invited as guests of honor.'

'We'd have been dead in the water if it weren't for them,' Sandecker said. 'Their discovery of the crew's remains helped sway the Italians to give us the rare earth elements carried in the submarine. Kept us from having a one-trick pony today.' He winked at Pitt.

'Speaking of rare earth elements,' Loren said, 'I heard a rumor on the Hill that the Chinese are lifting their export ban.'

'They've told us as much. Once the Australians stepped in and took over Edward Bolcke's mine at Mount Weld, the Chinese lost hope of monopolizing the market. And our rebuilding efforts at Mountain Pass are well ahead of schedule. Fortunately, the remnant materials we acquired from Bolcke's former operations in Panama and Madagascar have kept us humming.'

An aide materialized at Sandecker's side, informing the Vice President that the ceremony was about to start.

'Duty calls.' He bowed to Loren and shook Pitt's hand before returning to his seat.

A moment later, Ann Bennett worked her way down the aisle and took an empty seat next to Loren. 'Hello,' she said warmly. 'I wasn't sure I was going to make it.'

'Did you just fly in?' Loren asked.

'Yes. Dan Fowler's sentencing was this morning, and I didn't want to miss it.'

'Ironic timing,' Pitt said. 'What did he get?'

She gave a satisfied smile. 'Thirty years, as the prosecutors hoped.'

An admiral took to the podium and introduced the Vice President, who gave a rousing speech about protecting the seas from all forms of enemies. A string of Navy officials followed with the expected words of ceremony.

During the speeches, Ann leaned across Loren and whispered to Pitt, 'Is it in the water?'

Pitt nodded. 'Two nights ago, under the downpour they were waiting for.'

'And ready for sea trials?'

'All systems look good, I'm told.'

'I thought the *North Dakota* already had her sea trials,' Loren said.

'Yes, that's right, dear,' Pitt said, tightening his lips.

At the podium, the *North Dakota*'s honorary sponsor was introduced and sang out the traditional commissioning first order. 'Man our ship and bring her to life!'

The crew and officers of the *North Dakota* stepped aboard the submarine to the cheers of the attending crowd. Pitt's eyes looked beyond the vessel, focused on a motorized barge surrounded by numerous red-and-white warning buoys.

'Where is she?' Ann whispered.

'By the barge on the other side.'

Loren noticed that some of the Navy officials also seemed more interested in the barge than the newly minted *North Dakota*.

'What's with everybody?' she asked. 'You all act like there's something more important going on here than the *North Dakota*'s launching. And why is everyone staring at those buoys by the barge?'

Pitt smiled at his wife and squeezed her hand.

'The sea doesn't always reveal all her mysteries,' he said. 'Even under the threat of a rusty butter knife.'

He just wanted a decent book to read ...

Not too much to ask, is it? It was in 1935 when Allen Lane, Managing Director of Bodley Head Publishers, stood on a platform at Exeter railway station looking for something good to read on his journey back to London. His choice was limited to popular magazines and poor-quality paperbacks – the same choice faced every day by the vast majority of readers, few of whom could afford hardbacks. Lane's disappointment and subsequent anger at the range of books generally available led him to found a company – and change the world.

'We believed in the existence in this country of a vast reading public for intelligent books at a low price, and staked everything on it'
Sir Allen Lane, 1902–1970, founder of Penguin Books

The quality paperback had arrived – and not just in bookshops. Lane was adamant that his Penguins should appear in chain stores and tobacconists, and should cost no more than a packet of cigarettes.

Reading habits (and cigarette prices) have changed since 1935, but Penguin still believes in publishing the best books for everybody to enjoy. We still believe that good design costs no more than bad design, and we still believe that quality books published passionately and responsibly make the world a better place.

So wherever you see the little bird – whether it's on a piece of prize-winning literary fiction or a celebrity autobiography, political tour de force or historical masterpiece, a serial-killer thriller, reference book, world classic or a piece of pure escapism – you can bet that it represents the very best that the genre has to offer.

Whatever you like to read – trust Penguin.